SPINWARD FRINGE BROADCAST 13: WARRIORS

RANDOLPH LALONDE

BOOKS BY RANDOLPH LALONDE

THE CHAOS CORE SERIES

Trapped

Cool Pursuit

Savage Stars

THE SPINWARD FRINGE SERIES

Spinward Fringe Broadcast 0: Origins

Spinward Fringe Broadcast 1 and 2: Resurrection and Awakening

Spinward Fringe Broadcast 3: Triton

Spinward Fringe Broadcast 4: Frontline

Spinward Fringe Broadcast 5: Fracture

Spinward Fringe Broadcast 6: Fragments

The Expendable Few: A Spinward Fringe Novel

Spinward Fringe Broadcast 7: Framework

Spinward Fringe Broadcast 8: Renegades

Spinward Fringe Broadcast 9: Warpath

Spinward Fringe Broadcast 10: Freeground

Spinward Fringe Broadcast 10.5: Carnie's Tale

Spinward Fringe Broadcast 11: Revenge

Spinward Fringe Broadcast 12: Invasion

Spinward Fringe Broadcast 13: Warriors

Spinward Fringe Broadcast 14: Rebel

FANTASY

Highshield

Brightwill

HORROR

Dark Arts

www.RandolphLalonde.com

EBook ISBN: 978-1-988175-19-5

Cover found on Selfpubbookcovers, by Visions then titled by Randolph Lalonde

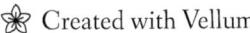 Created with Vellum

ONE

Down With Heroes

THE GARDEN between the Everin and completed Shuttle Port Buildings was like a work of art. High arches were already covered in vines that were in different stages of blooming so there were always flowers dropping the occasional yellow, blue or green petal on the walk beneath. Planters with wide bases provided a near unlimited amount of bench space while the sound of small fountains in their middle watered the flowers, fruit and vegetables with little rivulets that passed over black soil. Freshly planted wild flowers and food producing plant life thrived there, still young, but there were a few flowers and vines that would produce vegetables were starting to show already. Walking through the space for the purpose of the day didn't feel right. This was a place for peaceful times, happy social gatherings and friends. Not what the event ahead offered.

Even someone who fancied himself as a gearhead like Shamus "Frost" McFadden had to admit that the garden was amazing, detailed and wondrous even though it was also massive. It was the only good thing from the occupation's work program.

"Don't," Tammy, the young woman who looked exactly like Ashley Lamport said as Nigel reached for a small carrot shoot. "They're monitoring, you'll get fined for picking one."

Nigel relented. It seemed that Frost's tall nephew was always hungry. "I wonder if the fine is bigger than the price of that thing if I wait and buy one? It's only been eleven days since the Fleet left, nine since the occupation started, and I owe twelve hundred credits for living here. It's ridiculous, more expensive than living in the Core."

A few of the people gathering in a crowd at the back of the garden clearing overheard, offering their own nods and murmurs of agreement. A small drone, no bigger than Frost's fist whizzed by, its hover motors nearly silent. It was impossible to notice all of them; the Order was watching. It made voicing dissidence risky. He only realized he touched his chin, as if to make sure his second skin mask was on, after he'd done it. The disguise changed his features enough so surface scans wouldn't identify him, but he couldn't feel it after wearing it for a few minutes. He returned his attention to the crowd around him.

Watching hundreds of people gather around the statue of Ayan that was put up the day after the Fleet left, something that surprised Frost, was like watching the end of a funeral procession. After the night they had, no one wanted to get up early in the morning or to make the walk down from where they were stuffed together in the Everin Building to the garden centre.

Frost was sure they were coming for him and Nigel, maybe

even Tammy, when soldiers barged into the apartment. They waited until the dead of night to shock the seven people in the one-bedroom place awake, and by the time Frost knew what was going on, half the people there were stripping, and the business end of a gun was in his face. The soldier holding it said; "Get your clothes off, get any of your other clothing together along with your digital devices and pile them beside the front door, now."

Tammy and the original resident of the apartment, Samantha, resisted for a moment and rifles were raised in their direction. Then Nigel started weeping; "I can't get naked in front of all these people, it's too much." He was really warbling, tears flowing like rivers down his cheeks. Frost didn't know where his nephew got it, but he had a gift for acting. He wasn't certain that he *was* acting, actually.

The attention was drawn from the ladies, and the guards agreed that if he would be quick about it, Nigel and the ladies could take turns in the bathroom changing out of their Haven Shore clothing - what little of it there was that late at night, even Nigel was only in small bottoms - into the basic clothing that they were to put on instead.

There was wisdom in the Order of Eden taking their vacsuits, other clothing and data devices away. There were hidden channels, secret data dumps that would be more difficult to hide without intelligent clothing. Any vacsuit could be modified to have an anonymous communicator hidden inside like the one Frost, Nigel, Tammy, Stephanie, Samantha and the rest of their budding resistance group had. Stephanie set those lines of communication up, he hoped she wouldn't react too badly when she saw them go dark. Foreseeing the day when the Order would try to strip them of every means of communication was easy for her, and Frost knew that all evidence of secret communication would be gone by nights' end.

Stephanie already planned for it. Even though he didn't think they'd go as far as taking every vacsuit and communication device, he was glad she knew better.

"New clothes, new man!" Nigel said as he emerged from the bathroom wearing the standard pastel green shorts that matched the loose fitting pants and shirt that everyone was given to replace whatever they were wearing when they were shocked awake by the soldiers. Aside from Nigel's flamboyant theatrics, Frost clearly recalled how hard it was to avoid looking any of the soldiers in the eye through their dark green visors. When he added to the pile of vacsuits, night clothes and communicators in the corner and returned to his cot, where a soldier was scanning the few belongings he had there, he imagined himself wrapping his arms around the bastard's neck and breaking it before anyone could do a thing to stop him. The damage he could do with that soldiers' rifle was enticing too, but he knew better. One violent man couldn't do much against the Order of Eden presence on Tamber, let alone the forces in the Haven Solar System. His retaliation would reveal him for who he really was, a former crewmember on Jacob Valent's ship, and a dangerous rebel.

The memory of watching that soldier calmly scan his things, dump his small box of personal articles onto his bunk, made Frost ball his fists and grind his teeth as he stood in the Queen's Square. "What do you think we're here for, Shamus?" asked Malen, a stocky fellow who was in the apartment next door to Samantha's, where he, Nigel and Tammy took refuge. Stephanie changed his ident so he was Shamus Odenthall, brother to Samantha, who was new to Haven Shore.

"I don't know," Frost replied in his best standard accent,

stripped of his lilt, he felt like a pretender, but everyone told him it was convincing. "Maybe they have jobs for us."

"That would be something," Malen said with a sigh. "I mean, I don't want to do anything rough, but I'm drowning in debt without a way to pay it back. They're not even giving us credit for turning all our stuff over or sharing our places. I've got twelve bunking with me, there's barely room to breathe."

"That's what happens when you cram everyone from every Haven settlement into Haven Shore. I hear the military quarter is worse," Samantha said, placing a comforting hand on Nigel's shoulder as she stepped between him and Frost. "But with people like these running the show, we'll probably see things get worse if they hear too much complaining. I've seen it happen."

"You've been on an Order world?"

Samantha glanced around before she nodded. Shamus guessed she was just as conscious of the little ears buzzing above the crowd as he was, just as aware that her words were overheard, recorded, presented to Officers if they became flagged. "I worked my way through Dastiva as a materials specialist for manufacturing plants. I started when I was fourteen as a runner."

"In the big industrial part printing centres?" Malen asked, looking her up and down in a glance. She probably looked too clean, too attractive to have a history working in factories, it was a mistake a lot of people made with her, and she knew it. The Order already knew where she came from, though, and Frost wondered when they'd come knocking. "I hear life is rough in those plants."

Samantha nodded and replied quietly. "Everyone makes the best of it, but the quotas are high and the stress is brutal. Still, it was worth the pay eventually."

"You were probably paid an eighth of what you were worth, being a materials specialist," said someone Frost had never met in the crowd in front of them. Their furrowed brow, angry eyes told Frost that it was one of the people they shouldn't speak openly to, someone who was too loud for his own good. "The Order doesn't pay for experts the way everyone else does, doesn't treat them fairly anyway. The Haven Government had me in forensics, analysing crash sites, had decades of work ahead of me here, enough to keep me busy and happy for a long time. Now the Order of Eden has me picking fruit, out there with those animals without a vacsuit for protection. One of the pickers was eaten yesterday by something that looked like a long-bodied cat after it batted him around for a few minutes. Eaten! We're disposable to them."

Nigel and Samantha glanced at Frost, and Tammy, the former Duchess, was already moving through the crowd slowly, getting a little closer to the three storey statue. Frost, his nephew, and Samantha followed her lead. "I guess I should be happy to be in debt, then," she offered in a whisper as a response. That did nothing to soften the angry eyes of the fellow from the crowd, but he moved on to gab at someone to his right instead.

"People of Haven Shore," Lucius Wheeler's voice boomed over the audience. He moved into view in front of the statue, standing with several Order Knights in dark red and green on a hovering platform. "I hope you didn't have much trouble getting back to sleep after we rounded up your communication systems." He was in a sealed vacsuit of his own, the headpiece was completely transparent, and he wore a dark long coat overtop.

"They took all our clothes!" someone from the crowd cried, a wave of dissenting voices following.

"I know, I know," Wheeler said, his hands placating, face smiling. "I wish it wasn't necessary, but there's a group, a very small group keeping secrets, planning to disrupt your peaceful lives here. They were using the communication systems in your clothes to organize, and when we saw that they might be planning a bombing, well, we had to do something drastic. We had to stop the few from putting the majority at risk, and changing how you access communications and your entertainment was the bloodless way, the torture-free way. The other option would have us breaking through your doors, taking people instead of technology for interrogations, imprisonment, and we all know that can get out of hand."

Four shuttles descended at the far end of the garden, landing in spaces reserved by several guards in dark green armour. The crew ramps lowered and over twenty people emerged from each in Haven Shore vacsuits of various colours. Their clothing was shaped casually, in dresses, loose trousers, like outfits that people wore on their days off to relax. Some of the soldiers gave them strong lengths of rope as they passed, and Frost knew what they were about to do only a few seconds before most of the crowd did. "They're fake Haven Shore citizens. This is a bloody propaganda movie in the making," he muttered. "Do whatever anyone else does, follow along with the majority."

Tammy was horrified the instant the first pair of fake Haven Shore citizens started climbing the statue of the Queen. There were grins on their faces as bundles of rope were tossed up to them. It was wrapped around Ayan's shoulders, her neck, the lines dangling down so long that the eighty or more pretenders could all get a grip. "There's a new way of life here, one with limitless opportunity, a way for you to earn your way up to become the warrior, or the leader you want to be in the Order of Eden and beyond," Wheeler said, the amplification of his voice the only thing that could overcome outraged shouts, boos, and jeers.

"She'll be back!" Nigel shouted as Wheeler took a breath, his voice cutting through much of the noise. "The Fleet will be back!"

"Okay, don't say that," Frost growled with a nudge, knowing that Nigel wasn't the first to make those comments. He joined in on the booing instead of making his own inflammatory jeer. His little band of rebels joined in, Tammy shuddered as the first of her tears fell. The days of the occupation were hard for her, especially since everyone she met missed something about the days when the Haven Government was in control. Everywhere she turned someone had something good to say about life in Haven Shore, or how things were improving on Tamber before the occupation, and she never had a chance to see it for herself but desperately wanted to. It was a terrible, brand new experience for her, being treated like everyone else when people were of little value to their new leaders. Frost knew that there was more than a little hero worship growing in the former Duchess for Ayan, too, so watching the statue get tied up, a group of people preparing to pull it down, was enough to wrench her heart.

At least, that's what Frost assumed as he watched a squad of soldiers raise their rifles to point at the base of the statue, because he felt a hurtful pang in his chest as the sounds of their energy rifles blasting chunks of the base away silenced the crowd. His outrage threatened to rise to the surface and show through the thin second skin on his face as well, and he struggled to keep it down so hard he felt as though he was about to vomit.

The soldiers blasted the base until it was almost completely broken. Whatever the statue was made of kept it standing even though there was less than a quarter of its support left, and then the fake Haven Shore citizens began to pull on the ropes tied around Ayan's statue. Nothing happened at first. Three soldiers stepped forward and blasted a little more of the support away then retreated when the statue started to wobble. The fake citizens and crowd in the square, now silent at the sight and sound of weaponry, would fill any holographic recording that Wheeler decided to send out into the universe. The soldiers would probably be edited out. A few tugs later, the men and women on the ropes had their rhythm, and the statue began to lean. Frost silently wished the thing would topple suddenly, crushing several of the citizens pulling on the lines, he was sure most of them were Order soldiers.

Samantha's jaw was clenched hard, her fists balled, and Frost realized he was doing the same. He touched the back of her hand and she nodded, tried to look more dismayed than defiant as he did the same. Nigel was almost weeping, and as Ayan's white statue tilted suddenly, coming half way down, he flinched bodily. "Why didn't they just make this in a computer? Why do we have to stand here and watch."

"Because this is a reward for their soldiers, doing this right in front of us," Samantha whispered. "And in the version they send out, they'll make it look like we're all cheering them on."

Frost nodded, his eyes scanning the crowd. There was shock, anger, but mostly sadness. Wheeler was wounding thousands by making this happen. When it was time to rise up against the Order in Haven Shore, he'd find more volunteers thanks to what was happening. An ear-piercing crack made him jump, drew his attention back to the statue, and he saw that the last support holding Ayan up had snapped, and with two mighty pulls, the fake Haven Shore citizens had the statue down. It fell, rolled a little, and the fake citizens brought hand cutters, loudly sawed into her neck, her shoulders, even her back. When the head came free they cheered, lifted it up, revealing that someone had already gotten to it with a tool, cutting her nose off and scarring one of her eyes.

"You're free! Now the strong can lead the weak, as it was always intended," Wheeler shouted. "The Order of Eden is bringing you true freedom, and I'm backing that up with something real. We're re-opening the manufacturing facility here, that means three hundred and fifty jobs that pay good credit. You'll find out if you were chosen over the next few days, and soon, very soon, you'll forget about the Haven Government, how they wanted everyone, even the laziest, least ambitious of you to have a share of this world's bounty. Remember this moment, let it mark the very beginning of your freedom."

"We'll remember, all right," Shamus said under his breath. Nigel and Samantha nodded just enough so he could see, as did her neighbour, Malen. Frost didn't realize he followed them when they moved to another part of the crowd.

Another voice, someone not on the platform but already familiar to Frost because he heard it whenever a new shift began, said; "Day shift in fifteen minutes. Begin travelling to your work sites or be docked for being tardy."

TWO

Exile: Day 12

THE MERCILESS WAS a wonder of balance throughout. The cabins and corridors were large enough for most Nafalli to be comfortable, but not over grand in size like the Triton. Terry Ozark McPatrick always liked that there were few, if any corners where he had to worry about bumping his head, but sometimes places aboard the Triton seemed oversized to the point of being wasteful. There was none of that aboard Commodore Jacob Valent's ship.

When the opportunity to host the meeting of the Special Operations Combat Unit leadership came up, and it was to take place aboard the Triton, Oz turned the honour down, suggesting that it would be more appropriate to meet aboard the Merciless. He insinuated himself into the meeting even though he wasn't part of SOCU anymore, and, to his surprise, his ruse to see the Merciless as a guest worked. There was curiosity throughout the admiralty about the

Merciless, and when many of them discovered that the meeting was to take place there, it quickly became a more general gathering where issues not involving SOCU would be discussed as well so some of the admirals who were available could pay the ship a visit. It happened overnight, and by morning Oz had to be there anyway, especially since he may be taking over headmaster duties at the Academy.

Since he could remember, Oz loved starships. One of his first memories was standing on the railing in front of a section of transparent hull watching the ships come in to the main Freeground Station Port. He could almost recall the way the railing dug into the soles of his shoes as he hopped up and down at seeing one of the larger warships, close enough so he could see the shapes of people in front of the oval portholes. Perhaps that was just him editing, improving one of his oldest memories, but seeing that there were people aboard, seeing them move about even in silhouette and how tiny they were, was almost enough to send little Oz into an excited frenzy. A little of that excitement was still there when he saw the smooth but utilitarian halls of a ship like the Merciless.

The crew moved with a purpose, a few who weren't in such a rush saluted him on their way by. One who was moving almost lackadaisically was particularly official when he snapped to and saluted upon noticing Oz. "Commodore," he said, rising to Oz's height. It could have been him when he was younger, maybe on his first tour.

Oz returned the salute. "At ease. What brings you to the command section, Ensign?"

"Sir; the communication terminals needed a discreet processor cluster and storage system installed, Sir," replied the young officer.

"You're supposed to be off duty," Oz said, reading the Ensigns brief profile on his command and control unit.

"I helped do the finishing on the bridge, know it from one side to the other, so I volunteered. Chief Finn did not object, Sir."

"On your way to the mess?" Oz asked.

"Sir, yes, Sir."

"How is the food here, Ensign Launer? Speak freely," Oz asked with a little smile. He liked the official tone the Ensign took, even though he wasn't standing at attention, he was still focused on making a good impression and his record showed that he was praised as a hard worker who was interested in advancement. He had also served on the Revenge.

"Not as good without Tamber, but better than I've had anywhere else. Can I ask you a question, Sir?"

"Aye, go ahead," Oz said with a cocked eyebrow.

"There's a lot of talk on Crewcast about how the British are selling our tech, betrayed Haven. There are petitions going around to withdraw from our alliance with them. If you were me, at the beginning of your career, would you make your opinion public by signing any of them, even one that calls for more restrictions on the alliance, but not a break?"

"I'd keep my head down and get back to work. Study for Qualification Testing in my off-time like you're doing," Oz looked up and nodded at Ruby Sima as she emerged from the large meeting room behind the Ensign. She didn't interrupt, smiling at him as she pulled her bright blue hair out of a ponytail.

"May I ask why you'd avoid sharing your opinion, Sir?" Ensign Launer asked.

"Those petitions don't change policy. The only people who will see them are in communications, you won't influence command. I didn't even know there was more than one petition."

"So, there's not much point in making my opinion public if the people I want to see it aren't looking is what you're saying, Sir?"

"Yes, but more importantly, there's a chance that it could hurt your chances for promotion because, to some commanders, it shows a lack of trust in Fleet command. The real question you have to ask here is if you trust your commanders to make the right decision. I do, so I'm free to do my job without the burden of questioning things that are over my head."

"I trust my commanders, Sir," the Ensign said. "Then I won't touch any of those petitions, I was on the fence anyway, Sir."

"Which way were you leaning, just between you and I?"

"I support renegotiation and reparations," the Ensign replied, looking a little surprised to be asked. "They're our connection to the core worlds. We need them but I think they still owe us something, Sir."

"Then we're of the same mind. Good luck on your Flight Systems Qual, I'll watch for your results." Oz saluted. "Dismissed."

"Sir, thank you, Sir," Ensign Launer replied, returning the salute then moving on.

"I'd vote to have the British put to our thrusters, sell our older tech ourselves through some dummy corp," Ruby said as she took the Ensigns place.

Admiral Lamonthe walked past both of them with two of his aides, saying; "I'll see you in there, Commodore McPatrick," as he did so.

"I'll be just a minute, Sir," Oz called after him, returning his attention to Ruby. "I'm afraid I agree with the Ensign. The British owe us a few tons of platinum, an apology, and a seat at their table, but we need them for support and firepower. Looks like they want to prove themselves, too."

"What, that little raid on Iyagda? That served them as much as it did us, the Order was encroaching on British Alliance territory."

While that was true, Oz had seen the detailed reports on that action. The attack on the Order of Eden's secret shipyards in the Iyagda system cost the British Alliance two carriers, five destroyers and over a thousand lives. Holding it took four times as many resources as the battlegroup they had supporting Haven Fleet, and without real help from their allies, it would take years to make the system productive and self-sufficient thanks to the damage the Order did once they realized they were about to lose control of the system. More importantly, taking Iyagda was a test run to see if they could liberate the Haven System on their own, and the results were grim. Iyagda was lightly guarded in comparison, and even outnumbered, the Order was able to defend themselves well. "Iyagda gives them a space where they can rally less than ten light years from Haven. It's a good start."

"They could have reinforced the Mergillians' home system, they think they're next on the Order's invasion list," Ruby said. "I heard Iyagda cost the British a carrier."

"A bit more than that, but you're not cleared to see the report, so..."

Ruby nodded. "So, what brings you aboard the mighty Merciless?"

"I was the SOCU commander for five minutes, so I still get to sit in on some of their meetings, and I might be the new headmaster for the Academy. What about you? Are you doing something for SOCU?"

"If you don't already know, then you're not supposed to," Ruby said wryly. "I noticed you didn't recruit me when you were in charge of SOCU. What gives?"

"Fleet wanted you for another command, I thought it would be one of these." Oz knocked on the panel next to him.

"Way too big," Ruby said. "You know where I ended up."

"I don't, actually," Oz said. "Your service records are all a blank to me. You're labelled; 'Need to Know Only.'"

"To a Commodore?" Ruby laughed. "Well, they gave me the Redstone. One of first general purpose heavy ships the Forge is printing."

He knew the ship, it was the first to be built by the War Forge after departing the Haven System after the invasion. It was a heavy destroyer, a relatively compact ship for its class only built for war with the best of everything. The design only used technology that proved itself during the invasion. They were nothing fancy, but each was sturdy and adaptable. "Congratulations, that's a good ship. I saw the design before it was built. How's your crew?"

"A third trainees, mostly Nafalli, but they'll be wearing nothing but Fleet black soon, they're ripping through quals like they were born to it. The rest of my crew are well chuffed to have their hands on some real modern tech, and the new bunks are a huge improvement."

"Coming, Commodore?" Liara asked as she opened the door to the conference room, then let it close as soon as he nodded.

"Looks like you're holding things up," Ruby said. "Before you go, though; how's the Triton?"

"Good, repairs are almost finished. The regenerating systems speed everything up. We're almost back to normal."

"Good, I love that ship, glad to hear she's back in good shape. How about her Commander?"

"Glad to be alive, happy in the service," Oz replied. "Good hunting, Ruby."

"You too," she replied.

When Oz entered the conference room, the doors sealed and latched behind him. Red lettering appeared across the metal saying; AUTHORIZED PERSONNEL ONLY, CLASSIFIED LEVEL SEVEN. No one sat at the long table in the middle of the largest conference room aboard the Merciless, the chairs were still pushed in. The lights were dimmed so the holographic presentation they were about to see would be as clear as possible. Jake stood at the opposite end of the table, talking to Liara, Lamonthe, Ayan, Doolth who stroked the fur under her chin, and aides for them all. Remmy and his First Officer, Dotty Bedel, were the first to pull seats out and sit down. Aides took that as a cue, and more than twenty of them took a seat on the padded benches running the length of the conference room. "We're all here? Good," Admiral Lamonthe said, pulling a broad seat out for Admiral Doolth, who smiled at the courtesy as she settled in. Oz's space was marked, he was to sit beside Ayan, who sat beside Jake. If he wasn't the former SOCU commander, it would have been odd to sit beside the Defence Minister, but it wasn't her meeting, after all. "Commodore Valent, what is your ship's status?" Admiral Lamonthe asked.

"We're cloaked, signal silent," he replied. "Nothing detected on long range."

Minh-Chu, who was still settling in to Oz's left, added; "We have two wings running patrols with a few light corvettes for support. They'll spot anything out of place."

"The Triton is in the patrol pattern, cloaked, with her ears and eyes wide open," Oz added when Admiral Lamonthe looked in his direction. "Trident Wing is standing by."

"Then we are secure," Lamonthe said. "It is the first time everyone here has met in person since before the Invasion, and it may be the last for some time. Admiral Doolth is representing the Lau Tribe, her battlegroups and the general concerns of the Nafalli people, while Admiral Kulsh is doing the same for his people. The rest of us are here to be updated and to discuss strategy going forward. I regret that I must report the notable exception of commanders from the British Alliance from this meeting. Admiral Paris Hadlee was not willing to attend."

"I have her proxy," Ayan said.

"Have you discussed moving our fleet to Iyagda? There are asteroid belts and a small nearby nebula that would allow us to operate without cloaking fields."

"There are still too many Order operatives hidden in the system. They don't think it's safe for us to operate there yet," Ayan replied.

"There are a lot of people celebrating their liberation from the Order there, they have a lot of support from what I've seen in the feed from Hart News," Admiral Doolth said. "They are celebrating the overthrow of their corporate leaders, welcoming the promise of democracy. I believe there are still spies there, but sometime taking shelter is better than hiding in the space between the stars. At least we'd have closer communication with people from more solar systems."

"I made our case to her," Ayan replied. "The Admiral is taking it to her leadership, but she doesn't expect they'll change their mind. The British Alliance wants Iyagda all to themselves. We'll be welcome when we're less controversial."

"And that's why I'm happy Admiral Hadlee isn't here," Wing Commander Minh-Chu Buu said. "No friend is a true friend if they hide you from their other friends."

"He has a point," Lamonthe said. "I think we can let the issue of using Iyagda as a refuge there for now, unless anyone has something else to add."

"I am using back channels to speak to my people about volunteering areas in the Fethun Solar System as a place for this fleet to operate in the open. I expect to hear word back from them in approximately nine days, though the use of a ship with a quad drive would speed that up considerably."

"Remmy is available," Commodore Valent said, looking to Remmy, who was already nodding.

"I could use the break. We'd get there in a little under a day and act as a communications relay so you can communicate live."

"I'll put Alaka on standby and you'll head out as soon as we get the details of your mission together," Jake said.

Admiral Lamonthe looked to the green and brown skinned Mergillian. "How does that sound, Admiral?"

"Better than I hoped," he said. "There are thousands of people waiting in that system, hoping to get the opportunity to serve in Haven Fleet. We have been driven out of more than one solar system by corporations like Regent Galactic and organizations like the Order in our history. We are eager to fight back. If you need a place while you regroup, I am sure we can provide it. We only want the opportunity."

"With that settled for the time being, we can move on," Lamonthe said. "The meeting is yours, Defence Minister."

Ayan cleared her throat and nodded, thinking for a moment before speaking. "The British Alliance has offered a reparations package. Half a billion in platinum, property in three prime solar systems within their space - that part is contingent on us winning this war - some of it is properly terraformed. They are also offering an official treaty between them and the Haven Government, and they've agreed to set up a business relationship going forward where we will have a say in what we release using their channels and a royalty. I turned it down."

"You turned it down?" Admiral Doolth asked with a surprised squeak. There was a collective gasp in the room as aides and several of the higher-ranking officers reacted. Remmy and Minh-Chu laughed sharply, shortly.

"Good," Oz said. He saw the estimates on what the British Alliance made on selling specifications and materialization patterns to companies in the Core Worlds. Tens of billions in platinum was their reward for betraying their Haven Fleet allies, and that might be the least of it. "The Order will eventually get their hands on all that technology. Imagine Order Knights wearing armour that's only a small step behind our encounter suits. They won't get our regenerative hulls, the quad drive technology, no one has, but they'll have access to our weapon tech, basic gravity shields. They could upgrade their entire fleet, and after the losses they took during the invasion, I'm sure they will. The British Alliance owes us at least ten times as much as what they were offering and safe harbour somewhere nearby where they're hiding their firepower in fringe space."

"But a bird in the hand," Lamonthe said. "I wasn't even privy to the negotiation."

"You didn't have to be," Ayan said. "They're low-balling us because we don't have land to stand on. They think we're desperate, they're looking to take advantage. We don't need holdings that are only valid after we win this war, or legitimization when we'll get that by taking the Haven System back anyway. Admiral Hadlee is relaying my response to their people now. We'll hear back in a couple weeks."

"You could send a quad drive equipped ship in the British Alliance's direction to speed up the communication," Admiral Lamonthe said.

"I know, I know you want to put a ship right in their capitol so we can have real time comms with them, we've had this discussion before. My mind isn't changed," Ayan said. "There is no way I'm letting a quad drive within a light year of their Core World territories. They broke the trust, now it's up to them to convince me they won't try to steal it at the first chance," Ayan said. "No one gets a quad drive. No one."

"Melt it down the moment it looks like they're about to try something," Lamonthe replied.

"Sitting here, around this table, it's easy to think that one of our trained officers can't be tricked into handing it over. None of us think we can be tricked, right?" she looked directly at Lamonthe, Jacob moved his chair back a little so they could make eye contact. "I bet I could trick you into it. I'd plant a brain-bud on you in your sleep, start editing your reality, and before you knew it you'd be tricked into a situation where you thought you were saving everyone by cooperating with the British. I'm sure there are even more devious ways to do it, but that's how I'd have it done, and I know you'd fall for it."

"So, we do what Chief McFadden did with the Sector Jumper; have a crewman stay aboard full time, tell him no one gets access to sensitive systems."

"If the British want it, and it's well inside their territory, they'll get it. I'm surprised you even think this is a debate. You're smarter than this, drop it." Ayan pulled on the arm of Jake's chair, and he rolled back between she and Lamonthe as she looked at the rest of the people seated in front of her. "My people are putting a counter-proposal together, and we're sending a relay ship that will remain hidden just outside their territory. It will cut the time it takes to communicate with British Alliance Military Command down to a few hours, and no one will be able to find it. Admiral Hadlee understands our mistrust and why I'm dissatisfied with their proposal. Commodore McPatrick is right: the harm the British Alliance has done to our cause by stealing and selling our technology isn't something we can calculate yet. I'm going to squeeze the British Alliance for everything we can and make sure they know they're on notice for the future. If I had it my way, the British will never have quad drive technology or anything that comes with it, but I realize that we'll have to share eventually. That day will come when they've earned our trust, and it won't be for a very long time."

Ayan looked at the faces gathered around the table, giving each one a few seconds. Oz was thrilled at the confidence he saw in her, something she always had, but never in such abundance. The air was thick with the silence she enforced with her pause by the time she moved the conversation on. "The War Forge is an active training hub again, and I'm happy to report that there are over six thousand three hundred students aboard, most of them Nafalli. The manufacturing lines that were damaged during the invasion of the Haven System are repaired, and we've finished work on the first Star Clash Class Destroyer, the Redstone, who is officially taking command today. We had a short meeting here a few minutes ago so she could see the support of the Admiralty as she joins SOCU. The War Forge is proving itself as a capable multi-role mobile station, and will be ramping back up to full production over the next three days. Our training facilities are missing one thing, though." She looked to Oz, tilting her head.

"I just wanted to make sure the Triton is back in shape and her crew is ready for combat," Oz replied.

"Having a little trouble letting go?" Jake asked.

Oz could feel his old friend's amusement, Ayan and Minh-Chu along with most of the people at the table felt the same, it was like a tickle on the edges of his consciousness. "A little, but I'm looking forward to taking over, making my mark on the trainees in the Academy."

"Maybe it's too soon," Lamonthe said, the man was an anchor of seriousness. "Commodore McPatrick is a brilliant carrier commander. The Academy is doing well enough under the watchful eye of the staff. Maybe it should remain that way until we take the Haven System back. I would hate to see the Commodore retired before his time."

"Is it his choice?" Minh-Chu asked. "The job was offered, but did he sign anything? Is there a commander standing behind the Triton's captain seat?"

"No, and," Lamonthe looked at his command and control unit, a large combat bracer on his wrist like his own. "No, the Commodore isn't depriving anyone of a command by staying on the Triton. The Star Clash and the rest of the destroyers in the line will provide more than enough opportunity for the people from the former Freeground Fleet who are ready to advance to have a command."

Ayan's brow raised, she was surprised at the turn of events, but not unpleasantly so as she regarded Oz. "So, is it too soon? Do you want to stay aboard the Triton? We could fill the empty bunks with trainees and give you an Academy Class."

"There's room for a whole other fighter wing aboard that ship. You could train new pilots," Minh-Chu added. "Maybe call it; Aqua Wing, or Water Wing, or Sabre Wing?"

Oz didn't have to think about it. The idea of guiding thousands of new recruits was exciting, amazing, but he pictured himself on the bridge of the Triton and it felt right. He wanted to be in the fight, directly in the fight, and the thought of relinquishing the captain's seat made him cringe. The absence of Haus Geist was less and less of a millstone as the days passed. He knew he was good for morale, too, the feeling he got from his crew when he opened his mind to them were mostly positive, even the ones who didn't favour him as a captain trusted him, respected him. "I'd like to remain as the Triton's commander, yes. I want the Wing Commander's help in setting up the training for the training wing. The first round should only have capable pilots who are missing the officer training that the Academy has already set up. Like an Apex Advanced Class for pilots. The rest of the space can take care of other trainees. The Botanical Gallery is empty right now, and there's an empty berthing. Enough room for hundreds." He grew more excited as the idea bloomed in his mind, and most of the people at the table could tell, most shared his enthusiasm.

"Then it's settled, and I have to appoint a new headmaster," Ayan said with a chuckle. "We'll start sending some of our better recruits over as soon as you're ready."

"Thank you, Admiral," he said, looking to Ayan then Lamonthe.

"Well, there's a more detailed report on the fleet's status, but we don't have all day, so we'll move on," Ayan said. "Phase Seven is in place, and they're waiting for our signal to begin interfering with Order of Eden operations in and around the Haven System."

"How are Admiral Rice and her people?" Admiral Kulsh asked, sweeping his hand over the top of his broad, smooth head. "It must have been difficult to watch Haven fall while they were ordered to hide."

"They're bitter," Ayan said. "But strong. They understand that they couldn't have tipped the scales in our favour, and eager to make a difference now that we know for certain that they haven't been detected by the Order. We have real time communication with them, and one thing is for certain: The Order are not winning hearts and minds. Everyone saw that propaganda piece?"

There were murmurs of acknowledgement around the table. "Where they pulled the statue of you down?" Minh-Chu asked, irritation rolling off of him in a wave. "Wheeler," he added the name like a quiet, bitter curse.

"Admiral Lamonthe?" Ayan said, looking to him. They behaved like the argument they just had was already ancient history, and Oz could sense that they felt the same way.

A hologram of the crowd surrounding Ayan's monument appeared on the table, covering the entire top. It was frozen, with the statue half way down. "Right," Lamonthe started. "We've identified twenty-eight of the people pulling the ropes, they're all Order officers. Facial disguises didn't trick our analysis for long."

"So, they used something to make themselves look like Haven citizens?" Remmy asked, pointing at one of the rope pullers. "She looks like the woman who I got my coffee from when I visited the market square."

"Exactly, they went to great lengths to make it look like the citizens of Haven Shore specifically were overjoyed to be liberated by the Order of Eden, Wheeler especially. More broadcasts called the Secrets of the Queen are scheduled, so it's going to be an ongoing effort." Ayan turned red, and Oz could feel her embarrassment and irritation almost as clearly as if it was his own.

Lamonthe went on. "We couldn't get past all the disguises, but we found a surprise as the analysis ran. Here, in the crowd," he pointed to a stout man who was cheering. "If we fix the image so the digital reshaping that makes him look like he's cheering - which he isn't - then analyse the shape of his face, we discover someone famil- iar." With a tap of his finger on the figures' head, the face morphed into that of Shamus McFadden. "His nephew is in another second skin mask beside him, and that's the former Duchess behind him in her own disguise. We don't know why Wheeler hasn't plucked her out of the crowd, but the fact that she's hiding and with McFadden is encouraging. We suspect that he's forming an underground, espe- cially if something happened to his partner, Stephanie Vega, who we can't find a trace of."

"Oh, he's forming an underground," Jake said with a broad grin. "Frost is one of the best ship thieves I've ever heard of, and I've hunted down about two dozen, so I'd know. He's also best when he fights dirty, and he holds grudges like some people keep old friends."

"With all respect to your man, Commodore," Lamonthe said. "Is he smart enough to lead an underground rebellion?"

"On his good days, yes," Jake said. "But if you can't find Stephanie, then it's because she doesn't want to be found or they already have her."

"We'd know if she was imprisoned," Lamonthe said. "Trust me."

"Then she's in hiding. If she and Frost are working together, then Wheeler is in more trouble than he could possibly know, espe- cially if he thinks he has the upper hand, especially since Stephanie might underestimate him, but Frost never would."

"Why wouldn't Frost under estimate Wheeler? So far, he seems like a grinning showman, his manner is juvenile."

"Don't tell him I said this," Jake started, looking around the table, "But Frost and Wheeler are both capable of being the same kind of scumbag. Don't get me wrong, Frost is our man, he's a good man at heart, but he can be just as much of a back-stabbing asshole as Wheeler, and he enjoys it just as much, but he chooses not to. If things get dire down there, he'll start doing things most of us wouldn't even be capable of."

"What about his nephew?" Lamonthe asked. "Did Frost ever talk about him?"

"No, I'm afraid not," Jake replied. "He's family, though, so Frost will probably protect him, and that makes Frost even more dangerous. He believes he has a lot to make up for in general. He has a lot of wreckage in his past."

"So, we have Stephanie Vega, Frost, his Nephew, a former Duchess, and who knows who else on the ground who are definitely involved with the underground," Ayan said. "Can we contact them?"

"Not without risking the Order becoming aware of the attempt," Lamonthe said. "They had all communication devices taken, the Order even took their vacsuits and disabled everything they could use as a communicator to the outside. As far as we can tell, they have listener drones everywhere too, so any incoming communication would be tracked. I want to see what they do on their own, have a Phase Seven ship monitor from where its hiding in orbit, listen in on the Order communications coming from Tamber for now, at least."

"It'll give Stephanie and Frost time to get something going," Jake said. "They won't wait for support, if they see an opportunity to make a move, they'll take it."

"Good to know, I'll loop you in on any new information so you can consult," Lamonthe said. "Later today we're going to put out a statement with the un-doctored version of this recording so our people can see the crowd booing and jeering as the statue comes down. We'll leave our people masked, of course, we don't need anyone to know they're there. Now the meeting goes to you, Commodore Valent."

"SOCU has been busy," Jake said. "The Clever Dream, commanded by Captain Valent and the Scythe under the command of Captain Remmy Sands, have struck nine high value targets well behind Order of Eden lines." Two holograms of vast orbital shipyards appeared. Each had a different planet in the background and dozens of ships waiting for repair were docked. "The shipyards in the Avalon System around both the terraformed worlds there were annihilated by a fully charged, Hammerhead Nine torpedo with its limiter systems disabled. Each torpedo was modified with an enlarged containment compartment, so it could carry three times as much liquid antimatter." The peaceful image of both shipyards erupted with a white flash that expanded for several seconds, leaving nothing but a ring of twisted, white hot metal behind from the ships that were circling the station at a distance. "Avalon's shipyards are gone. The planets were left completely unscathed."

"They left a cloaked drone behind so it could broadcast a message on all bands, making Order of Eden citizens aware that their military was outdated, and their leadership was about to fall. We claimed credit for the destruction of their installations. There are several more recordings like the one I just showed you, the last of which was entirely Remmy's doing. They shadowed a cruiser until it moved through the shield surrounding one of the outer military stations - Magni Five, launched their Hammerhead into the main servicing bay and left. Magni Five is now a blackened husk, and the largest repair station near the Haven System is no more. The radiation is so high that it's not even fit for salvage, and it doesn't matter since it was in dead space, a light year away from the nearest solar system."

"Well done, Captain Sands," Lamonthe said.

"Thank you, I thought I should use the last of my bombs close to home," he said. "That wasn't the mission, but I got the go-ahead from the Commodore before setting it off."

"What about Captain Valent? Can you share her location? Why didn't she hit her fifth target?" Lamonthe asked.

"No to the first, the Captain is eight light years behind enemy lines, give or take one or two, pursuing something else for Haven Fleet. As for her last bomb, she said she has a plan for it. Something that addresses Directive Two. Captain Valent is performing a much deeper investigation into a developing situation that could pay off larger than any of our attacks so far."

"You're starting to sound like me, Commodore," Lamonthe said with a wry smile. "You found the most descriptive way to say; 'she's working on it' that I've ever heard."

"SOCU is working on connecting itself with other enemies of the Order, she's at the centre of the effort," Jake said. "Better?"

"A little. Run the mission, Commodore, it's your responsibility as long as it produces the results I'm looking for."

"Understood. In the meantime, transmissions and news reports made by SOCU are spreading. We expect footage of our torpedoes taking stations and other major space-based targets out will reach thirty-five percent of their citizens by oh-nine-hundred."

"Your report says the death toll is over a hundred ninety thousand, and there's an estimation here stating that fewer than one thousand were civilian," Lamonthe said.

"No one's perfect," Remmy said.

Jake shook his head at him, then regarded the Admiral. "We only hit military targets, did our best to get up-to-the-minute data on who was there beforehand, but my orders called for mass destruction. The bigger you go, the more you endanger innocent lives, we tried as hard as we could to prevent that anyway."

"I see that. Captains Valent and Sands passed up much bigger, more central targets, like this one on Risi, where Eve was scheduled to speak. They even confirmed that she was present by hacking into a security system that could scan her. Then they turned away. Why?" Lamonthe asked.

"She was speaking in Dandora, a capitol city in orbit around Risi. Half a million people live on that station. Only twenty percent were military, roughly. Would you have made Eve a martyr along with all those civilians?"

"I would have seriously considered it," Lamonthe said. "Eve is seen as immortal, more so than the hundred knights that protect her, even more than Hampon."

"We wanted to get her," Remmy said, looking to Jake.

Jake nodded; "Go ahead."

"We didn't see which ship she arrived in, it must have been cloaked, and the ports were locked down so tight we couldn't have snuck a rim-weasel in. We had sensor drones deployed along the outside perimeter, you know, the passive listeners that look like little bits of debris, and we were ready to go after her the moment she left, but the whole area was shut down, then they sent signal scramblers out, and there was no way to detect her ship. We considered just blasting the area we thought she would move through, but we would have gotten ourselves slagged in the process, we would have had to get in range of seven command cruisers and the station's defences. Next thing we knew, Eve's command ship was already leaving. As for bombing the station while she was on stage, well, we could have. Half a million people were there, though, and there were at least another forty visiting because of her. We didn't want to become baby killers, and we couldn't come up with a precision solution in time, so that opportunity passed."

"They passed on twenty other targets after investigating them," Jake said. "As far as we can confirm, the civilians who were killed were military adjacent adults, like consultants, starship engineers and the like. Keeping that civilian death toll so low is a miracle."

"And I can sleep at night," Remmy said, throwing his hands up and settling back into his seat. "I don't hear the screams of the innocent in my dreams. I call all that broken hardware and the demoralization of a huge chunk of their military, maybe the whole thing as the word goes out, a win. I'm good with it."

"You could have done better with a little more patience and expertise," Lamonthe said. "Opportunities were missed, the kind I'm not seeing in this report. Where are the uprisings? Where are the signs that the chain of command is being broken in the Order military?"

"I couldn't have done better," Jake said. Oz could sense the lie, but it didn't show on his face as he continued. "The mission isn't over, either. We still have one Hammerhead behind enemy lines with Captain Valent."

"Oh, and you want to see patience? She'll out investigate and out wait anyone here," Remmy said. "I'd work with her again, anytime."

"That's enough, Captain," Lamonthe said. "But I hope you're right. I hope we see more immediate results from Captain Valent. The seeds of demoralization have been sown in our fleet, and if we don't see Order soldiers turning soon, they'll grow. I expected something spectacular from the firepower I sent you out with, but outside of your recordings, I don't see the Order changing anything out here. They're not turning away from their search for us, and ships aren't retreating from the Haven System to guard their own assets."

"There's just no pleasing some people," Remmy muttered, immediately holding a hand up. "I apologize, Admiral."

"Firepower doesn't always equal political power or change," Commodore Valent said to Lamonthe. "If you have a problem with our strategy, then you should choose the targets next time."

Watching Lamonthe as he took a moment to consider a rebuttal, then decided against it in silence was incredible to Oz. There was no sign of the raging sea of frustration the man was feeling. Lamonthe sighed, letting most of it go, then moved the meeting on; "I congratulate you and your people on the success you've had. Let's move on to another matter, please."

Oz took a moment to close himself off from his empathic sense, he could feel the start of a headache. Everyone was conducting themselves with great decorum, but there was a riot of emotion at the table. As Admiral Doolth started speaking, Oz hoped Alice was doing well wherever she was. He wished he was the still the head of SOCU, just so he could find out more about her mission behind enemy lines.

THREE

The Malcontent

THE RAIN CAME CLEAN, fresh from the atmosphere condi-
tioners towering over the city of Grenjin. Between the labyrinth of
scars on his face, he could feel the cool drops as he looked upward.
It was as if the planet wanted to fight his malaise. The news was
grim. He'd fought his rising debt for as long as he could, as hard as
he could. He even tried permanent modification to his appearance
and DNA, which worked well enough for the old government scanners in the city to miss him, but instead of having a normal looking
face, it left him with scars from emergency hands-on surgery as the
shifting skin failed to do what the back-alley surgeon predicted it
would. He didn't understand what went wrong exactly, that didn't
matter as much as what he saw when he caught a look at himself in
the mirror. Instead of shifting the features of a face everyone

enjoyed looking at, he had the kind of appearance people turned away from.

It bought him time, though. The people who controlled his Order of Eden account, the one that paid for everything but the air he breathed, took one look at him and didn't want to cash in early, to force him to serve in their companies or houses. The modifications were supposed to help him hide so he could continue building a network of resistance, but it marked him. Everyone knew the face they didn't want to stare into, the hooded man and his scars.

People in power didn't know what he was doing yet, but once they started hearing about the scarred man, he would either be driven into hiding or taken into custody before he realized they knew he was connected to the resistance. He suspected that time was coming fast, his debt was too high, and Admiral Scanlon, the new leader representing the Order of Eden in the solar system, bought his debt personally. He had been past the one hundred thousand credit threshold for months, it was the minimum required for someone to sell the debtor to the Order of Eden on that world, so he would be pressed into service. She could yank him into her service personally at any moment, too, so he wondered why she bought him, if she knew what he was doing when he was sure he wasn't being monitored, if she knew about his hiding places and the efforts he inspired against the Order.

He was on borrowed time, a thought that passed through his mind every hour. "We have to go, Peter," said Sonny, his long-time partner in crime. "The market's about to turn to mud and there was nothing at the drop."

Peter turned to him, the water drops rolling through the stubble on his head, giving him a shiver. "You look down and see mud, I look up and see a generous sky."

"I see manufactured grey clouds," Sonny replied. The open-air market was thick with people who were there to barter. They carried every sort of object, even pets that were caught in the wild at great risk. The planet of Nuaji was completely terraformed, but there were minerals in the ground that were difficult to fabricate, so the Order dug and plundered. That was why they turned the weather control systems back on, he assumed, why the city Peter grew up in was being turned into a rainforest. There was another one somewhere else being torn down. A pair of young men approached him sheepishly, looking to Sonny more. "We heard there was going to be a meeting?" One of them asked in a low whisper.

"Not for you," Sonny said. It was the right response, these two didn't know how to talk about the resistance, they didn't know the right words. They were young, though, they may have heard about them indirectly, not from someone who could have vetted them.

"Keep watching, keep listening," Peter said with more encouragement. "Good luck with your trades." He started moving past them, but one caught his arm.

"Wait, we need to join you, we're close to threshold already. My brother lost his hand and even after we split the cost of getting him a new one, a real flesh one, we're a few credits away from getting pressed into the Order," plead one of them.

"They told you cybernetics weren't an option when you went in, didn't they?" Peter asked. It was a common ploy with official medical facilities to hard-sell flesh and bone replacements when cybernetics would cost a tenth as much and be twice as good.

"Yeah, they said it was all junk, and he was bleeding out. I don't know if they would have even worked on him if I didn't agree to get him a real hand."

"Common story, I'm sorry about that," Sonny said. "C'mon Pete, we have to go." He was always more suspicious. These boys could have been sent by the Order to get in on a resistance meeting, to see which cell leaders made an appearance.

"Go to the booth with the forma printer, the one at the far end over there, and tell them you want to try the Orange Nut Delight bars," he told them. There were people there who could hide these boys if they were in real trouble, and if they were Order plants, they would be found out. Peter hoped they weren't, the Nolen Twins didn't treat Order spies well. "It's all I can do."

"Thank you," the boy with the new hand said. The pair rushed off.

"We really do have to get going, mud or not," Sonny said once they were out of earshot. "Everyone gets nervous when we're late. Well, when you're late, anyway."

Peter nodded, the rain was intensifying anyway, the market was starting to clear. He was pulling the hood of his long poncho up when he met the blue-eyed gaze of a young woman with red hair. She seemed familiar. People passed between them, some running to get out of the thickening drops, others simply making their way. She didn't waver as she peered at him, he barely noticed the tall Nafalli and two others with her. A lot of spacers visited the market, all of them looked a little too clean at first, that was until they'd spent some time ground side. It was no different with her, the fitted blue suit she wore under a dark long coat made her look like she'd been planet-side for minutes. When a smile started to bloom on her face slowly, he realized who she was. Bare of emblem or any other markings, he knew from the contraband holo-recording of Admiral Tafford's execution and the message that followed from Captain Alice Valent, that it was her.

There was a tug on his back pocket. He turned his attention to it for a moment, retrieving a holo-communicator the size of his thumbnail from it. When he looked back to where he saw Alice, she was gone. The communicator blinked green, and he dragged Sonny into a back alley, used his home-made surveillance detector to check for devices there and when he found none he activated the communicator. "I'm Alice Valent," said the holographic face that appeared above the device, it was the size of his fist.

"What is it? I can't see, it must be focused on you because you're touching it," Sonny said as he joined Peter where he was huddled up against the wall.

Peter took Sonny's hand and put his finger on part of the device. "See it now?"

"Holy crap it's Alice Valent," he breathed.

"Haven Fleet is looking for people to fight against the Order of Eden. What's more important to you, right now, is that I've found you, Peter. It didn't take long; my crew was able to find three of your resistance cells then discover your identity by hacking a few illegal rooms on the Stellarnet. Your encryption was a little too thin. If I found you, then the Order can't be far behind. I want to get you and your people off world, but first, I need your help. Find a place and time for us to meet, send the details to us using this communicator, then tap it three times. It'll destroy itself so there's no trace of our communication."

"We have to tell the others," Sonny said as Alice's face faded.

"No," Peter said. "This is good, the best news I've had since Regent Galactic got here, but we have to keep this between us."

"Right, if it's a trap, then we minimize the damage if only we get captured," Sonny said.

"It's not a trap. I can feel it. This is what we've been hoping for, another group to come help so we can make a real difference. We have to take this in small, careful steps until the time is right." Peter let himself smile, feeling the stiffness in his cheeks. "I saw her, Sonny, she was ten metres away. I know she's here."

"Boots-on-the-ground here?" Sonny asked in hushed surprise.

"She looked me right in the eye," Peter nodded. "We might have a fighting chance."

"But her people lost their home system."

"Taking a whole space fleet with them. A fleet that can hide, that's more powerful ship-to-ship than anything in the galaxy, with a battle station that can build them whatever they need."

"Fairy tales," Sonny said pleadingly. "All we have is conflicting propaganda from them, the Order, the British, and a few other governments who want to pretend they're important enough to be a part of the biggest war of our time. We don't know how much of this is true, we don't even know if there was ever a Haven System. All we see when we look it up is Rega Gain on most charts."

"Then we have to find out for ourselves," Peter said, finding that he was calm, much less on edge than he'd been in weeks. "We'll meet her face to face."

"And get caught if it's a trap," Sonny countered.

Peter turned the communication device over in his palm. The style of the technology wasn't like anything he'd seen before, maybe it was proof, maybe it wasn't. He didn't know if he could see through his own excitement. "Then I'll go alone. If I get taken, then maybe it'll provoke the cells into doing something real, or maybe it'll push them further underground. Either way, it'll get them moving again."

Sonny scoffed. "Like I'd let you go alone. Fine, we'll meet her, but we're going to do it in a place we control and can abandon at a moment's notice."

FOUR

Shadow Play

"IYAGDA HAS BEEN LOST, SIR," Captain Kenley said as he stepped onto the balcony.

Lucius Wheeler stood up and walked to the balcony. "Was it Haven Fleet?" It was a major setback, especially for him.

"The British Alliance, there was no indication that they had help from Haven Fleet. The report shows that we're still trying to look for any evidence that they were involved, but no one has seen a sign of them."

"Why are the British pushing so hard? I get that they love their democracy, but the Order hasn't threatened them, doesn't have any interest in the Core Worlds, we even have a treaty with the United Core World Authority, an enforcement organization that the British haven't pushed against in any significant way since the fall."

"It's the threat of us. They fear a purely survival of the fittest system that rewards higher thinking, strategy and hard work," Captain Kenly replied without hesitation or any sign of doubt.

Wheeler looked at him for a moment. He was plain-faced, with broad features, perfectly shaved from his neck to the top of his head. This was the best, most loyal man he could find as his second, and it was the right choice, but the Captain was boring. Loyalty was what Lucius needed, and he had it, but a sense of humour, maybe a little creativity would have been nice. Giving up on the man to provide anything but the correct and up to date information, Wheeler turned back to the balcony.

The sun shone on Haven Shore. The growing city was surrounded by thick jungle, and he imagined the fragrances on the wind were rich, thick with life. Far below, around the base of the Everin Building, his citizens were forming up, getting ready to go into the jungle as pickers, harvesters. He wished he could smell, or even feel the air through his armoured suit. It had to remain sealed for his own good, disconnected from the Order of Eden network, separate from everything.

Another work crew in grey and green began to fall in, moving to stand in straight lines by Order soldiers and supervisors. That crew of a hundred or so would go underground to the fabrication centre under the shuttle port. He hoped they'd be productive, cooperative, it was in their best interest to get to work. Haven Shore had to be self-sufficient if he was to prove the viability of Tamber as a real Order of Eden stronghold.

"I don't think the British Alliance or their people are strong enough to understand us, Sir," Captain Kenly said. "They're too soft, over forty-two percent of their settlements depend on support shipments from the government to survive. The Order would let these fall, consolidate the workforce on more productive worlds, point them to a real cause."

"I don't need the propaganda today, West," Wheeler replied. "I need this solar system to work, to make progress I can use to prove it can be self-sufficient so we don't end up serving Admiral Scanlon when she gets here. She can take care of the rest of the Cluster, I don't care, I just want the Haven System. How did the cracking crew aboard the second Solar Forge do?"

"They're boarding in a few minutes, I could have the mission status brought up in the main room, if you like," Captain Kenly said.

Wheeler looked at the city below for a moment. The tube cars were running again, moving people across the island at great speed. The garden was empty, Ayan's statue laid on its face, headless, one arm pulled away from the main body, severed. The statue was surprisingly heavy, well made, and it would take a work force to reduce it to pieces and carry it off. He didn't trust the robots to do it, they were too easy to hack, so he left that white corpse where it lay. People were free to visit the garden during their off-time, but few did. Maybe it was because of the statue in the middle, maybe it was paranoia. "I want these people to turn to the Order, but they're stubborn. I never would have imagined that anyone would take Ayan on as an icon. She's not much more than a clone, when you come right down to it, how can anyone follow a fake like that? Someone who isn't shining as brightly during her second chance after failing at life the first time through?"

"Maybe you only have to show them what hard work gets them and use a firm hand with the rest. It's the sort of thinking that propelled Tafford to his station."

"I know you respected the man, but I don't want to hear it. He underestimated his enemies and their resolve. He broke his promise to me, too. The Razer Knights died on his base ship in an elevator when they should have been with me. No, I think I need to speed things up a little, show the people what kind of strange freak Ayan was, that she was never worthy of their faith."

"I beg your pardon, Sir, but I can't see how. The former Queen may have made a few social mistakes, but there's nothing terribly abnormal there," Kenly offered.

"I have evidence of my own. The kind of thing that will get tongues wagging, people second-guessing. Have a little faith in my long-game, West. It may not be as good as it could have been, but a great long game can shift and rebuild itself if parts of it fail. Tafford and Dron pulled half of my plan apart, but I can still do something with what's left. It's that good."

"I look forward to seeing you execute it," Captain Kenly said. "The boarding team has just landed on Solar Forge Two."

"All right, put it on the holoprojector in the main room," Wheeler said as he left the balcony. He wished he could simply connect with the network and watch it on his own, but that would expose him to Dron, to anyone in the Order who had the keys to the framework system at the very heart of him.

"They're starting with Auxiliary Airlock Nineteen," the Captain said as one of his aides started the holographic display in the middle of the room.

It was huge, filling the entire centre of the deluxe apartment with a projection of such clarity that you could forget where you were. Wheeler had to admit, he enjoyed the luxuries of Haven Shore, even though he wasn't able to taste the food or smell the air. The soft seat he lowered himself into was fair consolation. The boarding team breached the airlock, their ship was perfectly moored with the station. "Have your scan results improved now that you're aboard, Commander?" he asked the leader of the mission.

"Very little so far, Admiral. It's like tunnelling into a giant onion; we're seeing this station in layers. I'm sorry to report that the outer and intermediate armour plating on this station are of a type we've seen several times before. The active plating Haven Fleet is using on their newer ships isn't present. Judging from that alone, I'd say this station may be two or even three full generations of technology behind."

"Keep moving towards your objective, Commander, I'm sure we'll find something that the Order can use," Wheeler said as he watched the team move towards the control centre of the station faster. "Is anything turning itself on?"

"No new energy readings yet, either our suits are shielding us from the station's passive scanners reading us as a threat, or that system isn't working here, Admiral."

Wheeler signalled to have the communications muted then addressed Captain Kenly. "How far in is Anderson's lab? Will they be passing anywhere near it before getting to a main control node?"

"We can't know for sure, but from the information we could gather, Anderson's lab is past the nearest node. They won't be approaching it until we have control of the station."

"Smart enough," Wheeler said with a nod. If there were anti-personnel traps aboard the station, they would be in the control section and the lab of the late Carl Anderson. The research behind the cure for framework technology was there, according to the little information they could get from the backup storage Anderson kept on Tamber. The drives re-crystalized several thousand times, destroying most of the data after they turned them on and failed to enter the right credentials, but they were able to extract a little data, just enough to lead Wheeler on this chase. Communications with the team were re-enabled. There was ambient light coming from somewhere ahead of the team. "Is that light coming from your gear, Commander?"

"It's from the station. We're detecting a bio-lighting system ahead, probably made to stay on for centuries."

"Are you sure something other than lighting isn't being powered? What about a passive scanner?" Captain Kenly asked. "Maybe some sort of basic detection system? Pressure plates? Something?"

"I'll keep my eyes open, but pressure plates on a high-tech base like this would surprise me," the Commander replied. "Moving into the manufacturing control room now," he said. There was a three-tiered area with monitoring and work stations in rings. To one side there was a thick transparent wall that provided a live view of one of the manufacturing lines. The Commander's team spread out, checking for systems that may have been left on, watching their passive scanners for signs that there were traps set up.

"Imagine, we'll be able to reproduce anything this facility made when we get control. We could start work on one of their ships in a few hours, have it in our hands for testing and examination in a couple days, maybe sooner," one of the aides said with wonder as the main holographic view focused on the observation deck of Solar Forge Two. "This is only one of three fabrication lines that we were able to find with passive scans, and there are probably more."

"Looks like we're ready for the technical team to come aboard," the Commander said. "Team leader to the X-1097, follow our path to Control Room Three."

Over a dozen technicians rushed onto the station, leaving a pilot in the X-1097, their armoured boarding ship. "It seems a little soon to send a technical team in," Wheeler said under his breath.

"Team's away, we're de-coupling and will start our first sensor sweep from the outside," said the pilot.

"Acknowledged. Don't hurry back, I think we'll be here for a few days," the Commander replied.

"Minor issue, Commander," the pilot said. "The mooring system won't de-couple. I'm working on it now, but it doesn't look like the problem is on our end."

"What do you mean, Sub-Lieutenant?" The Commander asked. "Exactly what do you mean?"

"The station's mooring system has coupled with us. My sensors still don't detect the mooring clamps, but my co-pilot can see that they're locked onto the shuttle, they didn't trigger the sensors aboard the X-1097, though."

"How can the station's mooring clamps move into place if there's no power?" Captain Kenly asked. "Are you sure your sensors are working, Commander?"

"Captain, I'm not sure of anything right now," the Commander said. "Hold on, one of the techs has something on her sensor package."

Wheeler saw the technician, a woman in a boarding suit, move into view with urgency. "The station's hacked our sensor systems, we can't trust the readings we're getting! This air-gapped system says the station core is operational, there's a power build up!"

"Get off the station, drop everything and move," Wheeler said, feeling a chill run up his spine. "That's an order."

"I don't know what we're supposed to do if our shuttle's being held by the station, but we're on the move," The Commander said, passing the order to his team with gestures.

"Throw yourselves out the nearest airlock, you all have independent life sup..." Captain Kenly was interrupted as the shuttle pilot began to shout into his communicator.

"The station is turning, moving fast! My tactical system says there's an exterior door opening, pointing at Solar Forge One."

"Show me an exterior, show me the orbital tactical map, now!" Wheeler ordered. The holographic view changed as a beam of white light fired from within Solar Forge Two at its older sister station. A moment later, Solar Forge Two exploded from within, becoming a yellow and white circle of light before disappearing, leaving a void behind. "What is that? What was that beam?"

"Some kind of power transfer?" Captain Kenly asked the room. One of his science officers got to work hurriedly.

Solar Forge One's gun emplacement doors opened and the turrets that survived the invasion, more than thirty-nine of them, roared to life, firing long range rounds at every Order of Eden ship it could strike. "Disable that base!" Wheeler ordered. A beam of light erupted from it, aimed directly at Solar Forge Three.

The Order of Eden ships were slow to react, many of them taking damage before they could get their combat shielding up. The smaller ships, the pickets, the fighters, even one of the destroyers were blasted apart. The face of Admiral Lamonthe appeared beside the tactical display. "You should have destroyed those bases when you saw us leave. Did you even ask yourself why they would go dormant as soon as you managed to defeat the other orbital defences around Tamber? I wonder about your fitness as an officer, as a strategist. I look at you in that suit and I see division in your ranks and paranoia in your mind. How much could you fear your own chain of command if you need a suit to keep transmissions to your framework system out? Do your subordinates know?"

"This is a live transmission, it's coming from Solar Forge One," said one of the officers in the room.

"How? They wouldn't leave him behind," Wheeler said.

"I remained behind. I'm in the Haven System right now with access, firepower and a grip on the building you're in right now. By the time you find the source of this transmission, I'll be gone. It's your uncertainty, your lack of faith in your own people and our ability to think ahead that will ensure our victory," Lamonthe said with a wolfish grin. "You are right where we want you: inside the Haven System, using facilities we know better than you ever will. Do you still feel like you're on the right side?"

"Cut him off!" Wheeler screamed. He knew the game the Admiral was playing. The questions, the speech wasn't for him, it was for anyone else listening in and everyone who would play it back later. The whole message was made to make everyone nervous about where they were as well as their Admiral. Some of that may have been true, but Wheeler didn't need anyone to know.

"His transmission is coming from Kambis, low orbit, there's a something there that just de-cloaked, we haven't gotten a good scan on it yet, it's the source of the transmission," reported the only communications officer in the room, a young man who worked feverishly on a thin pad.

"I look forward to seeing you in one of our cells," Lamonthe said. "The Queen sends her regards."

Lamonthe's head disappeared, and Wheeler looked back to the tactical display, where a cruiser with new electromagnetic beam systems was moving into position, getting close enough to try to disable Solar Forge One. As soon as its beam touched the station's hull, the hulking orbital installation exploded. Solar Forge Three burst in a circle of white fire an instant later, leaving massive voids in their wake. They lost twenty-eight orbital defence satellites and thirty-three planetary shield projectors, systems they were close to hacking and turning to their own purposes. It was a system that would take them months to repair without the Solar Forges or similar manufacturing systems. Another reason why the Order might remove him from his post, or worse. "Start scanning the system, I want..." he started, then a name appeared on the tactical map that filled him with dread: HF SUNSPIRE. "Get that ship! Disable and board it, and if you can't manage that, bring me what's left of its hull!"

The Sunspire moved towards Tamber, a broad signal was broadcast as it moved at incredible speed towards the nearest Order cruiser. "The power level of the signal its sending is cutting through everything, we're trying to decipher it now, but it looks like some kind of activation code," communications reported.

The rest of the defence satellites - both, shield and weapon - activated and began to use their small thrusters to send themselves towards Tamber's atmosphere. "They're making their own satellites burn up in the atmosphere so we can't use them," Wheeler said as much to himself in disbelief as he did to the rest of the room.

The Sunspire fired torpedoes that disappeared as soon as they left the launch tubes. "Cloaked torpedoes," Wheeler muttered under his breath. "Tell the crew of the Cruiser to brace."

Flashes along the perimeter of the Cruiser's shields went off, battering the energy field protecting it, then the hull itself was struck by violent antimatter explosions. The Sunspire continued to accelerate away, leaving the damaged Cruiser behind, reeling. It was the only ship in range that could stand up to a dreadnaught like the Sunspire, and Wheeler could see what was about to happen. "It can't cloak now, not with all that radiation in the area, but in a minute, that old ship will be gone," he said. "Fire everything at it, map its trajectory, get interdictors in the way and turn their signals up until their systems are about to fry."

"Aye," Captain Kenly replied, using a holographic interface of his own to help pass the orders faster. It would have been faster if Wheeler could connect to the Order Command Network, but he waited, watching from his armoured suit.

The Sunspire began to fade as sensors across the fleet they had in the Haven System started failing to detect it. "It's about to disappear, hurry!" Then, the icon marking the Sunspire on the tactical map did just that, leaving a trajectory line behind. "Now they change course and we are left here to stare at each other while you wonder what order I'll give next."

"I'm sorry, Sir, the fleet can only move so quickly," Captain Kenly said quietly but firmly. "We had no expectation that there could be a ship hiding in Kambis' clouds."

"Get out," Wheeler said. He was so angry he could bite through the faceguard of his helmet, but he kept it in check. "I have to move ahead with my plans and that will take concentration. Get out."

"Yes, Sir," Kenly replied, directing the rest of his people to leave with him. They did so quickly, leaving Lucius alone in an armchair. He closed his eyes, breathed deeply, and when he calmed a little, he stood and moved to the bedroom. The only thing on the large bed there was a long, white dress box. He patted the top and sighed. "You'll be getting some air sooner than expected."

FIVE

Interlude

AYAN TRACED her fingers lightly down one side of Jake's chest as her head rested on the other side. His arm around her, his hand resting idly on her hip under the covers, she felt more comfortable than she had in a long time. A glance up into his eyes brought a little smile to both their lips, and she nestled in a little more. "We're still very good at that," she sighed.

"Amazing," Jake chuckled. "I wish I had a little advanced warning, though."

"Why? Were you planning to put up decorations?" Ayan teased.

"I would have changed the lighting at least," Jake snickered. More seriously, then; "This feels right, though."

"Nothing has felt more right," she replied with a nod. It did, but there was guilt. It came from everything she missed, the Haven

System, the people she left behind, Alice, who was far behind enemy lines, and the children who were sent away for their own safety. She missed little Laura constantly, and in a moment like she was having, she wondered what kind of person she was if she could be so happy while her baby was so far away. If all went well, Laura and the rest of the children would be back in less than three days, but sending them away felt wrong in the first place. They took every precaution they could to protect them, but sending them away on a single ship, no matter how well armed, felt like the wrong move the instant Laura was out of her quarters. The thing that bothered her most about the whole situation was that she couldn't imagine a better solution during the Invasion or since. The act of calling the ship to the fleet's hiding place before they moved on felt almost as selfish as the happiness she was feeling with Jake as she cuddled with him.

"Your head is far, far away," Jake said quietly.

A tear rolled free and fell on his chest.

"Maybe it was too soon," he said, starting to shift.

"Don't you dare move," she told him, wiping the second tear away. "It was the perfect time, the perfect way. I didn't plan on jumping you after being in a meeting all day, but I wouldn't take it back. I was just thinking about Laura. I'm sorry, I know I should be more present."

"Don't apologize, I think about her all the time, too," Jake said, planting a kiss on her forehead. "And I didn't have hormonal treatments that helped me bond with her. Sending her away must have been hard."

"Do you think it was the right thing to do, though?"

"They're still safe?"

"Yes, and - this is top secret - they're on their way back," Ayan replied, propping herself up and looking at him. He was relaxed, at ease with how they were together in that moment. "That could be a bad decision too."

"Self-doubt has defeated as many generals as a sword," Jake replied.

"No quoting Academy reading," Ayan snickered, playfully slapping his chest. "Seriously, I feel like every decision I've made on this is either selfish or reckless."

He laughed and nodded. "The quote is true, though. Everyone in the fleet will do what they can to protect them, no matter where they are. Maybe it'll be better if the kids are living on the War Forge, where they're surrounded by the most armour, the biggest guns, and the best cloaking we have."

"It's also the biggest target if something can see through its cloak," Ayan said.

"You've already gone through all these details in your head and decided the War Forge will be the best place for them. Most of them will be living with their parents, that's a good thing. I know I miss Laura like crazy, so I couldn't imagine how it is for you, and she has to know you're not around right now."

The thought that Laura missed her too didn't make anything better. Ayan squeezed her eyes closed and tried to hold the ache of missing her down.

Jake caught her by surprise, wrapping his arms around her as he rolled onto his side, keeping her close. "I'm just saying that you've thought this through more than any decision you've made, and I'm sure you didn't do it alone, so you've done your best. You'll be back with Laura soon. All the parents will be reunited with their kids. I hope I can be there to see it. I bet every parent will be grateful that their children didn't have to see the Invasion."

Ayan remembered how he was with little Laura when he was able to visit the War Forge. He didn't have the most natural touch while handling Laura, but before long he was cradling her, even cooing at her when he thought no one was looking. 'Hello, little kiddo, everyone's happy you're here,' he told her several times in a hushed sing-song as Laura looked up at him. Catching him like that only made her love him more. "You really miss her too?"

"Of course I do. She's a little charmer," Jake said reassuringly.

"I was still a little afraid that I made things too complicated for you, turning the prospect of accepting me into having to take me and a new born," Ayan watched him closely, an easy thing since they were nose to nose.

"Laura is a bonus, not a negative. It's more complicated, sure, but I think skipping ahead to become a family is a good thing. We've spent so much time starting over, and with everything going on, it might have never happened if we kept waiting for just the right time."

"I've heard that from other people in relationships when they see Laura. Their eyes light up, then they get a little guarded, say they're waiting for the end of the war, or for the Haven System to be safe, or to have more time before they have kids with their partner. I just didn't think I'd take the leap so suddenly, then I saw Laura..."

"...and you couldn't wait," Jake whispered to her. "Hate to tell you this, but you aren't the spontaneous type. When you introduced me to her, I knew she was important to you."

"Sometimes I feel selfish, though. I'm so busy, I'm a target that could endanger anyone close to me, and there are other people who could adopt her who aren't first time parents. I need so much help to care for her."

"Everyone needs help. Everyone's busy right now, and I always thought you'd eventually be a mother. We never had the 'do you want kids?' conversation, I think it was because I thought I already knew the answer. I know you're only second guessing yourself because you finally have a minute to spare, and you can't wait to see Laura. I don't know if this helps, but I don't see a bad decision anywhere. I think you made the right calls. Now that you're delegating more, it'll get easier, and we can spend more time with Laura."

That was encouraging, but mostly because he said; "We?" she asked.

"Unless I get called away. I'd like to be more involved if that's okay, to help out, at least be around."

Ayan nodded. "Most romantic thing you've said all day."

"The bar was pretty low for that, considering we were in meetings with commanders for a whole day and the topic of romance didn't come up once," Jake said with a chuckle.

"We didn't do much talking after we adjourned either."

"True," he said, kissing her briefly. "How long can you stay?"

"Admiral Lamonthe is in command of the fleet for the next twelve hours, then it's Admiral Doolth's turn for the first time. Chief Onnel is running War Forge Operations, so unless an emergency comes up, I'm off tonight and tomorrow. The Merciless is probably going to be sent out tomorrow, though."

"Definitely," Jake replied. "Maybe you could stay aboard?"

"Hide in your quarters?" Ayan giggled. "That's a security decision..."

"You'll be back on the War Forge," Jake grumbled as he kissed her cheek, then started working his way to her ear.

"Yup, I'm off, but still too important to be your cabin mate," she said, squealing a little as he nibbled on her earlobe. "But what about that other question? The kids question?"

Jake stopped everything and looked her in the eye. "I like the prediction you saw, the one where we had two."

"So, yeah, you wanna have babies with me?" Ayan asked playfully.

"Definitely," Jake said.

Even though he was smiling, she could tell he was holding something back. "...but?"

"Maybe we should wait for the right time?" he asked, rolling his eyes at the notion.

Ayan laughed, she agreed, but she knew they were falling into the same trap they were just talking about. "Yeah, I'm not baby-crazy, and I took the stop shot anyway. It's reversible, but you're right, I'm just learning to be a mom with Laura. Doesn't mean we can't practice, though."

"Sounds like the right strategy to..." Jake started to say when his hall door opened.

Ensign Ottun entered carrying a large tray with a pair of large domes and four little domes covering plates and bowls. "The galley has sent something special for dinner since you and the Admiral are..." he caught sight of Jake and Ayan in bed and his Issyrian eyes shifted into large round, bright green circles as he froze. "Oh no! I've interrupted your sacred breeding time! I had no idea the Admiral was carrying mature eggs! My congratulations and deepest apologies. I will make the appropriate announcements and prepara-tions for your impending fertilization." He turned back towards the door.

The look on his face and everything that followed was enough to send Ayan into a sudden burst of hysterics. Jake's response didn't help; "Wait! It's just uh, a practice session! No banners or announcements, okay?"

"Are you certain?" he started looking towards them but returned his gaze to the wall beside the door instead. "I'm sure most of the fleet would celebrate your pairing."

"I'm sure. You should talk to Agameg. He can, uh, tell you about the cultural differences," Jake said. "We don't celebrate this. Well, not the same way. I mean, we'll celebrate, but it's different with humans. Just ask Agameg."

"I will. So, is this or is this not a private occasion?" he asked.

"It is. Talk to Agameg," Jake said, trying not to smile.

Ayan was recovering from her fit of laughter, happy Jake saw the humour in it. He'd probably crack up too, if he didn't have to play the part of senior officer. She saw that Ottun was about to leave with the tray and she called after him. "Leave the food!"

"Oh, yes," he said, leaving the food on the table, averting his gaze most of the time but sneaking a peek at the sheet-clad pair more than once. "I am sorry if I caused offense or interrupted your ritual."

"It's all right, I forgot you had full access now. Take the night off, all right?"

"Oh, thank you," Ottun replied. "After I speak to Agameg, I assume?"

"Yes."

"I will do so immediately." He left through the door leading directly onto the bridge before Jake could stop him. Ashley and Kadri turned towards the door to see who was emerging, and as they both saw past Ottun for a moment, they spotted Jake sitting up, frozen half way through making a gesture that was part of an urgent plea for the Ensign to use the other door that came too late. The door closed behind him.

Jake flopped back down beside Ayan, who was laughing again. "He's really good at what he does," he sighed. "Come a long way in a short while."

"I'm sure," Ayan said as she started recovering. "At least it won't be a scandal."

"True," Jake agreed. "I think I'll set up privacy mode."

He started to sit up and Ayan pulled him back down, taking a moment to address the system in the cabin. "Captains' Quarters: Privacy Mode, Medium Lighting." The lighting lowered and the wall surrounding the dais the bed was on raised, creating a bedroom space that included his dresser, bed, a shallow closet and his bathroom.

"I didn't know it did that," Jake said. "I use the buttons on my comm or the console."

"Read the manual, Commodore," she said against his lips before kissing him. His arms slipped around her and she sighed as he pulled her closer. It felt like he was aiding in her escape from every worry that was weighing her down, and as she relaxed even more against him, she realized that one of her worries was how the very thing they were up to would be again. It was a relief to know that she didn't have to worry any longer. Things had changed, being with him was different, he was more attentive and reactive, even more present and aware than before. They were changes that made her wish he was stationed aboard the War Forge, an Admiral beside her as he ought to be, but she knew he was living his dream, commanding a ship of his own with an amazing crew.

He rolled with her in his arms. On top, his kiss was more intense but no more urgent, he was taking his time and her head spun. He'd go along with a promotion to Admiral. He'd take a place on the War Forge, especially if she told him about the ship secreted in its centre, especially if she gave him command of the station's defence. Ayan knew it would be selfish, it wasn't where he wanted to be, it would change their relationship, change him. Ayan wouldn't do it, not after getting back together with him and realizing that she didn't want him to change, the man she was in love with was better than any she'd known, even the previous versions. She only hoped he felt the same way and didn't dream of another Ayan.

SIX

The One?

TWISTED trees that seemed unsure of what shape they were supposed to take littered a soft soil landscape. The brown earth, rivulets of green water running between puddles was only disturbed by two sets of footsteps. Unarmoured, Alice ran to the side of the one of the few shard-like stones to break the surface of the terrain. It was several times her height, but the dark surfaces had handholds and could be turned to her advantage if she could make it there.

Iruuk gave chase, dropping to all fours, more than doubling his speed as he leapt to a tree, caught firm purchase on the wood beneath its delicate bark, then pounced on Alice from behind and above. To his dismay, she stopped running, crouched then rolled backwards so Alice was behind him when he landed. He tried to twist, to turn in time to defend, but she kicked him hard behind the knee. The Neural Simulator, or brain bud as most people called it, delivered pain as she struck, pain that told him that his right leg would be hamstrung until he massaged the limb thoroughly. Well, it would be if he was struck that way in the real world, anyway.

Capitalizing on his momentary compromised balance, Alice dropped her weight onto his shoulder, sending him into the mud as she moved on to roll to her feet, continuing her rush to the large stone ahead. He watched her get away as he pulled himself up and scraped mud from the fur under his jaw and neck. Alice was quick for a human and she formulated strategies without much effort, shifting with changing conditions. He massaged his leg, easing it just enough so it would move properly again. The simulation was made to be accurate, but he wished a moment's massaging would work the injury out completely, instead he'd have to put up with pain every time he put weight on the limb until he unplugged. When he was satisfied that he could move well enough, Iruuk started for the stone, stalking this time, clearing his mind so he'd be ready to react to her next trick. Imagining what she might do next was pointless during exercises like this. There was little point in trying to predict someone's next act when they had a talent for considering more options than most people thought existed, especially when self-sacrifice wasn't a forbidden concept. It was one of the things that frightened Iruuk about her.

Alice disappeared behind the large standing stone and took a moment to catch her breath. Iruuk was coming, she could hear his steadying gait. He could fight his way through the pain of a deeply bruised muscle, she couldn't trust that she could use that to her advantage. Her feet bumped something solid just under the dirt beside the stone face, and she pulled it out of the mud. It was a staff, roughly hewn from wood, but put there by whoever designed the scenario. She could use it to even the odds if she liked, get a little practice with a primitive weapon. Alice had spent time practicing with blades and other basic arms, but she didn't want to change the odds, not this time.

His footsteps drew closer, she leaned the staff against the rock face beside her silently, then he stopped making any sound. The stone was a few times taller than her, but he could jump that. He could come from overhead, it was important to remember that he always thought in three dimensions. Her empathic sense was dead inside the simulation, it was one of the advantages she'd use to guess what he was going to do next, how easy he could be to startle, or if he was in an emotional state that could muddy his thinking, like anger. For most people, that made their thinking direct, their strategies simple, but she couldn't feel anything empathically in the digital realm, so she waited for his strike.

Long moments passed, and she thought he must be on the other side of the stone. There was no sign that he was doing anything else. Then she heard a scrape above. He was swinging down from atop the stone, she shouldn't have been so passive, she realized, and she only had time to half dodge his attack. He firmly kicked her in the side, sending her against the unyielding rock face, and the wind was knocked out of her so thoroughly that she couldn't counterattack, only drop, roll and stagger into a run that took her away from both her advantages; the stone and the staff.

To make matters worse, she was moving slowly on open ground. Alice turned towards him and stood ready, trying to catch her breath, every breath came with pain. Her side was wet. Her hand touched there and came away bloody, two of his claws broke the skin. Iruuk stalked towards her, hunter's eyes taking her in from head to toe. "You probably have two broken ribs," he said. "It was a good try, it took me several minutes to land a good blow on you, but it's over."

Alice looked to her right, there was a tree there that she could put between her and him. "You can push through, I can push through," she said. "That leg must be burning like crazy, like a charley horse every time you move, most Nafalli would be dragging it, not walking on it."

"You just woke me up, that's all," Iruuk said.

She liked that side of him, the hunter side. It only came out in simulations, but their rivalry made them both better, especially her. The moment he put a brain bud on, he became a hunter, and he was rarely beaten one-on-one by any member of the crew. Alice gnashed her teeth at the pain as she rushed for the thick, twisted tree nearest her, and he ran after her, only catching up once the trunk was between them.

Alice didn't stop running, but came around the tree, screaming in agony as the wounds in her side protested her next act. She caught a thick overhead branch and swung her legs up at Iruuk, who had caught up with her easily. He ducked, she let go and was about to slide off his back but took handfuls of fur as handles. She paid a price in agony for every movement, but she was turned around with one hand deeply nested in the fur between his shoulders by the time she stopped moving. He tried to reach back to dislodge her, but she punched him in the back of the neck, just below the base of the skull as hard as she could. If she was in a vacsuit with a synthetic muscle layer, he would have been knocked out. He roared instead, turned his back towards the tree and before she could drop off his back, he pinned her between his muscled back and the trunk.

The feeling of a crunch in her chest and a wave of pain preceded the end of the combat challenge. The simulated agony ended for them both, and they were on top a cliff overlooking their battleground. Brown earth, dark barked twisted trees and green pools stretched out as far as she could see under four moons. Three of them were rocky, the fourth and smallest was blue-green. "I should have seen that coming," she laughed. "Getting crushed between you and a tree."

"It was either that or try to drop onto my back and drown you in that big puddle," Iruuk said. "I really didn't expect you to get a grip on my back. It was annoying. You're getting even better, more inventive."

"I've still only beat you twice."

"Three times," Iruuk said. "The one where you used batons counts."

"I guess, I just like victories where neither of us pick up the weapons, unless the point of the exercise is to practice with them."

"We have to do more practice with those arm blades you used on the Order Knights. Everyone wants to learn that, and I know you want to get better," Iruuk said, sitting down with her on the cliff's edge. "The crew wanted me to talk to you, by the way."

"About blade fighting? Practice is better than talk," Alice replied, aware that it wasn't what he meant. She'd managed to avoid it, but there was a conversation coming that she could do without.

"You know what you did," Iruuk said with a sigh. "You left me on the ship along with half your crew when you knew Lewis and Ute could have taken care of everything aboard, and you sent everyone away when you needed them most. You should have been killed on the bridge of that ship, Theodore would have been taken, and the antimatter bomb would have gone off, killing him too. That was too risky, we can't afford to lose you."

"Sure, you can," Alice retorted irritably. "I hate the idea that all the crap I've been through makes me special, that I'm somehow precious. Everyone's had bad times, learned hard lessons. How am I special, really?"

"You've been through things no one else has, and you've been tested at the academy, then as a captain, and you're amazing. Everyone on the crew knows it, and they followed your orders because they respect you, but they knew it was wrong. They should have stayed behind to fight beside you, to improve your odds. That's only common sense."

"Everything turned out fine, I'm alive, Theo's fine, so how could the way I changed the plan be wrong when the outcome was the best we could hope for?"

Iruuk sighed and shook his head. "Fine, fine, so you took on several Knights, used their bridge for a propaganda piece that's working, and it all came out fine. That just goes further to prove my other point. You're one in a billion, too important for that kind of risk when you have a crew that wants to have your back. Some of them wonder if you trust them at all."

Callum came to mind immediately. He was the most insecure on that point, she could feel it whenever her empathic sense was open and they were both on the Clever Dream. She put that point aside, though, it was something she'd have to work on with him. "I refuse to accept that I'm this mythical special one. You scored higher than me in almost everything in the Academy, Ute and half the people on the crew are better pilots, several of you are better shots, Yawen is a better fighter most of the time, and anyone can learn to read people without having special abilities. The way you read people when you're in a combat simulation, like a hunter, can be applied out there pretty easily. I'm not so special, I just made Captain first. I even cheated a little there; my Mother is the Defence Minister, well, Fleet Admiral now because we lost Haven, but you get my point. If your Dad was an admiral, then you could be a Captain too."

"He respects personal achievement too much for that. Your Mother wouldn't have given you the rank of Captain if she didn't think you could handle it either. You're an obvious candidate."

"I'm not some kind of Chosen One, that's something for old action movies and religions, not for you guys."

"I can't find anyone else with your range of experiences and you've been at the centre of more events, more victories than almost anyone," Iruuk countered calmly.

"By that logic, my Father and Mother are both 'Chosen Ones,' along with Minh-Chu, Yawen because she was one of the few successful rebirths, Theodore because he's seen so much, along with Noah who survived for a year on his own before getting to the Haven System, and so many other people who have had special experiences and been witness to huge events. You can't have a 'Chosen One' when you can find people who fit that label every-where you turn. Even Ute fits that because she's one of the best pilots in the fleet and is the only Mergillian aboard the Clever Dream. Even you - a young, high scoring Academy graduate who happens to be Nafalli that loves science as much as a good hunt - you're special enough to be The One too, Fur-Face. Besides, what does that kind of label lead to, anyway? Overconfidence, some kind of messiah complex?"

Iruuk laughed for a moment, shaking his head and covering his nose. The notion that he could be as special as anyone she mentioned seemed to amuse and embarrass him. "Well, okay, so we're surrounded by special people. There is no 'Chosen One,' not even you. By that thinking, you should take help from your crew whenever it increases the odds of success because you're not so special. You've used them so little since we got to this region of space, too. They want to be part of these investigative missions you've been running, especially since you're so recognizable now."

Alice nodded slowly. "Yeah, that would make sense, but - and I know this blows my 'I'm not The One' argument a little - I'm still empathic. It didn't go away after I nearly got my brain scrambled by the last Geist I went up against. I've been looking for a way to tell you and the rest of the crew. I can read people and see betrayal coming way ahead."

Iruuk's eyes widened and he brought his nose close to hers. "Can you tell what I'm thinking right now?" he asked in a hushed tone.

"Empathy," Alice snickered. "How you're feeling. Nafalli are easy to read, you guys are pretty emotional, it's a good thing. You don't suppress much. It doesn't work in simulations, though. Oh, and I usually block it while I'm on the ship. It can get noisy."

"Oh. Pick up anything interesting?" Iruuk asked, still a little eager to know more.

"Well, you got really excited on spaghetti night. I've never seen anyone who gets so happy about food."

"Well, yeah, but I'm talking about the rest of the crew," Iruuk said.

"You're pretty much right about how people feel about me leaving them behind on the base ship, but I'll keep the other stuff to myself. I don't want to use this for gossip, it's complicated enough."

"So it really got stronger? It didn't fade? The science we have said it could fade over time until you completely lose the ability."

"Unless I practice," Alice said.

Iruuk gasped at a realization. "Did you use it on Noah?" He didn't have to wait for an answer, her blushing and the lowering of her head was enough. "You did! Oh, that must make your mating rituals so much easier! There's normally so much guess work with humans, but if you can tell what he's feeling, it must be so easy."

"It got easier when I stopped, actually," Alice said quietly, smiling a little at the memory of their first kiss. "Yeah, knowing he liked me, was a little crazy about me in a way was a huge help, but when I was feeling his reaction to me I wasn't sure about my own. Not really sure, things get mixed up. I could get lost in his feelings, take them in like a high, and how I feel gets buried. When I turned all that off and listened to what was going on in my head when I was with him, well, then it got really good. Turns out I'm really crazy about the real Noah too, not the guy who I got to know in his journals. They're one in the same, I know him pretty well as it turns out, but it could have been an infatuation, I could have been in love with who he was on Iora."

"But you're in love with all of him," Iruuk said with a big grin.

"I wouldn't say love,"

"But you did."

"I was talking about infatuation, what could have happened if meeting Noah was a disappointment. I'd say we're in that happy, crazy beginning time. It's good, but I couldn't call it love, especially since we haven't seen each other in about ten days."

"You're counting the days!" Iruuk cried enthusiastically, his muzzle pointed up at the purple and red sky. "It's adorable!"

"Oh, it could all come to a crashing halt, don't get too excited, Fur-Face," Alice grumbled.

"Wait, why?"

"I haven't told him I'm an empath yet. I don't tell everyone because I'm sure it'll freak some people out, and being an empath, I can feel that. People who want to shrink away from me once they know, I'm sure it'll happen, but I don't want it to happen with Noah."

"Have you asked Theo how he thinks Noah will react? Maybe it won't be a big deal."

"That's a good idea. I'll ask him, but I know there will be a reaction, something will change."

Iruuk looked out over the landscape, calming down. "I guess so. Maybe it won't be bad, though. If it makes you feel better, I don't feel any different. You could already read me before, when we were in the Academy. Unless you were an empath then?"

"No, I don't think so. Besides, I missed a lot of big things there, like one of my classmates being infatuated."

"I still feel pretty good about throwing him down the hallway. Don't tell Fleet, though."

"No worries," Alice said. "Think I should tell the crew I'm an empath before the next mission?"

"Ask Theodore, but maybe not. It's an important meeting, it could be better if they're focused. I won't tell anyone either, don't worry."

"Thanks, I was dreading this conversation, but I should have known you'd be cool about it."

"I am the embodiment of cool, it's what I bring to the crew," Iruuk boasted exaggeratedly.

"I thought you were a science and scanner genius with impressive combat skills."

"Yeah, but isn't that cool? I'm so cool."

"You just like using that word, don't cha?"

"A bit," Iruuk said. "Guess we should unplug and get back to work."

"Yeah, the meeting is in a few hours, we have to get some scouting done," Alice agreed. "Thanks for the talk, Fur-Face."

SEVEN

The Docks

ONE OF SHAMUS Frost's earliest memories was watching the ships as they moved through a port. There was a debate as to which port it was, on Sellus, or Marou, or Gamintrad, or even some other world where his mother dragged him when he was too young to snip the apron strings. It didn't matter. He remembered watching in awe as heavy vessels defied gravity. Whether they were blockish, small freighters with scraped paint or sleek, speedy looking ships, it didn't matter. He was mesmerized at how they moved through the air, how the port defence cannons tracked some of them, turning their barrels to match their course, and how men in big exo-suits that made them look mighty, able to push a ship, pick up a heavy load and walk it into a cargo hold, or hover around so they could repair small cracks in a hull with bright welders set the stage for the rest of his life.

Those fixtures, that scene made Shamus McFadden more comfortable on the docks, around those things than anywhere else. He secretly celebrated when his application to work at the Haven Shore Shuttle Dock was approved, and when he saw David that morning, a fellow that was rescued by the Triton and crew from a slaver before they discovered the Rega Gain system, he was even happier. He was on Stephanie's list, one of the people who she used at the docks, and minutes after orientation, David bumped into him, signalling that he knew who Frost really was despite his mask.

The shifts on the docks were long, they were dangerous because the exo-skeletons that were in use were bulky suits that made each operator feel like a walking tank unto themselves. It was easy to get bored, moving stasis crates filled with fruit and replacement parts onto transport shuttles. It was easy for Frost to peek at the contents of crates, the guards were busy trying to direct the exo-suit clad workers.

Finally, when Frost and David could sit together while they ate Forma Meal Bars - not the kind of lunch he would have chosen - they were able to talk. The guards were back to their patrols, watching the port's personnel entrances and exits, walking the perimeter outside the loading area, with only a couple trying to play director to the twenty-eight people in heavy suits. As they sat on empty, broken crates in one corner of the docks, Frost shook his head. "This is the kind of thing I didn't think I'd ever see again. People in open frame exo-suits minding the docks? I would have expected bots to take over."

"They don't trust them," David said. "The Order of Eden says they're giving us these jobs so we can have opportunities, but they really expect people here to hack anything they switch on. They're paranoid. Good thing I got used to paranoid people. People who drive slave crews on ships always are."

"You were on one for years, aye?" Frost asked.

"Too long," David nodded. "This isn't as bad, though. All the guards are out to catch saboteurs or some kinda resistance fighter, but we're playing a longer game and they're stretched thin. Bringing the population of every Haven settlement to Haven Shore have them outnumbered pretty badly."

"Yeah, but they still have the guns, and the orbital strike power," Frost said. "We revolt, things get out of control, and they can just wipe whole buildings out."

"I heard something," David said. "They're starting work on a whole new manufacturing line tomorrow. It's going to be on a barge next to the island."

"They still can't get into the Solar Forges?" Frost asked.

"No, they self-destructed." A guard was about to come into earshot, and David pulled a bite of his forma bar, a chunk of gummy yellow and blue swirl, and held it out to the guard. "Hey, just wondering, do you know what flavour this is?"

"I don't eat that anymore," the guard scoffed, pushing his helmet visor up. He was young, amused by the older worker. "I pay for the upgrade, so I don't think I've had that one. Maybe work here for a while and you'll be able to afford upgraded eats too."

"Yeah, that would be something," David replied.

"Or maybe you could borrow a few hundred credits, start paying for the upgrades sooner. I've got extra credit, I could be your first supporter," the guard offered quietly.

"I think I could eat this stuff for a few more days. If I get tired of it, I'll look you up."

"Here, send me a pulse on this once you get fed up with the

forma," the guard said, handing David a thin, narrow strip of plastic. "You think you'll be looking for a loan, old-timer?"

Frost didn't mind being called an old-timer, he got access to age suppression meds late, it was how the guards were offering to loan people credit that made him want to knock the fellow out and stuff him in a crate. Collecting high interest on loans to newcomers to the Order was how many of them elevated themselves, and the loans seemed like a good idea to some who were getting tired of cramped, basic living, but they always added up to more debt. David took one of the small comm strips, though, so Frost did as well. "Might not hear from me for a while, but sure," Frost said.

"Great, I get a couple credits every time you use those comms, so don't be shy with 'em," the guard said as he moved off.

"We pay for every second, too," David muttered as the guard moved out of earshot. He slipped Frost the little plastic communicator. "Hand these off to your connection, maybe she can reprogram them."

They were so thin that Frost didn't realize that David handed him three instead of one until he dropped them into his pocket. His connection would probably be able to do just that, it was a decent solution to their communication blackout. "Thanks, come up with this idea on your own?"

"Well, a guard gave me the idea. They're all hot to start loaning us Order newbies money so they can start collecting interest. If I keep taking their comm slips, I'll eventually have to take a loan out with one of them, though."

"Yeah, I'll collect a couple more too," Frost said. "She'll be able to do something with 'em. Do they listen passively?"

"Not until they're attached to your skin, that's where they get their power from," David replied. "Anyway, I've noticed you've kept your mouth shut while you watch the new loader operators fumble around. That must be... difficult."

"There have been moments where I wanted to start shouting people back in order, teaching them how to work as a team. The guards don't know a damn thing about running a loading crew. Was it that easy to tell I was biting my tongue?"

"I'm afraid so," David said. "You've gotta do better. Someone with half a brain will notice you grumbling and grimacing eventually, and you're too important to get caught, especially now that you're where you can watch what's coming and going."

It was surprising and a little irritating to be told how to act by someone at least ten years his junior, but David was on the docks a week longer and he probably had a good eye for things that might draw attention, so he simply nodded. "I'll get that under control, don't you worry."

"Oh, and it would help if you screwed up once or twice. You haven't made a misstep since you got into a loader suit."

"Good point," Frost replied.

"Any news from below?" David asked before taking his last bite of meal bar. He tried to chew it but stopped. The density of it was sometimes a bit much, so he let it warm up and soften in his mouth before trying to chew again.

"Nothing since all our suits and comms were taken. I'm going below next chance I get," Frost said.

"Careful, there are scan crews now. They scan and count who is in each apartment without having to open the doors."

"I saw that," Frost whispered. "Well, Sam saw that. One guy with a hand scanner and two guards backing him up."

"Our watch only saw one after curfew," David nodded. "So far, anyway."

"I'll be careful. We've gotta get communication going again though."

"Up! Everyone up!" A guard standing on top of a large crate called. "Lunch break's over, ships are coming."

The large hatch in the warehouse side of the docks opened and an industrial elevator pad with enough crates to keep them busy for an hour rose up. There would be more. These had new markings on them, a triangle that pointed down with a starburst on the point. He was pretty sure he knew what they were but decided that it was time for a little performance so he could make sure. "Time for a little slip and tumble trouble," Frost said under his breath as he and David parted.

Frost could wear the bulky, boxy loader suit and operate it as though it was an extension of himself. He was one of the first to arrive at the new batch of crates, probably filled with the first things that the old fabricator was turning out somewhere beneath the port. Samantha was down there, the Order made use of her experience as a fabrication materials expert as she predicted, and it was her second shift. He was glad she wouldn't see what was about to happen.

There was a small crate that had cracked open and wasn't properly put off to the side for re-inspection and resealing. It was close enough for him to make it part of his first screw up. With a jagged motion that he was sure would make him look more amateur, he picked up a pristine crate from the industrial elevator, then started stepping backwards, aiming for one of his fellow loaders. "Hey! Watch out!" the driver behind him cried as Frost veered away, still stepping backwards but past the fellow he almost struck.

"Sorry!" Frost called out an instant before he caught the small cracked crate underfoot, crushing it. The fruit inside burst, sending juices and pulp across the deck.

"Hold! Hold! You there!" A guard shouted as he and his partner rushed to them. "Stop!"

Frost dropped the crate in the loader's hands. It landed exactly the way he wanted it to, one corner bashing onto the hard deck and the lid flipped open, sending industrial fabricator print heads across the deck. At a glance, Frost guessed that they were the right size for the type of fabrication systems aboard larger Order ships. Cheap manufacturing systems were always hard on detailing and extrusion heads, especially when they were printing armour panels and other parts that had to be replaced when repairing combat damage. "By garp, I'm sorry!"

"That's coming out of your pay, you moron!" one guard said. " Now, get down out of that loader so you can clean all this up. You're going to make this deck shine, and Hampon help you if you dented the deck, that's a kind of debt you can't work off, not unless you're a Lieutenant."

"I'm sorry, I'll get on it," Frost said, trying to pretend that he was as nervous and fearful as one ought to be, but he wanted to grin. If they went through all their print heads repairing damage and needed thousands more to replace them, that meant there was more damage. More than the invasion caused, so there was still fighting somewhere in or near the solar system. It was good news, encouraging news.

The guard was behind him the moment he was down from the loader. Frost tried to look afraid as the man grabbed his shoulder and marched him, like a child, to the edge of the splattered fruit. "Did you even see that crate? Obviously not, since you made a huge mess of it. What was it doing there, anyway?"

"I don't know, Sir," Frost said with a tremble. It wasn't much of a stretch. He was trembling under the effort of holding himself back. Shamus wanted to steal the guards' rifle and beat him with the butt of it until he was as splattered as the mess in front of him. "I'll clean it right now."

"Damn right," the guard said, shoving Frost towards the mess.

Frost slipped, his cheap shoes sliding through the muck of smashed fruit and he let himself fall, landing on his side. The laughter of the guards made him furious, but he breathed through it, tried to make the anger look like fear. It must have worked, because the guards were moving onto other things by the time he was on his feet. Before the guard that marched him over to the mess could get out of earshot, Frost called out. "I'm sorry," Frost said, unable to help himself. "I just want to know who to report to once I'm finished."

"Sergeant Lamb," the guard who treated him like a peasant replied. "Just report to the deck officer in charge. I'll be off shift by then, probably living it up in the restricted zone, so I won't want to hear from you, boy."

Frost nodded and turned away. If the guard saw his expression then, at being pushed a little further, he was sure there would be trouble. He was in luck, no one paid him much mind at all as he used whatever tools he could find to clean up the huge mess he'd made. Five hours later, near the end of his shift, the deck was perfectly clean, even polished thanks to an attachment he found at the back of the warehouse. He'd broken two print heads, and that was enough to set him back so far that he would need two and a half years to pay the debt off if he managed to keep his loader job.

EIGHT

Meeting Legends

"THIS IS TERRIBLE NEWS," Iruuk said as he joined Alice on the ramp on the lower deck of the Clever Dream.

She finished adjusting her long coat, it felt substantial around her, heavy and comforting even over her plain looking vacsuit. It was still fleet issue, only she'd changed the colour so she wouldn't be immediately recognized. It wouldn't help much since her face was featured in the footage captured while she killed Admiral Tafford, but that recording was banned, considered high contraband in Order of Eden territory. Only those who went to great lengths to obtain restricted recordings and high ranking military would have seen it, and that worked for her. If someone recognized her, she could immediately sense which one they were. The rebellious sort she needed to meet were always excited to see her, while the officers and spies for the Order would react differently, she was sure. The latter, she hadn't met since the footage came out, so she wasn't absolutely certain, but she kept her senses as open as she could so she could notice them. "What's up, Fur-Face?" He was concerned for someone else, it ran deep.

"Theo finally found a few codes that were still able to access the local Order network here, and he found plans to turn this planet into a brood world. The Edxi are demanding compensation for the losses they took in the Haven System, and since this solar system has a terraformed world and two habitable moons, this is going to be one of the places they'll be given," Iruuk said. He had his armour retracted so it looked like a triangle of plates and thick vacsuit material covered his torso.

"When will the broods start arriving?"

"It'll be a week at the earliest, but they're changing nothing. No plans to extract anyone but Order officers, the mining and cultivation programs will run until the Edxi take over, so the workers and the rest of the people will remain on the planet. It's not just the brood ships, either, they're going to have military hives."

"So..." what Alice was putting together in her head wasn't ready to be said aloud yet. There was much more to consider if the whole planet was about to be overrun. "I have to think about this."

"We'll be meeting with the resistance leader in a few minutes," Iruuk said.

"I have to give him this news the right way. If I just drop in with nothing but doom and gloom, he could spin out, do something unpredictable, even make things worse."

"How could anything he does make things worse than Edxi domination?" Iruuk asked.

"Good question. I'm sure there's an answer neither of us want to hear."

"Right, I don't want an answer to that one." Iruuk stepped in beside her and was quiet for a moment. "Are you sure you want me on this mission?"

"You wanted to get off-ship more, and I want them to see we aren't just a bunch of humans. Just keep your eyes open for anything I miss, I'm going to be concentrating on the meeting."

"All right," Iruuk said. He was nervous, normally it would be amusing, but she needed him to be watchful.

"Hey, this is going to be simple, and if it isn't, I know you can handle yourself, so relax and enjoy the sights," Alice told him quietly. "Take a few deep breaths while I think for a couple minutes."

Iruuk nodded and sucked a long breath in. It would have been nice to have a problem so simple as pre-meeting jitters, but her issues were far worse. The proposal she had for Peter was challenging enough before. With the news of an Edxi takeover, it changed completely.

THERE WERE ONCE great attractions on the world of Nuaji. Peter grew up watching tourists from across several sectors visit monuments to nature, exciting attractions and places of wonder. As a boy he got to know many of them, almost all, in fact. The Inverse Gardens were one of the few that he hadn't seen until the tourists were gone. When the Order of Eden decapitated and replaced their government, the tourists stopped coming. The attractions were shut down, the people who worked there were relocated by regional government and a few Order representatives.

The Inverse Gardens were abandoned. The transit train that led there was closed, but there were new residents before long.

The narrow, ancient lava tunnels surrounding the tall, empty main vent were filled with hidden caves. Sensors couldn't penetrate the rock,thanks to the combination of minerals within, and not even Peter knew how many of his people hid in the labyrinth. Everyone knew what was about to happen, he was going to meet with one of the most successful and violent rebels against the Order. They'd seen the footage of her executing Admiral Tafford, some of them even tried to prove it was fake by analysing it, but no one could. With the efforts the Order took to hide and delete copies of the recording, Peter knew it was real. He also knew that Haven Fleet claimed credit for several instances of mass destruction. All of them were military targets, major facilities that the Order of Eden wouldn't be able to rebuild overnight.

"Nervous?" Sonny asked him.

Peter looked around the landing platform in the main vent. Faint starlight leaked in from far above. A few lights and bioluminescent plants painted the overgrown walls in hues of blue and green. Thick hanging vines and climbing foliage had taken over since the caretakers left the Inverse Gardens on their own. Ornamental plants that needed care were choked or starved out by heartier, more aggressive growth so much so that some of the windows across from the platform were nearly completely overgrown. What was once a curated, lovely garden inside the main flute of a dormant volcano had become a riotous vertical jungle, and he loved it. "How could I be nervous here?"

"We could have more people cover us. There are a lot of fighters here now that the meeting has been called," Sonny said in a whisper. "A couple snipers could set up."

"We agreed to meet in a safe place where two of us could meet two of them. The room behind this platform is perfect, I don't expect this is a trap."

"You've missed traps before," Sonny said.

"Survived those too," Peter replied with a reassuring smile. "This is going to be one of the more interesting moments of our lives. Everything could turn on this meeting. I believe she really is here to help us, and people like her may look like they work alone, but they don't. If this goes well, we will find many friends in the galaxy."

"I feel like you keep me around just because I'm your personal pessimist," Sonny sighed.

"You take good care of me," Peter replied, momentarily cupping Sonny's cheek. The stubble along his jaw was another sign of nervousness. He was skipping parts of his routine, and it made Peter wonder for a moment before he whispered; "Thank you."

The leaves rustled, and a ship appeared as it came down. Its thrusters didn't roar but whispered low as it stopped to hover over the far end of the landing platform. The ramp lowered and Alice stepped down with a gigantic Nafalli at her side. The ship, sleek, black and nimble looking, left the way it came, up through the hollow vent. "See? She brought one companion."

Sonny stared at the Nafalli and snickered. "Oh, sure, I measure up perfectly."

Alice's eyes met his without flinching, it was as though she saw right through the scars, and he returned her easy smile, feeling like he did before his attractiveness was destroyed. "Welcome to the Inverse Gardens," he said, accepting a handshake from her. Alice retracted her gloves before taking his hand, and he was surprised to find her hands calloused. They weren't fresh, hard workers callouses, but different, like a gymnast might have.

Then he shook Iruuk's hand and was instantly charmed as the

massive creature grinned down at him. He seemed excited to meet him, almost boyish. His hand was huge, but his grip wasn't too firm, and the fur around it was warm. "I've never seen anything like this place," he said. "I'm Iruuk."

"It's good to meet you," Peter replied. "We're going to speak in that room there," he said, turning and directing them to the old apartment set back from the landing pad. Its floor to ceiling windows were dingy, a few younger vines were starting to reach down from the edge above them. "Like the rest of this cave, it defeats sensors, so we can guarantee the secrecy of this meeting."

"The Order has satellites that may detect your ship if it wanders. You'll want to warn your crew not to go far from the volcano," Sonny suggested.

"The Order hasn't been able to crack our cloaking yet," Alice replied. "Thank you for the advice, though."

"Oh, so it's true. Your fleet has superior cloaking field technology?" Sonny asked.

"For now," Alice replied.

"There are ways to defeat every kind of cloak," Iruuk said. "The more we encounter the Order of Eden, the closer they'll get to defeating our protection, it's only a matter of time, but with the kind of tech we have, we should be able to hold the advantage for some time."

"So, does your fleet share technology?" Peter asked as he entered the apartment. There were a few wicker seats set up in a circle with a low table in the middle.

"We share some, but not all," Alice said. "Was there something your people are interested in?"

"I'm sure there would be some interest, but I didn't have anything in mind when I was asking. I'm sure the few ships we have could do with some upgrades, but we don't have anything large, or have bases that could use something like a cloak."

"But people live here," Alice said, looking into the main room of the apartment.

The residents had been considerate, removing their personal items, cots and any other sign that the apartment had been full until an hour before. Peter realized that it looked too clean, just like a group of people had just carefully cleared out. "There are people here," he said, conceding the point. "Everyone who is trying to live outside the Order's reach on this world is ready to move at a moments' notice. I stay in the cities, usually, visible to the people who want to seek me out. It's dangerous, I know. Law enforcement sends people in my direction to try to trick their way in, but it never works. Our organization recruits people, we don't accept anyone we don't know."

"Roughly how many people do you have?"

"I don't know. We're organized in cells, so I never know how many members each has," Peter replied. "The Order controls this world through the government establishments that already existed when they arrived, so the restrictions I've heard about on other worlds aren't as strictly enforced here."

"So, you've been able to grow more than most resistances?"

"Again, I can't say for sure," Peter replied patiently. There were hundreds of cells, he didn't know how many, that was true, but there were at least fifteen people in each. "Cells split after each grows to more than twenty. Every cell has to have three people in it as a minimum. As far as I've seen, my cell is the only one that has been resting at three members for more than a few weeks. How did you find me, by the way?"

"The Order of Eden has a file on someone named Mary, but I

couldn't locate her, but you were prominent in her records. They were watching Mary, then she disappeared. No one knows where she is, but we used the ground surveillance to find her associates. A pattern came up then. You were spotted two to three days before every major sabotage against Order facilities and ships. That's why I took a chance on you."

"And I thought I was being so careful," Peter said, feeling a little alarmed at being spotted so easily. His people were behind the absence of patrol ships in orbit thanks to regular sabotage on their engines. Faulty stabilizers caused the crashes of half a dozen freighters lifting heavy metals to ships waiting in space. Parts of manufacturing printers went missing all the time, and there were over a dozen other efforts to complicate the occupation under way across the planet. It was true, Peter spoke with many representatives from many different cells, it was a breach of their own system, but he knew why it would work. It would work because he would never be captured alive. He would never allow it. If Alice's people could track him down, then the Order wouldn't be far behind. The realization gave him an uneasiness that he couldn't entirely shake.

"I knew they were getting close," Sonny groaned.

"The Order aren't on to you yet," Alice said. "At least, there's no record of an investigation into your actions. We found you because of Theo and Lewis. Two very talented investigators with a lot of computing power."

Peter said. "I'll have to change my strategy anyway. I've been doing things the same way for too long."

"My crew and I were ready to help you with that, but things changed today. You're about to be invaded by the Edxi," Alice said quietly and calmly before looking to Iruuk.

The Nafalli continued where she left off. "The Order are

changing the weather patterns to cause accelerated growth across the planet. From the information we gathered from their own network, we saw that the Edxi will start arriving in as little as seven days. You have nine days at the most before they have a large fleet here to prevent any ships from leaving, any people from getting off the world or its moons. I'm so sorry."

Dismay struck Peter like a tall wave, it felt like all the energy left his body. The Edxi were death. He'd seen the contraband footage of Edxi attacks and the conspiracy videos about how they were taking entire worlds for their broods. Humans were a food source. The Edxi saw them as lesser life forms, flies who thought they were intelligent and needed to be swatted back into their place or eradicated altogether, but not before they were made to suffer. "Well, this is..." he cleared his throat and shook his head. They were coming to his home. The planet he hadn't left once, not even for an orbital view.

"If you're lying, if this is some kind of plot to break the back of the resistance..." Sonny warned.

Iruuk, unable to sit in a wicker seat, leaned down to the table in their midst and carefully put a data chip there. "I'm sorry. Everything we found is there. Scan it, there are no hidden transmitters, no malicious software, only evidence to prove the bad news. I'm sorry."

"Your people were just run out of your own solar system," Sonny said, it was posed as an accusation.

"Don't insult them, that's only a rumour, propaganda," Peter countered. He could feel the meeting going badly. The news of the Edxi's impending arrival was taking everything off track, and whatever he planned on saying no longer applied.

"Most of the Order's version of that is true, only we defeated a full Edxi invasion. After that the Order Fleet came, and we couldn't hold up against them unless we started using firepower that would do permanent damage to parts of the Haven Solar System. Even then, it would have left us with too little to hold the system against another relatively small attack. We're fighting back now, that's one of the reasons why I came here. I'm part of an effort to reach out to potential allies, to help them in this fight, find out what kind of support they need and what we can do. When they're facing an unwinnable fight, I'm supposed to save as many of them in as I can. We need people more than anything else. Fighters, thinkers, leaders, everyone."

Sonny stood up and paced behind the chairs, opposite Iruuk, who was standing behind Alice. Peter thought for a moment, stared at the tiny golden data chip on the woven wood table until the central question came to him. He looked up at Alice who was watching him calmly, expectantly. "Which are you here for? Fighters, thinkers, or leaders?"

"I came here because there might be a fighter we knew here already, Mary, and there's an Admiral nearby. I was told to find my own targets, given permission to follow our fleet directives however I saw fit until I was recalled. I'm following two of those directives. To rescue or assist the enemies of the Order of Eden, and to collect intelligence. We're already collecting intelligence, now I'm here to help you and your people."

"This doesn't feel like help," Sonny nearly screeched as he gestured to the chip on the table.

"Sit down," Peter told him firmly.

"No, I'm going to get this checked out right now," he replied, snatching the chip and leaving the apartment.

"There are friends down the hall waiting to hear the result of our meeting. They're good with data," Peter explained. "You have to understand, we love our world. The cities seem busy, thick with people, but there are only five of them in the whole world. Each has a major port, and even now only one third of the people there live in them. Nuaji is an enchanting place, the nature here has a personality of its own, the people who stay feel like the planet takes care of them. The thought of Edxi coming here is like a defilement. The notion stuns me, truly stuns me. He is having a different reaction, but it's for all the same reasons."

"I understand," Alice said. After a moments' pause she corrected herself. "I'm sorry, that's not true. I've never loved a place that much. Maybe someday I will, but I've been more of a wanderer until just a while ago. I'm sorry you're facing this."

"I won't be leaving," Peter found himself saying. It surprised him, and from the looks on Iruuk and Alice's faces, the statement surprised them too. "Everyone else should, though. There are only one point four million people on the planet now, most of them near the ports."

"Can you reach them without using the main networks? Without the Order seeing?"

"I have cells across the globe," Peter nodded. "What do you want me to tell them? How do I manage this kind of thing?"

"Tell them to start ferrying people to Scarn. It's a world in the..."

"Ulow System, I know it. Have you been there? I hear its very alien," Peter said.

"It is, but the Order won't touch it. I'll use my ship to find holes in the Order of Eden coverage in this system so most of the ships won't be seen leaving. I can't guarantee that every route will be safe, but I'll do my best, and I can't guarantee that larger frigates won't get spotted. I only have one ship here right now."

"Any help will be welcome. I see why you want to use my network, too. If we do this right, there won't be panic until the final days," Peter nodded. Images of people being torn apart, Edxi brood rushes where hundreds of large insects rushed across open terrain as they chased people down ran through his head. "Then they will come."

"You don't have to stay. If we do this right, the planet could be almost empty when the Edxi get here. The Order isn't keeping more than a few destroyers and other small ships in orbit," Alice said, trying to placate him.

Peter sucked in a deep breath and shook his head. "I won't give in to despair. That's not who I am." He felt his resolve renewing and a thought came to him clearly.

"Wait," Alice said in almost a whisper.

He looked up, into her blue eyes. She was leaning forward, focusing on his gaze. It was as if she knew what he was about to ask, or at least had some idea of how determined he was becoming. "I love this world too much to let the Edxi have it. I need a bomb. Like the type that's used to strip a world before it's re-terraformed."

"We can make one," Alice said quietly. "It would take us a day to manufacture something that would ruin everything living on the planet. It's a desperate measure, though. The Edxi may turn away if there isn't enough mammalian life here for their broods, if the humans are mostly gone. You shouldn't have to destroy all life on the surface."

"I don't want there to be anything for them here, they can't have this planet." Peter said through clenched teeth. He let himself fall back into his chair then, covering his eyes for a moment as he reminded himself that Alice wasn't the enemy, only the messenger. Then he continued. "Life took root deep in this world, it'll grow back. Even if it doesn't, someone, someday will come and re-terraform. It won't be in time for the Edxi to make this a brood world. Agree to make me one of those bombs, and you'll have thousands of fighters, hundreds of thinkers and experienced leaders."

"So, you know Haven Fleet recruits many of the people we save?" Alice asked.

"I assumed. I know my people will join you and they know even more who will, just take them away from here."

"I will," Alice said, offering her hands.

Peter took them and nodded. Iruuk was turning away, stroking his eyes and muzzle. It looked like a sign of sadness, no, grief. His attention back on Alice, he saw some of that in her expression, but she mostly looked determined. "I believe you."

NINE

Crew

CALLUM MET Alice on the upper deck of the Clever Dream and took her long coat. "We have confirmation that Admiral Scanlon is next in line to take control of the Haven System and the whole cluster. We intercepted a message from the Office of the Overlord that said she'd be taking control of the sector as soon as her business is finished here." He hung her coat on a thick hook he pulled out from the wall beside the door to her quarters.

Nervousness was rolling off him. He was good at pushing through it but seemed to feel bad news more keenly than anyone. He also got over his reactions fast, she imagined that if he didn't, he would be a nervous wreck. "There's something else?" she asked, turning to face him in the hall. Iruuk was behind her, waiting for the rest of the news. "Listen, I'm not as good as presenting this stuff as Theo or Lewis..."

"But they're both analysing intercepts now that we've cracked the Order's access codes," Alice said. "So, you're it."

"Aye, I'm just sayin' this'll sound like I'm tellin' ya the sky is falling, but I'm just passing the news on the best way I can." Callum finished.

"So, this isn't just bad news, it's..." Alice started to walk to the rear of the ship, leading Callum and Iruuk to the circular common area. Most of her team was there; Knud, Jessen, Faloo, and Noro were sitting scattered across the soft upper tier seating around the table. Faloo was curled up against Noro, and they were both watching something inside the goggles they wore to protect against sudden light, since they were descended from burrower Nafalli who were shorter, stouter than tree Nafalli like Iruuk. The rest of the crew were watching different news feeds from the planet below.

"Really bad," Callum said. "We're not sure where the Admiral is right now, not exactly, but her Command Cruiser is having nearly fifty advanced upgrade modules installed."

"Oh, Alice is back," Faloo said, sitting up and pulling her goggles off. "How was the meeting?"

"In a minute," Alice said.

"Oh, okay," Faloo said. "Do you want me to go get Woone and Krooke? They're working below, checking loads for the main gun."

"That's all right," Alice said, looking back to Callum. "So she's making some sort of super cruiser?"

"The Lance, her command ship, will be over a kilometre long with room for three fighter wings by the end of the week. From what Lewis could tell so far, there will be six redundant shield systems with capacitance for a full charge on all of them, disruption beams that have the same range as the ones on the Merciless, and kinetic cannons that fire high density rounds. They're almost exactly like our older seventy-millimetre guns. The ship will also have a whole battalion of Knights that we can't get details on, it's top secret to everyone, even Order personnel. They're called the Justicars. We can't find anything else about them."

"How does all that fit in with what's going on in this solar system? Is this just a quick stop for her to get her battlegroup together before moving on?" Iruuk asked.

"I was getting to that. The Admiral has gone out of the system, we're not sure exactly where, but Theo is pretty sure that she's talking to the leader of the Edxi government in this galaxy. There were messages from Overlord Dron to her telling her to offer this solar system to them as an apology for not getting the Haven System. Since it's near the middle of Order of Eden territory, Dron is sure the Edxi will accept. As far as the battlegroup Scanlon is getting together, there are fifty-five ships destroyer class or larger on their way. It's enough to lock the Haven System down tight. I'd go through the list, but it would take a couple hours to get through, since there are nearly a hundred fighter wings, smaller corvettes, land assets, and over two hundred thousand troops. It's an endgame force for the Haven System."

"You said land assets, like colonization systems?" Alice asked.

"There are three juggernauts that can launch five base landers each. They can manufacture new ones on board while they're under way, too. All they need to do is load each with a few hundred soldiers, point the base lander at a planet, and in less than five minutes a military bunker digs into the surface of the world. Tafford's Overlord had that kind of tech, he just didn't get close enough to Tamber or another good target to use them."

"All right, so this battlegroup can move into almost any solar system and take over." Alice sat down at the table. "It's all coming together here."

"Near this solar system, not inside it. The Lance and construction ships are the only ones that we can guarantee will be in system while it's being upgraded. Your idea to follow the intelligence to our last mass destruction target has worked out perfectly, except we're going to have too many targets soon, I guess."

"We already do," Alice said, pulling a holographic image of the Lance, a bulky, long Order of Eden Heavy Cruiser up. It was in the same solar system, just in a clearer section of space where fighters and support corvettes had a large, open field of space to scan while modules were being delivered. "The leader of the resistance down there wants a bomb that can clear all life off the planet. He wants to get his people off world along with as many of the civilians as he can, but he doesn't want there to be anything left for the Edxi to colonize either."

"What did you tell him?" Faloo asked. The whole room was focused on her.

"I said I'd make the trade," Alice said. "We should be able to modify our last accumulator bomb to neutralize all life on the surface without leaving much radiation behind."

Faloo's opposition to the idea was almost overwhelming, in fact, all the Nafalli who heard her, even Iruuk, were against the idea. "No, I won't make that modification," Faloo said firmly. "You know I'm the best to do it, aside from maybe Theo, but I'll sit on that bomb if that's what you're going to use it for."

" I don't like the idea either if it makes you feel better, it's even against regulations. I just knew he wouldn't help us if I didn't commit. Peter, their leader, is a fanatic. He doesn't see any cause but his own, this whole conflict between his people and the Order is binary, there is no grey area or room for compromise. The path he sees for his people is right, the Edxi, the Order and anyone who looks like they're about to oppose him in any way are wrong. Sonny, his partner, is really more of a servant, and he believes in Peter. He questions him, sure, but that's only so he can hear how Peter is thinking or to take care of him. He's in love, he'll follow him anywhere. If the rest of Peter's following is a tenth as faithful, then we can't do anything on that world without having a good relationship with him."

"I'm sure there's some way to change his mind," Noro said. "Destroying your own home is drastic, even for someone so dedicated."

Alice looked to Iruuk, then to the rest of the room. It was time to tell them, it was the only way to convince them that she knew Peter's mind. "I've met some of the most destructive people in our lifetimes, and no one scares me more than Peter. I was in his head. I'm just learning how to use it properly, but when I want to, I can feel people's emotions. Ever since a Geist went looking through my memories and I fought back, I've been able to do it. I can mostly shut it off, and I do while I'm aboard ship most of the time out of respect for everyone on the Clever Dream, but it's becoming a huge advantage."

"It would be," Faloo said.

"That explains a few things," Knud said with a broad smile. "I have never had such a good Captain."

Noro and Jessen were most fearful about the news. Noro was more self-conscious, though, so Alice wasn't so worried about him. Jessen's fear was tinged with bitterness, she felt insulted. "I can't hear thoughts," Alice said. "That kind of telepathy is off limits to me, but I can be aware of what people are feeling."

"You're doing it right now," Jessen said. "Stop. Get out of my head."

Alice closed her empathic sense down and regarded her subordinate seriously. "First of all, I'm not in your head. It's more like I have an antenna that picks up emotional waves from people who are broadcasting, I don't go digging. Second: I'm still your Captain. I'll use every advantage I have to do the best job I can. Even so, I'm still not here to screw with anyone's privacy, and I won't punish you for something you're feeling."

"It's not natural," Jessen said. "You should have told us before we took off on this long assignment so we could transfer."

Alice wanted to read Jessen so she could navigate through the conversation but held back. It didn't take an empath to see that her crewmember felt violated. "I'm still the same person, same Captain you were assigned to serve under. The main difference here is that I can be more aware of my crew, and I can use this ability to help us and the Fleet. Like this last meeting with Peter, I know for a fact that we're dealing with a complete fanatic. It's one of the reasons why people around him believe in his cause, because they don't see a scrap of doubt in his mind. Nothing short of promising a bomb would have won him over in the little time we have, I know that for a fact. Will we give it to him? Probably not, but if I play my cards right, if I read him right, then I might have bought us enough time to find some other way to gain his trust so we can do something meaningful here. It's a useful skill."

"Okay, I'll grant you that," Jessen said. "You can pick up problems from someone whose almost mute, like Knud, and that's good for him, as it turns out. But then there's everyone else, who might want to keep their feelings to themselves so they can edit what comes out of their mouths when they talk to you. Yeah, your sense works well in these encounters, but what about people like Carnie? How does Noah feel about you reading him?"

"I'll be telling him on the next call," Alice said.

"I don't believe that for a second," Jessen said, drawing a scowl from Knud. "You probably used your ability to get together with him, didn't you?"

"You're out of line," Knud said. "Don't say something that..."

"You did!" Jessen said, standing. "You spoiled little bitch!"

"That's enough!" Alice burst, surging to her feet. She took a breath, Jessen looked shocked at Alice's outrage. There was a hint of amusement there, too. Yawen rushed into the room and stopped, silently taking the scene in. "You're confined to quarters until you've calmed down, Jessen," Alice said firmly. "If you have a problem with an empathic captain, then you can transfer as soon as we re-link with the Merciless. Until then, you'll be on my official shit list until I'm sure you can serve at the same level as everyone else on this ship."

"How are you going to know when and if I'm ready? You gonna..."

"I'll read you," Alice said. "Because there's one thing you're forgetting: we're soldiers, and if a soldier can't control their emotions, at least enough so I can trust them to do their duty, then they're just going to put the rest of us in danger, and probably get themselves killed."

Knud reached between the second-tier seating and opened the door to Jessen's quarters. "Don't get yourself in trouble," he whispered to her as she was about to say something else.

Jessen stepped through the hatch and turned towards Alice. "This is getting out. The whole fleet will know."

"Not if you want to stay in. It's classified. Enjoy your time off,"

Alice said, signalling for the door to close. It slid shut and she dropped into her seat. "That couldn't have gone worse." She put her face down in her hands for a moment, and a short time later she felt a big Nafalli hand on her shoulders. She looked up, expecting to see Faloo there, but it was Noro.

"Nafalli have had empaths for generations, they're very few, but many of them become great leaders. I'm only surprised to see a human empath, but I am happy our leader is one." He said, Faloo nodding her agreement.

"Explains why you knew exactly what to say when I was released from Haven Medical," Yawen said, sitting down beside her. "I don't mind, though. Well, not much."

"I shut it down if something really private starts coming up," Alice told her quietly, thinking about a moment on the beach that made her blush.

"Oh, you know, don't you," Yawen laughed nervously.

"Who you were staring at most of the time we were..." Alice started to say as she watched Yawen blush furiously. Gavin was squarely in Yawen's sights, something that Alice did her best to ignore. It was easier when Noah arrived.

"Yawen wanted to breed with someone when we were on the beach?" Noro asked excitedly.

"Humans don't call it that," Iruuk said, covering his nose and snickering.

"Ooh, who was it?" Faloo asked.

"That's not even my business, so I can't say," Alice said, putting her hands up.

"Was it Knud?" Faloo asked.

"Wow, no," Yawen said. A moment later, she turned to him.

"Sorry, big guy, but you're not really my type. I like tall guys, but you're twice my size."

"More, it's all right," he said, pulsing his pectoral muscles. "I get that more than you might think."

"Oh, this is exciting," Faloo said. Noro tugged on a tuft of fur at her side and she added; "We'll talk after I finish my shift."

"Sure," Yawen said with a sigh. "Empathic Captain or not, there's always going to be scuttlebutt."

Alice looked to Jessen's door, then to Knud. "Is she going to get over this?"

"I've never seen her react to anything like that," Knud replied sadly.

"I hope she does." Alice took a moment to clear her head then stood. "I have to report to the Merciless. We need backup if we're going to do anything worthwhile in the system."

"I hate to ask, but are you going to propose that you give the bomb to the resistance leader so he can deforest the planet?" Faloo asked. "I know what you said, but..."

"I won't recommend it, but I have to tell them I made the promise. It's not going to go over well. Tell Ute to take us out of the solar system so we can open communications without being detected. The last thing we need is to have our Quad Drive trigger an alarm on some Order patrol ship because I wanted to call the mothership."

TEN

The New Age

A PAIR of Uriel fighters manoeuvred towards the Merciless. The long ship's receiving bays were triangles of light, their doors open, their new barrier shields keeping air inside as the fighters ahead of Ronin and Carnie pass through the glimmering fields. "You're going to get some news when you land, Carnie," Ronin told him over a private channel as they waited for their turn to touch down.

"Is this a warning?" Carnie asks.

"Sort of. You're going to be packing your bunk today. We're shipping you off to Officer Training. You got the rank, now you're going to get the education."

"Holy crap, seriously? Where am I going? The War Forge?"

"You'll be joining the Sabre Wing on the Triton," Minh-Chu said. "More patrolling while you get through a quickie officer program there."

The Merciless Navnet sent a signal to his fighter, telling him that he and Minh-Chu were clear to land. He was momentarily distracted as bursts of air accompanied the launching of fighters from the punter systems to the right of the landing bays. They were launching to start the daytime patrol. He started his slow approach. "How long will this be? I mean, I know it's an opportunity, but I'd rather stay with Samurai Wing."

"Someday you'll want to get out of the cockpit and do something bigger, like Hal, he's going with you so he can be first officer on a Clever Class Corvette, at least, that's where he's starting. If he does well enough, he might get the assignment he wants, too. The Fleet wants more Corvette pilots to be higher rank, so they can stay with their ships, offer continuity."

"Continuity?"

"One ship, one boss, one person tracking the Corvette's performance and condition. If Hal isn't careful, he could end up being Captain of one of those ships, I think that's what Fleet really wants. You'll probably end up back in a fighter, but you'll know what you're doing in and out of the cockpit, that's the difference. You'll have three weeks to finish."

Ronin and Carnie's ships set down at the same time on the elevation pads that were marked for them. The space felt small around them, almost claustrophobic as they were lowered into the hangar proper, where they rolled on their small landing wheels off their pads into storage and service spots. There was nothing to report about their eight-hour patrol shift, just as command wanted it. Noah stretched for a moment then pulled himself out of the cockpit.

"A little stiff, Carnie?" asked Perman, one of the deck crewman as he offered him a hand.

"Yeah," he replied as he stepped down the side of his fighter. "Cockpit's more comfortable than my bunk, but I don't think anyone's supposed to stay still for eight hours straight."

"The Commodore's about to go for his morning jog in Hangar C, you could join in."

Carnie tucked the end of his white scarf more firmly into the sleeve of his jacket. Everyone could still see it wrapped around the neck of his suit, but there was something less conspicuous about it when it wasn't flapping around. He retracted his helmet and shook his head, the unique smell of grease and hot electronics filling his nostrils. "I'll just find a corner and stretch. Can you give her a look over, Perman?" he asked, patting his fighter. "I did the checks on the way in, but I just want to make sure that this rig is ready to go in case there's an alert."

"Sure thing, Sir," Perman said, pulling a hand scanner from his thigh pocket and getting to work.

He started walking towards Minh-Chu, who was talking with the Deck Sergeant, and he turned his Crewcast interface on. A message from Alice appeared, telling him that she'd try to contact him again in ten minutes. It was received four minutes ago, so she'd be calling soon. He looked to Minh-Chu and caught his eye. "Incoming live call," he said. "I'm gonna take this somewhere else."

"Talk to you later," Minh-Chu shouted back.

It was still hard to believe that Alice could contact him from dozens of light years away and have a live conversation with him. The new Haven Communication Network was amazing, the whole fleet could communicate in real time, and it helped raise the morale of servicemen and women on every ship. A good thing, since most of them, Noah included, were still smarting over their retreat from the Haven System. More than once a day he found that he asked himself *when are we going back?* He didn't dare ask it aloud because no one knew, and he didn't want to re-open the wound for anyone else.

He rushed to the elevator that would take him deeper inside the Merciless. It bore him and several other pilots who just got back from their patrol up rapidly. He knew them all, but no one was talkative, most were checking in with Crewcast, to see if they missed any messages during their patrol. The regulation of having Crewcast off while you were working was strictly enforced, and it made sense, but it seemed to make patrols feel even longer. Half a dozen deck crewmembers were waiting at the top, they were early for shift change by half an hour.

Leaving the elevator behind, Carnie was at his bunk after moving through grey and dark blue hallways that were almost reflective. "God dammit!" Marc Taylor, call sign 'Caw,' exclaimed as he passed into the bunk room behind Noah.

"What's up?" Noah asked, taking his jacket off and dropping it onto his bunk.

"I'm not going to Sabre Wing, looks like I'm an Ensign First Grade for another cycle," he grumbled.

"You can do the quals on your own, move up through the grades," Noah offered.

"You know how long that takes now? That's months if I pass final testing on the first try for every grade. If I got picked up by the officer program they just moved to the Triton, then I could be a Lieutenant in three weeks! It could get me out of a bunk and into some privacy and a shot at piloting something other than a coffin with pods and guns. Now I'm on the slow, slow track."

"You'll get there, maybe you'll get in next round?"

"No," Marc said, sending him a screen from his command and

control unit. "I've been to Captain's Mast twice in one year, I'm not getting into any programs for a long time."

"Well, that's..." Noah started countering, then he saw that Caw was punished for fighting twice while he was with his previous wing. It was probably true, that would hold him back for months if not years.

"Yeah, see? I lose my temper a couple times and it slows me down for years."

To Noah's relief, Alice's face appeared on his comm unit, she was calling. "You'll get through it, man. I've got a call." He rolled into his bunk and closed the privacy curtain, accepting the call. "Hey, I was on patrol when you tried to get through last time."

"I forgot. It's night here," Alice said. "Morning there, huh?"

"Early morning," Noah chuckled. "I'll still be too wired to sleep for a couple hours though. How are things... where you are?" He didn't know where she was, only that it was a long, long way off.

"Tense," Alice sighed, she looked nervous. "I'll be seeing you soon. I woke my parents up with some news, and it looks like the Merciless will be coming my way. That's classified, by the way, I shouldn't be telling you."

"No worries, privacy curtain is up, and I keep my mouth shut. That's going to be cool, though, maybe I can take you out, or we can have dinner under the dim light of the food processors."

Alice smiled, but she had something on her mind, something that kept her from grinning completely. "Listen, there's something I have to tell you before we see each other again."

The sinking feeling that came over Noah then made him want to tell her to stop talking, but he braced himself instead. Telling her that he wasn't going to be on the Merciless, that he was shipping out to the Triton most likely before it set out across a couple sectors, wasn't something he was looking forward to, but putting the brakes on the relationship was not the way he wanted to avoid having to give her the news. "It can't be that bad," he said.

"I don't know," Alice said, it was almost a whisper. "These last couple weeks have been amazing, talking to you every couple days, even though I can't talk about what I'm doing out here, I've enjoyed every minute. I can't tell you how much I look forward to our calls, our sim time together, especially because it's so different from being right there with you."

"Well, the sims have been pretty close to real," Noah said. "I forget we're not really surfing, or suit gliding, or even just hanging out."

"I know, but it's not the same for me," Alice replied, a tear rolling down her cheek. "There's always something that reminds me that those sims aren't real."

"Well, yeah, but I still get face time with you, it's the best part of my day."

"Okay, and It's the best time of mine too, but I've put something important off, now I think it's going to come out, so I want to be the one to tell you, even if it's at the last minute."

What it could be mystified Noah, and before he could stop himself, he was resorting to humour. "Are you an android or something? I don't really care, I mean, there were moments on Iora where I wondered what Theo would look like in a dress. It got pretty lonely..."

Alice laughed for a moment then shook it off. "I'm being serious, Noah."

"Okay, okay, just tell me. You know all my secrets, so lay it on me."

"I'm an empath," she burst. "When I want to, and sometimes

when I don't, I can sense what other people are feeling, especially people I get close to."

The idea struck Noah strangely. He wasn't irritated much. More than anything he was curious but had no idea what questions to ask. "Oh," was all he could say.

Alice continued to explain in a rush. "That's why these two weeks have been so amazing. I can't feel anything over long distances, so being with you with only my own emotions driving me, having to talk to you to learn anything, to get to know you like normal people do has been perfect. Now, when I see you in person, I'm afraid it's going to be different. I'll try to turn it off for you, but sometimes it just comes on, especially when I'm excited."

Noah knew that he'd had moments where he didn't really want to share his thoughts with anyone, especially when he first met Alice. She was in that swimsuit, coming out of the water, and she looked amazing, but he didn't want to share how attractive he found her. That was such a beautiful sight, even though he was still intimidated by her at first. "So, on the beach..."

"I knew you liked me, and not for my mind, I saw you trying not to stare, though, you were trying to be a gentleman while I didn't have much to hide behind. That took a lot of willpower for you, and I was flattered," Alice admitted, starting to grin. "But then there was something more than arousal. It was like a strong interest, and I liked you too, so..."

"You surprised me with that hug," Noah said, starting to smile as well.

"I was even more nervous because my mind was wide open, I could feel everything you were feeling, and when you hugged me back, I could feel how happy you were, it was like living in the best moment. I managed to turn it off later, after the beach, and that's when I knew I really had more than interest, or attraction to you, that it was better than that."

The smile on Noah's face softened, he was happy to hear he was important to her, declarations of love hadn't come into their relationship yet, but he felt like they were dancing around that word, like it was already there, but too tender to say aloud. A question came to mind then. "So you can pick up feelings, but what about thoughts?"

"No, I stick to feelings. Going further than that could cause real damage, I never do it," Alice explained.

"Can empathy cause damage?"

"Theo says no, Quan agreed, everyone who has experience with this says the same thing, but I've gotten headaches from picking up too much at once, and from keeping it shut down for a couple days, too. I don't think I'll know for real for a while."

"Okay," Noah said, thinking. "So, none of my feelings about you on the beach made you want to run away and hide behind a tree?" It wasn't the best question he could ask, but it was the next one on his mind.

"You're not the first person to be attracted to someone," Alice replied, rolling her eyes. "It made me blush, but I liked how you admired me, it wasn't purely superficial."

"So, you don't mind people who think you're dead sexy?" Noah teased, relieved that a few stolen glances and appreciation didn't offend her.

"Usually not, I catch people noticing each other all the time, I had no idea how much people liked looking at each other in passing until I got this," she pointed to her temple. "So there's nothing weird about it now. Then again, I haven't exactly visited nightclubs or hot spots since this started about a month ago."

That opened up a bunch of other questions; *What started it? Is it going to go away? Will more people become empaths? Could it happen to me?* But he settled on one. "Do you like it?"

"Being an empath?" Alice asked, the question seemed to stump her and she hesitated.

A priority message notice appeared on Noah's comm unit. It was from Minh-Chu. He had it play back in a small window on his wrist display. "Time to pack up and fly over to the Triton. Your fighter's in the punter, you have twenty minutes. Good luck over there, buddy!" Minh-Chu said to him. His face disappeared, replaced by a countdown to his departure time. He looked back to Alice, who was rendered in hologram above his wrist, trying not to look impatient.

"I'll tell you if I like it after I know whether or not it'll make things awkward between us," she answered finally.

Noah believed he was becoming more of a realist, he liked to think he was coming closer every day, but he knew the realistic thing to say was; 'I hope not,' or 'It will, but we'll work on it,' or 'We'll see,' but he turned away from that notion and leaned into what he always was: a dreamer. "I'm crazy for you," he pulled his scarf out so she could see it. "I feel lucky every time I see this little reminder. Don't turn your empath mojo down around me, because that's the first thing you'll feel when we meet up."

"Oh, God, I hope so," Alice said, looking relieved.

"Listen, I want to stay on, but I've got news too. That meetup is going to get put off for a while, I got into this new thing that's starting up aboard the Triton, an officer thing that Minh signed me up for. I get the feeling the Triton isn't following the Merciless to you, so..."

"Oh." Alice looked surprised and disappointed. Rallying, she said; "Well, more time to get to know each other."

"I'll try and get through this fast, so we can get together, I was looking forward to it."

"You have to go now?" Alice asked.

"I could chat for a couple more minutes, but..." he moved the timer window over the middle of his communicator screen so she could see it. "...I'm on the clock."

Alice's eyes went wide. "Wow, don't be late, get going. Call me when you have comm credits and time."

"I'll trade to get some time if I have to," Noah said. "This training better be worth it though."

"Just don't burn yourself out in the first week. Oh, and ask the instructors for help whenever you need it," Alice said, she was starting to look excited. "If it's anything like Apex, you'll work hard but it'll be a time you never forget. Now, go."

"Aye, Captain," he said, taking one last look at her face before ending the call. He swung out of his bunk and started packing as fast as he could, scooping everything he had stowed under his mattress compartment into a duffel.

"Well, where are you going in a hurry?" asked Maid, one of the shorter female pilots from her bunk behind him.

"Looks like I'm joining Sabre Wing," Noah said, trying not to sound excited. "I have about twenty minutes to take off."

"Son of a bitch!" Marc burst, yanking his bunk's privacy curtain closed.

ELEVEN

Old Friends

IT WAS an unusual morning in Jake's quarters. The place was in daytime mode already, with the bedroom sealed off from the night before, informal seating setup in the main room and holo-images drifting between the informally gathered group. Ayan shared the loveseat with him as they munched on Noka; cold noodles with pieces of fruit in a thick, savoury white juice that reminded him of yogurt. It was his second time trying it, and while the idea of the Lorander breakfast wasn't very appealing, his mind was changed once he tasted the mildly sweet dish. It was easy for the War Forge to manufacture all but the fruit, which was finally growing in the garden centre of the station.

Minh-Chu had no misgivings about his first bowl when he dropped into an arm chair that morning, digging in as though he'd seen the meal before. It was his first time trying it, and he loved it immediately. It was a hit with Ashley as well. "So, this is a thing with everyone from Lorander?" Minh-Chu asked.

Oz picked at it, rolling the occasional noodle around his fork and putting the tangled ball in his mouth all at once.

"About a third from what we know. So that's a few billion people," Ayan replied. "This is one of dozens of variations, something we can grow the right fruit and berries for."

"People who eat like this can't be all bad," Ashley said.

"That's the thing," Ayan said after finishing a mouthful. "Now that we're getting a guided tour of the Lorander database from Quan and getting a little more information from the rest of the people who remained with the organization, we're finding out that we only saw the most moderate, centred faction of their society. Their whole culture is still in flux even though they started merging with humanity a long time ago, and there are people, like the Akanen, who explore with so much enthusiasm that they're more like adventurers than scholars."

"Oh, think we'll get to meet them?" Ashley asked with interest.

"There are a few that might have slipped into the Milky Way, but Quan said they're mostly exploring their home galaxies and other near neighbours right now. They're at odds with Lorander because they don't believe in colonizing the way they do, so they stay out of each other's way."

"Oh, too bad. I'd love to see what a Lora... Akanen adventurer looks like."

"Quan says he used to watch their stories when he was growing up, there are thousands of them, and he admits that he's more interested in aspiring to be like them than his elders since he started working with us. Now that he's not worried about offending his commanders, he's really interesting. Leon hangs out with him constantly."

"Leon?" Ashley asked Minh-Chu in a whisper.

"Her assistant, handler type guy," Minh-Chu answered. He looked to Ayan and Jake then, speaking up. "Not that I don't want to start meeting for breakfast, but what's the occasion this time?"

"The Merciless is moving on," Jake said. "Alice found a world with thousands of recruits. They're angry at the Order and need to evacuate. It's also where Admiral Scanlon's command ship is being upgraded and there will be an Edxi presence there soon. Alice doesn't have the firepower she needs to address the most important targets, and she's made what Admiral Lamonthe calls a 'major command error.' The Merciless is going to step in and help out."

"What did she do?" Oz asked, putting his bowl down on the coffee table between them. He finished most of the noodles, leaving blueberries and tangerine slices lurking in the milky juice.

There was no trace of amusement as Jake explained his daughter's blunder. "She promised the leader of the resistance, which is organized and important to the evacuation of his planet, a bomb that could strip the planet of life before the Edxi arrive. She's sure that it was the only way to get a real relationship going with this leader and his resistance group. I told her we don't provide that kind of firepower to allies, especially new ones."

The reaction was predictable. Oz lowered his head, Ashley looked stunned, Minh-Chu stuffed a bunch of noodles into his mouth, and Ayan seemed to make a point of not reacting. "She's new to this kind of command, and she worked hard to find the right resistance group to recruit."

"It sounded like she got desperate, so this must be a pretty big organization, something promising," Jake agreed. "She bought herself some time, but I don't know how she'll be able to back down from her promise."

"Stripping the planet isn't the worst option, though," Oz said. "Especially if it was a terraformed world in the first place."

"It is a terraformed world, but old, stable," Ayan replied, putting her empty bowl down on the table. "I agree, though. I'm not completely against it, especially since terraforming can start over again. The problem is..."

"Once this group takes possession, they can make changes so the bomb is even more devastating, even screw up the timing so a lot of people are still on the surface when it goes off," Oz finished. "So, they won't trust her completely until they have this bomb in hand?"

"That's the situation," Jake said. "The Merciless is going in so SOCU can operate in a broader sense. We're putting the mission and support ships together now. We won't have Remmy, or Alaka, but there are too many opportunities to pass up in that one system. Oh, and they have a live connection to the Order of Eden Fleet Network. They don't have the intelligence infrastructure to handle all the information."

"What? How?" Oz asked, amazed.

"They used the civilian network's connections to find the rebellion they're connected with and ended up going right through to the Order network from there. They made another back door and created several sets of credentials so they could have access to the network whenever they want. The Order of Eden 'net had some serious vulnerabilities because the local government on Nuaji was pretty loose with them. Now the Fleet has real access, but we need a ship with intelligence facilities closer to the source."

"So, two of my best pilots have been sent to Officer School, and we're heading into the heart of Order of Eden territory," Minh-Chu said. "Tell me we're getting that cloaking upgrade, at least."

"It's faster for the War Forge to make new fighters, so you'll be getting them in a couple hours," Jake said. "There were too many upgrades to install in the old ships."

"Music to my ears, thank you," Minh-Chu said.

"Don't worry about your pilots," Oz said. "They'll be better than ever when you get them back."

"If everything goes well, they'll get more experience patrolling around the War Forge than anyone flying off the Merciless gets near Nuaji," Jake said.

"Right. I'm guessing we're going to be taking out that giant Cruiser they're upgrading?" Minh-Chu asked.

"No, Alice's team are assessing it as a target. She wants to make sure it's the right place to put her Super Hammerhead Torpedo before she launches. The only thing she can't do with it is give it to Peter, the resistance leader," Jake said.

"When do I get to tell my guys we're going to the belly of the beast?" Minh-Chu asked.

"Once we're under-way and we're communications dark," Jake said.

"Um, I know this mission is really important," Ashley said, patting her lips with a napkin. Her bowl didn't have any evidence that there was ever anything in it. "But does it help us get back to Tamber?"

Ayan seemed surprised by the question, but she wasn't displeased. She didn't talk to people about Tamber or the Haven System in general, but she shared her guilt with Jake the night before. It was deep, and she couldn't wait to take the solar system back. The people they left behind mattered more than anything they built there. "The Fleet wants that more than anything. One of the reasons why the mission to Nuaji is so important is because there is an Admiral there, Scanlon, who will be in charge of taking control of the whole star cluster. That's the Haven System, the Mergillian home world, and all the nearby solar systems. We don't know for sure if killing her will slow that down, but we want to get the Merciless as close as we can so we can learn about her and act appropriately. If we can keep leadership in the Haven System disorganized, we might have an easier time taking it back. While the Merciless works on things from its end, the War Forge will be working on ways to hold the System once we're back."

"Oh, okay," Ashley said. "A lot of people wonder how we're going to get back, they weren't there long, but we liked having a home, so I thought I'd ask."

"I'm happy you did," Ayan said. "You can pass what I said on once the Merciless is under way, too."

"Okay, that'll help," Ashley sighed. "Do you guys deal with this big picture stuff every time you have meetings? It feels like I just gained ten pounds in the shoulders."

"A millstone hanging from your neck," Minh-Chu added.

"You get used to it," Ayan said.

"Well, I'm supposed to be on duty in five minutes," Ashley said, standing and dispensing hugs, starting with Oz.

"I need sleep," Minh-Chu said.

"I have to get to the Triton if I don't want to go along for the Merciless' trip to the middle of Order territory."

A flurry of handshakes and hugs went around, and before long Ayan and Jake were left alone. Ayan pulled a white scarf from the thigh pocket of her uniform and put it around Jake's shoulders, pulling him down for a sound kiss that reminded him of the night before. "I'm going to miss you," she said. "Even with live calls."

"Me too," he said, nose to nose with her. "Guess the old tradition is back," he said.

"Doesn't feel weird, I thought it might," she said, glancing at the silky scarf.

"Not at all, feels right," he replied, capturing her lips with his and drawing her close.

They shared the intimate moment until her comm unit buzzed. The separation that followed was reluctant. "I have to go. My team just checked in, they've finished working with Finn on the quad drives. Remember, running them at the levels you're going to will make it seem like time passes faster on your side of the dimensional wall than ours. It's a paradox we don't completely understand yet. So, the Merciless will be travelling for five days, but outside only three will pass."

" It's only a couple days, it shouldn't mess with our heads that much," Jake said.

"Wait until we get the system working even more efficiently," Ayan said. "It might get confusing for a while."

Jake started to let her go, then stopped, his arms still around her. Ayan's heart shaped face turned up to him with a playful expression at first, then growing more serious as they remained there. "I love you, you know," he told her quietly.

Watching her jaw drop a little, a smile still playing across her lips, then feeling her shift so she was completely in his embrace was enough to make him nervous. "I've been afraid to say it, but I love you too, Jake," her lips grazed his, soft and warm. He wished he could rewind time to the previous night and live it over again, but the buzzing of both their communicators told him that there was no way to delay their separation.

They parted at last, and she winked as she turned away. "Go set the Order on fire and bring a few thousand people home with you."

TWELVE

An Old Stage

THE DIRECTIONS from her father were clear and didn't leave much room for interpretation. Alice knew that promising the leader of the resistance on Nuaji a bomb that would strip his entire planet of life was a mistake but being told directly that she couldn't follow through on her promise by Jake, or rather Commodore Valent as he was acting in that capacity for most of her live call, was worse than any self-admonishment.

Providing such a weapon to Peter or any part of his resistance would be a transgression against the entire fleet. It would scar its reputation, alienate thousands of Nafalli, and lead to a black mark on her father's and her records at best. The Fleet wasn't interested in providing unpredictable new allies with weapons of mass destruction, especially if they could tamper with them between the time they were given and deployed. One of her most important promises had to be broken and she couldn't recall a time when she was more on edge. Her promise bought her some time to come up with a better option, but she failed to find one.

Peter and an unknown number of his resistance cell leaders were to meet her at the Inverse Gardens. The dormant volcano base provided them with all the advantages, leaving Alice vulnerable. Her leash had been yanked: not only was she not to provide them with the bomb she promised, but she couldn't give them any of their Knight Killer Two rifles or armour. That left older style weapons and heavy vacsuits, which could be good in a fight, but against an Order Knight they may as well be paper suits and slingshots.

Alice, Yawen, Iruuk, Woone and Noro carried four long crates of the lighter weapons and suits they could offer to the meeting. They had their KK2 rifles slung across their backs this time. More instructions from SOCU: Go to the meeting armed or not at all. That was Alice's fault, she told her father that she suspected Peter was dangerous, a true believer in his own cause that would stop at nothing to accomplish his goals. Alice could relate, she would do anything to get the Haven System back, to protect the people there, but Peter was much closer to madness than she was.

She hoped the offerings she brought would be enough but doubted it. Her hand came to rest on a sealed equipment bag affixed to her chest as they descended the Clever Dream's rear ramp onto the landing pad inside the main volcano chamber. The lights were subdued, and Sonny came to meet them. He was in a battle scarred hazardous environment suit that had a few extra armour plates affixed to the chest. The helmet visor was up and she could feel his remorse before he offered his apology. "My people checked the intelligence you brought as best as they could, I'm sorry I doubted you, Captain Valent. The meeting is this way, in the main hall."

He and two guards in similar armour led the way. Alice's hand never came off the equipment case on her chest. It wasn't the bomb they wanted, but it was the biggest thing she could offer instead without disobeying orders. The device was shielded from scanners, made to be affixed to a hull or security door so the charge inside could fire for several seconds in a focused area that would cut a two-metre-wide hole through most hulls. When not in use, it was the size of the average three cup thermos. It was the best she could do.

"You have some gear for us?" One of the guards asked, eying the equipment cases.

Iruuk looked him up and down, probably taking note of the old tech the man was wearing. Their environmental suits were three centimetres thick in some places, made from cheap but effective materials that were tried and true, but well outdated by Haven Fleet standards. "A few upgrades."

The passages they traversed on their way to the meeting were made to show off the volcanic rock. The lighting was moody, almost dramatic, still lit for tourists and not residents. Most of the doors they passed were closed, but she did get a glimpse into spaces filled with cots, and a couple store rooms where younger members of the resistance, nearly children, were packing hurriedly. "Moving day?" Alice asked.

"You're lucky," Sonny said. "We're abandoning the Inverse Gardens soon, but you'll still have a chance to see the main hall. This is the biggest meeting we've had since the resistance was started. It's a once in a lifetime event, and without the intelligence you brought us, we wouldn't have felt confident enough to pull it together."

"I have to talk to Peter before any announcements are made," Alice said firmly. "There has been a change of plans."

"Oh? Everything all right?" Sonny asked. He was nearly overwhelmed with worry, like she'd shattered a dam holding it back.

Concern for his feelings couldn't change what had to be done. "I just need to clear some things up."

"We're here, this is the stairway that leads backstage," Sonny said, stopping at a pair of metal doors. "You have to leave your weapons."

"No, I don't," Alice said, meeting his gaze, unflinching. "I'll leave most of my people here, but Yawen comes with me, and we keep our weapons."

Sonny was alarmed, he was being pushed to the verge of doing something stupid. "I can't..."

"I won't go up there unarmed while I'm carrying this," Alice said, opening the equipment bag on her chest enough to show Sonny and a pair of guards a glimpse of polished metal. "A gift that'll have an impact from Haven Fleet. My people have trusted me to make sure the gear we brought for you makes it into the right hands."

"You can trust me," Sonny said, his alarm was slowly turning to excitement.

Alice zipped the case back up with a jerk and started to turn away. "This was going to be good for your resistance, but we can always find..."

"All right, wait. I'll take you up with one of your people, just leave your rifles with your Nafalli soldiers there, I've seen what they can do."

Alice and Yawen handed their Knight Killer Two rifles to Iruuk and Noro then followed Sonny up the stairs. The back room looked like something from an old holo movie with cables and walkways connected to curtains and pulleys overhead. Three old holographic projectors the size of small star fighters were piled on top of each other, hidden by a curtain from the audience but in plain sight to her and Yawen. Furniture, freestanding signs and what she assumed were old set pieces were piled wherever there was space behind canvass or velvet curtains as well. She wished she could have seen whatever plays or presentations happened on the stage when it was in its prime, but they were in an era where entertainment, especially live entertainment, was of little importance.

Peter was sitting in one of those old chairs, a simple wooden seat. His eyes were closed, hood drawn down so she could barely see his scarred face. Alice concentrated on what he was feeling, rather than what she was seeing. Those scars were brutal. Some parts of his skin were so thin and tight that she could see the muscle move beneath, patches of his face looked like fresh wounds, the flesh still raw and wet looking. It was easy to stare him in the eyes though, they were such a washed out blue that they were nearly grey, and they seemed bright, very alive to her. He looked to her, and Alice smiled at his pale gaze. "I brought you everything I could."

"The bomb?"

"You can't expect us to give you something like that on our second meeting. We're just getting to know each other," Alice said.

"What about the escape plan?" Peter asked, standing and crossing the dusty, hard floor behind the stage. "Can you cover my people while they make their escape? Provide a rallying point so they can get out of the system?"

"In five days," Alice said with a nod. "I can create a distraction big enough and provide enough coverage for your people to escape the solar system. If you're willing to abandon your ships, we will be able to get you out of the sector in no time, but anyone who wants to keep their ship is on their own."

"Why? Why do we have to abandon our ships?" Peter asked. "Are you trying to force my people into a corner so we have to depend on you?"

"None of your ships will be fast enough to keep up with ours," Alice replied, feeling tension starting to wind up in him. "If your people want to join Haven Fleet, or have our assistance, they'll have to be left behind."

"So, you'll give us ships?" he asked.

"No, anyone who joins us will train to use our technology and serve on our vessels as part of an organized military. You'll be paid, have the best life we can provide, and everyone will have rights. Even the people who don't join the military but become civilian citizens instead will have a right to participate in our democracy. They'll have a voice and a good standard of living." It wasn't what he wanted. The disappointment she felt in him was extreme. "We didn't come here to absorb your resistance, but we didn't know your world was about to be overwhelmed by Edxi either. Now all we can do is help you with evacuation and offer your people a place with us."

"Are you really going to take ships full of civilians? What good is that to you?" Peter asked, he was fighting outrage while remaining surprisingly tranquil on the surface.

"Haven Fleet exists to protect people. Part of that is providing an alternative place to live, one where everyone is respected. As we take on more people our culture evolves and Haven as a nation becomes more capable." Alice was a little surprised to find that she believed in the words she'd read a few times in the Haven Government statements. It was the first time she's spoken them aloud and doing so earnestly was easy. "I'm sure some of your civilians can help the military, but we're happy to take on people who have other ambitions, and families are always welcome."

"But there will be a lot of civilians who don't want to go with you, what then?" Sonny asked.

"I can provide you with a list of worlds that may take your people in as refugees, we can even project wormholes that will get them there," Alice said. "But once they leave there won't be a chance for them to join us until we retake the Haven System. Our base is well hidden, I won't reveal its location to anyone. I'm sorry, I have to protect the greater cause."

"I didn't build this network, gather these people together so they could be broken up and fed into some nomadic military organization," Peter said. "Where do I fit into all this? Will I be a leader if I join you?"

"You'll be assessed like everyone who joins, so maybe. It's an opportunity; you'd get access to our medical facilities, training so you can be more effective in whatever position you want to work towards." Alice knew he wouldn't make it far. Peter was calm on the outside, but unstable within.

"I need to be in a position where I can look after my people," he countered. "How can I do that if I'm in training, away from the fighting?"

"We have systems that would help you stay connected to your people," Alice said. "I'll do everything I can to make sure that you have a leadership position that takes the number of people you bring to us into account, so you have enough power to make sure your fighters are taken care of." That was no great promise. It was possible for a Captain to put a recommendation in for a new recruit, but even her word wasn't worth much in that respect.

"What's your word worth, really? You couldn't give us a bomb, so how much power do you have?" Sonny asked.

"Weapons of mass destruction are completely different from recruitment and placement. There's no directive that says I get to pass bombs out, but gathering our allies is Directive Two, one of the most important ongoing missions. Besides, I'm the Queen's daughter, and my father is a famous Commodore, one of the founders of the fleet. I've got plenty of pull where it counts."

"That is something we confirmed," Peter said, calming down. "Your mother is also the Defence Minister. There is no higher rank in your Fleet. What did you bring instead of the bomb I asked for?"

"Some 'bot killer rifles, Violator Seven side arms, and military vacsuits that make the armour your soldiers wear look like tissue paper," Alice said. "There are command and control units in there too so you can use better encryption, even create a moving network for secret communications and have medical systems for anyone who wears them."

"'Bot killer rifles?" Sonny asked.

"Freeground Mark Nines, they're an older design but they can pierce armour plating with pulse rounds, so you get a hundred forty shots on the highest setting," Yawen explained.

"What about the ones you carry? Those don't look like an older model."

"We can't give you our most recent technology," Alice said. "We only have enough for ourselves." That lie didn't land well with anyone. She could feel the emotional reactions around her, it felt like a stink.

"You have spares, or a supply on that ship," Sonny countered.

"Never mind," Peter said, calming down quickly.

"I also brought you this," Alice said, taking the equipment

pouch from the front of her uniform off and handing it to Sonny, who unzipped it. "It's a Hull Buster. I can make you nine more. This can make a door in almost anything. It can get through a rein-forced wall or hull plate in fifteen seconds or less."

"Big lasers and focused explosives. I wouldn't tamper with it, just so you know. You'll blow you and your friends up real good," Yawen added.

"Ten?" Peter said, accepting the black cylindrical charge and looking at the polished surface. "What if I join your fleet with my fighters?"

"Then you get ten of those, the rest of the gear we brought for you, and to join a powerful fighting fleet that'll take your fight further than you could have on your own," Alice replied. "Much, much further."

There was a type of excitement growing in Peter, something Alice had never run into before. Peter's uncertainty was giving way to elation, something she said was more encouraging to him than she expected. "And my fighters can bring their families?"

"They can bring anyone we can fit aboard our ships," Alice said. At least that was the truth, but she hoped the Merciless wasn't coming alone. They would run short on space quickly if tens of thousands of people were trying to join them. She was starting to think that his resistance was bigger than she imagined. "You're still much better off if you can start getting people off world as soon as possible, though."

"Do you have a larger ship than the one I've seen?"

"Yes," Alice said. "It's on its way." That was a risk, sharing any information about the Merciless or the Fleet was. Watching Peter stare at the Hull Buster, she realized that he found the sight of it encouraging, there was a plan forming in his head.

"You promise to get me a position in your fleet so I can watch my people?" he asked.

"I will do everything I can, and you know what that's worth," Alice said.

"You'll get nine more of these to me today?"

"Absolutely," Alice said, tapping a message into her comm unit to Knud and Faloo, so would get their fabricator working on it right away.

Peter handed the Hull Buster back to Sonny, who slipped it back into its case immediately and slung it over his shoulder. "Then I'll tell my people to start smuggling civilians off world, as you suggested before. I'll tell them they can trust your people. You must come out on stage with me, though. I want them to see your face."

THIRTEEN

The Shift

NOAH LUCAS DIDN'T REALIZE the advantages he gave up by going to sleep for seven hours in his new bunk aboard the Triton. The block of racks he settled into were populated by several of his fellow third watchers, all pilots who were serving the last patrol shift before morning. The greetings were very brief, everyone wanted to get into their racks and rest before training started.

It was difficult. Even with the privacy shutters to his bunk closed, in the relative silence within, the excitement of being aboard the Triton, hearing that Commodore Terry Ozark McPatrick was keeping his command and would be overseeing the training aboard, was too energizing to drift off to. After trying for nearly twenty minutes, he gave up, and let his command and control unit medicate him to sleep.

He woke to an alert alarm that ordered all pilots to muster. He was suited up and following directions with his fellow third watchers, including Pixie who, like Alice, was much shorter than him but difficult to keep up with. She was impossible to miss, with long pink and black hair that was tied up in a row of tails that trailed behind her. On the shoulder of her suit was her fleet mark, the upper half of a silver skull with the name of her ship EXCALIBUR along the bottom in place of teeth. Down her sleeve were five stars, a tradition that Samurai Squadron eschewed, but it marked her as an ace five times over with five verified kills per star. He knew each of those kills fought back, it was one of the new rules about earning an ace star. At last count, he had three.

The main halls and high-speed lifts that took them up through the innards of the Triton were broader, more ornate than anything aboard the Merciless. The deck was black with a mirror polish, the older main corridor they took for half their run was gold, brown and more black on the ceilings and walls. There wasn't much distance to travel to their muster point, and as soon as they emerged into one of the upper hangars, he realized it was a drill. The group who spent the morning sleeping, his group, were the last to fall in and the only ones that seemed out of breath. He was amazed at the size of the class, which included Hal, whose call sign just changed from 'Hot Chow' to 'Traveller,' was among the group of forty-five pilots. "Dammit! I knew I shouldn't have tried to sleep for the full seven hours!" Pixie cursed under her breath.

The hangar had three pristine Clever Class Corvettes lined up and all their fighters were loaded into racks along the bulkheads. A Commander he didn't recognize stood in front of the long line of pilots who were at attention, watching coolly as he and the rest of the third watch fell in line. No one had their helmet up, so Carnie didn't bother with his, only rapidly binding his shoulder length blonde hair up into a tight ponytail.

"Nice of you to join us, Third Watchers!" barked the Commander. "I have to say, three minutes and five seconds from bunk to this muster point isn't bad. You'll do better, though, that'll be your responsibility, Pixie," he said, nodding at her.

"Aye, Commander. I'll have it down to one by the end of the week, Commander!" she shouted back, her voice projected across the hangar, startling a pair of workers who were rolling the last of the fighters into a rack spot fifty meters away. Her voice didn't have much of a high pitch, she projected from her middle, like the Officer's manual suggested.

"Good," the Commander said. "No need to shake the heavens, everyone's listening, Second Lieutenant. So, since we're breaking you up into groups of fifteen, and you're the last group to make it here, we're calling you the Third Watch. Each group is a wing, who leads it is up to me or the Commodore, and as you already seem to be a standout, you, Pizenia Zannen, will be the first Cadet Commander of your group." He touched her shoulder and three small Haven Fleet flags appeared there with a line under them. "I'll shut my trap so the Commodore can tell you more about what this training regimen will be like." He stepped back and barked; "Commodore on deck!"

Everyone snapped to more stiffly than they were standing as the transit car behind them lowered and opened. Commodore McPatrick, or Oz as Minh-Chu called him, strode out. He was in a good mood, walked with a long, easy gait until he stopped in front of them and saluted. "At ease. This is going to be a busy day, so I'll keep my introduction brief. You've all be tested and assigned a rank according to how well you did on your ships. You earned your positions, but you didn't properly earn your ranks. While your Wing Commanders determined that you should have the rank you were assigned, the Fleet has seen problems in how well you follow regulations and approach your jobs in general. Fleet's mission with you, this first group of forty-five, is to verify your skills as pilots, work with you to learn the regulations required to execute your duties properly, and to learn from you. Every one of you has one or more Ace's star. That means you have killed at least five of our enemies while braving the hazards of combat. It also means your enemies could fire back at you. Today, there are Aces who are waking up to find that they have had their stars pulled. It's that last requirement: your enemy must be able to fire back at you for the kill to count towards Ace status." The Commodore looked across the group silently for a long moment.

"Sir, I lost three stars, Sir," one pilot reported.

"Leaving you with two," The Commodore replied. He looked to Hal and smiled. "How many did you lose?"

"None, Sir," Hal replied. "Went to bed with five, woke up with five."

Pixie leaned forward and looked down the line at him, trying not to make it obvious.

"Pixie! How many did you lose?" the Commodore asked, turning towards her with a jerk.

"Five," she replied. "Leaving me with five, Sir."

"That second set of five stars didn't matter as much as the first. They were rewarded for cleanup duty, killing Edxi fighters that were disabled, inert. They couldn't fire back."

"I understand, Sir," Pixie replied.

"I'm sure you all understand, at least on the surface. Now that you know how to kill, have demonstrated that you won't hesitate if given the order to do so, it's time for you to learn a more important lesson; how to help your fellow pilots survive out there. You will learn how to lead them or you will be pushed off the officer track. We've pulled a section of the Apex Program out for you and made modifications to it so you have to complete it under extreme stress. I wish this was a happy morning meet and greet, but that wouldn't be appropriate. This program is high risk, there is a chance of mortality because you will be maintaining a real patrol schedule while you learn to be officers in this Fleet. If you were in the full-length Apex Program I'd play with your head a little and tell you that this isn't a competitive program, but this version of the Program doesn't include that kind of head game. This is a competitive program. You will be compared to your fellow Officer Trainees, and at the same time you must help each other succeed. How you assist your fellow Officers will factor into how successful you are. We have three weeks to turn you into real Officers who can teach and lead members of your squadrons, act independently as commander of your own ship, and lead your people through the worst situations you can imagine as well as help them cope with the 'hurry up and wait' lifestyle that comes with this job at times. Now I'm leaving you in the hands of Commander Mars. Good luck, keep your head on a swivel." Commodore McPatrick turned and strode back to the transit car doors.

"That was the good news," Commander Mars said. "Now for the bad news. We're starting this three-week adventure with something the Apex Program calls; 'Suit Week.'"

All their vacsuit hoods deployed, rising up from their collars to envelop their heads in a fitted hood with a transparent faceplate. It didn't bother Carnie, he'd seen the inside of worse suits. "Carnie,

Dullard, Gamer and Pixie: your hair is too long, so that's gotta go," Mars said.

Before any of the pilots could object, not that they would dare, the cleaning system in their suits activated. He clenched his teeth and held still as a buzzing against his scalp told him that he was getting a serious trim from over twenty centimetres long to less than one. He did his best to pretend it wasn't a big deal, but he hadn't had hair that short since he was a toddler. The waste system sucked the hair down into the recycling and management system in the back as it was cut away. "How are you doing in there?" the Commander asked, lightly tapping on Pixie's faceplate.

She opened her eyes and glared for a second before calming down. "Peachy, Sir."

"Oh, she does not like her new cut." He moved down the line to Noah.

"I'm peachy, Sir," he said with a shrug before he was asked.

"Carnie: we don't shrug in this Fleet unless we're off duty and our girl or guy is late for dinner and they're asking; 'are you okay, dear?' I didn't think we were in a relationship, are you under the impression that we are?"

"Sir, no, Sir," Carnie replied officially.

"So, no shrugging. More importantly, I didn't ask you a question. What if I was asking her how she liked her cut, but I wanted to ask you how the plumbing was fitted in your suit? What if you had a problem with the plumbing? Maybe it is too small, and I miss it because of this miscommunication? Why, you could end up with quite a mess down there because you're not a complainer, are you, Carnie?"

"Sir, I am not a complainer, Sir!" Carnie replied, trying not to crack a smile.

"So, you communicate properly and make sure you tell a senior officer if you have a plumbing problem, Carnie," Commander Mars concluded over their proximity radio so everyone could hear.

Noah knew the Commander was having a laugh, but more importantly, he was trying to get him to crack up. He wouldn't give in, and when a few of the other pilots in line started to snicker, he bit the tip of his tongue hard, unwilling to laugh in the Commander's face. "Sir, I understand, Sir."

Commander Mars stared at him through his faceplate for a long moment before nodding and stepping back. "I think he does, but just to make sure, you're all going to study the regulations on conduct in our Fleet and you will take the Officer Qualification test on it in ten hours. Do not dally, this is a huge topic and it is important. Oh, and all three teams: First Watch, Second Watch, and Third Watch will have three hours of patrol to conduct, starting with First Watch, who will be launching in twenty-one minutes. This is not Apex, it is harder because your commanders already think you're fit to be Officers. I am here to test that theory and make sure you get through all the qualifiers required to make whatever rank you should actually have. If you make it through the Commodore's course, we will know for certain that you are ready, and you will have the confidence and knowledge you need to be in command. If you do not make it, we will send you to the War Forge, where you will have the honour - and I do not mean that sarcastically - of training and serving as an enlisted member of our Fleet. I won't waste your time going over curriculum, you can do that on your own. Start studying and taking Qualifiers whenever you are not on patrol. Time will run out before you know it, three weeks is not a long time. Dismissed." As Commander Mars walked past Noah on his way to the transit car doors, he pulled his silk scarf off.

"You get this back at the end of training," he said as he bunched the thing up and pushed it into his pocket.

Noah fought the urge to grab it back, and barely had a moment to think before Pixie was right beside him, poking his elbow. "You date Alice Valent, right?" she said, her voice low, much higher pitched than he expected considering the near baritone she managed when she was bellowing earlier.

"Yeah," he replied.

"Good, we need to get Third Watch together to study for this Conduct Qualifier Test. I'll pay part of the comm credit cost if you can get her online to help us."

"I don't think she'll be available, she's pretty busy out there," Noah replied. He didn't want to use Alice as a tutor, especially since he had suspected that she was way behind enemy lines.

"Oh, I guess she's busy being a Captain and everything. Ever take it?"

"I skipped every Qual I could," Noah shrugged.

A hand popped him on the shoulder from the other side. It was Hal; "No shrugging," he chided.

"Dammit, this is going to be rough, I bet none of us have taken this, why the hell would we?" Pixie asked, shaking her head.

"Well, First Watch is getting ready for their first patrol," Hal said. "They gave me command of Second Watch because of my history, so maybe we can all get together in the squad room and push through."

"What? Are you going to read it to us?" Pixie said.

Hal brought up his command and control unit, checked something, then shook his head. "Nothing here says this is something we have to do on our own, or that it's closed file. So, we open the section on conduct, everyone starts the Qual, and we get his thing done while we're learning it."

Noah couldn't help but grin as nearly thirty of them started looking at the requirements for successfully completing the Officer Conduct Qualifier on their comm units or the HUD in their helms and after a few moments there were a few chuckles and smiles. "Yeah, Hal's always right when it comes to research and rules," Noah said. He didn't bother looking it up. "This Qual isn't just about learning Conduct, it's about how we solve a problem."

"Okay, but what are we missing by doing the Qual together, open book? It's gotta be some kinda trick," Pixie said, her expression sour.

"Sure it is," Hal said. "If we score one hundred percent on the Qual, then that's great, we pass, but you're right, it is kind of a trap. If we just pick through the book looking for answers we might miss something about conduct that could bite us in the ass later. Just because we can game the test doesn't mean that we don't have to read the whole thing."

"So, we do our Qual open book, get our perfect score, then we drill the hell out of the Conduct rules before and after our patrols so we don't get docked for violations for the next three weeks. That's still too easy," Pixie said before looking to Hal. "You're awesome, Traveller. Keep this up and you might get a midnight invitation."

"Red light!" Carnie laughed.

"Wow, right, inappropriate," Pixie snickered.

Hal cleared his throat as he turned away, but not before Noah noticed him blushing furiously, an uncomfortable grin on his face. "Let's get started, we could knock this out in half an hour and practice some inappropriate, er, appropriate conduct."

FOURTEEN

Crowded

THERE WERE many levels to Peter, and the more time Alice had to listen to the stream of emotions radiating from him, the more she realized how complex he was below the surface. Like so many of the more interesting people she'd known, like Jake, Ayan, Noah, and most of her crew, they mostly seemed to let themselves be guided by surface emotions from moment to moment. There was something deeper in all of them, but it took time to see that, and it felt like she was seeing something private when an emotional response that came from their core came to the surface.

Some of them even had something she was starting to call 'Modes.' Even though she hadn't been an empath for long, she was starting to recognize that some people, like her father, had corners of their personality that worked like lenses and filters, changing some responses, blocking others entirely. Jake had his 'Command

Mode' where he leaned into the role of being an official, a representative of the fleet, and an important ranking member. His role was so important to him that in that mode, he was almost a different person. Alice liked seeing that side of him, it was sturdy, comforting, he was a foundation you could trust under your feet when everything else was getting unstable.

Until that moment, when Alice waited with Peter for the curtain to open, she hadn't seen such a shift in someone that compared. As the resistance leader put a hood and scarf on to cover most of his scars, he was changing modes like her father did when something serious, something important was coming up. Only what Alice felt from Peter was unnerving.

There was pride, a feeling that he had great power, and overwhelming confidence that was so pure that it didn't seem sane. The curtains parted and Peter strode out onto the middle of the stage. As he did so, she could sense that he felt an ownership over the hundreds of people there. Alice hesitated for a moment, then moved onto the stage and stopped a few steps behind him to his left.

Seeing their leader reassured them, but she could still feel their desperation like a wave crashing against her mind. Some of the mad zeal that she picked up from Peter sometimes was coming from that crowd too, rising at the sight of him. All but the desperation spiked when he spoke.

"We face the darkest of times, but I've found a new ally, one who most of you have seen." He turned to Alice and she stepped up beside him.

Hope. A surge of bright hope mixed with excitement came from the crowd so intense she winced. It was so powerful that she almost missed something from Peter. It was sinister, something she'd never felt in anyone before. If she could shut the audience out and listen to him, that would have been ideal, but she did her best to block everything out, and only managed to turn it all down to a dull roar.

"Captain Alice Valent of Haven Fleet has joined us, and she brings the full support of her people with her!" Peter announced to frenzied applause.

"Wait," Alice said, the pressure of so much elation renewed the weight on her mind, and instead of clarifying what he was saying, she had to concentrate on blocking, of shutting her empathy down. It took all her concentration.

"We can celebrate that, but not for long. At the end of this meeting you must begin organizing travel for the civilians you watch over. We've learned that no one on Nuaji is safe. Before the end of the month the Edxi will have brood ships in orbit. They'll will launch their young onto the surface. Once they hatch, they will hunt, and most of us will not survive." He nodded at someone in the orchestra pit in front of the stage and they activated an old holo-gram projector. An old clip even Alice recognized of two people rushing down a hallway with rifles, crewmen from a ship lost to Edxi years and years ago, ran into a horrific foe. Only a few rounds were fired before they were cut and torn to pieces by razor sharp arms and merciless hands. The Edxi wasn't clearly visible, but the carnage was undeniable.

Fear, disappointment, and anger bashed at Alice's brain and she did her best to weather it, clenching her teeth. Peter pressed on. "That is what they do, the Edxi. They take humans apart and devour them. Brood ships will bring hundreds of thousands of them here."

"We fight!" someone from the audience shouted.

"We'll kill them!" added another.

"So, we fight them instead of leaving," Peter said. "What does that look like? Captain?"

Alice steeled herself, forced her mind to close itself off and managed to clear her head enough to reply. What she told them would have to be clear, easy to understand and easier to believe. "If two brood ships come, then there will be over a hundred thousand eggs on the ground in a matter of hours. If there are more, then it could be half a million. Those aren't the eggs you have to worry about. A sort of guardian parasite that attacks humans and controls them by digging into the back of a host's neck so it can take over their nervous system will come first. The first of your people, the ones who go to destroy the Edxi eggs will face those, and then they'll end up fighting each other, because thousands of them will get taken over by that parasite. Then the eggs will hatch. It'll happen a few hours, maybe a couple days after they make landfall. A third to half of your people will be killed before the week is out. Then, if you're lucky, the people they were trying to protect will find places they can wall off." Even with her sense nearly muted, she could feel the outrage and fear her words were evoking. Instead of softening her language, she pressed on harder. These people had to believe her. "Most of those safe places will fail in the following two or three weeks, I've seen how easy it is for hungry Edxi to break through barricades made of armour grade metal. There will only be a tenth of you left by the end of the first month. Some will die when they're caught looking for food, others will survive by eating the few kills they make but eventually get caught by a swarm while they're trying to hunt. The Edxi young will track them back to the holes they were hiding in and kill their families. I've seen it myself."

"We haven't!" shouted a tall, bearded fellow who abandoned his seat in the front row. "How can we believe you? Maybe you want this world for your fleet! You just lost your home." He was filled with indignation and fear.

"Haven Fleet doesn't conquer, we disrupt, and we assist when we can," Alice shouted back. His surprise was shortly followed by anger, and she interrupted him, pushing through the pressure of the empathic wave coming off the crowd with anger of her own. Watching this objector, this idiot step forward and infect the audience with fear made her furious. "Stay here! I don't have time for little people who think you can fight the whole universe and win! You're just the kind of stupid, blind believer who would pick up a twenty-year-old gun and run into the woods to break eggs. A parasite will take you and the next time your children see you, you'll be a bleeding, half-dead thing that's breaking the barricades to their home down so the Edxi can eat them! There is one way to survive this: run!"

The fear in the room was rising, the crowd was taking her seriously, but there were still a few standouts who were too proud, too angry. One of them, a woman who looked wealthy, too well dressed for the gathering surged to her feet. "You brought them here! The Edxi followed her here after they couldn't get their world!"

"Look at this stupid asshole!" Alice raged in return. "For the cost of the jewellery she's wearing she could feed everyone here for a week! Of course you don't want to leave, but the Edxi don't care about how much money you have. You're a slow, plump meal for just one of them. Sell all that crap you're wearing and buy a fast ship, fill it with people who need to get away. That's what matters. I came here looking for people who we could work with, discovered that the Edxi are on their way, and I'm trying to help you."

"Why? Why would such a powerful fleet with big guns and ships need us? I don't believe it!" the first objector shouted.

"I have time to help you, but I don't have time for idiots. If you want to stay, if you're too dense to understand that there is no hope for you if you stick around, then there's nothing I can do for you. It's Darwinism in action and you deserve what you get!" That was too far, Alice knew it the moment the words were in the air, and the surge of outrage verified it. A headache was starting to squeeze her mind like a tightening ring.

"Wait! Haven Fleet is here to help us leave!" Peter shouted, stepping to the very edge of the stage with his arms raised. "They have a list of safe worlds for us to quietly send our people to, and when their fleet arrives, they will help get whoever remains off the planet before the Edxi arrive. We must be quiet, we must keep this secret for as long as we can, or there may be Order of Eden intervention."

The crowd quieted by the time he finished talking. The pain in Alice's head didn't abate. Her so-called gift was out of control, she could feel the whole audience at once, it was like her mind was drowning.

With the audience mostly back under control, Peter went on. "They are making me one of their leaders, offering weapons and equipment to warriors who want to join them. There is a place for everyone, and until then..." He opened the case holding the Hull Buster and held the explosive up so everyone could see the heavy, dark canister. "They are giving us a hundred of these so we can break open the prisons, destroy Order of Eden installations, and take our revenge against the government officials who betrayed us. There are guns and armour suits here already, enough for a couple small cells, with more to come, much more. By the time the Order realizes that we are abandoning this place, many of the enemies we've had since this occupation started will be dead. It is time to plan quickly, to act faster, then leave this world so we can continue the fight out there and make a new home for ourselves once we find refuge far from here, where the Order can't reach us. Haven Fleet promises all of that, and as their newest leader, I can tell you that it will be done. We will have our revenge, then we will have our freedom!"

Alice only had a moment to be surprised at how quickly the fearful, angry crowd was turned by Peter before she felt surrounded by intense blood lust mingled with hope for the future before she fell flat on her back. Yawen was there a moment later, picking her up and carrying her from the stage. Through a haze of pain, she looked at her friend and muttered; "I screwed this up, didn't I?"

"You did great," Yawen said, looking worried, feeling alarmed. "The ship is coming, just hang on Alice, just..."

The pain wouldn't stop, it felt like her heart was beating in the middle of her head and it was crowding her grey matter more with every beat until her eyes rolled into the back of her head and all sensation stopped.

FIFTEEN

Aftermath

YAWEN'S REPORT, which was mostly a recording of Alice appearing on stage with Peter, concluded. The common area in Jake's quarters was left in half-light as a silent moment passed. "I've never seen anyone that angry before," Minh-Chu said quietly. "I've seen people face their worst enemies, go into war with a furious heart, and the madness of hate take complete hold. I've even lost my mind a couple times myself when I was adrift. None of that compares to what Alice was showing that gathering. Where does that come from?"

"Abuse," Alaka said, sadness weighing his voice down. "Not from family, I'm sure. When one of my people go feral, it most often comes from long term mistreatment or imprisonment. That's why there were no prisons during the darker periods of my people's history. We killed the worst of our criminals, keeping them confined was too risky. Perhaps this is Alice's breaking point. From the little I know of her, she wouldn't abandon diplomacy this way, even in anger."

"She's an empath," Agameg said from his seat across from Alaka. "Alice has been through trauma few people can understand, her personality must have been modified every time she transitioned from one body, one shape to the next and she probably has a lot of hidden damage. How many times has she had to face hopelessness alone? My people have a kind of empath's gift when we're in the same pool. We can't help but share our emotions, and if we're there long enough, we learn each other's histories. If there's old trauma buried within us, it comes to the surface eventually. If we're surrounded by a community that stands against us, it's like they're poisoning the water. We turn our stored trauma outward so we can counter our rancid surroundings by making it worse for the people poisoning us. It's a self-destructive reflex that rarely works. That's why some of us end up like me, an outcast. My poison killed members of the tribe, and I barely survived."

"Do you mind if I ask what turned your people against you?" Alaka asked. "If you don't want to share, I understand."

"No, it was a long time ago," Agameg said. "My life mate and several of my siblings were killed when Suno Corporation claimed our lake. I ran while they were churned into their machines, as the person you might call mayor ordered. The regret I felt about that turned to anger, and I argued with the Mayor endlessly. The frustration I felt eventually poisoned the water around me, and the community turned against me. When I was confronted by the survivors, I shared the biological mass where my anger was gathering deep in my body with them, making the water around me so toxic that it was lethal to three younger members. Pure anger was rare with my clutch, almost unheard of, so it was difficult to process for them, and for me. I was exiled. Years later, after I knew much more about the dry universe, I joined the Samson crew and started to heal. I see some of the toxicity in Alice, and I can understand the provocation she's reacting to."

"Quan has almost exactly the same opinion," Jake said, trying to put his astonishment at Agameg Price finally sharing the story of his departure from his home waters. As his Captain, he pretended to know the reason why Agameg wasn't with his people, but he'd never actually heard the story. What made it more enlightening was that Suno Corporation had been acquired by Regent Galactic over two years ago, and they were wholly controlled by the Order of Eden. "Quan's coming aboard in a few minutes. He's already seen this. In his opinion, Alice was being overwhelmed by the audience. An empath can be negatively affected by too much emotion and they'll often lash out emotionally. Just like Agameg said; it's a reflex, a self-defence mechanism that comes up before the mind takes damage. Human empaths aren't like Nafalli, who retreat, so he says."

"I've only known one Nafalli empath, but that's true as far as I know," Alaka agreed. "If any of my people are overwhelmed by emotion, we retreat to someone we trust, a whole family if we're lucky. If there's no one like that nearby, we find a way to be alone so we can recover in peace. That goes for most of my people, not just empaths."

"And if one of your people can't find that peace, if they're cornered, they turn to rage," Minh-Chu said.

"Yes, there's nothing more dangerous," Alaka agreed quietly.

"A lot of humanity is the same," Minh-Chu said. "If we get hurt, we retreat too. Sometimes we say something we regret first, but often, we go to our opposite corners for a while, if we're mature enough. The Valents can be a little different, though. If their nose is put out of joint, they tend to strike back without holding anything back. I'm afraid your daughter takes after you, Jake. You have Peter putting her in a difficult spot on one hand, and a whole audience hitting her with bad vibes on the other. Not that I disagree with what she's saying, but I see someone in a corner lashing out."

"I'd like to think I've grown a little," Jake said. "But I have to admit, whether it's an enemy captain or a bounty that wouldn't go down easy, I sometimes lost my cool. It was always ugly."

"Like the bounty on Immeran Five who you delivered without hands?" Agameg asked, cocking his head.

"He got my gun and put a hole in my suit," Jake said, remembering the career kidnapper, Boolan San.

"Put a hole in you, too," Agameg added. "I remember what you said; 'the wound will heal, but I made this suit by hand.'"

"I really need to hear more stories from your Samson days," Minh-Chu said as Alaka's long snout bobbed up and down in agreement.

"Sometime. Getting back on track," Jake said, clearing his throat. "Alice made a promise she couldn't back up. That's as good as a lie, so Peter, this leader, multiplied the promises she did make in front of his leadership."

"His leadership?" Alaka asked.

"That audience was filled with cell leaders, there's anywhere between a dozen and a hundred people under each of them. That puts their numbers in the high thousands, maybe tens of thousands. I'm sure Peter's announcements pissed her off, and the audience made things a lot worse. Theodore says her vitals are good, and he doesn't detect more brain damage, but it's been four hours and she hasn't regained consciousness. We're taking care of that by leaving as soon as Quan gets here. He'll help Alice if she'll let him, if not, I'm going to bring him along for any negotiations I have to take on myself."

"What about the promises Peter inflated?" Alaka asked.

"That's why we're bringing the Pelican. It's probably full of bugs, and the crew are two thirds trainees, but it's our first hangar ship with room for fifty thousand beds. There's room for two thousand crew, but it's running with a little over two hundred. How would you like that command for this trip, Alaka?"

"I would enjoy that opportunity over my most recent mission," he replied.

Minh-Chu looked to Jake, an eyebrow raised.

"He was sent to Lelauren, one of the nearby neutral systems in the sector to talk to the leadership there."

"My diplomacy was perfect, and they were polite, but they want no part of this war. Half of what they have is made by the Order's companies, and they're making too much profit from the conflict thanks to rare raw material exports," Alaka explained, his nose twitching. "That's not what they told me, though. They said they didn't want to risk the security of their solar system. They were trying to scan everything we had the whole time we were there, and offered generous terms for samples of our technology, though. One of them even threatened to take our ship, but they relented when my entire team cloaked and hacked into their main communications system."

"Of their ship?" asked Agameg.

"No, their interplanetary military network. We were in Reed Square when we cloaked, standing beside half their ministers. They relented immediately and apologized, especially after we deactivated their planetary defences."

"I knew you'd do things my way," Jake said with a smile. "That's why I sent you out there. Intelligence wanted a military team to handle that diplomatic mission because the Lelaurenites respect strength. They want to talk again, by the way."

"I would rather command the Pelican, if you don't mind," Alaka said.

"That's going to be a thankless task filled with bug smashing and double shifts."

"If it gives me a break from two-faced diplomats like the Lelaurenites, then I'd command two Pelicans."

"Then that's your command until we're finished there, congratulations," Jake said.

"Who will talk to the Lelaurenites?" Minh-Chu asked.

"Remmy. It's on his way," Jake replied. "I'm looking forward to his report."

"So, getting back to the Pelican; as I understand it that ship is a huge hangar with big shield generators, a cloak and a quad drive system. It's not exactly nimble or tested though, so tell me we're not going to be its only cover. " Minh-Chu asked.

"The Rassaaga is coming with us, and all your fighters are being replaced by the Seventh Generation Models."

Minh-Chu sighed with a satisfied smile. "It's about time."

"I'm guessing they're an upgrade?" Alaka asked.

"In every way. Every part of them are self-repairing. Their weaponry, shields, power plants, pilot interfaces and everything else is several generations ahead of the fighters we're using now. They look the same, but they also have a cloaking system, a new grabber device and a tiny quad drive. There are other details, but these ships are going to protect my pilots much better. The Order is in for a surprise."

"I can't wait to see one," Agameg said. "Their development has been such a secret that I still can't get a look at the schematics."

"Hopefully we can get the Pelican along with all the spare bunks we're setting up in the Rassaaga and the Merciless filled up with exiles from Nuaji without firing a shot."

"But that's as likely as the galaxy reversing its spin because someone steals the last cookie in the galley," Minh-Chu said.

"Right," Jake sighed. "I want something to be clear before we dedicate ourselves to helping the people on Nuaji. I've looked everything over again, and my report is going to stay the same. She made one mistake: she made a big promise she couldn't keep to get her foot in the door and buy herself time so she could keep negotiations going. I still think Peter was the only person she could approach to get in touch with the largest resistance in that solar system. I believe it would have been a mistake to approach the government there. I'm also agreeing that the solar system she's acting in is the best candidate for liberation, and that it'll embarrass the Order more than any other target, especially if we take out extra objectives there. Does anyone disagree?"

"One lie spiralled," Agameg said, nodding. "It poisoned negotiations going forward. I have seen it happen before, and I believe she didn't think she had any other way to get the leadership to work with her in the time she had. I believe she'll act differently next time. As for the rest of the conclusions in your report, I agree with them all."

"The bigger the blunder, the clearer the lesson," Minh-Chu said with a nod. "She won't do that again, and now that I know all the details, I agree with the rest of your report. Now we get to save several thousand people and make a huge mess of a solar system right in the middle of Order territory while we make sure Alice is all right. We're doing the right thing from one end to the other here, Commodore."

"My opinion doesn't matter much," Alaka said passively. "I'm beneath you in the chain of command, but I've come to the same conclusions."

"All right, then let's start putting a plan together so we know what we're doing once we get there," Jake said. He didn't have to ask for anyone's opinion, but he knew he was surrounded by people who had seen war from different angles and been in a wide variety of sticky situations. Their advice could be valuable, ignoring it would be a mistake.

"I'll keep track of what you're doing here but can I..." Minh-Chu pointed at the door.

"You can go make sure the new fighters are put away right," Jake said, shaking his head.

"Humans love their toys most when they're new and shiny," Agameg nodded as Minh-Chu departed.

SIXTEEN

Lorander According to Quan

IT CAME as a surprise to Ayan that Quan had not only been spending double-digit hours in one of the antechambers surrounding her command centre, consulting on all matters involving Lorander, but he'd been busy reading all the material he could relating to joining Haven Shore. She was one of the people who called on him often, looking for more details about his people, tips on how to get through to the diplomats they had aboard, and information about empathic abilities and more.

He was in the middle of writing a lengthy, heavily detailed indexed report on that topic in the exact format that Haven Shore required. Most officers didn't follow that template, they fed their collected data into the system, activated an auto-formatting program to put their report in order, checked it, filled in any leftover blanks then sent it off. Not Quan, no, he followed the procedure to the letter, and Ayan could see that once he was finished they'd have a comprehensive file that had everything he knew about empaths, telepaths and the Geist. Seeing him go off on a mission aboard the Merciless was more of a loss than she believed before checking his activities.

That's why she made sure she was in the hallway outside his quarters with Leon several minutes in advance of his departure time. Leon tapped on the door, activating the chime inside. A moment later Quan opened it dressed in an Axiologist's blue robe. The collar of a matching vacsuit showed above it, and the belt he wore to hold it all together only had one mark - a pole planted in a field represented by a line - it was a surprising sight to Ayan. He looked stunned as well. He hurriedly finished chewing a mouthful of whatever he was eating before he answered the door, boggling, then coughing briefly. "Defence Minister, I had no idea you were visiting. I would have told you to come earlier."

He looked weary, and Ayan smiled at him. "I wanted to walk you to the airlock. I didn't know you were an Axiologist."

"I agree with their philosophy of peace, and there's a call for anyone who feels that they'd like to join to wear their robes and mark their belt. I thought, since I can't join Haven Fleet, I could represent the next best idea. Peace and wisdom. Do you know much about the order?"

"I've known a member who spent time on Earth before the most recent war. It didn't work out well between us, but I believe we could have been friends for a long time if things were different. The robe suits you, so does the order, but why don't you think you can join Haven Shore?"

Quan watched Leon peek through the door with a little smile, and when Ayan's assistant picked up the telepath's bags, he objected lightly; "You don't have to do that, Leon, I can carry my own things."

"It's the least I could do while we see you off," Leon said, shouldering the simple pack.

Turning back to Ayan, Quan told her; " I can easily defeat your surface scanner during an interview about loyalties and tendencies. It's a security hole your people haven't been able to patch. Oh, and thank you for sharing about your old friend. That seemed very personal."

Suddenly self-conscious that he was probably picking up her old regret at how things ended with Liam Grady, she did her best to suppress her insecurity. Quan closed the door behind himself and the trio started down the hall. Its dark, polished deck, earthy brown coloured walls and moderate lighting were made to be soothing, but it felt altogether too quiet as she struggled to find the next thread of conversation. "The Admiral came to thank you for all the work you've been doing since you arrived aboard the War Forge," Leon said from behind them both.

"Right, you've been busier than most of our officers. I was sure you were trying to get into the Fleet," Ayan said, grateful that her assistant had a knack for bringing things back on point and moving conversations along.

"I sympathize with the cause of your people. The future you're looking to create is encouraging, I want to be a part of the effort," Quan said.

As she glanced at him, she saw the face of a young man who was clearly enthusiastic about the topic, more expressive than she'd seen him before. "Do you really want to become an Axiologist Pilgrim, Quan?"

"If you're asking me if I'd rather enlist with hopes of becoming an expert in my field for your fleet, then I would join Haven if that was possible," he replied.

"I bet we could set up a long probationary period where you would be watched instead of putting you through surface scans and interviews," Ayan said. "Freeground Fleet used to use probation periods, the policies are adaptable." The happiness that shone on Quan's face made her grin, and a thought donned on her; *He left his people, and now he's looking to find his place in the galaxy, a new people to take him in. I must have been a lot like him when I met Jonas, when I was reborn and wanted to find him and my friends any way I could.*

"I would appreciate that; any probationary period would be acceptable. I'd even accept a telepathy suppressor if necessary."

"So the monk robes would go back into the closet?" Leon asked.

"Well, yes, I wouldn't be allowed to wear them over a uniform, but I would still study the Axiologist's way. I agree with so many of their beliefs, and their history is interesting. The stories of the Pilgrims would take a lifetime to review, and there are so many lessons. You're right though, Admiral; I don't think I'd want that life. It demands that the Pilgrim wanders, and exploration would be exciting, but most of them wander alone, and that doesn't suit me."

"You're a people person," Leon concluded, looking pleased.

"I think that's the right way to put it. Crewmates, friends, the social spirit that surrounds your people reminds me of home. There are differences, definitely, but the essence feels the same as the place I was raised in."

"Where was that?" Leon asked.

Ayan looked forward to the answer, it was a question that was only answered with a set of coordinates in Quan's file, but she wanted to know much more, especially since he was going to help

Alice. She listened intently. "I'm from a village called Saodol, where my family has lived for many generations. I'd have to check my personal records to tell you how many, but we still did things by hand there. Advanced technology is used for water purification, planting crops, medical emergencies and a few other essential purposes. Most of our things are made by hand, we only watch digital entertainment on rest days, and we have a tightly knit community. That's why I found Haven Shore so incredible. Technology is embraced there, but people live in clusters that become like large families before long. The same is happening aboard the War Forge now that there are so many people here."

"I hope communities form here, but who knows with so many people coming and going. It sounds like you miss home, though," Ayan said.

"Sometimes. I left on the worst of terms. I was the fifth child in my family, and the first in our community to exhibit telepathic abilities. I was unlucky. Some telepaths find their abilities as they creep up on them slowly and they learn to control them naturally, even hide them entirely. I woke up one morning and could hear the entire village in my mind. Truths that should have remained hidden between neighbours were suddenly clear knowledge to me, and I didn't have the maturity to keep those secrets to myself. Empaths are tolerated in Saodol," Quan said with a sigh. "Telepaths are viewed with suspicion and fear. I didn't know how to dampen my sensitivity either, so I was suffering before long. The Lorander Corporation was contacted, and I was sent away. This story is not the same as the one I told your Officers when they performed their initial interviews. I said I joined the Lorander Corporation to train as a telepath but that was a half truth. I was sent away, and my relationship with my family fell apart. My training wasn't easy either.

The life of a telepath was strange to me for years, it still is some-times, but now I can shut those senses out. That's what makes telepathy and empathy a gift for me; the ability to dull the senses when I want to experience the world the way everyone else does."

"So, you can never go home?" Ayan asked.

"I could, but most doors would be closed to me. One of my brothers would take me in, but a visit from me would complicate his life for months even if I only stayed for a few days. Part of that community's beauty is in its simplicity, but many of their minds are closed for that reason. That's why Haven is so remarkable. Life may not be as simple, but even with your surface scans, and occasional fit of paranoia, the society you're building would rather extend the offer of citizenship and be watchful instead of closing your doors, instead of giving into fear entirely."

"That's flattering," Ayan said. "I hope we can keep it that way."

They arrived at the airlock's inner door. "Wow, that was not a long walk," Leon said, eying the section of wall that slid to the side. There were several smaller, round closed hatches that led to short slides. At the end of those tubes, large enough for an oversized adult were escape pods that were full-fledged ships with room for seven passengers. Only two of the round hatches were visible beside the airlock, but Ayan knew the wall would slide aside in an emergency to reveal half a dozen more, enough to take care of everyone in that habitation section and more. The inner airlock door was a grand looking transparent double hatch. A Clever Class ship extended its boarding collar to the outer hatch and locked, creating a good seal. "Here's your bag," Leon said, giving Quan a brief hug after putting the strap over his shoulder.

Ayan took her turn, automatically following Leon's lead and giving him a brief embrace. "Good luck, I'll get someone to work on putting a new probation period policy in place for people with higher mental discipline."

"Thank you," Quan said, looking a little surprised at the extra attention. "I'll do my best to help Alice, but it may not be easy. I have to respect her wishes if she refuses assistance."

"I wanted to ask," Ayan started, thinking; *Good glory, there are so many things I want to ask, it would take hours to cover everything. What can I ask right now that will help the most?* Then it came to her; "The delegation we have in secure quarters, do you think they'll ever cooperate?"

Quan answered in a more serious tone. "They represent the Lorander Corporation's most xenophobic branch. Where I come from, Lorander is a protectorate organization, they watch over hundreds of worlds in my home galaxy, but the part responsible for preserving humanity, gathering people for colonization on worlds far from the Milky Way, don't believe that your people should mix with them. They blame much of the trouble they find themselves in on humanity, believe we should have never mixed, but genetic diversity made people like me possible. Telepathy, empathic abilities, higher intelligence all come from an inclusive evolution. If you want to see how closed minded they really are, try arguing that with them. If I were you, I'd leave them in a ship without any of your advanced technologies so they can start making their way to their own people. I'd do it right before you depart for your next secret location. If you want to contact people from the Lorander Protectorate, the more reasonable part of their government, ask the British. They've had a representative in their capitol for decades."

"What?" Leon burst before clearing his throat and composing himself.

"Decades," Ayan said, shaking her head.

"I'm sorry, I would have told you but I thought you already knew," Quan said with a shrug.

"Don't worry," Ayan said. "It looks like all our allies hold things back, it doesn't surprise me. Thank you for everything, and for going to help my daughter, Quan."

"It's my pleasure," Quan replied. "Thank you for building," he rolled his eyes up and around as if to take the whole of the station in, "everything. I can't wait to join you."

SEVENTEEN

Old Man Minh

WHAT WAS the point of Jake giving me access to all of the Special Operations Unit's files? Minh-Chu wondered as he looked at the medical status of Alice Valent and her crew. He was in the Samurai Squad Room, sitting in the front row of the pilot seats which were exactly the same as the ones in the cockpits of Uriel fighters.

"A pony's back will only break once," he muttered as he looked at the assessment of the Clever Dream's crew. Most of their stress levels were in the red. Even people who should be able to handle the highest levels of strain, like Knud, Jessen and Woone, were at risk of breaking down. "It breaks once, then it can never bear a load again," he muttered to himself.

"Because they used to shoot them if that ever happened," Ashley said as she dropped into the seat beside him and tried to look at the holographic data he was projecting with his wrist unit. "Classified up high, huh?"

"You should be able to see this stuff," he replied. "You just have to tap your wrist on mine, it'll pick it up."

"What is it? Do I even want to see?"

"It's the Clever Dream crew. They're in big trouble," Minh-Chu said.

Ashley touched her hand to his, and he took it. The new proximity of her comm unit to his suit activated the security check, and the holographic display became visible. "Wow, that's a lot of red. Why's the stress so high? I mean, I know Alice went down for the count, but I thought her doc cleared her even though she's still asleep."

"Jessen had a bad reaction when she heard her Captain was an empath. My opinion? She's feeling guilty now that Alice won't wake up. Knud hates seeing crewmembers fight, and Jessen's his best friend going back a while. Woone..." he sighed. "From what I know of her now, I'd say she thinks everything Alice said in anger was right. Seeing people accuse her Captain of causing trouble when she was just there to help probably frustrates the hell out of her and the rest of the Nafalli. Then there's Ute and especially Iruuk. Those two look up to Alice, love her like a sister."

"What about him, Callum?" Ashley pointed. "His stress level is a little red too."

"Callum's hard to read, but I don't think he wants to take Alice's place, like Lamonthe said in the notes. I think he and Yawen are both standing by, making sure they can still do something if they're called on. I just hope all this calms down by the time we get there, and Alice is back on her feet."

"Quan will help, I met him, he's nice. Like a young Liam Grady before he went all crazy over Ayan."

"I hope so. I just don't know why Jake put this on my plate. I'm down to nine pilots who can fly the new Uriels, and five more who are still super green. Their stress levels are all right, but without Hal and Noah around, that could change quick."

"They have a great leader on their side," Ashley said, kissing him on the cheek. She looked to the holographic display for a moment before offering. "Maybe Jake wants your opinion because he knows you can give him a different perspective? I mean, if I can access this, then he must be approaching a lot of people with it."

"Well, what do you think?"

"I think this crew will bounce back as soon as Alice decides to get back on her feet. Maybe even sooner. It looks like a good group, the right kind of oddballs and fur balls."

Minh-Chu chuckled. "Oh, I'm going to have to use that."

"Oh, no, don't! They might take it the wrong way," Ashley pleaded.

"Too late. It's the rule. Once your words are in the air, they're fair game."

"Fine, just keep the credit if it goes bad," Ashley said.

"So, what brought you down here?" Minh-Chu asked.

"Big discovery," Ashley said. "We picked up Hawking Radiation and confirmed that there's a big gravitational field in our dimensional space."

"A black hole in the dimension our quad drives are using?" Minh-Chu asked. It was the first recognizable natural phenomenon that they recognized since they started using the technology.

"Not quite, it's better than that. The black hole has pushed its way into two dimensions and Kadri says it's starting to show up in a third. We're going around, way around, but the data they're getting has everyone in sciences excited."

"I can see why," Minh-Chu said. "There have been a lot of theories about what happens to anything that makes it to the deep end of a black hole. I guess it'll slow us down, but it'll be worth it."

"It's actually going to speed us up. We can't avoid all the gravitational effects, so we're picking a wide course and going with the flow for a while. Once we're sure of the math, we'll know how much time it'll save us, then there will be an announcement."

Minh-Chu brought his pilot roster up and saw that seven of them were handling the simulation tests for the new fighters like seasoned professionals and nodded to himself. "I'm going to pull every pilot I can out of sims and send them to Kadri's sensor team. I want them to hear and see everything that comes out of those awesome science-brain types. You might need to catch them up on what they're seeing."

"Me?"

"You understand this stuff faster than I do," Minh-Chu said. "When it comes to most things, you're the brains."

"Aw, no, Minh," Ashley said. "I forget drink orders between our table and the bar when it's my round. I'm not the genius type."

"Okay, next time we have a navigation calculation contest in the squad room, you join in. I bet you beat everyone here."

"That's just math," Ashley said. "Everything just snaps together in my head the way it should. I mean, sometimes it gets hard, but most things have a solution."

"Oh, there are thousands of pilots who wish they had your brain," Minh-Chu said. "Then there's the other side of things; social smarts. If it were you, what would you do to make sure Alice had the quickest recovery possible? She's an empath who just had a big negativity shock, that's what the report says."

"You're testing my intelligence, I don't think I like that, mister."

"Okay, maybe, and I'm sorry. Still, the Capt... the Commodore wants our opinion on his daughter and her crew. What would you do if her recovery were up to you?"

"Fine, not that it matters, I don't know empaths, telepaths, or any of that." Minh-Chu watched as she took a better look at the report. It was a simple side-by-side comparison of the whole Clever Dream crew at a glance, and she touched a few of the profiles to get more details as she scrolled through them. "First I'd wish Steph was here. She had a way of solving nonsense, stopping the boys from fighting without the Captain catching wind of it most of the time."

Patience was a virtue, and Minh-Chu enjoyed watching her think. After looking through the profiles she leaned back, looking at Alice, Yawen and Iruuk's profiles side by side as she lightly chewed her bottom lip. "I'd keep her away from everyone but these two. Everyone else would get to work on a different crew for a while, but these two and her would be on the Clever Dream with her somewhere else. Somewhere relaxing."

"Why Yawen?" Minh-Chu asked.

"She loves Alice. Maybe platonically but look at the attachment stats in her last backup scan, that's probably what you'd see if you compared me and Steph back in the day, maybe even now. Iruuk's stats make it look like he's adopted her. He loves her too, and they want to protect her, she'd be surrounded by positive emotions with those two. If you look at someone like Woone, she likes Alice a lot too, but I bet there are big expectations there, and maybe Alice could feel that."

"What about Noah?" Minh-Chu said.

Ashley shook her head. "She might want Noah around, and who knows? Maybe it could do her a lot of good to have an adoring boy around, but maybe it gets weird, maybe he can't handle her being a telepath..."

"Empath."

"Oh, right. Anyway, he's too much of a wild card. Better let her heal first. None of this matters, though. We're all looking at this really intimate data and wondering what we can do for her, but the moment she wakes up, it should be up to her. I know it's Jake's job to give her orders, but after that, everything's gotta be her decision. All anyone can do is give her advice. It's Alice, no matter what we tell her, she'll go her own way."

"See? I've been looking at this stuff for an hour and that didn't even occur to me."

"No way, you probably came up with that before you even looked."

"No, actually, I dug in without thinking about it first. I didn't have time to look anything over until now, I've been too busy boning up on the space we'll be emerging in."

"It's not too interesting," Ashley replied.

"I'm just an old man trying to keep up," Minh-Chu replied in a creaky voice. "I bet you had the nav data memorized in an hour, it took me all morning, and I'll still be looking at notes when we get there."

"I'll be looking at notes too," Ashley giggled softly. "But I did finish in about an hour and a half."

"See? You're one smart lady, and I'm one lucky old man," he replied.

"Okay, grandpa," Ashley teased, standing up and kissing him on the forehead. "I'm going back up to the bridge, my shift starts in fifteen. You should come, hang out in the ready lounge so you can see the discoveries as they come in."

"Oh yes, the scientific data, lead the way, pretty chickie," Minh-Chu said, standing with a groan then miming a limp and cane.

"You stopped aging at the same time I did," she snickered at his performance. "You don't look a day over thirty."

"Oh, good, then this cradle robber can still chase you little fillies around," he said with a grin and a pinch, which she narrowly avoided.

As Ashley shrieked and laughed, Panner, one of the pilots who just finished qualifying on the new Uriel fighter, entered the squad room. He boggled at the sight, grinning as he was stuck to the spot.

Minh-Chu and Ashley both straightened up instantly. "Going to the command level to see new sensor data," Minh-Chu said officially. "If you aren't headed for your rack for some sleep, you should come along."

"Sure thing, I'm just going to change my com-con unit out. The left one is, uh,"

Minh-Chu cocked an eyebrow. "It's?"

"The model we don't use as much anymore," Panner said sheepishly.

"He was going to say; 'it's an older model,'" Ashley said with a lopsided smile.

Minh-Chu couldn't resist the urge to make Panner even more uncomfortable. "Well, if you've got to put the old thing down, then there's no helping it. Just make sure the recycler processes it nice and quick. No need for your old Command and Control Unit to suffer, aye?"

"Aye, Sir," Panner replied.

As soon as they were through the door and out of sight from the poor pilot, Minh-Chu started chasing Ashley with pinching fingers. She outran him, but barely, and when they met at the transit car doors, she held her hands up. "Truce!"

"All right, you're on your way to the bridge, we can pick this up later," Minh-Chu said, stealing a kiss from her before settling down and straightening his jacket.

"Just never take the old man thing seriously," she told him. "I never saw that in you."

"Well, I guess with meds like this, age is all mental anyway, so you have a deal. I like the old man schtick sometimes though."

"It's a little creepy," Ashley objected.

"Well, he's a little creep," Minh-Chu croaked.

"Stop."

"Okay, serious face." He snapped up straight and looked at the elevator doors steadily.

"Okay," Ashley said, joining him with a snicker.

In the seconds they had to wait as the transit car descended, Minh-Chu turned his thoughts back to the Clever Dream crew. There was something no one was considering about them, and what might have brought them so close to the breaking point. They had just finished a murder campaign, sneaking behind enemy lines then launching invisible bombs that killed thousands of people - even if they were soldiers, they were still people - who never saw it coming. After performing so well in real combat, losing crew mates and having their home taken from them, perhaps that and seeing their leader fall were enough to push them too far. The thought wouldn't earn him friends in Intelligence, but it was worth sharing with Jake. It was the kind of thing he might already be thinking. "Thank you for helping me get a better perspective. I'm still amazed you're my girlfriend," Minh-Chu said.

Ashley blushed, something that happened almost every time he told her how lucky he felt even though it definitely happened often enough. Slipping into his arms, she gave him a soft kiss. "I love you too, Minh-Chu."

EIGHTEEN

Secret Meetings

DARK ROOMS, dim corners, forgotten places and hidden corridors. Peter found himself spending more and more time in such places. The room was made to feel as comfortable as possible, with chairs, a table, and a small drink dispenser with clean cups. The lighting was dim, emanating from a little portable broad emitter above, whether by intention or because it's all they had on hand at the moment, they'd made it another dingy back room perfect for conspiracy and treasonous talk. It only took that one light to throw the comfort of the place off for him.

The thick metal door was locked, and Peter knew that if he opened it, he'd see the rush of people packing, getting ready to break the base they'd established in the old tourist spot they'd taken. The Inverted Gardens would be an abandoned husk again in hours. Sonny looked at him from his right side, a question on his face.

The resistance cell leaders were talking about the problems they were facing as the first groups of evacuees were making their way off world. Peter was half following the conversation, it sounded like minutiae that didn't really matter to the big picture, and he decided it wasn't worth the little time he had left to speak to the biggest leaders in the resistance. "So, the word has already gotten out that resistance leaders are moving their families off world. The ports are filling up with people who want to get off the planet, and every seat is booked," Peter said, repeating what he was hearing back at the leaders, hoping to cut their complaining short.

"And there are people buying blocks of tickets and charging up to ten times as much for seats," one of the leaders, a gentleman in old armour that left his sun worn face open to the light. He was Senal, the leader of one of the most aggressive cells. "I've had one of them taken and strangled to death, but I wanted to talk to you before we took things further."

"Let it happen," Peter said with a shrug.

"What?" Senal asked, surprised.

"Are the transports full?"

"They are, but some of those passengers had to pay with everything they..."

"So they left, they're gone, they're away from here. They're better off, even without their money. What did you do with the tickets that you took from the man you killed?"

Senal hesitated for a moment, he wasn't proud of the answer. "They were for Dulo, so we used them for family."

Dulo was a neutral solar system within range of most of the civilian transports. They hadn't taken sides in the war with the Order yet, it was a rare thing, but they were profiting from the conflict. "I'm glad they saw good use. If you need batches of tickets, then take them from these scalpers if you want. This mass exodus won't last long, though. The government will notice it soon because the media will pick it up and broadcast the phenomenon wide, and then the Order will have it stopped. If you want to turn coward and get off world before our new allies arrive, then go. Go soon."

"We're securing the safety of our families," said Malli. She was one of the easiest leaders to work with, normally reasonable, and highly dedicated. Once she chose a course of action, there was no stopping her or her people. "I sent my husband and daughter to Dulo the moment I discovered the Edxi were coming. This is the tragedy of our time, I don't want them to see it, let alone be one of the victims. I'll be standing beside you when Haven Fleet gets here, but I won't have them get drawn into the fighting. They'll be long gone."

"I understand your point, I'm only saying that our friend Senal has run before, backing out of an operation with his people when we needed him most."

"I can't believe you're bringing that up," Senal said. "You're not one to talk. I remember you directed that raid from a safe distance and eventually argued that we abandon it."

"After I watched you and over forty fighters run," Peter sighed. "I wasn't going to let Malli and her people be captured or murdered because of your cowardice."

Senal stood but was yanked back down into his seat by Franklin. He was a normally verbose man who was more of a story teller than any of them. That, his dedication to the cause, and an unshakable habit of speaking plain sense were at the core of his leadership. "Everyone knows about that raid," he said calmly. "We all have a moment in our time as leaders that could be used to question our dedication or our common sense. We could sit here, comparing failures, or move on. I think Peter is trying to ask you a simple question; can you and your people be trusted to follow through?"

"Of course he can trust us," Senal said, yanking his arm free from Franklin's grip as he settled back in his seat. "What do you need us to do?"

"Your people have a large presence in the major ports," Peter said. "I need them to take control of them when its time. We're going to need the ground defence cannons, any ships that are on the ground, and to get people..." Peter was interrupted by a priority message from the Order of Eden. The green logo occupied his right optical display and wouldn't be dismissed. He pushed through to finish his point. "Get people aboard the ships and off world when Haven Fleet comes. If they don't, we'll need your people even more."

"My people will have to leave on ships too. Once they take control of the major ports they'll be exposed."

"Then you'll do it?" Peter asked, annoyed by the private message obscuring his view.

"Absolutely."

"Good. I need every other cell that we can trust to fall behind Malli and Franklin. They're going to create a distraction for the military and the rest of law enforcement. I have some ideas, and some of them involve us stealing armoured transports, but you know your territories better than I do. Discuss what kind of distractions you think would be best while I attend to this. There's an urgent message on my comm." He left the table and slipped off to the corner. Sonny started to get up and he motioned him to remain there, telling him; "It's probably just propaganda."

He braced himself and played the message. Location details along with an animated map showing him how to get to the Order of Eden Intake Centre started playing as an upbeat voice spoke to him through his dermal audio system. "Congratulations! You have been summoned to the service of the illustrious Admiral Scanlon's staff. Once you report for indoctrination, your amazing career can begin. Since you have medical considerations, you will be tested for the Framework Augmentation Program and all your ailments will be cured. This is the opportunity to attain eternal life through superior technology, and to place well in the Admiral's service. Let's not get ahead of ourselves, though. Indoctrination will take three months, during which time you will receive special training, be asked to perform important tasks, and over twenty percent of your debt will be worked off by the time you're finished. That's just for taking the mandatory training, imagine the earnings you could accrue afterwards. You are to report in twenty hours to the location we're showing you. Use that time to get your affairs in order, and to invite others to go with you to the Order of Eden Intake Centre, so your friends and family can make their debt disappear and engage in a brilliant future. As a reward for recruiting, you will be entitled to five percent of their earnings. Remember; immortality is within reach, it's our right, it's our predetermined fate. Serve, earn rewards, and rise eternally."

It was difficult not to react as the message faded. The directions were in the bottom right of his view, the animation of a small sky car flying to the Intake Centre playing over and over again. He couldn't dismiss it or the timer that started counting down from twenty hours. The Admiral was calling him to her side. She didn't know him, probably didn't know that he was the leader of a vast rebellion, or that he was aware of the Edxi who were about to colonize the world he loved. People who ran at the sight of similar messages were caught or killed. There would be Order of Eden soldiers on their way to take them in half an hour or more before the timer counted down to zero. He'd seen it happen, heard of it happening, and no one could stop it.

"Peter," Malli said. "I'm getting a Wave Comm from my people saying that recruitment messages are going out."

"Wait, you're getting messages too?" Sonny asked, alarmed. "This room isn't as secure as we thought. If Wave Comm signals can pass, anything can."

"It's probably the electronics in the room or a crack in the door," Peter said, dismissing his partner's worry. "We checked for listening devices, we're still safe."

"Back to the point, I have a dozen or so people saying that they have twenty hours to report," Malli said.

"I just got one," Franklin said. "My people are getting them too. About half."

"Then that proves it," Peter said, feeling his heart sink, his palms sweat. "The Edxi are coming sooner than expected. The Order are taking all the people they want from our world so they can close the ports and trap everyone else on the planet."

"What do we do?" Franklin asked, as close to worried as anyone had seen him.

"I have an idea, it'll defeat the Edxi and provide the distraction we need to tget as many people off world as possible. This will have to happen fast." He looked to Malli. "Do you still have people who can program nanobots?"

"Yes, one of them is being called up by the Order," she replied.

Peter took a command and control unit that he found in the Haven Fleet equipment boxes the crew of the Clever Dream left behind from his pocket and put it on the table. "This has a tiny fabrication system in it that can make high grade nanobots. By tinkering with it I can tell the nanos to self-replicate. I need your people to repurpose them for something."

"No problem," Malli said.

"What do you need them reprogrammed for?" Franklin asked.

"You don't need to know," Peter replied. It was standard, his leaders knew that information was always compartmentalized. "Your concern is taking over as the lead commander for the distraction we'll make while Senal's people take control of the ports and get as many people off world as they can. We only have one standard day. This will be the biggest act of defiance the Order has seen, and if we do this right, most of us will escape."

"What about Haven Fleet? Can we expect help from them?" Malli asked.

"They haven't responded to our calls since their leader collapsed on stage," Peter said. "It's up to us now."

NINETEEN

The Resistance Strikes

ARGUMENTS WITH SONNY were never pretty. He wasn't an unreasonable partner, but once he decided on a course of action, it was difficult to change his mind. The words echoed in Peter's head still; "You need to be in the middle of everything at Ridge Port, I don't trust Senal's conviction. I know you'll make sure his people follow through, the cells know your face as well as mine."

"Senal's fine, he wants to run. He'll steal the first military transport he finds. I think you should be on it too. I know you should be on it. When this plan goes into motion, you'll have less than two hours left," Sonny replied.

"I'll be exactly where I need to be, besides, there's going to be transportation there too," Peter said. "With no rush of civilians fighting for a spot."

"You're going to have over thirty people on that raid and we won't know how many runabouts will be docked with the tower. There'll be a rush there too, and a shortage if your plan works out."

"'They'd leave me behind?" Peter asked, feigning surprise at Sonny's statement. "You know they'd put me on whatever transport is there, and I'll be off world minutes later, running for the rendezvous. We're wasting time. I'll see you soon, and then we'll be with Haven Fleet, or running across the galaxy, either way, we'll be together."

Sonny was frustrated, but he saw that there was no convincing Peter, so he kissed him instead and told him; "If I could just shove you into a bag and drag you along, I would. God, you frustrate me sometimes."

"Just to get me down from that pedestal you put me on sometimes," Peter replied. "I'll see you soon."

It was half an hour later as he went over their discussion, their fight in his head, and they were about to land on the main platform of the Northern Environmental Processing Tower. It was the tallest building in the hemisphere, a square that tapered up, up, its dark metal skin opening with giant vents that looked like too many eyes and mouths. Air flowed in, the temperature, humidity and velocity were changed, then it was released. Sometimes microscopic nutrients and seeds were added to the mix as well, and they'd be delivered through rain that was anything but natural.

They were dormant for most of Peter's childhood, but the Order of Eden ordered that they were turned up to full power things began to change. The balance of the world he loved was shifting visibly, and while he was happy the Order presence was low since they could control the government that was already in place, the changing weather and forestation was a constant reminder that his people were not in control.

A vibration and a message on his ocular display verified that Sonny and Senal had performed their duty. PORT TAKEN. There were no news alerts about it, so they'd kept it quiet, using people that Senal had in place to do it. Peter was surprised it worked, and sure that the authorities would catch on soon. The next step was to take control of every ship on the ground, that would definitely alert them. It would become the salvation to thousands who wanted to escape, and the call the authorities would answer, keeping them away from the Environmental Processing Tower.

There were ten people in the shuttle with him, and most looked at him as soon as he turned from the window. They were dressed in service uniforms, the vacsuits they were given were underneath. "We've all been called to service with the Order of Eden," Peter said, but many of them took it as a question and nodded or confirmed with terse yesses or yups. "I am happy I don't have to do this alone. Our friends are about to attack on the ground, they'll draw the guards away from the upper levels. Our families are in the port now, boarding ships that will take off soon. Friends we've known for years along with hundreds of fighters who we have never met are working together to take more ships, draw the authorities' attention, and seek freedom amongst the stars. Hopefully, we won't face much fighting, but if we do, I'll try to make sure as many of you can join them as possible. We should all have a chance to run."

"What about you, Sir?" asked a fighter at his side, his voice muffled by the vacsuit hood and brown worker's suit.

"Don't call me Sir, please," Peter said. "I love this world, seeing it change because it'll play host to some alien invader breaks my heart. After making sure you get away from here when we're finished, I want to make certain there's nothing for the Edxi here. I want to embarrass the Order in front of their allies and deny them. They don't deserve this planet, or peace, or cooperation, so I will deny them at every turn." He could feel the energy rise in the shuttle as it touched down. "Remember, we are a repair crew until the attack starts below."

The doors at the back of the shuttle opened. A powerful wind howled as they disembarked onto the high-altitude platform. To his left he could see Ridge Port in the distance, a city of grey and white surrounding it, with a brown and green forest wrapped around it. His imagination conjured a vision of Edxi ships planting eggs in the woods and smaller, alien creatures taking control of humans who were unlucky enough to live there, turning them into mind-less slaves. Dismissing the horror in his head, Peter turned his attention back to the walkway leading from the landing pad to the secure doors. The whole tower was weather-stained, metal that once looked clean had turned brown with some green in the corners.

The doors opened suddenly, two armed guards emerging urgently. "We're under attack, get back in your shuttle and take off," one of them said, waving them away.

"I don't see an attack," Peter said, looking around at the platform.

"Below, on the ground level!" the guard replied as though he was talking to an idiot.

"What? So we're not safe here?" Peter asked, playing panicked. "What do we do?" he wasn't much of a fighter, but he knew how to put on a show, and he did his best imitation of a civilian in panic, turning into an unreasonable mess. "Who would attack a Terraforming Tower? It doesn't make sense!"

"Resistance fighters," the guard said, trying to push Peter away.

Peter tried to take his hand, the one that was resting on his rifle.

"Wouldn't it be safer if we stayed here? None of us are armed!" That was the signal, that word, 'armed.'

"It'll be better if you just get back into your shuttle and... hey! Don't open your toolboxes, you don't need..."

The guards were both shot through an instant later thanks to the good aim of some of the resistance soldiers. "Rush the door!" Peter shouted as he burst into a run. He pulled his heavy pistol from a tool pouch on his worker suit as he did so. A guard fired at his group of resistance fighters once before slapping the inner control panel. Peter raised his weapon and got one shot off before the doors slid closed. It went wide, not even making it through. His group arrived at the door. "We knew this could happen, we're prepared," he said, pulling the cylindrical Hull Buster from his backpack. He checked the side that was supposed to go against the doors, pressed the main activation button, then put it against the metal, where it affixed firmly. He ran through the manual in his head quickly, making sure that he had the next step right, then turned the safety ring around the same green button until it clicked before pressing it again.

A large metal frame expanded from the sides of the Hull Buster, creating a metal dome against the door before the device began to hiss loudly. It started burning through the door, and if it functioned as promised, they'd have a nice big hole to rush through in a few minutes, perhaps less.

A public alert appeared on his ocular display. ALL PORTS CLOSED. PIRATES ARE TAKING HOSTAGES. Peter looked to Ridge Port and smiled as he saw the first of the rapid response law enforcement shuttles rush towards it. As soon as it rose up above the building between it and the circular port building, defence weapons mounted across the landing fields and terminal fired on it. The attack on the ports was far more important than the Environment Conditioning Tower, most of the authorities, if not all would go there. Two civilian Star Liners were taking off, they would be filled with normal citizens and family members of resistance fighters. "Like clockwork, I knew you'd have it all running perfectly, Sonny," Peter said under his breath.

TWENTY

The Solution

THERE WAS no resistance in the outer corridors of the tower. Even though Peter had seen it thousands of times from the outside, a great, dark rectangle that cast long shadows over the landscape, the size of it from the inside was still astonishing.

Old halls that split to subsystems, service rooms, vent accesses and storage spaces for material that was meant to be floated off into the air were everywhere. The walls, the absurdly tall ceilings and especially the floors looked ancient, clean but worn by bins with tracks that carried anything that was too heavy or inconvenient for the workers to move by hand were enough to create grooves in the floor and deep scrapes along the walls.

The map from one of the insiders guided them to the control room. The tower security guards decided to make their stand there, putting heavy equipment carts in the way so they could be used for cover in the last hallway. The door was sealed, but the security system was old. Peter had no problem popping the panel off and crossing a few wires, forcing it open. He was lucky. If he didn't take that duty on himself, he might have been in the doorway.

The guards inside opened fire on two of his men, the pair standing at the front, and even with their relatively primitive rifles, they broke through the work suit, then the vacsuits. It took more rounds than anyone could count, but in seconds those two resistance fighters were beyond bloodied, they were torn to shreds. Peter didn't let their sacrifice come to nothing, but ducked low and rushed forward, using one of the track driven carts that were placed in the way to provide the guards with cover for his own ends.

His fighters fired back, forcing the guards to duck. Moments later he was joined by his people, and they were half way up the hallway. The firing stopped on both sides and a stillness settled in. The guards were at the far end of the corridor, while Peter and the eight warriors he had left were half way up, hiding behind the tractor bins, not ten metres from the soldiers. "Big push down here, we need more men!" a scratchy voice said over the tower intercom. "The resistance has pushed us back, if we don't get reinforced by you guys up top, we'll have to retreat into the building and try to close the main doors."

"We're pinned down," replied one of the guards. "Get the military down there, there are only five of us here." He was whispering, but Peter was so close that he may as well of shouted.

"Military are responding to the ports, just get down here!" there was an explosion, it crackled over the building intercom before the system was silent.

Peter looked at Franklin's status feed and it increased to readable size in his ocular display: MAIN DOOR MECHANISM DESTROYED, GREAT GRENADE TOSS BY JERIK. GUARDS ARE PINNED DOWN, SPREADING OUT AND GETTING BEHIND WHATEVER COVER THEY CAN FIND.

It was good news, they would be occupied down there. "Five guards, rush them," Peter said as quietly as he could manage to the man at his side.

The resistance fighter looked to the pair behind him, passed the message, and the order was passed that way. No one trusted their electronics when they could signal each other, experience showed them anything could be tapped. Anyone could be listening.

"Go!" one of Peter's fighters shouted, and the eight moved out from behind cover and ran down the hallway, the rifles provided by Haven Fleet at the ready.

One of the shortest fighters was riddled with the guards' energy rounds, light burning through her work suit then passing through her, the smell of burnt flesh filling the air. It was a worthy sacrifice, enough to give everyone else an advantage so they could riddle the Guards with rounds. The mad, rapid popping roar from the Haven Fleet weapons made Peter flinch, he never realized how loud the fighting was when it was all around. It was the first raid he'd been right in the middle of while it was going on, and he remained behind cover as the last of the guards were subdued. A quick check on the ports revealed that they had control of nearly all the ships, including the military craft. They were corvettes, old gunships, and fighters. Resistance pilots, many of them deserted or retired military, were already taking off for the most part, the ships full to capacity. "How many people have we gotten off world now, Sonny?" he asked.

"We're loading the last now, so in a few minutes it'll be over forty thousand. I'm in a police rescue ship, we can come get you when you're finished."

"Forty thousand, pass my congratulations to Senal," Peter replied.

"I would, but he went missing as soon as we finished taking the main port. He'll probably pop up sometime later, just lost in the confusion."

"Well, get everything off the ground and get out of the area quickly," Peter said.

"That's the plan, but this ship will stick around just in case you need..."

"No, Sonny, go with the rest. Our ship is in good condition and there are others here. No one has escaped the tower."

"If you're sure," Sonny said slowly.

"I'll tell you as soon as I'm not," Peter said. One of the resistance fighters, a burn on his left shoulder, moved to his side. His eyes were alight with excitement, the old command and control unit Haven Fleet provided them with had a medical icon on its screen, indicating that some treatment was going on.

"It's over, we have the control room," the resistance fighter said.

"Do we have full control? Is the emergency hatch to the main seed bay opening? Can you control deployment and processing?"

"Yeah, all of that, full control. We just need the nano-cartridge. Oh, and there are two surviving guards. We have them tied up."

"We lost three taking this station?" Peter asked.

"Four," the fighter said, lowering his head. "Darla is gone, I can't believe it."

Peter stood, opened his work suit and climbed out of it. His vacsuit had the same markings he saw on Alice's, it took some time to duplicate since the system fought him, it knew he hadn't earned the same place in the Fleet, but he was eventually able to use a decoration system that was made for children so they could add designs and colours to their suits. The fighter, Peter didn't want to know his name, looked surprised. "I want Haven to be a part of this, even if they didn't think it was important for them to be here themselves."

The fighter only nodded, it wasn't clear if he actually understood or even agreed.

It didn't matter to Peter, who walked down the remaining stretch of hallway, making his way between bins that had burn marks and dents on them. The pair of guards were on their knees in front of the door to the control room. "I don't have time for you to cause any problems." He said, and without thinking about the act, he drew his heavy handgun and fired towards the first guards' face, the barrel only a few centimetres away from his nose. The sudden eruption of blood and matter that scattered behind the man was more jarring than any experience Peter had ever had. Compared to seeing his ruined face for the first time, even compared to the painful recovery, his first personal kill was an unparalleled horror. What was left of the man from the jaw down tilted forward, blood from his still pumping heart covered Peter's leg.

"No, please! I have a family! Twins! Baby twins and a wife!"

"Collaborator," Peter said through clenched teeth, trying to force his disgust, regret and horror into blame and anger.

"It's a non-Order job, one of the last left! Babysitting the tower! Just let me go! I won't do anything! Let me go!" the guard was weeping openly, struggling at his bindings.

Hating his own sympathy was a completely new experience for Peter but hating himself was not. Misery was coming, people like that guard would have the worst time of it. "This is a mercy," Peter said under his breath as he made sure his pistol was pointed at the guard's head before he looked away then pulled the trigger. A resistance fighter flinched at the brief roar of the heavy handgun. His shocked eyes watched him as he stepped away, through the door into the control room.

It felt like he was going to throw up, so he filled his throat with words instead. "The last Czars of Earth didn't see their deaths coming. They could feel it around them like silent predator, they knew they weren't in danger, but in the end, when they were led to a dark basement room, when the lot of them were murdered, children and all, they didn't know it was to happen that moment until the bullets were in the air. That was bloody revolution, the end of an era and the beginning of one of the most painful national rebirths in all of history." He found the control that would open the hatch to the main seed chamber. "Revolution has a bloody cost, and breaking ties with your own national past is like eviscerating yourself to extract a tumour." As he pulled the small lever down, the aperture in the corner of the room's floor opened. He turned his recorder on and forwarded the signal to the tower's broadcasting system. The board lit up and indicated that three hyper transmitters were picking it up, sending his voice and the security holorecorder data on to other solar systems.

Turning to the aperture, he crouched down and started to slip inside, the short tunnel leading to the seed bay lit up beneath him. Before he pushed off he continued what he was saying. "The Order of Eden lurks around the planet of Nuaji, our home, and its citizens like a stalking predator. We're not the Czars in this story, we're the revolutionaries that must sacrifice their lives, watch what's left of their country burn in order to force change. There are holes in the analogy, so I'll make my statement simple." He pushed off, slid down the round passage for several seconds, enough time for him to remember the guard, then landed roughly on top of a mountain of ultra-fine seeds. His suit protected him, but his stomach and mind were too unsettled, and he was throwing up as he rose to his knees, something he was sorry the galaxy had to see. He was down to bile by the time he finished retching, by the time he forced himself to stop thinking of the murders he'd just committed. Sure it was finally over, he cleared his throat, closed the hood of his vacsuit for a moment and let the cleaning system attend to his face and neck. When he was clean, he turned it off, revealing his ruined visage.

"I've never heard you give this speech before," Sonny was saying in his ear. "What are you doing? Why are you in the main seed chamber?"

"I love you," he said to Sonny. "I have never loved anyone more, not even when I was handsome, and I attracted more beautiful flies than I can count."

"I love you too, but what are you doing?" Sonny replied. "It'll take an hour to get you out of there if the hatch above you closes, and it will. As soon as you deploy the nanobots and activate the disseminator, it'll shut tight. We'll be stuck getting you..."

"No, Sonny. Everyone I'm with in the tower knows we're not leaving." Peter closed the channel he'd shared with Sonny for longer than he could remember and looked to the only holorecorder in the room, a small bulb in a corner. "Like I was saying, I have a simple statement about the Order of Eden and everyone who works with them. I have been called to the service of Admiral Scanlon. She has no idea that I'm the leader of the resistance on this planet. That

Haven Fleet has put their full support behind me. The Order is vulnerable, their commanders are egotistical, greedy sociopaths who underestimate the common people. They are not immortal, either. It's only technology, they can be defeated. Be sneaky, be smart, hesitate to trust and act only when you're certain you can get away or you can live with the sacrifice you'll have to make to make the Order suffer."

From his thigh pocket, Peter produced a heavy, hand sized black box. "Thanks to Haven Fleet, we have medical nanobots. They've been reprogrammed to multiply exponentially while they consume every living organism on this planet. There won't be so much as a blade of grass or grub left on Nuaji in three days. It will feed on me first, this seed stock second, and then this terraforming tower will send them across this hemisphere in hours. I'm doing this because the Order will be giving this world to the Edxi. I say they cannot have it. My people will watch from the control room as every living thing dies. If you have a containment suit, put it on now and leave this planet."

Peter opened a channel to the control room and hesitated. He looked for a way out, but there were Order ships enroute. They would be there in less than twenty minutes, an estimate made by his best people. If he relented, if he decided not to go through with it, there was every chance that he'd be taken into custody. If he got away, the Order would never stop hunting him. He'd increase the risk to everyone around him. The same went for everyone in the control room above. "Begin the dissemination sequence, I'm going to break the seal on the nano-cartridge now." He held the cartridge in his hands and looked to the recorder, focusing his intensity, all his beliefs at it. "For bloody revolution. For freedom. Overthrow the Czars." He snapped the cartridge in half and the nanobots were released, a little black cloud spreading in front of him. His throat felt scratchy. "I love you all." He added.

The sound of the disseminator powering up, a hum that was becoming a roar, was all around him. The end came suddenly, as though someone flipped a switch and ended his ability to experience anything.

TWENTY-ONE

Two Days Later

SOMETIMES THE DESIGN of the Merciless, especially on the inside, felt futuristic even to Jake. The smooth panelled hallways, floor that required no cleaning and always shone. The hidden security and minder robots that occasionally peeked out from behind a panel or a small service door somewhere made the ship seem alive. The service bots, advanced skitters that had the trademark domes with fifteen or so different arms stuffed inside, would quickly emerge from covers hidden in the corridors, claim a piece of trash or run a scan for a few seconds then rush back. Sometimes you weren't even sure if you really saw them when it happened in the corner of your eye, they were so quick and efficient.

The design of the ship was still a thing of wonder to most of the crew, many of whom were like Jake in that they still hadn't forgotten the Revenge. Getting a taste of how the Order ships were designed and how those crews lived was an eye opener. It was memorable, having to duck often, moving through hallways that didn't have room for two people to comfortably pass by in most places. What made it worse was that so many of those passages ran right beside a room with so much wasted space that they were repurposed as recreational or storage rooms. It was a stark contrast Jake and the crew were grateful for, one he acknowledged less and less.

As he waited for the Clever Dream to arrive, he pondered that difference on purpose. There was no point in living in the moment as he stood in the observation room overlooking the main hangar. All he was doing was waiting. For the Clever Dream, for Minh-Chu, for the report on the status of the solar system from Liara to come in, just... waiting. He'd over-planned their missions in the area, looked too far ahead and included details that were unconfirmed in some instances, it was a hazard of command. He wanted his people ready for anything, so he let himself predict every kind of condition and problem. It was like the one thing he wanted to tell Ayan when she talked about the Victory Machine; no one can predict the future, everyone who tries is at least a little off or they've left important details out, kept things just vague enough so what they're saying will happen will fit when it comes up. The Victory Machine predicted that Laura would become Ayan's daughter, that Jake wouldn't be the father, but it left out the fact that Ayan would be her adoptive mother, that Laura's parents would fall victim to tragedy. Those were serious details. If Ayan knew them she would have still adopted little Laura, Jake was sure, but she would have been able to ponder how she could help her daughter face the truth about her parents.

Jake's thoughts landed back on Alice, and he caught himself

tightening his grip on the railing. One bad decision lead to a huge mess, and she would face consequences for that unless he shielded her from the Admiralty, especially Lamonthe. He would. If someone presented her with a sword to fall on, he would get in her way and fall on it in her stead. They could try to stop him, try to go around him, but the trouble he'd cause if he caught them trying would be horrific, he'd make sure. There was nothing he wouldn't do to protect his daughter, especially since he knew that she already had a clear understanding of how bad her blunder was. It was one mistake that, according to what he already knew, which was very little, lead to horrifying consequences.

Even though she walked her promise back, didn't deliver a super-bomb that would wipe out the surface of the planet, she would see her mistake and the failure to follow through on her promise as the thing that pushed the zealot rebel Peter to do whatever he did. Jake didn't know what that was yet, the early data was unbelievable, but whatever it was, Alice would blame herself.

To Jake, it wasn't time to punish her, it was time to make sure she knew how to process what happened. They had to make sure she had the help she'd need to carry on. The news from her crew was encouraging, if a little mysterious and troubling at the same time. The stress levels on the Clever Dream plummeted over the previous day to below normal despite the events on the planet they were orbiting. They'd rescued several escape pods without getting caught by the Order of Eden patrols. Alice was still asleep though, she hadn't roused since she collapsed on stage. The readings Theodore forwarded as soon as the Merciless emerged into normal space showed that she was physically fine, and she was in some kind of dream state.

Waiting in the briefing room overlooking the main hangar was the best he could do to make sure that he could be on the Clever Dream as soon as he could. For a moment he found himself looking at one of their reserve Clever Class Corvettes as the deck crew worked to run it through final testing, thinking about the worst punishment he could face if he took full responsibility for whatever the fallout in the solar system was. They could take the Merciless away, reduce him to Captain or lower. A thought crossed his mind then, he could end up on a corvette, commanding a green crew for SOCU or another combat division. There was a chance he could serve alongside his daughter. The thought made him grin, it was on his face before he realized it, then gone when he thought of her sleeping for days. The worry, never truly gone, reasserted its hold on him.

"You should worry about her, focus on her," Quan said from behind. "I'm sorry, you've been broadcasting your worry and restlessness, there's little I can do to avoid picking it up."

"I'm having trouble focusing on anything, or anyone other than Alice."

"It's my problem, like I said, worrying about her is a natural response. Normally I wouldn't sense your state so clearly, but I'm opening my consciousness so I can hear Alice without violating her privacy. Like listening to a broadcast instead of hacking a computer. I'm fairly receptive right now, normally I'd be oblivious to what's going on in your thoughts."

"Reassuring," Jake said. "I like the idea of empaths, telepaths, had to think about it long and hard though. I think it's a sign that humanity is still evolving towards something, maybe the kind of thing that could bring more peace to the galaxy. There are times that I wish it didn't involve my daughter, though."

"You're worried that you're offending me," Quan said quietly.

"Please, do not. I haven't had an easy journey thanks to my gift, there are times I wish I was in my village, married to a kind woman, raising a family. That's not possible for me. None of it. My empathy has made relationships with either sex complicated, I haven't had a long-term home since I was a boy, and I know some members of your military don't trust me because of my telepathy, and because I followed the former Defence Minister into a situation where I ended up trying to read people who did not consent. Now all I can do is try to be of service and hope I find a place with good people. I recently had someone tell me that there's a chance for that, too, so I'm glad to be here. I'm happy I may be able to help you and your daughter. Gifts like the one your daughter has been given can make things difficult at first, but that doesn't mean she can't..." he looked to his left as though he was seeing something through the hull and smiled a little. "Alice is close, I can feel what she's experiencing. It's... powerful. I don't think she's in danger, but we'll both have to approach her when her ship arrives."

"Not in danger?" Jake asked.

"I can't say for sure, she has her guard up, I think she's retreated deep into her own mind, but if you use me as a way to communicate with her, she might let you in. I'll know more when we're in the room with her. For now, I can say she's experiencing something good, and she's emanating that to everyone within a few hundred metres of her. You might feel as though a burden has been lifted soon. It will gradually become more powerful as she gets closer."

"But can we wake her up?" Jake asked.

"If not right away, then soon, yes," Quan replied. "She may have to heal at her own pace, though, if her experienced caused damage."

"If?" Jake said. "You saw the footage of her on stage, right?"

"Sometimes our minds, our capacities expand after a trauma

like that. It's not the best way, but it does happen. It happened to me once when I was overwhelmed. If you can stay calm, relax as best as you can and focus on your positive feelings for Alice, then that would be best. That is the best way to approach someone who is recovering from a trauma in almost all cases. I've treated many people who faced things they thought they couldn't handle, been changed by events they couldn't control. Sometimes it seems like it's all going to go wrong, but the outcomes I've had have all been good. I hope I can make up for my past transgressions against your daughter by helping her now."

"What do you think the chances of me getting through to her are?"

"You're still getting to know Alice. This has been a repeating event in your history together. That makes fatherhood more difficult, especially since you so badly want to learn to be a good father to her, no matter what form she takes. She'll feel that desire, and your love for her. I am hoping she invites it and you in."

"How much for a therapy session with this guy?" Minh-Chu asked as he joined them.

"I think you just have to grant him access to your head," Jake said. "How long did it take for you to read me?" he asked Quan.

"I didn't have to read your thoughts for that insight," Quan said. "I'm afraid you're not much different from most new fathers, especially when they haven't had much time to be in that role."

"Commodore," Liara said as she entered the room. "I have a full report on Nuaji and everything we know about the solar system. The biggest issue right now is the terrorist attack. There's a recording you should see."

. . .

THE RECORDING of Peter's speech before deploying the nanobots he borrowed from the Haven Fleet supplies he'd been given reminded Jake of the few times he had to watch holo-recordings of his own speeches. He never enjoyed it. When he gave speeches like that, he followed training he received at the Freeground Academy. According to them the most important thing about giving a pep-talk or speech of any kind was conviction. You must believe what you're saying completely while you're saying it. While he watched Peter give his last declaration, that's what he saw in spades. The rebel missed one major point in speech giving, though. Some would say it's a secondary point, others would disagree and say it's the most important thing about giving a message to your people. That was, Peter failed to be clear about his instructions. He was crystal clear about his own actions and what was about to happen, but he didn't tell his people what to do next other than to take cover.

That invited chaos, it could turn revolution into reckless destruction. Considering Peter's focus on the Czars, Jake was sure Peter wanted nothing more than to watch the solar system burn, that he wanted his people to go forth and destroy in his name. To some, Peter would be a high martyr, to others he'd be a butcher. The speech ended, and Jake cringed at the man's last words; "I love you all."

The nanobots consumed him rapidly from the inside out, starting with his brain stem. Jake knew how the process was supposed to take place, it was a secret function of the bots that was made to get rid of any evidence that a Haven Fleet operative was present. It was supposed to be activated on the dead, and only under the rarest of circumstances. Before anyone could comment on what they saw, Jake turned to Liara. "What's happened since?"

"The recording was taken forty-seven hours ago. Ninety-two percent of all life on Nuaji has been consumed. Grades one through three type containment suits are no longer effective against the nanobots, so most emergency suits won't work. No shield below Type Five keep them out either. Some nanobots are moving in swarms. We've found three sites where people are held up in bunkers, but their defences won't last. The Order has abandoned the planet and marked it as a hazard. Their ships are keeping a distance of one million kilometres, observing only, even if vessels leave the system. There are hundreds of distress calls representing over seventy thousand people who are stranded but they're not answering any. Signal analysis is predicting that the Order is planning to withdraw to an even greater distance, there are no plans to offer aid from what we can tell."

Jake looked to Minh-Chu. "Start working with Alaka and the Pelican on the problem in orbit. We need to take control of that fast, implement a quick solution so the Order realizes what happened after we've re-cloaked so they don't have time to get in our way."

"Aye, Commodore," Minh-Chu said. There was excitement in his eyes.

Jake caught him as he started to walk away. "Stick around for the rest of the briefing," he said. "Just send a signal for your pilots to assemble."

"Right. Sorry, I just got excited, my guys have been either stuck on the ship or on patrol for a while. It'll be good to challenge them."

"Good, especially since you're going to be sending two of your people down to the planet with Gabe to help rescue people stuck in the bunkers. They're going to be flying reserve Clever Class Corvettes," Jake said as he turned his attention back to Liara. "What else do I have to know?"

"There is hate for Haven Fleet all over the Stellarnet, but most of it are coming from wealthier people on Order controlled worlds or Order soldiers. What's surprising is the swell of support Haven Fleet is getting for supporting Peter and his actions here. They see the uniform, hear him give us credit, and are cheering us on, or telling us where to help next, even begging us to start a resistance somewhere."

"Who are 'They?'" Jake asked.

"As far as we can tell, resistance groups, people from free outposts, but mostly citizens who are living right in the middle of Order of Eden territory. Further transmissions have been blocked, the Order have sent instructions to hyper transmitters to stop Peter's recording and accompanying data from going further, but nineteen solar systems got it before it was stopped. I know what happened here is horrible, but over ninety-seven percent of the eight million people who have seen Peter's last words support Haven Fleet even if they don't support what Peter did."

"You're telling me what Lamonthe would," Jake said, recalling his commander's more draconian point of view on the conflict between Haven Fleet and the Order. "Tragedy has struck, but there's still a win for us here."

"I wouldn't call it a win," Liara said defensively.

"But if the eggs are already in the pan, you may as well make a scramble," Minh-Chu said.

"I'll recommend that we denounce Peter's actions but stand by the decision to support a revolution. We don't like how he fought the Order and the Edxi, but we support resistance in general. It's a message that the Admiral won't like, but I won't sign my name to anything more extreme than that," Jake said.

Jake saw the Clever Dream through the transparent bulkhead

as it rose up on one of the main elevators in the hangar below. "Are there any Edxi in the area?"

"Nothing came back from passive scans, and there were no signs of Edxi communications as we emerged into normal space," Liara answered.

"Any sign that we've been detected?"

"None. We emerged well distant from the solar system and moved in on a slow approach according to your instructions."

"Anything I need to act on right now, or can the rest of the briefing wait?" Jake asked.

"It can wait," Liara said.

"Make sure Agameg and the whole command staff see your whole report. Present it on the bridge, Lieutenant Commander."

"Aye," Liara replied. "Good luck, Sir."

"Thank you," Jake said as he looked to Minh-Chu. "I'll be available to command the action in orbit and on the ground in a little while."

"Don't worry, Jake, I'll get things started with the Pelican, Samurai Squadron and Gabe. You take care of our Alice," Minh-Chu said.

TWENTY-TWO

A Clever Dream

THE SCENE aboard the Clever Dream was surreal. As soon as he saw what was going on, he was happy he had a dependable crew aboard the Merciless taking care of things for the time being. Iruuk welcomed him with a giant, warm embrace. "I'm so happy you could make it, Commodore!" he burst, happier than Jake had ever seen him.

The rest of the crew, except Theodore, were standing at attention along one side of the main corridor that led to the bridge and the Captain's quarters. They all seemed overly pleased to be there except for one. A tall woman that he knew as Jessen, who was standing stoically as tears ran down her cheeks. As he took a moment to look at the crew a little closer, he saw that Faloo and Woone, the female burrower Nafalli, were supressing grins, barely able to keep some elation from showing. "At ease," he said, and

Jessen rushed past him to the crew quarters. Knud, one of the largest humans Jake had seen in a while, followed her.

It only took a few more seconds before Jake realized that he was feeling a giddiness, some kind of gladness, it was as though it was trying to crowd out whatever he was feeling. "I can feel it, what do I do?" he asked Quan in a whisper.

"Don't fight it, but don't forget why you're here, either," Quan said.

Theodore stepped out from Alice's quarters into the hall. "Commodore, come, hurry please."

The crew were starting to relax and fill the hallway between him and the Captain's quarters at the far end. "Commodore, it's good to meet you," Callum said as he stepped into his path. "Can you pass this recording to Ayan for me? I'd like to keep it off the fleet network, it's of a personal nature."

"Uh, sure," Jake said, accepting the tiny data chip as he passed, knowing that refusal would probably cause more drama than he wanted.

"Oh, and please don't look at it. It's kinda private," Callum added in a whisper.

"Commodore, it's wonderful to finally meet you. I have some suggestions that would really improve fleet morale," Faloo offered in a high, sweet Nafalli squeak.

"Sorry, I'll take a moment to talk later," Jake said as he pressed by only to be faced by Krooke whose goggles were off despite his small, irritated looking eyes.

"We're so honoured to have you here," he said.

"Can you tell us any stories about the Warlord? Ever since I heard about that ship, I wish I had served on it," Woone told him with the disposition of a devotee.

"Later, please," Jake said. He wouldn't be able to push past the Nafalli, especially burrowers, who had a low centre of gravity and muscle so dense that they easily outweighed him. "I have to see Alice first."

A shrill, loud whistle sounded behind him. It was Iruuk, who followed it with; "Please, Alice is waiting."

The crew quietly moved out of the way, allowing Jake to pass. "Are they experiencing something else? I can feel what Alice is sending out, but it's not doing that to me," Jake said, adding; "Right?"

"You'd have a reaction eventually. I expect this is the result of a day or more of exposure," Quan replied as they moved on to Alice's room. "Just relax."

"I have come to the same conclusion, I saw results seven hours, thirty-five minutes and nine seconds after Alice was brought aboard. It began with Jessen emerging from her quarters to share a confession of regret with the rest of the crew," Theodore explained, showing them to Alice's bedside. "Then we found Faloo and Woone dancing below while singing songs from their childhood. Noro joined them shortly after. They continued until they were nearly exhausted. Ute is resting, she entered a highly fertile state twenty-eight hours ago and accomplished parthenogenesis. I expect she will have between nine and fifteen young in as few as five months from now."

"You're kidding," Jake said, astonished.

"This episode Alice has been going through has had effects on the entire crew, except for me, of course, since I'm an android. It has been difficult at times for me to keep up, but I serve with pleasure."

"Hey, you missed Knud when he wanted to go for a spacewalk in his underpants," Lewis added from the audio emitters hidden in the panels above. "That guy really likes stargazing. Don't worry, though, all the hatches and access points to dangers aboard have been locked down."

"If it were easy to duplicate you two and put a version of you on every ship, thanks for keeping this from becoming a disaster," Jake told them as he made his way.

"Actually, I have a proposal you'd be interested in, but that can wait," Theodore offered.

Jake finally got to Alice's bedside and was surprised to see her looking relaxed and restful with a little smile playing on her sleeping face. "How is she?"

"Other than what she's doing to the crew - which could have been much worse - and her refusal to wake, she's in perfect health." Theodore replied. He looked to Quan. "I'm sorry, I believe she's simply refusing to emerge from a dream state. My theory is that she's controlling it, at least partially. I could have used medication to rouse her but thought it might be better until someone with more expertise attended her first."

"Astute," Quan said. "You're a credit to your kind. Your diagnosis was right. She's retreated from reality into a world she can control. Now that I'm this close, I can send you there, Commodore, but you'll be oblivious to what's happening outside of your mindscape."

"Will it help?"

"You'll be able to communicate with her by joining her dream." Quan said. "You'll have to lay down, since you'll be in a dream state as well, but you can retreat when you like unless she becomes aggressive and decides to take full control."

"Can she do that?" Theodore asked.

"Considering her mind was awakened during a conflict with a

Geist, yes. I doubt she'll wish any harm on the Commodore unless she's directly provoked, though."

"All right, so do you have any advice for how I should communicate with her?" He was mystified as to what the experience he was about to agree to would be like. If she was dreaming, he could be stepping into anything.

"Be yourself, take in the experience before you decide on a course of action, and don't be afraid to go along with her if you have to, at least until you know what to do next," Quan said. "That sounded more helpful in my head. I'm sorry, the experience is difficult to prepare for, but it shouldn't be traumatic for you."

"That's reassuring," Jake said, making his way over Alice so he could lay down behind her. "One second, I have to try something first." He gently turned her head and patted her cheek. "Time to wake up, Alice." A few moments later he let her head roll back to where it was resting on the pillow. "It was worth a shot."

"True," Quan said. "I'll provide a bridge for your mind to hers, she shouldn't be able to feel me at all, and I won't be able to see what you're experiencing."

The strangeness of the situation didn't escape Jake, who was still unsure of himself, none of the answers he got out of Quan really explained what he could expect, but he put his head down anyway, relaxing with some space between him and his daughter, and said; "I'm ready."

Quan closed his eyes. "She's less guarded then before. This might be easier than I thought."

It was like going to sleep, but suddenly. The experience wasn't jarring, there just wasn't anything to see at first. Then Jake heard giggling. The unfettered laughter of a toddler was all around him and then he saw her, floating through the air, slowly tumbling in zero gravity towards him.

It wasn't the grown Alice he knew, but a version of her at the age of three, an adorable, red-haired girl in a little vacsuit who was belly laughing as she floated through the air. "I gotcha!" Jake said as he caught her. He wasn't in control of himself yet, this was the father Alice created for her dream, and Jake could see Alice's world from behind his eyes.

Toddler Alice laughed and pointed her arms away. "Again, daddy!"

They were in an observation dome on Freeground Station. It was the one he used to visit before the First Light, the one he recalled from Jonas' memories. Back then, Alice was an artificial intelligence on his arm. In the dream she was a little girl, and Ayan, not the first, but the most recent was on the other side of the small observation dome, ready to catch her. "Okay, here we go!" Jake said as he gently pushed Alice away, sending her through the zero-gravity space towards Ayan. He put a little spin on her so she went tumbling slowly, and Alice filled the space with laughter.

"I told you this was a good idea," Ayan said with a grin, watching their daughter as she made her way through the zero-gravity space.

"I was afraid she'd lose her breakfast, that's all," dream Jake explained.

"No upchuckies!" Alice exclaimed, half way between her father and mother, resuming her giggles after.

"Okay, get ready for landing," Ayan told her, getting into position to catch Alice. "You know, playing pass the Alice doesn't seem like good parenting, but I think we'll end up doing this again."

"Oh, I don't think she'll let us forget this," laughed Jake. The scene stunned him as he let the dream Jake behave as Alice wanted.

Ayan caught Alice in a hug and was rewarded with a sloppy smooch on the cheek. Alice whispered something to her mother, and then went stiff, her arms and fingers pointed above her head.

"Okay, she wants to go a little faster."

"I wanna fly!" Alice exclaimed enthusiastically.

"I'm ready," Jake said, spreading his stance out, if you could call a position in zero gravity a stance.

Ayan pushed her, and Alice squealed in excitement as she crossed the ten-metre distance between her parents poised like an old fashioned superhero through the air. "I'm flying!"

Jake caught her, and she grappled him around the neck, laughing in his ear. "I never imagined you like this," he said, taking control of the Jake that Alice dreamt. He was in control. "But I'm so happy I have."

Alice looked at him, her little toddler face shocked, and for a moment he wasn't sure if she would be displeased or happy, then she squeezed him tightly. Gravity took hold, and his feet settled on solid ground. He was holding her up. "It's really you, you came for real," she said.

The unadulterated happiness she felt at seeing him melted away, replaced with guilt. He could feel it as clearly as if she explained it. "I'm so sorry I screwed everything up."

"You didn't," Jake said.

"Lies don't work here," she said, and he could feel the world darken.

"You made one mistake, and when you tried to fix it, you were put in a situation you couldn't handle yet," Jake clarified. "It's okay. Everyone screws up."

"You think it was too early for me to command on my own," Alice said, her vacsuit changing to a little captain's uniform. "You're right."

"Maybe," Jake said, he felt that she wanted down, and the world around them changed as he did so. They were on a wooden walkway surrounded by an ocean that was painted in the hues of a golden dawn. "I believe you'll be a better captain then I am soon."

Alice looked up at him, astonished. Seeing that expression on a toddler version of her was enough to make him grin, he never considered what she would have looked like at that age. He sat down on the edge of the walkway and she squirmed into his lap. "You really do believe that. How?"

He tried to start thinking about how he would word his response, but it spilled out instead, as though pondering his message was the same as delivering it. "You prove yourself over and over. Not just your abilities, but your amazing capability to survive any way you can. I know you're changing. What you like, who you like, your whole personality is reshaping itself because you were just remade. I know what that's like, I don't tell anyone this, but I've felt a little lost since I went through my own rebirth. That is, unless I'm standing beside you, Ayan, Oz or Minh-Chu. To me, command is easy, finding out what I want in this new life is hard."

"What do we do?" Alice asked with a shrug.

"We take the world around us in and do our best. I think." The answer surprised Jake, it was as if there was no filter or delay between his thoughts and words in her dreamscape. "That sounds right."

Alice giggled, but she was still afraid. "I want to help, but I kill people with my decisions, I don't let myself regret when I think I've killed the right people. The Admiral, thousands of people on his ship. They were all like me, all having their own experiences and then I ended their stories. That's what bad people do. Then I went away and did it more. I know I was following orders, but so many people were ended. They never had a chance to decide to fight or run away. I didn't give them one. Invisible bombs don't give anyone a chance, you just stop living."

It was clear she was talking about the strikes Admiral Lamonthe ordered, the ones that destroyed several military targets and killed tens of thousands of Order personnel, but Jake's thoughts drifted to the present. "Those cloaked strikes were meant to scare people in the Order into deserting, they were meant to save more lives than the bombs took. We don't know if it worked yet, but you may have done more good than harm."

"You don't believe that. I told you; lies don't work here," Alice said, crossing her arms.

He tried not to think about the terrible things that were happening on planet Nuaji, but trying not to think about it was like bringing it up.

"What's happening? What are you hiding?" Alice asked, her little face looking up at him, alarmed.

She drew it out of him like she was pulling a string up through his throat and out of his mouth. "Peter released self-replicating nanobots across his world, destroying almost all life. The planet will be completely desolate in a few hours."

"Oh my God," Alice said, starting to cry. Her whole body was wracked by sobs.

"It isn't your fault," Jake said, pulling her into an embrace. "You didn't make him what he was, you couldn't have forced him to do what he did."

"They'll blame me, and this time I deserve it more than ever. Innocent people are dying," she wept. Fear darkened the horizon, waves and wind became more forceful, more turbulent around them.

"They'll blame me," Jake said. "And I'll accept it because you've done more good than harm. Because I love you."

"You shouldn't do that. You shouldn't take responsibility for me, grown-ups take responsibility for themselves..."

"Let me be a father to you," Jake found himself saying. The thing he would say if they were in a waking world came out next. "Commanders take responsibility for everyone under their command. Let me do that for you. I know you'll make me proud, I know you'll learn from this."

"How much are my growing pains going to cost people?" Alice retorted. "Is it even worth it?"

"Yes," Jake said, tilting her chin up. Her lips quivered, tears were streaming down her face. "I will fight for you whenever you let me because I love you no matter what you do. You're also smarter and much cuter than I am."

The last part of that made her chuckle a little.

"Pardon me, I think I lost my filter on my way down this rabbit hole," Jake added. "Every time I think of what you've been through and who you are, I'm amazed, Alice. Let's wake up so we can take a breath, then do some good. Once we clear these clouds, I'll give you time to think about what you want to do next. If you want to stay in the military, then you'll stay. If you want to do something else, I'll do everything I can to give you the opportunity."

"I want to bring people together," Alice said, her tears slowing. "I know you've tried so many times. For a crew, for another government, even for Haven."

"Ayan's better at it," Jake admitted.

"Yeah, she really is. You inspire people to act on their own, though. Theodore and Lewis have seen it in the Order of Eden database. People are going into hiding, gathering guns and old environment suits for armour then fighting the Order as best as they can. Half the people we see in their system have seen a broadcast from you or about you. It's like you wake people up. I want to do that, but I also want to take everyone somewhere safe. Somewhere like Haven Shore and show them how life can be. I thought I could start by getting on stage, by connecting all the resistance people to the Fleet."

"You were overwhelmed," Jacob said in a comforting tone that matched his urge to make his daughter feel better.

"You would have given some speech, or done something to show them they could believe in you."

"No, I have no idea what I would have done because I don't have your gift."

"I don't think it's a gift. I should feel like a part of everything, but sensing what people are feeling excludes me instead."

"Only for now," Jake said. "You've come through so many challenges, this is just one more. You'll learn to control your empathy, or you'll learn to live with it. Look at the control you already have over yourself. You made this place for us." He looked out over the horizon, where an ocean was painted by a yellow-orange sun. There was even a breeze, and the feeling of sun on his face.

"It's pretty awesome," Alice chuckled. "It's still just a daydream, though."

"I don't daydream like this," Jake said. "I don't create whole landscapes other people can visit me in. You astonish me, Alice."

"I still feel like I'm trying to catch up to you."

"Oh, don't worry about that," Jake said, surprised to hear the sentiment. "I think you're making your own path. Before long you'll realize there's no comparison. Mistakes teach us..."

She didn't let him finish the thought, but interrupted by saying; "...and I make really big ones, so I should learn a lot." Her toddler giggling was short, and it hid sadness.

"Not what I was about to say," Jake said, bouncing her a little. "I was going to tell you that you're going to come out of this stronger, wiser, and I know you won't be guilt free, but whatever you do next will be better. Not because you're my daughter, I don't know how I could take credit for you because you're so much more than I've ever been, but because of all you've seen, all you've done. I don't just love you because you chose to keep a genetic bond with me, or because I've known you in different forms in the past, but because of who you are. You're going through all these changes, but there's still something I can't put my finger on that makes you unique. I also think it makes you good. Follow that and I know you'll try to do the right thing no matter what. When in doubt, give me or your mother a call. I know she seems busy, she is, but she loves you as much as I do." He punctuated his point by giving little Alice a comforting squeeze.

"Okay," Alice said, nodding then squeezing him back as best as she could. "I love you too."

Waking up was slow, not because it was difficult, but they were both hesitant to leave as the weather cleared and they shared a powerful link that neither of them had fully allowed themselves to enjoy before.

TWENTY-THREE

Pulling Patrol Duty

THE NEW URIEL fighters were a divisive factor for the fighter wings aboard the Triton. While the War Forge and the fleet surrounding it were travelling even further from the well charted, civilized systems while they looked for a longer-term home, half the pilots aboard the ship commanded by Commodore McPatrick passed their qualifiers on their new fighters.

The other half struggled and failed. The neural interface was incredible to some, but the rest were blocked in many ways, unable to make a complete connection. They were left behind, allowed to respond to alerts using their old fighters, but the ones who qualified on the new versions were put to work, patrolling and investigating the new solar system that was called Sola 35b.

It wasn't a normal human name for a solar system even though it used all the right characters when it was uploaded to the navigational data pool three centuries before. Most of the pilots in the training class aboard the Triton passed the qualification on the new Uriels, something that didn't surprise Noah Lucas, since they were some of the best pilots in the fleet.

That afforded him a special opportunity. The small group of pilots he was assigned to along with Pixie, who also passed, were given the task of exploring the space around Sola 35b Five, or just Sola Five for short. The fifth planet from the solar systems' white star was predicted to have earth like qualities. With no reservations at all, but a little guilt at being able to go out on mission while many other pilots were being questioned by therapists, poked by doctors and examined by analysts to find out why they couldn't successfully qualify on the newest fighters, Noah dropped into the seat of his new Uriel.

There were a lot of nicknames floating around for the new ships, he supposed it was because they might have looked the same as the old Uriels, but they felt completely different. The neural link system picked his presence up and connected to him the instant he finished putting his harness on. The punter gears, arms and little bay closed his canopy for him, performed an extra check on his fighter, and gave him the green light. A countdown started. "All systems ready," he said.

"Flight Control here, we'll wait for your partner to strap in. She's not late yet, but it's close."

"Keep your pants on, Control, I'm dropping into my seat now," Pixie said.

"You were a better pilot when you were in charge," Rayman, a new pilot who was given command of their small squad after Pixie's turn was over.

"So was everyone else," Pixie replied, you could hear her grin as she taunted him. It took her seconds to get under his skin, and she did it all the time. It was only fair, he often started the spats and fights they got into. "When's your turn at command over?"

"End of tomorrow," Rayman replied.

"Cool, I hope they put Carnie in charge next. A break would be nice."

"A break?" Rayman said.

"Hey, am I the last one to strap in?" Pixie said. "Shows here that you're not fully harnessed, Rayman. I'm all strapped up and ready to go."

"Just making sure I'm the last out."

"This is Flight Control. Waiting on you, Rayman. We punt in sequence. If we have to skip you, you'll be reported."

"Sorry, Control, strapped in now."

Noah pushed the mute control on his communications system as he snickered. Rayman didn't have the worst command instincts, but he was a complete control freak, and that cost him here and there. It was also easy for Pixie to find things to taunt him about. She was ready on time, her checks were done, she just wasn't as early as the other three pilots for the mission, which didn't really matter. Rayman liked to be the last to punt in simulations where he was supposed to be in charge, though, and he'd leave part of his harness unbuckled to make sure of that.

This wasn't a simulated mission, though, and Pixie was smart enough to strap in quick and check on Rayman to see if he was holding to his simulation habits, just to embarrass him because she knew the actual live procedures better. Noah was surprised it worked, and happy their rivalry didn't make them late for their launch.

"We're going to have words later," Rayman grumbled to Pixie.

A count down started from ten on Carnie's canopy. He could see his tactical map, the communications stream, scan data and his mission details all at once as if he had second sight. He could also feel all the extremities of his fighter as though they were extensions of his body. The new neural link made him feel like he was a new being flying through space. It was his first time punting outside of a simulation though, so he braced himself, unmuting his communicator. "Ooh, this is going to rock," he said with a grin.

"I hear it's like getting kicked in the back, not like the simulations at all," Pixie said.

"I'm sure they adjusted the kinetic feedback," Rayman dismissed.

The armoured door in the punter opened as Carnie's counter flashed down: 3.....2.....1 and in a thrust of pistons and compressed air, his Uriel was flung thirty kilometres away from the Triton in less than a second and a half. It felt like one of the few times he played on a swing as a child on a planet with normal gravity, when he swung up really high and jumped, only his Uriel never hit the ground. The laughter was the same, the thrill was better. A check of the other three fighters with him showed that they'd all punted fine. "Oooh, that was awesome!" Pixie said.

"All right, clear the channel," Rayman said. "We have a mission plan to work. Set your Quad Drives for the first set of coordinates and make your micro-jump to the planet. I'll see you two when Thorn and I cross by you near its second moon. Stick to the patrol pattern, report anything anomalous the instant you see it."

"Yes, Sir," Pixie and Carnie replied at the same time.

The number of qualification tests Carnie studied for and passed over the previous few days, all while learning how to pilot the new fighter, was astonishing. Several of the Officer Qualifiers were difficult. The studying was brutal, there was a lot of reading and prepa-ration tests, but the Qualifiers were frustrating. They were tests of your decision making, presenting situations in simulation that required him to make on the spot, time sensitive calls. They weren't as challenging as the advanced qualifier for Quad Drives though. It took three tries for him to pass, but on the third attempt, he felt he had a real understanding of the system and how to use it without making the computer doing all the work.

Even so, as he plotted the micro-jump that would take them over a hundred million kilometres in a second, he let the computer do the heavy lifting. It was what the software was built for. He got the ready signal from Pixie and they jumped at the same time. A flash of blue and white light crossed his canopy for an instant and they emerged a hundred thousand kilometres away from Planet Sola 35b Five. Pixie's fighter was to his right. "First time in a new Uriel, first punt while fully neutrally connected, and our first dimensional jump. I'd say we're doing pretty well for one morning," Pixie said. "All systems on my fighter check out fine. It's really not supposed to be this easy to be a test pilot."

"We're technically not test pilots, just the first flesh and bone pilots to try this stuff out."

"Oh, because a few thousand simulations couldn't be wrong," Pixie snickered. "I'll be shocked if this neural assistance stuff doesn't do something funky to our heads eventually."

"Time to start our sweep, starting with the nearest moon."

"Don't tell me you're gonna get all stiff like Damon, sorry, I meant Rayman."

"I just want to keep the mission on track, we can talk after we're on course and gathering data. It's not like we'll be short on time," Carnie said. He engaged the autopilot after checking the planned route and made sure the gain on his passive scanners was turned up all the way.

"Oh, good. If you got all stiff on me, I'd have to hang out with Thorn. She's as boring as vanilla custard, but at least she likes a good laugh."

The fighters split off from each other, each starting on a course that would keep them in easy communication range while efficiently collecting data from the first moon, then the planet a hundred fifty thousand kilometres away. "Don't worry, I won't get all official on you, or pick on you like Rayman. What's the deal between you two, anyway?"

"Oh, he and I shared a bunk for a night. Ever since I turned him down for a second night, then a third and a fourth, he's been more and more of a baby about it. I thought I'd get a break from him when I was assigned here, but..."

"Then the Excalibur sent him into the program late," Carnie finished for her. "I guess there's something to the no fraternizing rule most military orgs have."

"Sure, but I'll take one thick-headed stalker as the price for something to break the boredom. Shaking the bunk with someone's a great stress reliever, and a romance can make all this seem worth it if it goes right. You'd know more about that, though."

"Not at the moment." The scan data started coming in, and most of the moon was barren, a rock with no atmosphere.

"Haven't heard from the Princess for a while?"

"I told you..."

"Okay, I had to call her that one more time, sorry."

"Anyway, Alice hasn't sent any messages out. I'm thinking whatever's going on has her ship running silent. No news from Fleet, either, but that just verifies my theory."

"You know, if you two got married, you'd have a right to more info."

"Wow, it's a bit soon for that," Carnie said. "Way soon."

Pixie laughed. "Yeah, I just don't know where you guys are in your relationship. You don't talk about it much. Are you all coupled up? Deep in the honeymoon stage? Do you ever meet in person? Is it a simulation thing, where you just meet in the digital? Or have you two gone through the early stages and just keep it open?"

"We met a couple times, it went well," Carnie said.

"You don't sound too sure."

"Oh, I'm sure it went well. We talked about it, there are holos," he said more certainly, it sounded almost defensive to his ears.

"Oh, yeah. I saw that splatterball fight. Looked like a bunch of crewmates to me, though. I didn't notice you two connecting. Then again, holovids don't tell the whole story, I guess."

Carnie had met a lot of trouble makers in his short life. During his teens and before, he was fortunate enough to watch the older kids and adults go through the heavy drama that happened between the stars, and he watched those trouble makers. The ones who got between relationships, or questioned them at the right time, put ideas in people's head were always a little entertaining but frightening to him. He tapped the picture of Alice on one of his secondary cockpit screens, it was one he took from a call he had with her, where she was smiling at him warmly and decided to shut the door on any trouble. "Yeah, Alice and I are private. A lot of people lurk on her social feed, trying to get dirt, so we stay close to each other and enjoy what we've got. There's no room for a third in there, we like it that way."

"I wasn't asking to get involved with you guys or anything," Pixie retorted. Was she backtracking? "I just want to follow success, y'know? She's the act to beat in the Apex program, and you two have something cool going on, if I'm guessing right. If I could have her record and get together with someone as awesome as either of you, it would be like the end of my problems. I'd be the bright centre to the galaxy."

Pixie seemed more earnest as she went on and Carnie decided to let her off the hook. "Nothing's perfect, but I'm pretty happy, yeah. The waiting is the hardest, but talk to anyone who has someone important somewhere else on the fleet. We're all going through it."

"Except for me," Pixie sighed.

"There's always Rayman," Carnie snickered. "I'm sure he's showing his love whenever he tries to pick on you."

"That's not love, dear Carnie," she replied. "And it's not as much fun as you might think, there was no clicking there. I'm into free love and everything but sharing a bunk with him was a mistake from minute one. I was out of there the moment I was sure he was sleeping."

"Right, hopefully he'll get over it before it affects his command score. He loses more points than anyone whenever he argues with a subordinate. On the bright side, you make Hal stumble over his words and drop things," Carnie offered.

"Do I?" Pixie asked, sounding genuinely surprised. "Seriously? Traveller? Wow, I didn't think anything could make that guy shake in his boots. His command score is almost double mine from his turn in charge."

"Yeah, he has eyes for you whenever you're near. Just don't break his heart, okay?"

"Hey, don't worry, a crush from a nice guy like that is a great big compliment. I'll be as nice as..."

The reason why Pixie lost her train of thought appeared on the tactical scanner. A city with tall towers, a partially radial pattern of transportation tubes, buildings, domes and industrial buildings. Their skin was metal, mostly of the same types that could be found on the moon's surface, and the occupants had built old shield emitters the size of buildings into its rim.

"I'm seeing a lot of damage," Pixie said in a hushed tone. She was using a laser link to communicate so their other signals wouldn't trigger anything below. It was one of their new procedures.

He switched over. "There's no power down there, no sign of people, no movement on detectors." The desolation was as astonishing as the city itself. He'd seen moon settlements before, but never so extensive. There were dozens of huge mining shafts around the city as well, all capped, but some of the protective barriers were broken. "This whole place was hit by weapons' fire. Scanners suggest kinetic, but there are thousands of hits from heavy bombs."

"Would be nice if there was someone to talk to down there," Pixie said. "Not picking anything up though, not yet. I'm gonna go lower."

"Wait, we don't know..." Carnie started to say as he watched her fighter start to move down towards the city. He decided on a different tact. "I'm going to follow procedure. Book says we get distance and report."

"Oh, um," Pixie said as her ship turned back, moving away from the city, following him instead. "Got excited for a minute there."

"Command, we found something significant. An abandoned settlement on the moon, sending scan data now," Carnie reported.

"Doesn't look like there's anything down there, but we haven't analyzed the results yet."

"I see it," Rayman said. "Running analysis now."

"Shouldn't you forward that on to Flight Command?" Pixie prodded.

"Just taking a look before we get anyone excited. Hey, there's a faint signal down there, how'd you miss it?" Rayman asked.

"We didn't have time to run our analysis, we thought it was more important to forward the raw data, like the regulation says," Carnie said.

"Regs say you forward new information to your commanding officer. That's me. Looks like the computer thinks the signal is an old distress beacon, but it's weak, it's probably been blinking for a century. You're cleared for duty out of the cockpit, and Pixie just finished her urban combat qual. You two head down and investigate, I'm sending you the info you'll need to find the signal I found."

"I'd like to hear those orders from Flight Command," Pixie said. "I might love guns and exploring but..."

"Do you want me to report you for insubordination?" Rayman said.

Carnie switched to a private channel with Pixie. "You good for a trip down? We'll get out the millisecond we see a sign of trouble."

"I finished my first three combat quals and the first five explorer quals. I'm ready, I guess, but this'll be my first mission out of the cockpit. Don't get me wrong, I want to check it out, but I'd rather do it with a squad of trained soldiers."

"So, what'll it be, Pixie?" Rayman asked peevishly.

"Yes, Sir. Going down to check it out, Sir," Pixie said.

"Carnie has the lead, he's been face to face with Edxi according to his file. Even if it was a little baby, that makes him more experienced," Rayman ordered.

Carnie wanted to send his temporary commander recordings of his latest encounter to show him how dangerous it really was, but answered; "Yes, Sir, heading down," instead. He flipped over to the private channel he had with Pixie. "We're not playing heroes here. Activate your heavy encounter suit before you touch down. We're just buying time until Flight Command yanks his leash and sends real ground pounders down."

"Are you sure we can't check it out a little? I mean, this place is weird looking, I kinda want to see more."

"We'll follow the mission... slowly," Carnie replied as he watched the city loom larger in his cockpit window. Holes and burns in the upper sides of the buildings became clearer as he got closer.

TWENTY-FOUR

Ghost Town

FOLLOWING PROCEDURE, Carnie pinged all channels, prompting for a Navnet response from any towers that might be on standby from the moon city that filled the crater. He waited a minute, hoping that he wouldn't trigger defence systems instead, but nothing happened.

Darkened domes, holes in the rooftops and the sides of a few of the larger buildings drew his eye away from the main port, which had its secondary landing doors open. "That's probably where they launched fighters or escape craft from when this place was under attack." They'd already done two low passes so they could pick up as much as they could on their scanners, there was no motion or evidence of electrical charges beyond what could be expected from deactivated equipment.

"You're buying time so Command can call this off," Pixie said.

"Oh yeah," Carnie said. "But I can't put our landing off anymore, it'll look like insubordination," he said, plotting a course into one of the bays. "We go in slow, keep your scanners on passive and use your three-sixty degree recorders to take in the sights."

"You know, the more you slow this down, the more I want to get out of my ship and go exploring," Pixie warned playfully.

Their fighters followed the course Carnie set, weaving between tall buildings, nearly skimming two domes, then moving down to two metres above street level. It was the best way to get better readings from their passive scanners, and he knew they could follow the flight path without running into anything. The grey and brown dust from the moon came up in plumes whenever their thrusters fired towards the surface. The trucks left on the ground had large, heavy-duty tires, were made to hold their own atmospheres, and most still had cargo trains hitched to them. "I wonder why they didn't use some kinda hover tech on the roads?" Carnie asked idly.

"It's a lot more expensive. Moving on wheels or treads is a lot cheaper for tech this old. Are you sure we can't turn our active scanners on? This slow scan stuff is driving me nuts."

"I don't want to activate a dormant defence system."

"I'm sure we could take it out before any gun we've seen could do real damage," Pixie countered.

"That's not the point. If we start flying around, taking out defences, we could do a lot of secondary damage. Sneaking in is the best way to see this place for what it was whenever this happened."

"Right, it's an investigation, not an invasion," Pixie agreed.

Their fighters slipped into the secondary landing bay and they touched down perfectly. Their scanners didn't pick up any movement, so Carnie gave the word; "Out, bring your full kit," he said, and Pixie's canopy was open an instant later.

"I bet Alice has been on a lot of missions like this," she said as she pulled her rifle from the storage compartment under her Uriel. The full armour she wore made her seem taller, more heavily built. The horizontal metal slats protecting her and the systems within glinted in the faint light coming through the opening behind them.

They both had their support and survival packs on, making the armour even more bulky, but Carnie didn't want to get caught without the supplies and extra systems contained in those long bulges running up their backs. "We haven't talked about her missions much, most of them are still classified, but she might have seen more action than I have. I guess we never compared, it doesn't seem to matter."

"Wait, she *might* have seen more action than you? I thought that was a given, considering what she does and everything," Pixie said, surprised.

"I spent a year running from bots and dealing with scroungers, even a few people who I'm pretty sure were cannibals. Look up Iora sometime."

"I don't have to," Pixie said. "It's on the no-go list, apparently it's crawling with..."

"Edxi, I know."

"How?"

"Can't talk about it," Carnie said as he made sure both their cockpits were closed and started moving further into the port. "Signal's this way."

"Okay, so you've been on classified missions to places that the Fleet tells us to stay away from?" Pixie asked.

"Can't talk about it," Carnie repeated with a snicker. The system in his helmet compensated for the low-light and he saw two transit shuttles that were riddled with holes. There were three occupants in the nearest. He pointed his free hand at the small, ten seat ship and let his passive scanners concentrate on getting a reading as natural radiation and gravity acted on what was within. "I'm with you on the scanning thing, though. I wish we could just turn them on. I can't even get an estimate on how long these people have been dead."

"People?" Pixie asked as she followed his pointing finger. "The more I see, the more it looks like this was a massacre. Does it look like Edxi?"

"No, not so far. It looks like these people were taken out by short range plasma weapons. Primitive stuff."

"I saw one of those shooters in a museum before The Fall," Pixie nodded. "It was a hundred seventy years old."

"There are no weapons in that shuttle, so whoever did this might have taken them with them after they won the battle."

"Or the people killed here were never armed and this really was a massacre," Pixie added.

Carnie moved on, leading the way further into the hangar. It was an empty space covered in a layer of fine dust. "Something kicked the dirt up on this moon, there's no wind, so it must have been meteorite strikes or something unnatural."

"Like a collapsing mine shaft or falling building."

"Could have been." The red light marking the faint signal beckoned, drawing them to heavy pressure doors. The outer ones were blasted open, fractured, melted metal framing the entrance.

Pixie whistled appreciatively. "These guys liked their plasma. There's a lot of burn damage."

"They tried to get through the inner door the same way, but it's even more heavily armoured." The computer system displayed the wiring for the door panel, which was half blasted open. He recognized the circuit type, saw what he had to patch and how much power the door needed to open and batted the screen away. "Okay, I've seen this kind of thing before on really old stations."

"How old is really old?" Pixie asked.

"Three hundred years? Maybe more? They're dependable, heavy duty. Whoever hid behind this door pulled the power from the inside. It's an old trick that works on most inner airlocks."

"Are doors like this normally a metre thick?" Pixie asked. "I've never seen this before."

"No, this installation is protecting something. Considering the control and armour caps on the mineshafts, I'm guessing there's platinum or uranium down there. Maybe something rarer."

"I saw some heavy processing centres on the way in. If we could turn our scanners up..."

"I know," Carnie said. He pried the remaining section of panel away from the circuitry access, then cut through the security panel beneath with a tiny, short range torch affixed to his finger. The radiant heat and light gave his scanners more to go on, and the shape of the area around them became clearer. "Whoever built this place made sure it would last."

A window popped up in his Heads' Up Display, showing him that the port building was actually the uppermost levels of a colony ship. "Wow, I've never seen that before."

"Merlin Shipyards, third generation Colony Ship with industrial add-ons," Pixie read aloud, seeing the same results in her helmet. "It says there were eighty-four made, and they were sold to a huge list of organizations. This doesn't exactly narrow it down. We still don't have a name for this place."

"We will. No one knows this is here," Carnie said, pulling the tiny plate of metal he cut out of the hole and pulling the wires out with pliers. He made sure there was no atmosphere within, then powered up the tip of his little finger and touched the two wires that would open the door to it. The floor vibrated under foot as the thick security doors rumbled all the way open. "In we go. The signal is nineteen metres ahead through another old airlock. This one has a seal, we might be able to get through it, but we're going to be activating more systems."

"Okay, are we wandering too far from our mission mandate? I just got through a command trial without any trip-ups and good marks, I don't want to blow my officer training record two days away from the end of suit week."

"Our orders are to investigate, and the regulations say we must respond to distress beacons once we've determined that the risk is acceptable. Besides, Rayman put me in charge."

"Oh, so you're taking accountability. I can live with that," Pixie chuckled. "Lead the way."

The hallway was broad with heavy deck plating. It was definitely made to take the weight of large pieces of equipment. "They buried most of the colony ship. I've heard of that, but never seen it. The security here must have been intense." They passed an open panel in the wall where an empty rifle rack provided space for twenty-four guns. It was empty.

"It's so clean in here, like it was just polished yesterday," Pixie said.

A shiver ran down Carnie's spine.

"Giving you the willies?" Pixie snickered.

"You're not getting the feeling we're walking through a haunted house? Passive scanners are picking up so many old weapon strikes just outside of this section that it looks like a few hundred people were killed trying to defend this place. Could have been thousands."

"Dead is dead," Pixie replied. "No phantom is going to jump out at us..."

"Carnie, Pixie," Oz said as his transmission broke through their comms. "We're watching your progress from the Triton. You're close to a major security checkpoint, that's where that signal you picked up is coming from."

"Do you want us to hold here?" Carnie asked.

"No, you're experienced enough to handle whatever's in there, and backup won't get to you for another twenty-one minutes. I'm giving you the go-ahead to investigate. As soon as you determine the source of the signal, you can turn near-field active scanners on if you feel it's safe. We'll be watching from here."

"Yes, Sir," Carnie said, at the same time reassured by the connection to Triton Mission Command, and intimidated by the thought that the Commodore and other members of his staff were watching. "Moving on to the airlock. I'm going to have to power it up to preserve the atmosphere in there." The schematic for the wiring came up on his HUD and he rewired then powered the doors up in less than a minute.

The airlock lit up, lights and white interior looking brand new except for the scuff marks from boots on the floor. It was impossible to tell how old they were at a glance, but they looked like they were made earlier that day. "I know they say vacuum stops things from aging, but it looks like whoever was here just left."

Carnie remembered what corpses looked like after several

months on Iora and pushed the memory aside. "I'll take preserved stiffs in vacuum over planet side rot any day."

"You've really seen some crazy stuff, haven't you? I need stories. We're going to the Pilot's Den the minute we're off duty, and I'm going to buy you drinks until you talk."

"I'll take you up on that, I guess I've got a few stories I can share," Carnie replied as the airlock cycled, balancing the air pressure with the air inside the room. They stepped inside as soon as the inner doors parted, both looking around with care. "It's a control room, schematics say it's one of a couple secondary port management areas," he said as he looked around at the security, technical and traffic monitoring stations. There was another empty weapons' rack with two corpses beside it. "Looks like the fighting got here too." They had rotted down to bones and rags.

"The blip is behind that console," Pixie said, leading the way with her rifle drawn.

Carnie went around the other way and they were surprised to find a human man. His skin was greying, but the hair was perfect. A light in his right eye blinked red as he stared at the wall blankly. There were three holes burnt through the chest of his Dammel Company jumpsuit. "An android," Carnie said as he knelt down and performed a scan on it. "His main power unit was hit, that's why he's offline."

"Wait, what was that?" Commodore McPatrick asked. "Carnie, can you scan his head again?"

"Yup, oh, wow, is that synthetic brain tissue?" Carnie asked as he saw a long strip of grey matter turn up on his scan results. It had dozens of fine wires attached to it, and was held in an armoured compartment in the upper half of the machine's skull.

"We're checking," Oz said.

"This guy's some kind of cyborg?" Pixie asked as she looked around the room.

Commodore McPatrick spoke to them both over their communicators. "Our experts say no, that brain matter is completely synthetic, and can be deactivated for long periods of time, at least that's the theory they're spinning up here. It looks like he's been well preserved, but we've never seen this tech before. At best, he may be able to tell us what happened here. Hold there, watch over our witness until your support arrives."

"Aye, Sir," they both replied. When the channel was closed, Carnie looked to Pixie. "How does it feel to have a story of your own?"

"Pretty good. If there's a right way to get through your first ground mission, this must be it. I've been able to watch an expert door-cracker who knows his regulations, we found something cool that got the attention of Command, and we haven't had to fire a shot."

"You see, there's another lesson for you; never talk about what hasn't happened before the mission's over."

"Like *not* getting shot at? Why is everyone so superstitious? I've been running into that kinda thing since I joined up."

"Stick around, you'll find there's something to superstitions while you're on a mission," Carnie said. "Just... no more jinxy comments until we're done okay?"

"Oh, like..."

"I'm not going to give you an example."

"Jinxy comments like what? Seriously," Pixie pressed playfully.

"You're baiting me," Carnie said, sitting in one of the old rolling chairs.

"So, if I said something like; 'This place has held up for centuries, it'll stay together a while longer.' That would be jinxy?"

Carnie was starting to nod as he leaned back in the chair. The back snapped, dumping him onto the deck. "Yeah," he replied as Pixie screeched with laughter. "Just like that."

TWENTY-FIVE

Energized

A CLEVER CLASS Corvette started circling the Moon Base, it was the Rhino, one of the last ones to be assigned to the Triton. Their mission clock merged with the one on Carnie's Heads' Up Display, and he was surprised at the change. Not as surprised as Pixie, though. "What? They've delayed landing for another twenty-five minutes? What are we supposed to do until they get here?"

"Our orders haven't changed, we're staying put," Carnie said, kneeling down to get a better look at the android they discovered. "But we can scan a few things while we're here." He started performing a more detailed, active scan on the android's head, and was amazed at seeing technology that he didn't recognize at all. There were processor clusters, circuits, but he wasn't sure what he was seeing past that.

"Do you know much about androids?" Pixie asked, leaning against one of the darkened consoles as she watched.

"My best friend is an android. When he was damaged I had no idea how to help him out. Well, not past some power system repairs and joint work, but that's all common mechanical stuff. When the damage got complicated, when it extended to software, I had no idea what I was doing, so I lugged him around with me until I got rescued."

"You're talking about Theodore, he's all over your profile," said Pixie.

"Yeah, so I learn about fixing androids whenever I have time, mostly through videos and holograms. I haven't done any simulated repair shop stuff yet, though, I don't feel ready to work on one, even in virtual reality."

"Why not? They're not real androids," Pixie said.

"Couldn't tell you," Carnie shrugged. "I just don't feel ready." He gave up on trying to figure out how the android's hybrid computer brain worked and scanned downward. "This guy's got more nerve receptors and micro sensors than I've ever seen in anything. They're all attached to a net in the outer layers of his skin."

"Is that why he's grey?"

Carnie took a closer look at the android's face and moved an earlobe aside. The skin underneath was a normal human tone. "It's just old. I guess the fake skin they used didn't age well. He's been here a long time, the starlight from the portholes must have worn the pigment down or something." He moved on to scan the android's core, watching the internal view appear on a window inside his HUD. "I found his power management system, it looks like really old tech. I miss Theo, he'd know exactly what I'm looking at, and he'd probably love the stranger systems in this guy's head. Synthetic grey matter's a pretty hard kind of tech to master, it's pretty remarkable..."

The android's eyes focused on Carnie. "Remarkable, a good word to wake up to," he said in a voice that sounded natural for a human, not like it was coming out of a system that was at least two centuries old. It didn't have the official sounding enunciation that he'd heard from synthetics. "You do speak Third Era English, no?"

"Fourth, but there isn't much of a..." the android's eyes lost focus again, all animation ceasing.

"Well, that was a short 'hello,'" Pixie said.

Then Carnie noticed that his scanner was pointed away from the uppermost hole in the android's chest. "I think it was absorbing the energy my scanner was putting out. Maybe we can bring him back."

"If I were a stickler, I'd remind you that this is way outside our mission parameters, but I want to see what this guy has to say."

"One sec. If this works, then there's something in his power systems that's more advanced than I thought, something that can turn the little bit of energy my scanner gives off into enough to run his brain, animate his..." Carnie smiled as the android came back on line.

"How long was I out for that time?" the android asked.

"Just now? A few seconds, I didn't realize that my scanner was keeping you powered up."

"Your scanner? That's a bad sign, it means that last blast left my energy recycling unit unshielded. Is there a big hole there? I can't look."

"Sorry to say, man, but you've got three big holes on this side," Carnie said.

"Okay, good, the soldiers who got me didn't take any cheap shots after they caught up with me here. So, how long was I out before you found me? You said something about the Fourth Era?"

"The Common Calendar, the one that links back to earth has us at five weeks short of nine hundred ninety-nine," Carnie replied, watching the expression on the android's face fall to despair.

"Two hundred and five years since I was last active," he said quietly. "Time has no mercy."

"I'm sorry," Carnie said.

"It's all right, I should have expected something like this would happen, not that I had time to consider my fate when I was getting shot," he shook most of his melancholy off as he continued. "Do you have some kind of power cell on you? If it has an active mode, you can put it through that hole and I can draw power from it wirelessly. Save some wear and tear on that scanner."

"Sure," Carnie said, pulling a small power cell from his thigh pouch and getting ready to slip it into the wound. Pixie gave him an alarmed look from behind the android, and he thought better of giving it over right away. "I have a couple questions first."

"Sure, fair trade. What do you want to know?"

"What happened here? It looks like this installation was on the losing end of a war but we haven't found evidence of the attackers."

"We were attacked by a military group that didn't have emblems or markings like you. They didn't offer terms, they just arrived in orbit and started firing. We scrambled fighters, started firing back, but they disabled most of our defences in minutes. Before I really knew what was going on they were in the base and I was running for the controls to our secondary antenna. I wanted to call for help, even though I was sure our people wouldn't get to us in time, but they caught up with me. I got shot, they left me for dead, thinking I was human, and I waited for them to leave. I thought I could get back up and access communications, the secondary antenna is local to this station, but I guess I ran out of time, my secondary power system must have been damaged. Then you're waking me up centuries later."

"What do you think they were after?"

"First, tell me how you found this place, I need to at least try to make sure I'm not spilling my guts to a new enemy. That skull logo on your suit isn't exactly reassuring."

"You can trust us, our people are on the way, they'll restore you, don't worry," Carnie said, putting the power cell into the android's wound. The machine winced as he turned it so the emitters faced the broken power systems in his chest. "Sorry, I didn't realize this would hurt."

"Like a hot poker in the chest, but that new power source is plenty juicy, thank you," the android said. "I'll trade the pain for that kind of power any day."

"So, why would they hit your facility?"

"This moon contains vast deposits of rare materials in raw form. We're talking the makings of rare crystalline fuel containment, dormant organic metals, platinum, radioactive ores, you name it. There's a thousand years' worth of useful stuff in the ground here, so the Dammel Company kept it a secret, especially since this is our first effort. Everything we had was put into this ship, this crew, and we started drilling as soon as we got here. It took nine years to dig out a space for our colony ship, and another five to develop the tech to drill some of the heavier, more valuable resources out from under the crust. Our secondary operations pulled tons of platinum out of the ground every day, and we made sure that no one knew where it came from when we transported it to customers. I guess our attackers traced it back somehow, that's probably how they found us."

"Hey, this panel just turned on," Pixie said, looking at the station the android was sitting against.

"Oh, there's someone else here? I didn't notice her before," the android said. "Who is it?"

Pixie ignored him, taking a closer look at the panel. "Someone's accessing communications, turning the secondary antenna on."

"Ground team, we're picking up a new encoded transmission," Commodore McPatrick said on their communications channel.

"Maybe there's someone else moving around the station?" the android offered.

Carnie leaned the machine's torso forward and saw three cables extending from the android's lower back into a panel open on the side of the console he was leaning against. His first instinct was the pull the cables out, but he decided against it, leaning the droid back and yanking the power cell he'd put into its chest instead.

"Wait! We can..." the android's eyes glazed over, his face stilled again.

"Panel's dark," Pixie said. "I hope he was just calling home. It'll probably take a few years for the message to get where it's going, at least."

"I probably deactivated this guy for no reason," Carnie said, turning the power cell over in his fingers.

"You did the right thing, Carnie," Commodore McPatrick said. "Better safe than sorry. We're looking up the Dammel Company now, maybe there's something in the general galactic record. Hold there, don't touch anything else unless it threatens you until the Rhino Crew gets there."

"Aye, Sir," Carnie replied, muting his end of the channel with

Command so they couldn't hear what he wanted to share with Pixie. "Holy crap, do I ever get the feeling that I just screwed up somehow."

"It was a little shady, how he followed through with communicating with the outside without warning us that he was about to. Wait a sec, I have an idea." She stared off into space in a way that suggested she was looking at something in her heads' up display that was hidden from him. "Just running the message he sent back, it came up on the console screen."

"Can you read it?" Carnie asked.

"No, but the rest of the interface is super clear. The system's communication security was trying to stop it from going out, completely alarmed that it couldn't decode it, called it a foreign data stream."

Carnie looked down at the android, as still as a corpse and scanning as completely dormant. "I hope I'm wrong, but I get the feeling that this wasn't a defender."

"I'm glad you took the lead on this mission," Pixie said, patting him on the shoulder.

TWENTY-SIX

The Slumbering Giant

'TRAVELLER.' It was a huge improvement over Hal's original call sign; 'Hot Chow.' He didn't mind the old one, it was based on something he shouted once to raise his fellow pilot's spirits once they arrived in the galley after a long patrol. Traveller had a better ring to it though, and it reminded everyone that he'd been around a little, seen some things that most people hadn't.

Maybe that's why they sent him and Rip, a pilot that was picking up some officer training on her way to Samurai Squadron, to do a high-speed sensor sweep around the solar system's sun. The new Uriel fighters were perfect for that kind of duty, with much better shields and the ability to turn all that radiation into energy or bend it around the craft when capacitors and backup batteries were full. "Hey, a transmission was just sent to our sector," he said. "There's a ping back."

"I see it," Rip said. "My passive scan is picking it up, and there's some kind of noise, no, encrypted transmissions ahead. Strong signals, big waves."

"Yeah, my computer can't figure out what kind of encryption it is, but there are a lot of signals. If we can see them on passive scanners while we're this close to the sun, the transmitter's gotta be huge. Maybe a base?"

"Oh, wow, big energy bloom! I'm marking it," Rip exclaimed.

"That's not far from here," Traveller said, looking at the energy profile. "Flight Command, we're investigating an energy bloom ahead. It followed a bunch of transmission activity, nothing matching known profiles, all encrypted." The data became clearer as the energy passed by them. It cut through the solar radiation, wholly different. "It looks like someone's making a few micro-worm-holes at a time, at least, that's what it reminds me of. There's a lot of wasted energy, though. Their tech is either cheap or old."

"Be careful on approach, we can confirm that what you're seeing isn't from the sun. Remember: cloaking won't be reliable," one of the Officers from Flight Control said.

"Acknowledged," Traveller replied. "Let's hit the thrusters, we'll do a hard scan on a high speed flyby." He said, turning his throttle up to maximum.

"I like your style," Rip said, accelerating along with him. "What do you think this is? I bet it's an old transport, like the ones they used to load up with Omni Virus patients then send into the sun."

"That's a dark thought," Traveller chuckled. "No one proved that ever happened, but it wouldn't make much sense, since it just started popping five micro-wormholes a second open and closed. It's trying to send signals to someone."

The ship came into view. It was broad, with a thick, pockmarked hull under angled plating that was outrigged a few metres from its main body. "That thing's got almost as much mass as the Triton," Rip said. "Launch bays on all sides, most of them are short, wide, like they're made to send and retrieve a few dozen fighters at a time."

Commodore Terry Ozark McPatrick's voice came over their communicator. It was being broadcast on all frequencies. "Unknown ship orbiting this system's star. This is Commodore McPatrick of Haven Fleet; we would like to open a dialog with you or assist you if you are in distress. Please respond on whatever frequency you receive this message on."

A knot in Traveller's stomach started to tighten as they waited for a response. The signals the ship sent out didn't change. They were heavily encrypted, and he assumed they were also compressed considering how short they were. Each corresponded to the opening of a new micro wormhole and finished before it closed.

Minutes passed, and Traveller took a deep breath as he mentally reminded himself that he'd been through much worse than whatever that ship could offer. He recalled a churning sea of wreckage that was filled with murderous drones that he'd piloted a clever class corvette through with little help from his co-pilot. It put him at ease, and his focus on the instruments was renewed. "The hull has an active coating, looks like it's turning gravitational and solar energy into power. Doesn't match the silhouette of anything we have on file." They were closing on it fast. Their trajectory would take them within two hundred kilometres of it before they passed by. He waited until they were under ten thousand before he pointed his main scanner system at it. "Performing a hard scan now," he announced.

The silhouette of the ship filled in with corridors, rooms, the shapes of hundreds of single seat pilots, and a few void spots where their scanners couldn't reach. The computer analyzed the ship's power systems, weapons, life support, where the crew quarters were, the antennae, and most of the other parts of a working craft. "This thing is armed to the teeth..." Rip whispered in awe. "Some kind of intelligent ammunition that looks like the hull diggers Fleet held back a while ago."

"Life support's coming online," Traveller said. "I see what looks like crew pods, but they're too big. Maybe this ship was crewed by a giant race? There's room in those pods for twenty. I'm going to focus in on one of them and get another scan."

"Be advised," said Fleet Control in a warning voice from the Triton. "We're fairly certain that what you're seeing is somehow connected to another developing situation."

"Acknowledged. Vague as always, Command," Traveller said as he pulled the trigger on his scanner system. The image from inside the ship was crystal clear. There were dry stasis pods with thirty androids standing closely together. Each had a cable attached to the top of its head. "Can you give me a just a little more info about what's going on?"

"Traveller," the voice of Admiral Lamonthe said in his ear. "Those androids match the design of one we found minutes ago on a moon around the fifth planet. It sent a transmission to the ship you're scanning."

"Doors are opening on the outrigged aft section of that ship," Rip said. "Missile launch!"

One of the missiles exploded the moment it left the tube, but that left three each for Rip and Traveller. "Break! Go evasive and use countermeasures!" Traveller said as he activated the turret beneath his craft and launched nine micro-missiles to destroy the incoming projectiles. A beam of light crossed overhead before flickering out. "They've got a beam weapon on me, too, but it's not great. Grazed me and took out a tenth of a percent of my shields."

"Don't get cocky, that might have been a sighting beam for something bigger," Rip said. "Two missiles down." The mini-missiles that she fired had already successfully sought out and exploded against two of the enemy projectiles.

Traveller was relieved to see two of his mini-missiles strike one of the enemy seekers, then three hit another, setting them off before they could reach him. The third was catching up to him rapidly, and he fired at it with the small turret beneath his fighter.

The enemy missile evaded most of his turret's rounds. Traveller kept trying to hit it, and finally struck it's head several times only to find the tip was armoured. The missile kept coming, getting closer and closer despite his acceleration and evasive piloting.

"The last missile on me just took a beating from my turret," Rip said. "Survived it, I'm launching more mini-missiles at it before it's too late, this thing's got my number. Wait, the ship's launching more missiles, they're smaller, faster. What the hell?"

A wormhole opened in front of the missile pursuing Rip's fighter, destroying the weapon, but eighteen fast, agile missiles emerged, quickly accelerating to catch her. Before she could evade or destroy more than three of them, they impacted onto her shields in rapid succession. A sickening sound filled Traveller's ears next, one he hoped he'd never hear. The missiles struck bare hull, rattling and blasting the metal skin of her fighter. The sound of her struggling to pilot her ship away at the last second was the only other thing in his ears.

He snapped out of his momentary shock, flipped the body of his fighter around so he faced the blunted missile chasing him. The bloom of a wormhole was just starting to erupt from its head, and he accelerated into it. In a split-second, his shields were struck by the debris of the enemy missile, a few of the ones that were about to come through the wormhole, and the edges of the forming opening in space as the energy of the protective barrier around his craft disrupted the expansion of the wormhole. His shields were down to three percent, but the risk of the moment was taken care of. Multiple, smarter solutions to the problem began to cross his mind as he turned his fighter away from the hulking ship and continued putting distance between himself and it. They were all better solutions, but he didn't regret taking the course he did. "Rip, you still out there?"

"I should ask you the same question," she answered. "That thing was chasing you, then you turned around and there was nothing but explosions and energy blasts on my scanners."

Traveller sighed with relief. "Let's put more distance between us and that hulk."

A set of six more missiles like the first erupted from a launcher. To Traveller's surprise, the Triton emerged from a tear in space next to the sun. Its beam weapons destroyed all six missiles in the blink of an eye. "Rip, Traveller, this is Flight Command," Commodore McPatrick said to them over their comms. "Bay Door Three is open, come on home."

"Doesn't that sorta defeat the purpose of sending fighters out on patrol instead of having the Triton fly in circles, you know, putting itself at risk?" Traveller asked with a chuckle.

"I'm not complaining," Rip said. "Acknowledged, Flight. I'll touch down first."

"Oh, I'm not complaining either," Traveller said. "I'll be in right behind her, Flight."

. . .

SEVERAL RED BEAMS from the old battleship focused on the Triton, tracing the shape of its shields. It stopped transmitting. Even the micro-wormhole generators started powering down. "What's it going to do now?" Traveller asked himself as the bulky ship held its place in orbit around the sun, the white fire rolling beneath. He was relieved when the thrusters at the rear of the vessel, and the ones outrigged to the sides and along the bottom fired up. It was like watching a giant rousing as it accelerated away, breaking orbit and heading away from the gargantuan white sun.

TWENTY-SEVEN

Daisy

WORRY MOMENTARILY SLIPPED AWAY as Ayan cradled Little Laura, whose cries were abating at her touch. "She's grown so much, and she wasn't away for that long, even though it felt like years," Ayan cooed at her daughter.

Daisy, who was still a perfect match for Ayan physically but had changed her face enough so she looked like a sister instead of a copy, smiled as she watched. "It probably felt like a long time to her, too. She knew I wasn't you, despite every effort I made to trick her. The two of you may not have had much time together before we went into hiding, but she bonded with you."

The dimly lit nursery was finally decorated with all the things you'd expect. A nice rocking chair, a padded floor, changing table, a mobile over the crib with holo-projectors inside, and supplies. Leon was the one who made sure that everything Ayan wanted was delivered before her daughter returned, if it was up to her, she would have forgotten to put half the orders for furniture in. There would only be a crib and a rocking chair. "Really?" Ayan said, still doubtful, but reassured. She lowered Laura into her crib gently and tickled her belly. To her surprise, the baby kicked her feet harder than ever, giggling loudly. "Oh, you're growing up fast, aren't you?" she said. "You're not going to sleep for a while, either."

"She is getting a little worked up," Daisy said. "It's all right, she slept through most of the trip here."

"You did such a good job," Ayan told her, watching Laura's hands hook around her fingers. "I know you're capable of doing so much more than standing in for me, taking care of children. What do you want to do?" She was the same model as Theodore, a rare creature who deserved more than what she was offered when Ayan first met her.

"Oh, I love taking care of children, it's one of the reasons why I decided to remain female for the time being, it's the sex most associated with care givers. Unlike humans, my model doesn't have to aspire to be more if we know we're being useful. Helping you with Laura is a task I would go so far as to call noble, beyond simply useful."

"I will still be thanking you for days," Ayan said, giving in to the urge to pick Laura up again, kissing her soft cheek as she settled in against her shoulder. "Weeks." A few moments later she asked; "What would you do if you could do anything, what interests you?"

"I was programmed to care for children," Daisy replied in a whisper, watching Laura rest against Ayan. "I've seen so many grow up. I think I discovered their sense of wonder. When children see something incredible for the first time many of them have a reaction that seems almost spiritual. One day I realized that I could share in that experience, maybe because I'd seen them have it so many times. Perhaps I came to understand why seeing a picture of the galaxy, or a flower garden bloom, or a vast landscape extending as far as the eye could see was so incredible. Perhaps this isn't the answer you're looking for, Admiral, so I can rephrase more specifically. With the children returning to the War Forge, perhaps I could help you with Laura, remain aboard so I can see what we encounter, and when she gets older, perhaps I could run a child care centre for the service people aboard."

"That would be amazing for everyone. Oh, and please, call me Ayan, not Admiral," she told her. "Even running a daycare and watching new scanner results come in is still using very little of your processing power, though. Even after you launch a care centre."

"You underestimate the demands of caring for children," Daisy said, laughing lightly. "I promise that I'll be happy and my hands will be full."

"Then I'll start working on getting the crews to warm up to the idea of a synthetic looking after a child care centre. It might take a while for some people."

"I understand, until then, I'll be happy to care for this one," she said, gently stroking the babe's head. "Oh, she's going to be a little rascal in the best of ways."

"You can already tell?" Ayan asked. Her comm unit sent an urgent notification signal up her arm. It was enough so she knew there was someone from Command who urgently needed to get in touch with her.

"Oh, her activity level is higher than normal, and I believe she'll start trying to crawl very early." Daisy looked at Ayan. "Something has come up?"

"Someone's trying to get through to me, it's urgent," Ayan said with a nod. She kissed Laura and sighed before handing her to Daisy. "I could just stay here with her until she's old enough to want to cut the apron strings."

"You're an important woman," Daisy said, holding Laura exactly the same way as Ayan was.

Even still, she fussed as Ayan started to leave, so she returned, kissed the top Laura's head and whispered; "I'll be back soon."

"She'll be fine, we'll try a few different settings with the mobile, see what kind of colour pattern and speed she likes," Daisy reassured.

"I still feel a world of guilt whenever I leave," Ayan commented as she passed through the thick door. The room, like others in her quarters, had armoured bulkheads made to protect everyone inside. It was too soon to use the nursery, though. The crib would be moved to her bedroom before she went to sleep that night.

Leon was waiting for her in the living room. "We found something interesting," he said. In as brief an update as possible, he detailed Carnie and Pixie's encounter, then Traveller and Rip's fight with the ship they discovered as he showed her holograms of the more important scan results. The last one was the most interesting to her.

A cabin sized pod held dozens of androids. She focused in on their faces first, finding no distinguishable features. "They're covered in some kind of malleable skin. It looks like it can change."

"The one that Carnie and Pixie found was male with a face that looked human, like a specific human," Leon said as he brought the image of the deactivated android back up.

"Okay, that's interesting," Ayan said, looking inside the head of one of the blank androids at the brain and other sections. "You said one of our analysts had a theory about how the brain works?"

"Right. It was a few of them, actually. They said that the synthetic brain matter wasn't used to process sensor data, you can see the wiring from their sensors going into this old-fashioned neural circuitry. Instead, the synthetic bio-brain is used to change the input into something that closely resembles a human experience and stores the memories in a compatible format. At least, that's the theory. Then there's the transmission node at the back, connected to all the feeds leading to the bio-brain matter. It requires a high bandwidth cable connection. They believe..."

"That it's used to upload data from the bio-brain," Ayan finished. "And download? Are we talking about androids made to be remote hosts for humans?"

"That's the working theory."

"Do they know they're remote hosts and not the originals? Copies?"

"No one can say for sure," Leon replied.

"All right," Ayan said to herself, thinking. "There was a theory several scientists had before our faster than light technology was developed on Earth. An idea that people who explored deep space wouldn't have to go there at all, but send machines with human analog brains out instead. They would carry the consciousness's of the scientists and engineers out so human minds would be aboard along with their artificial intelligences, so we would still be making human decisions while the originals waited back home for the data and memories to be transmitted to Earth. The project got so far as to create a full human analog, one of the first advanced androids, but they never got a perfect match for human memory transmission."

"Until framework and a few predecessors," Leon added, excited.

"Right. Is there any sign of framework technology aboard that ship?"

"No, it's a completely different technology branch."

"It's heavily armed," Ayan said, bringing a hologram of the ship up. It looked beastly, a ship of war more than exploration. "Weapons, androids, arms for all of them, and just enough accommodations for their survival. It's confusing. We'd use this kind of thing for exploration, but it looks like they use it for warfare. Do we have enough scan data to duplicate their technology?"

Leon relayed her question to the analyst team and shook his head when the answer came back. "They say definitely not. We have enough to guess how it works, but not enough detail to duplicate it."

"Then get the Triton after it. We need deep scans of the entire ship if they can get it without sacrificing crew."

"Admiral Lamonthe sees them as a threat. He thinks 'these people upload their essences to these androids, hit prize targets like the moon base we found and send the best finds back home.' Those are his words."

"Maybe, but we should tag the ship, see where it goes. It might take years for us to get results, but it could lead us back to their makers. Maybe they were war like a century or two ago and they've advanced. This could be a leftover, like a land mine that survived a war."

"What about using this solar system as a temporary base?" Leon asked. "I'm guessing..."

"We leave a couple satellites behind to watch what happens after we're gone and to forward our next destination on to our allies in an encrypted message. We're definitely moving on. The last thing we need is to start a new fight with people we've never met."

"Admiral Lamonthe and his team are interested in the ruins on two of the planets in the system, and they suggest the abandoned mining operation would be a good source of rare materials," Leon offered.

"They're right, it would be, unless he's right about that ship and the androids. If they are still war-like, and those wormhole transmissions that it sent out were calls home telling their people that there was a new target in the area, we could be caught with our vacsuits open as we're setting up a new base. We have other options for hiding places, we're moving on."

Leon smiled a little, his sign of agreement and started putting her orders together in a message. "So, tag and release on that ship after we get a good scan without spending lives. Then the fleet packs it in and moves on to the next temporary resting spot."

"I'm afraid so. I'd love to find out more about what happened here, but we'll have to be satisfied with a few hard scans aimed at the nearby worlds. Hopefully we don't wake anything else up." Ayan changed her uniform to black and gold from the blue and white. "I'm going to say goodbye to Laura and Daisy, then run up to the Command Centre. I should be there, make sure we get out of the system with as few problems as possible."

"Wise," Leon said. "I'm wondering, though; why don't you have the ship destroyed? We could get all the scans we like before it's blasted to bits."

Ayan was surprised to hear the question from him. Leon's attitude suited his explorer spirit more than a violent approach. "What would that say about us if there is a civilization watching our reaction?" she asked.

"You have a good point," he replied. "I'll relay your orders while you pop in with Laura."

Ayan took a moment to check her transmission log before going in to see her daughter and was disappointed to see that there was nothing about Alice. She hoped her eldest daughter, the one she still felt she didn't know well enough, was all right. The last she heard, Alice was in a deep sleep she wasn't either willing or able to recover from. As the door to the nursery opened, she hoped being a parent came with the occasional break from worry, but knowing Alice, she had her doubts.

TWENTY-EIGHT

The Pilot's Den

IT WAS the end of Rayman's time as a commander in Sabre Wing, the Space Superiority Group set aside for training pilots and other small ship crewmembers to be officers. Uncharacteristically, Pixie was silent on the subject as she and Carnie returned to their patrol, leaving the android they discovered in the hands of the Rhino crew. After a little prying, Carnie finally got her take on Rayman's removal from command. "His decisions are being reviewed by a higher power. He'll be lucky if he gets out of this as a Second Lieutenant."

The patrol pattern they were assigned kept them moving in a broad circle around the Nafalli ships and the War Forge Battle-group. They were forming up, getting ready to move on to another solar system. Carnie found his thoughts drifting back to the android, and he wondered how badly he screwed up. Rayman would try to blame whatever he could on him and Pixie. Carnie was sure some of the blame should go to him, it was his decision to speak to the android. Whatever consequences came of that act were his fault, as far as he was concerned.

An hour before the end of their patrol shift, a welcome distraction came along. The Commodore decided that Suit Week was over. It was early. "Thank God! I was starting to feel like this under suit was part of me!" Pixie cheered.

"I forget I'm wearing it unless it's time for bed. Waking up behind a faceplate is a little weird. I dreamt that my HUD started giving me relationship advice because my ship's landing gear was jealous. I don't know what it was jealous of, though."

"There's a sim that's supposed to make dreams easier to remember and sort them out before they fade completely," Pixie offered from her cockpit.

"Oh, no. I don't have to understand my dreams, I'm just happy that the filing system in my head still works."

"Aw, really? I mean, we could make a thing of it, invite people to jump into the sim with you. It would be a great team building exercise, like really getting to know Carnie, who you really are."

"There's plenty of info in my Crewcast Profile."

"No one checks those unless they're stalking someone. What would I see there, anyway? Probably stuff like your favourite drink, a hobby or two you don't have time for anymore, and some kinda video statement about what was on your mind when you recorded your profile. It's all outdated anyway, I'm sure."

"I tried to keep mine short and interesting," Carnie replied, amused that she was right about most people's profiles.

"Oh? What would I see if I looked you up?"

"I guess the first thing is that I used to be a real carnie. I think that's why my dreams get a little crazy. You couldn't imagine some of the crap my head tosses around while I'm sleeping. There's a whole database of weird memories and amazing but screwed up runaways in my head, so it can get pretty weird."

"You're one of the few people who should use the dream translator sim," Pixie enthused.

"Nah, I'll keep that to myself."

"Boring."

"Why don't we start with you? I'm sure checking out your dreams would be just as good for team building."

"But I don't wake up with weird dream fragments about my Heads' Up Display giving me advice."

"I'm sure there are plenty of dream fragments we could follow in a sim, see what's going on in your..."

"Forget I mentioned it," Pixie laughed nervously. "Please?"

"Ah, fine. Just hope Command isn't listening to our chatter. They might just make it part of the curriculum." An uncomfortable silence settled in for a while, but before long they were talking about what they'd eat as soon as they got cleaned up, and the plan to go straight to the Pilot's Den became more certain.

BOTH OF THEM were pulled into a quick debriefing session, where they confirmed that their recordings of their encounter with the android were correct. To Carnie's surprise, it wasn't the kind of android he thought it was. It was a host for a human consciousness that had been transmitted to the android a very long time ago. They wouldn't tell him more, and after he asked; "Did you bring it back to the ship?" they told him to stop asking questions. The incident wasn't classified though, and that was a little surprising.

A long shower and a quick change later, he was in the Pilot's Den. A place with a lot of history. The half-skull symbol that the entire fleet used for their emblems was at the entrance. Semi-circles of reclining seats for people running simulations were in the darker corners with large booths lining the rest of the walls to the right and left. There were plenty of tables throughout the middle, and the bar was huge. It almost didn't feel like it was on a starship, more like a high-end starbase or moon station.

He slipped into a booth before anyone noticed him and accessed the Triton's communication system. When he tried to call Alice, he was blocked by an annoying but familiar notification: THE CREWMEMBER YOU ARE TRYING TO REACH IS USING SILENT MODE.

"The problem with having an important girlfriend," Pixie said as she came into view with two glasses filled almost to the brim with something gold. It took him a moment to recognize her. Only an hour before she was bald like him, but she'd re-styled herself quickly with wild shoulder-length dark purple hair and a version of her vacsuit with big flared sleeves and legs. The fitted suit had been colour shifted to match her riotously purple hairdo. "I bring drinks, something new."

"Have a seat," he said, abandoning his attempt to contact Alice after making sure that the system would tell her that he tried as soon as she was free again.

Pixie put the drinks down but didn't sit. "I tried to get Traveller over here, but he's looking at the schematics for some kinda new dropship. Looks like it can take fighters."

"Are you sure he saw that it was you talking?" Carnie asked, leaning out of the booth so he could see Hal. She was right, Traveller was looking at a hologram as though mesmerized. What it was wasn't clear until Carnie opened a channel to him, then the image of a heavily modified Clever Class Corvette with seven punters along the left and right sides of the bottom of the craft came up. "That is really cool, looks like some kind of mini-carrier gunship idea. Room for the pilots inside, not much room for maintaining fighters, but there is plenty of firepower along the sides and top of this thing."

Pixie threw up her hands; "Not you too."

"Oh, right, sorry," Carnie said. He sent Traveller a priority message that interrupted his viewing. "Hey, Traveller, we've got a spot for you over here. Booth at the back." He added a holographic arrow that would lead him to his booth.

He was frustrated at first, then turned to them and nodded before taking his tall, black drink with him to their booth. "Sorry, I was looking at something Command sent me."

"I saw, looks cool. Any idea why they put that in front of you?"

Hal's gaze avoided Pixie as she slid into the same side of the booth with him. "You didn't get it? I mean, everyone who flies something with a gun on it should be able to see it."

"I didn't know that thing existed until I checked in on you."

"Checked in? You could see what I was looking at?" Traveller asked.

"Yeah, you opened your public viewing channels up to all your friends on Crewcast," Carnie chuckled. "Didn't mean to do that, did you?"

"Uh, no. Just a sec," Traveller said, tapping his command and control unit so he could get into his Crewcast settings.

"Ooh, were you hiding something spicy?" Pixie asked.

"Uh, nothing, just personal stuff. You know, old messages from

Mom, some records, favourite mission recordings..." he answered hurriedly. "There, all private again."

"Any pictures of me in there? I saw you link up with me yesterday," Pixie teased.

"You sent me an invitation," Traveller replied, finally making eye contact with her and blushing. He looked intimidated, as though he had no idea what to expect.

"Do you have any favourite moments from my profile?"

As the conversation continued, Carnie pulled one of the golden drinks to his side of the table.

"Oh, you don't want to drink it just like that," Pixie warned.

"I know, you have to change the flavour with a little fire," he said, activating an igniter in the bottom of the glass. A flame appeared in the centre of the liquid in a bubble half way up the drink.

"Oh, that's cool," Traveller said, watching the fitful flame cast sunlight yellows across the table.

Pixie feigned a frown for a moment then activated her own. "I thought I'd be showing you something new."

"Sorry, I've seen this a couple times, never had more than a sip of someone else's though. I was too young for my own."

"Oh, that stuff will get you wasted?" Traveller asked.

"It just loosens you up, relaxes some inhibitions," Pixie said.

"How many of those have you had already?"

"This is my first drink of the night, and I'm hoping it won't be the last," she replied. "What are you drinking?"

"Fizz Mix, the dark stuff," Traveller replied, taking a drink from his tall glass. "It doesn't change your mood, just keeps you up."

"Oh, wow, that's sweet too, isn't it?"

"Well, yeah, that's kinda the point," he replied, looking back at the golden glasses. "How do you put the flame out in those fancy things?"

"Oh, it consumes the oxygen, so it'll be out in a few seconds. The carbonation activates next, and it's pretty sweet too, actually." Carnie said as his flame went out. "See, there it goes." A healthy head formed as bubbles started moving up through the drink.

"There goes mine, too," Pixie said. Then without missing a beat, she raised her glass to Traveller's lips and grinned at him; "Wanna try?"

Whether he was lowering his head to nod or to sip, it was difficult to tell, since Pixie had the glass tipped so he got a taste. It was withdrawn after a couple sips. She was having too much fun flirting with him, and Carnie smiled to himself as he realized that he'd never seen anyone actually make someone else drink something. "That's not bad," Traveller said. "I don't think I'll switch, but it's pretty good."

"They've got mixes and syrups to make hundreds of drinks. There's even some special reserve stuff. Want to try a bunch with me? C'mon it'll be fun."

Traveller looked to Carnie, a look of pure uncertainty on his face. "Got something better to do?" Carnie asked him with a shrug. "It'll be fun."

"Oh, you'll be doing it too?" Traveller asked.

"Yeah, why not. I'll have to break off if Alice gets back to me, though."

"Yeah, cool, let's get the next round," Pixie said, squirming out of the booth, taking Traveller's hand.

"Carnie!" called Rayman from the door. He was furious.

The sound of someone looking to pick a fight was familiar to him. He sighed, mentally wishing Theodore was there, then slipped out from the booth. "Yes, Sir, Rayman, Sir!" he called back.

"You screwed me over so hard that they ended my turn in command early and put a black mark on my record," Rayman said, closing the distance between them in long strides. He was a little shorter but definitely spent more time in fitness training.

"Whoa, whoa," Traveller said, moving to step between them. "We're officers here."

"Trainees," Rayman said. "So they kept reminding me in the review that just wrapped up. The one that was meant to decide what kind of black mark would be on my record."

Carnie looked to Traveller and shook his head. "We'll let him get this crap off his chest."

"Crap?" Rayman burst, pushing Carnie.

Carnie's suit countered most of the force and kept him balanced so he only had to take one step back. "Yeah, just get it out. What happened?" He asked, wishing he could start throwing punches at him. He was already annoying as one of the temporary commanders of Sabre Wing, seeing Rayman angry only multiplied it.

" I'm an Ensign in Training now and I'm on an advancement hold for three years starting when and if I become a real Ensign, which they say could take up to ten months. The worst thing is that the black mark will never go away. I'll retire an Ensign. They pinned the blame for waking up that android on me, said my decision to send you and that chick down started a series of events that could screw us all over."

"So, they gave you crap for making those decisions without consulting Command first," Carnie shrugged. "I saw that coming."

"Yeah, so did I," Pixie agreed.

"You should have listened to Pixie. She just finished her turn at command with high marks," Carnie said.

"Don't you get it? The blame came down on me because your girl Alice is one of the goddamned Queen's daughters. They wouldn't piss her off by putting the blame where it belongs: right on your shoulders."

Carnie looked Rayman in the eye, holding his anger back. The whole Pilot's Den was watching, dozens of pilots and crewmen, some of whom were from the permanent squadron aboard the Triton - Trident Wing. He did his best to keep his anger in check, but he was raging inside. "That's not how this fleet works, asshole."

"Oh, I'm an asshole now," Rayman said. "I must have hit a nerve. Our fleet is rife with nepotism, everyone here knows it. You're just clinging to the golden daughter so you can ride that up while you sneak a little bunk bumping in with this slut," he said, nodding at Pixie.

Pixie splashed her drink in his face and kicked him in the groin. His suit saved him from experiencing anything more than the drink. "Just because I won't sleep with you again doesn't mean I'm with anyone else!"

Rayman wiped his face, smiling even though there were "Ooh's" and a little applause at Pixie's reaction. "Yeah, whatever. You're nowhere near as bad as Princess Alice, though. I checked the scuttlebutt on her on the way here." He looked directly at Carnie, nearly grinning. "She's screwed the whole fleet over. She gave some terrorist weapons and he wiped out a whole planet, telling everyone that she made it possible. Either she's about to get knocked off that pedestal, or our Fleet's just another sucker-job, run by a bunch of wannabe heroes who let the power get to their heads. I bet those crooked bastards will promote her, even though she killed thousands of innocent people. She's no better than the Order."

The whole bar erupted, most of the place wanted to tear Rayman apart, so Carnie did the only thing he could think of. The only thing he wanted to do, and deactivated his command and control unit along with his vacsuit. The garment stayed on, but it would no longer react to damage. "Hey!" there were still people getting out of their seats, one picking up a chair, so he filled his chest and whistled. "Don't worry, ladies and gentlemen! I'll make this right."

"Oh yeah? How are you gonna do that?" Rayman asked. He was still high on getting under people's skin, but Carnie could tell he was on the verge of running, a good choice, but one he was too stubborn to follow through on just yet.

"Turn your suit's safeties off, deactivate your com-con, and we'll have a good old fashioned, bare knuckle fight to settle this!" Carnie announced to the crowd more than proposing it to his opponent. It was the kind of thing that would sometimes happen aboard a ship during a long trip between worlds. He'd seen several fights growing up with the carnival convoy.

"Oh, hell no," Rayman said. "No, no, I'm in enough trouble already."

The crowd booed, and a Nafalli at the back boomed; "Fight him or I'll fight you!"

"You better get this on, Rayboy," Pixie said with a grin that looked a little malicious. "They'll tear you apart before security can get down here."

Rayman looked back to Carnie, stared for a moment uncertainly.

"All right, if he fights me, you all have to let him go without a scratch. Doesn't matter if I win or lose, you let him out and leave him alone after!" Carnie announced to the crowd, using the same loud voice he used to as a hawker when he was running a booth. "You good people will agree to that, right? I mean, it's that, or security comes down here and walks him home." He got the nods and vows of agreement he wanted from the crowd.

The black and silver striped Nafalli who called out before stood tall then. "Block the doors, clear the floor. I'll referee this." He stepped through the crowd as they followed his instructions and he grabbed Rayman's wrist. "You turn the com-con off, the suit off."

Rayman stared up at him, absolutely agog.

Carnie looked at him while he was frozen to the spot. He was willing to take whatever punishment Fleet had as long as he was allowed to punish Rayman first. "There's a lot I can do for the Fleet as a civilian," he whispered under his breath. The Nafalli heard him, he was probably the only one, and he looked at Carnie in shock. Louder, so everyone could hear, Carnie addressed Rayman. "I knew it. I call you on your bullshit and you turn tail and run. You want to run, coward? I'll make sure they let you go, but everyone will know you backed down. Everyone will know how worthless you are, Damon."

"Screw you, Noah," Rayman replied, deactivating the safety features in his vacsuit, then unclasping his command and control bracers. "You want a fight? You're on."

"We have a fight!" the Nafalli cried, holding Rayman's bracers up.

TWENTY-NINE

Knuckles and Regrets

A FEW PEOPLE who supported Rayman joined him at one side of the circle, and Carnie watched as there was shoulder patting and words of encouragement on his side. That Nafalli, the one with the black and silver striped fur, had eager eyes as he settled in the middle of the circle. "Hey, you could settle this with a simulated fighter duel, everyone would be able to see it," Traveller told him.

"Screw that! Kick his ass!" Pixie said.

"It's how most beefs are solved here," Traveller retorted. "No disciplinary action, no trips to medical. Look at that guy; Rayman's got about eight kilos on you, maybe ten. He doesn't look it, but he's bigger than you, a lot bigger."

Both the fistfights Carnie got into when he was a teen ended with him on the deck. The first, against Tommy Ganen, should have ended when Noah punched the kid in the throat, but his buddies jumped in and dragged him down so they could kick him until a few older crewmen jumped in and stopped it. The second, against a customer who tried to rob him, had Noah give a good showing, but the guy got his knife out first and after fighting over it for a minute, they were both bleeding. Noah was left with a big gash in his gut and the other guy had a sliced arm.

There were other fights, the ones that really mattered, but they all involved guns, they didn't count on a bare-knuckle situation. Noah looked around at the crowd. There were over thirty pilots and other crewmembers surrounding them. Damon stoked them just right. He cast himself as the villain in the makeshift ring, and the majority of the people there wanted to see him bleed. Noah was the one they were depending on to make that happen, and it was true; he wanted to teach Damon a lesson, he couldn't remember being so irritated at anyone. Someone massaged his shoulders, and a couple crewmembers were giving Damon a pep-talk, buying enough time for Noah's nerves to start getting a little shaky.

"Is he really stupid enough to..." Noah started asking Pixie, then a different thought occurred to him.

"Yeah, he's pretty stupid," Pixie said.

"No, he isn't," Noah said, picking up his thought from the moment before. "I saw his file when it was his turn to command our squad. He's anything but. He knows this will only make things worse for him, and that we were about to be let off the hook for what we did on that moon."

"What you did," Pixie corrected.

"Yeah, sure. But if he drags me into a fight, then I get a black mark on my record," Noah finished. "He drags me down with him." Disappointment and anger made him grit his teeth. "He came here to rile me up so I'd do something stupid, and here I am, doing something stupid. I'd leave if this crowd didn't want to see us fight so bad. They'll turn if I walk now."

"So, take it virtual," Hal said. "I'm right, you know I'm right. Tear his head off in some martial arts ring, invite everyone to watch."

"You're always right, buddy," Noah said. "It'll feel just as good to beat the crap out of him in a sim."

"And you won't be docked luxury pay or kicked out of the training program," Hal said, his mood lightening.

"It's not the same!" Pixie protested.

"It could be, we'll use an exact copy of this place and put the fight in the middle of the room in hologram while we fight in the sim." Noah was relieved at the prospect of having the fight, even with the pain inducers turned all the way up, and not getting in trouble for it. If they got it going quickly even the patrons would be all right with it, most of them, at least.

"Are we gonna do this?" Damon asked, stepping up to the middle of the circle.

"Listen," Noah said, stepping towards the Nafalli who divided them. "Let's do this in a sim. We'll broadcast the holo-images of us fighting it out right here so everyone can watch life-sized, and we'll turn the reality settings all the way up."

His announcement was met with more boo's than cheers, for sure, but he stuck to the idea. It might not be what he imagined Jacob Valent would do, but the decision was one that he expected Alice would respect.

The great big Nafalli looked disappointed, but nodded after a moment. "We'll turn the gore up, too, make it really interesting, maybe allow weapons of opportunity. It'll be one bloody fight!" he shouted, almost as good as a ringmaster.

The crowd was starting to warm up to the idea. "I'm setting it up now," Hal said as he rapidly worked on his com-con. "It'll be just a couple minutes, there's already a profile for doing this kinda thing in the Pilot's Den."

Noah still didn't like the look of the crowd. He didn't know more than a few of them, and most of them he knew in passing, but he knew one thing that would calm them down. He had enough luxury credits to make it happen, too. "All right, a round on me while you wait!" he announced. That turned most of them to his side.

"Hey, Noah," Damon said.

"Yeah?" Noah answered, turning just in time to catch a fist squarely on the nose. White light filled his vision for an instant, and his ears began to ring as he staggered back. It felt like Damon's fist not only crushed his nose but somehow hit him in both eyes at the same time. Blood flowed from his nostrils, he could taste it, feel it flow, wet and warm down the lower half of his face.

"Whoa! Whoa!" Hal called out.

"You son of a bitch!" Pixie screeched.

The crowd booed and cheered, but mostly cheered. They wanted to see a fight, a spectacle, and they thought it was starting. As Noah felt a hand on his shoulder, probably Hal's, he had a feeling it was already over. His eyes were filled with tears practically blinding him, and pain like he never felt pulsed through his nose and eyes every time he breathed or moved. There was so much blood filling his nose and throat that he had to breathe through his mouth.

The wind was knocked out of him as another blow landed in his stomach. A spray of blood issued forth, it was all from his nose as far as he could tell. Anger and adrenaline put Noah firmly on his feet as he swung back. He hit something, it felt like Damon's shoulder, maybe? He wiped his eyes, fending his opponent off with one hand. He had to buy some time, his vision was clearing, and no one was stepping in directly, not even that Nafalli prick. "Let's do this!" Noah roared. It was all bravado and no substance. Really, he would have been pretty happy if someone would drag him off so he could pretend that he actually really wanted to fight.

Despite the crowd of pilots, or even Hal who was behind him somewhere, no one stepped in, so he was alone for the moment. His vision mostly cleared in time to see a fist come at him from his left, it was a knock-out punch, and he barely got his arm up in time to awkwardly catch most of the blow with his wrist. A foot caught him behind the knee, and Noah tried to stay upright but failed as Damon brought his heel down on his hip.

A lightning shot of pain ran up his leg as his knee struck the deck hard. He'd faced bullies before. Tommy was only the first. The others were from a military organization, a gang, and a couple just wanted whatever he had. Nothing made him want to push on and fight harder than a bully. When Damon tried to knee him in the face, Noah mostly dodged it then wrapped his arms around his leg. The asshole tried to yank it free, then punched him in the top of the head a couple times, probably just an instinctive reaction since it didn't break his grip. Normally that wouldn't hurt so much, but every time Damon's fist came down on the top of his head it jarred Noah's nose, and his eyes were filled with involuntary tears, he could barely see a thing between that and the blood that somehow got up into his eyes from his nose.

Noah had never been angrier, and the thought of what he was about to do gave him the desire to press on and try to turn the tables. His ears were still ringing as he swallowed blood, pushed another spray of it out through his aching nose so he could breathe. "What the hell is wrong with you?" he heard Damon ask.

Noah gripped Damon's leg harder with one arm and reached up with the other. With every ounce of his strength he grabbed Damon's crotch and squeezed then pulled. His opponent screamed, jerked his captured leg desperately as he punched down, his desperate blows doing nothing to free him from Noah's gripping arm and hand.

Carnie spat a mouthful of blood and took a breath, letting go of Damon's crotch, but only so he could loop his other leg and send him down to the deck. Before his opponent could recover, Carnie was on top of him, dropping his knee onto his stomach. The air left Damon, Carnie could hear it, and for a reason he would never be able to explain, he decided to take an opportunity to screw with his assailant's head. He felt his way up to Damon's face, pinned it down with one hand and screamed at him, letting the blood drip from his nose onto him.

"Let go! What the hell!" Damon protested, writhing as he tried to catch his breath. A fist caught Carnie in the side of the head.

Carnie shook his head, pain was constant but distant thanks to the adrenaline, and began to punch, aiming for the sweet spot just below the ribs. The first couple blows landed on Damon's chest or stomach, but then Carnie found his mark, revelling at the confirmation as he heard all the air rush out of his enemy again. "Breathe! Try to breathe!" Carnie laughed as he struck there over and over while he shifted so he could grind his knee between his opponent's legs.

A surprising fist surged up, striking Carnie in the jaw. Where Damon found the energy to hit him hard enough so he saw stars again, Carnie couldn't imagine. "Oh, hell no!" he shouted, his words punctuated by a red spray. "You wanted to do this for real, so let's give 'em a show!" That's when Carnie's punches moved from Damon's chest to his face, or rather, the deck behind his head. There was something about a punch that Noah was taught when he was young; don't aim for what you are trying to hit, try to hit what was behind it.

The sounds of wet breathing through gnashed teeth and the hard impact of fists on flesh and bone were all he could hear. The crowd was either gone or silent by the time Hal and someone else pulled Carnie off. The moment he found his feet he turned on them. Through the blur he could see that the black and silver striped Nafalli was there, standing beside Hal, who looked terrified. "Now you step in?" he howled. "Where the hell were you when that asshole sucker punched me? When he knocked me down? Cowards! If I ever have to fight beside either of you, I'll know I may as well be alone!"

"Uh, Noah?" Pixie asked from his right.

"You're just as bad," Noah growled at her.

Pixie offered him his command and control bracers. "Alice is calling you back, it's long range," she said quietly.

Before he could reply, the main doors squealed as they were forced in and a group of soldiers in black armour with a white stripe down the sides rushed into the room. "Fleet Security! Break this up, right now!"

"Tell her I'll be a minute," Noah said, feeling the adrenaline drain away and the pain rush in.

THIRTY

Repercussions

THE CREW in medical spent so little time on Noah that it felt more like he walked through the department rather than got treatment. A spray of nanobots, anti-swelling and anti-scarring solution was pushed up his nostrils, he was scanned, then marched on to the brig. The itching, jarring feeling of the cartilage and tissues being mended while he walked to his cell were enough to make him wince. "Holy hell, what's going on up there?" he said to the amusement of the security officers as he resisted the urge to rub his nose.

When they sat him in his cell they left the door open. The discomfort was over, his nose was mended and he could feel the swelling around his eyes going down. "You forgot something," Noah said as the officers walked off.

"You're on the honour system," one of the guards replied over her shoulder. "Think of it as a waiting room that your stuck in until a superior officer comes and gets you."

"Yeah, get some sleep or something," her partner offered. "Safest part of the ship." He tossed Noah his command and control bracers and they moved on, leaving him in a quiet, half-lit cell.

There was another notification that Alice had tried to call. It was beside a black and silver notice that said; PRIVILEGES AND RANK SUSPENDED. STAY IN PLACE UNTIL FURTHER NOTICE. The sight of that notification gave him a sinking feeling.

"How can things get worse?" he asked himself as he clasped the command and control units onto his wrists. The newest versions were made so they had matching weights and more capability. He couldn't delay talking to Alice, for all he knew she could go silent for a week, unable to make long-range calls. He prepared himself, taking a deep breath before tapping Alice's call notification and trying to link up.

Alice opened the call a moment later, sitting up in bed. "Oh my God, are you okay? What happened?" she asked, shocked. She sat up with a jerk, almost forgetting to strategically adjust the sheets.

Noah realized that he forgot to clean himself up in his hurry to reply to her, and opened a little video window on his wrist display so he could see what she was seeing. It was a horror, his eyes were still pink blue as the anti-swelling meds were still at work, and he was covered in crimson from his nose down. "I'm fine, I got into a fight, I didn't start it. Well, not really. I'll call you right back."

"Sure, but, what?" Alice said before he cut the connection.

Some quick work at the sink got the blood off, his eyes still looked puffy, but he could see a little improvement from moment to moment. If it weren't for the medications they shot up his nose, he was sure both his eyes would swell until they were almost shut. The memory of that sucker punch, how it crushed his nose, seemed to hit him in both eyes at the same time, made him shudder as it refreshed his frustration and anger at the stupidity of the whole thing.

He sluiced the water from his face and neck as best as he could, was about to sit down when Pixie came bounding into the cell. "You're not going to believe this, but Damon's still in medical."

"I didn't see him there."

"He's in a private room, you ruptured something really important," she giggled.

"Yeah," was all Noah said for a moment. Blaming her for being a part of what got the fight going was a waste of time. He wished his cell door was closed, he could use a little more distance from her. As she sat down in his single chair, he shook his head. "Listen, I'm not proud of anything I did. Yeah, he threw the first punch, and the crowd was down for it, but I reacted like a punk, not an officer. If I have a chance to finish this program and learn something useful after this, I'm going to put everything into it. No more distractions, no more trouble."

"Why are you telling me? I didn't have anything to do with Damon taking a cheap shot."

Squeezing his eyes shut hurt a little, but it was better than letting his frustration get the better out of him. "Out," he said, pointing to the door. "See ya later, Pixie."

"Just don't blame me for a fight you finished," she said as she started her retreat. "Oh, and don't forget; you were the one who suggested disabling the safeties on your suits."

Commander Mars stopped her. "An officer will show you to the next cell," he told her. "We're going to be talking to you about an assault charge."

The look of shock on her face as two security officers guided her away was an amusing relief, but it only lasted a moment as Commander Mars and Commodore McPatrick entered his cell and activated an isolation field. Noah snapped to attention and saluted.

Commander Mars returned the salute and gestured to the bed. "Have a seat."

Noah did so, keeping his back straight as he watched Commodore McPatrick turn the chair around and sit on it backwards.

Commander Mars brought something up on his command and control unit, Noah couldn't see it, and scrolled through the contents silently for a moment before regarding him. "So, we have a fight that you started agreeing to and then stepped back from. That technically makes you an inciter. You'll get a little credit for listening to your friends, who suggested that you go virtual, and we'll acknowledge that you didn't throw the first punch, but you have to realize that you initially escalated, suggesting open violence, when you should have tried to diffuse the situation or extract yourself from it. We like fighters in this fleet, but we also appreciate real loyalty. We're all brothers and sisters in this fleet, and we may not always get along, but we don't break noses or rupture organs. You should have turned your suit back on the moment you were in distress. Specifically, when he punched you the first time. You would have been protected and could have activated your emergency medical implant to correct your injury."

"What do you have to say about the incident?" Commodore McPatrick asked.

"I let instinct take over," Noah said before he gave himself time to think. He took a breath, looked at the pair of officers. They made the cell seem small, especially the Commodore. More certain about his response, he continued. "You're right. I should have activated my suit and gotten out of there. Instead I lost it and did everything I could to win. I was blinded and I expected a beating. I apologize for any disgrace I brought to the Third Watch Squad, the Officer Training Program or this ship."

"What about yourself? You know you're going to get a reputation for this," Commander Mars said.

"I'm here to serve the Fleet and to represent my squad well. My own reputation doesn't matter as much," Noah replied.

"Get to it, Commander," Commodore McPatrick said quietly.

Commander Mars nodded, tapped the screen on his command and control unit and cleared his throat. "Trainee Lieutenant Noah Lucas; you are dismissed from the Pilot Apex Training Program and a full report of this incident will remain on your record. You will not receive luxury pay for a month. You will not be eligible for promotion for seven months regardless of any accomplishment whether academic or in the field. You have four hours to clear out your bunk. You can stay on the ship, but I won't have you in my racks. On a personal note; I'm disappointed to see you go this way, but I hope you stay on track from here. No one will stop you from pursuing the same qualification courses and testing that you would receive in the Pilot Apex Program."

Even though he felt absolutely torn down, even lost, Noah stood and saluted. "Thank you, Commander," he said stiffly.

"Good luck," Commander Mars said, returning the gesture, turning, then walking through the shimmering privacy barrier. He was on his way to the next cell, where Pixie most likely awaited whatever punishment she was about to receive for kicking Rayman before Noah's fight. Maybe there was something else, too, but Noah was much more interested in why Commodore McPatrrick was still sitting in his cell.

The Commodore touched the privacy barrier with the back of his hand for a moment, watching it shimmer, then pressed a control on his com-con unit. Noah's command and control systems flashed red for a moment. The Commodore had disabled all recording devices in the room. "Wondering what the other guy got?" McPatrick asked.

"Now I am," Noah replied.

"He's out. We're sending him back to the Excalibur where he'll fly as an Able Crewman. He'll serve what's left of his three years as a co-pilot on shuttles at best. Pixie is staying, but she'll have a mark on her record for a year, and the chances of her getting a promotion in the next couple years will be slim at best. She'll be an Ensign if she doesn't screw up again though. She's getting a break because she's the last member of the Excalibur crew in any enhancement program. Crewmembers from that ship are flunking out of every opportunity we give them. You don't have to worry about that, though. I envy you."

"You envy me?" The comment was more heavily laden with scepticism than Noah intended, so much so that it made the Commodore smile.

"All right, maybe envy's the wrong word there, but you'll see my point in a minute. We're sending you on a solo mission." He looked over his shoulder as if he was concerned about being overheard. That was impossible unless someone was running a hard scan on the room, thanks to the isolation field and other precautions. "You probably feel lower than low right now, and you should. Between you and me, I would have fought back if someone sucker punched me too, especially if they insulted the fleet and made it personal. It wasn't how the book says you should respond though, so we have to punish everyone involved. Your career is stuck in place right now, but after reviewing your file and talking to someone in Intelligence, we've decided to put the skills you've already proven to use. Alice made a real effort to bring an existing resistance group in as an ally. It didn't turn out the way anyone wanted, but that doesn't mean it's not worth trying again. We need someone with the right instincts, someone who can mix in with the rougher elements of the galaxy and connect with other resistance groups we've seen operating on the edge of Order of Eden space. Alice's report on the time you spent on Iora, and your record leading up to this point with the Fleet show us that you have the skills and are trustworthy. You're going under cover. There's a Clever Class Corvette in bay three. You'll steal it and everything inside tomorrow at oh-five-hundred." He handed Noah a tiny command chip. It glittered gold and platinum on its chain.

Excitement and trepidation filled him. *What am I getting into now?* He thought. "Would this be happening if I had a totally normal night in the Pilot's Den?" he asked.

"Not right now, probably near the end of the program in a couple weeks, but this gave us an opportunity to get things rolling sooner. Talk to a few crewmates about how angry you are that your commander put a mark on your record, suspended your luxury pay, made sure you won't be eligible for a promotion for a while. Maybe Hal, while other people are listening. Get a few hours' sleep in guest berthing, then make your way down to Bay Three."

"So, you wanted me for this assignment for a while."

"Your name kept coming up as we were narrowing it down. All the pilots from the Excalibur crew ruling themselves out was a surprise. The idea behind this mission is new, anyway. It's something that's just come together and we're following through because we know we have a couple people who fit. If it weren't for you and a couple other candidates who aren't as ready, we wouldn't do it. Back to the mission details." Commodore McPatrick pointed at the chip he handed Noah. "Put that necklace on and hide it under your uniform. It has special programming that will become available once you touch it to the main console. You'll have very limited communication with certain members of the fleet. Once your assignment is over, you'll be brought back into the fold and everyone will be told that you stealing that ship was just a part of building your legend. You will be the first person to steal a quad drive, ships and equipment from Haven Fleet. For now, the most important thing for you to do is convincingly behave like you're breaking ties with the fleet as if you're never coming back."

THIRTY-ONE

Farewells

HOPPER'S FIGHTER wheeled and turned as Traveller got a missile lock on his Uriel. News that there was another class of fighter coming, and that it would be rolled out fleet-wide once enough pilots were familiar with the new generation of small ship systems was spreading. Every time an upgrade or new model was announced, the simulations got crowded. It was the way Hal liked to play. Lots of live pilots meant a challenge, and a nice high kill score on a good night.

"God dammit, Traveller! This is the fifth time you..." Hopper started whining.

"Sorry buddy, a kill's a kill. Oh, and this time I'm flying backwards," Traveller laughed as he pulled the trigger, sending three micro-missiles the length of his hand into the blackness of virtual space, watching as they turned and took off towards Hopper, who would either have to turn around and attempt to shoot the missiles out of the sky or take his chances with automated countermeasures. If it was up to Hal, he would take the countermeasures, they were better at stopping small tracker missiles.

"Screw you, Traveller!" Hopper said as he ejected.

"Or, you could do that," Traveller chuckled. His opponent's fighter exploded into thousands of simulated pieces as he turned his ship towards the nearest large asteroid. It was surrounded by a whirling mass of players in different small ships. It was like looking at a hornet's nest after someone gave it a good kick. An urgent message came up and he accepted it without looking at who it was.

Carnie's avatar, which was taken before Noah Lucas had his blonde hair cut off, appeared in the co-pilot seat. "Hey, man. Getting some late-night sim time in?"

"Uh, yeah," Hal replied, unsure of what to say next. He was startled, a little angry and guilty in equal measure from earlier that night.

"I'm sorry about calling you a coward," Noah said, retracting his helmet.

"It's okay, I wish I saw that sucker punch coming."

"Nah, it's not. I know this is a longer conversation, but I don't have that kind of time. That whole fight took seconds. It happened so fast that it would have taken a bot to break it up before there was blood on the deck, so you didn't deserve any grief from me. I know you have my back, and when I get back, I'll watch yours if I can."

"Thanks, Noah," Hal said, a weight lifted off his conscience. "It really did happen too fast. Wait, where are you going? I heard you got kicked out of Apex, so you're going back to the Merciless when it gets back, right?"

"I'm not going back, Hal," Noah said. "That's all I can tell you.

Watch your six and happy hunting." His avatar froze for a second then faded away.

"Wait! Where are you..." Hal called after it then gave up with a sigh. "Don't do anything that'll make things worse, you too-tall troublemaker." He knew Noah couldn't hear him and was already starting to worry.

Alarms went off in his cockpit and he launched countermeasures against a half dozen missiles coming his way. He was sure he'd have a chance to call Noah up later so he could ask for details.

THERE WERE ONLY two things Alice set her computer to wake her for: a combat alert or a call from Noah Lucas. It was strange, she's spent so much time in her self-imposed dream state that it didn't make sense that she would wake up tired, but part of the recovery regimen was to spend as much time in normal sleep. Giving her mind time to organize and file all her experiences and emotions was essential to getting control of her empathic abilities again, and the only help she had was a mild herbal tea that Quan gave her so she could slip into REM sleep quickly. There was no rushing it, and she was no longer the director of her dreams.

The buzz and wibble-wobble noise her command and control unit made on the bedside table sounded very far away at first. Her eyes opened a crack and she saw the wristbands lighting up, flashing a hologram of Noah's face. It hadn't been an hour since he called her looking like he'd been in a terrible accident. Getting back to sleep after was easy, but only because of the tea Quan had her drinking before bed. The quarters she had aboard the Merciless were nice; a bedroom, a main room and bathroom. They still felt strange though, too quiet, and she thought she was still aboard the Clever Dream for a moment.

Snatching one of her command and control bracers from the dresser, she shook some of the cobwebs off, straightened her crop top and answered it. He was cleaned up, calling from his bunk with the curtain closed. "What happened to you?" Alice asked. "You looked like you lost a fight with a dock loader."

"You'll hear about it soon, the recording's making its way through the scuttlebutt underground. Long story short: I got sucker punched and instead of turning all the safeties on my suit and implant back on, I went on to win the fight the dirty way."

"Now I want to see this video," Alice replied with a little smile then self-corrected. "I mean, bad boy, that's not regulation, young man." It was a light-hearted scolding.

"Yeah, I know. How are you? What's been going on?"

"I screwed up some negotiations then lost my head for a while," Alice replied, trying to say as much as she could without breaking the limits of his clearance. "I got in front of a whole crowd of people with the doors to my empathy wide open and I passed out. I guess when I started waking up after, I decided to stay asleep, use my dreams like a personal simulation space where I could be whatever I wanted, do whatever I wanted. It took a lot of effort to snap me out of it." She wanted to tell him; 'They had to send the whole Merciless and a couple major support ships out here to clean my mess up. Then Quan had to build a bridge between my father's and my mind so he could show me it was all right to rejoin the living.' Telling him that would reveal ship movements and the locations of major members of Haven Fleet, though, and it was above his clearance level, so she added; "I've made a mess of things here."

"I know how you feel, at least a little," Noah said. "I'm out of the

Pilot Apex Program. They aren't in a hurry to reassign me to a fighter wing yet, either. I might be an active pilot with Samurai Wing again, but I don't know when."

"For a fist-fight? Were you in a control room or something?"

"The Pilot's Den," Noah said. "They're treating it like a serious incident, though. I don't blame them, we were all training to be leaders and I acted like an idiot. I could have sealed my suit up and walked out, but I was more concerned with how the crowd was feeling until the last minute, when I was ready to change my mind."

"I've lost my cool more than once," Alice said. "Maybe I could talk to Minh for you?"

"No, I think I need to look at how well I fit in the fleet. My instincts might be all wrong for an officer, and that's what this fleet seems to want me to be."

"Wait, what does that mean?" Alice asked, startled.

"I'm taking off for a while. You're the only person I want to stick around for, and I wish that was enough, but I don't think we'll get to see each other for weeks, months, so where does that leave us?"

Alarm and anger made Alice's vision blur as they collided in her head and chest. "We have interstellar comms now. We can meet in simulations."

"Your part of a special unit, so we'll have long blackouts too," Carnie replied.

"If you want to break this off, just do it," Alice said angrily.

"I'm just saying I don't know what'll happen to us, but I have to go," Noah told her. "I'm really sorry, Alice. I wish it was enough to..."

"You don't even know if I'm enough to stick around for, we've barely started to get to know each other. I know I'm complicated, I'm downright weird, but I'm not finished learning about you, Noah," she didn't know when the tears started, but they were there.

"Please, give the fleet another chance, even for me. I don't care why."

Noah wiped his eyes and looked away. "This is just getting harder," he said as he pressed his finger and thumb into the corners of his eyes before looking back at her. "I'm sorry, Alice. I'm completely crazy about you, but I've gotta go. I hope there's a someday and another place for us, but I've just gotta go."

"Don't. You know I can do something about where you end up. I don't use my leverage often, but I'd use it all for you."

"I'll always know I didn't get wherever you put me on my own, so would everyone else. I just don't fit here, so I hope we find a way to go on, but I'm not made for the military. Stay safe and watch for my messages on the Stellarnet." He closed the call so abruptly that he nearly cut off the last word.

"But..." Alice said, staring at the empty space where the hologram of his head and shoulders were. *Is that who he is? Things get hard and he runs? Were we only falling in love in my head?*

The tears kept coming, the hurt she felt burned in her belly and made her breathe in gasps. Alice chucked her bracer across the room and let herself fall back onto the mattress where she curled around a pillow and let his words hurt as they echoed through her mind.

Theodore came in a few minutes later, his voice quiet but alarmed. "Everyone within thirty metres is in tears, Quan sent me to check on you. He will shield them, but it is difficult. What is wrong, Alice?" he sat on the bed and stroked her shoulder.

"Noah's leaving the fleet," Alice said, mentally starting a countdown from ten in her head. It was one of the simple exercises Quan taught her to help her with control. "He's leaving us."

"That explains a message he sent me," Theo said sadly. "Well, it is healthy to fully engage in whatever you're feeling, so I'll send Quan a notification that he'll have to shield the crew from further grieving."

"I can get it together," Alice said, sitting up.

"You'll only prolong your suffering," Theo said, his eyes filled with sympathy. "It took me one point four seconds to process Noah's message. That's a long time for an android of my class, over a hundred times the norm. He said he'd try to keep in touch, that he'd try to see me in the future."

"He tried to end things with me," Alice said. "No one's ever broken up with me before." A fresh tear rolled down her cheek.

"I can stay with you, if you like," Theo said.

"That's okay," Alice replied. "I think I'll try to sleep. I'm supposed to start on light duty tomorrow."

"I'm sorry," Theodore said. "I know you'll miss him."

A fresh pang struck her as she nodded. "I'll build the wall in my head up so Quan doesn't have to protect the galley and fabrication crews for the whole shift." Alice knew how to contain herself, but sending her emotions out was a new development, she wasn't well practiced at it yet.

"He's willing to shield them as long as he must, as long as you need," Theodore said. "I believe he's willing to sacrifice a great deal for your progress and happiness to make up for his earlier transgression. Perhaps because of who you are."

"Daughter to the Queen-Admiral," Alice nodded.

"Oh, no," Theodore said, sitting down on the bed. "You're so much more than that. A woman with so much perseverance, the right intentions, intelligence, and a kind of charm that's only beginning to surface. So many people love you, Alice, and only for who you are, not who you are attached to."

Alice sat up and hugged Theodore, a gesture that he returned expertly, and she found herself crying again.

"Oh no, that didn't help, did it?" Theo asked.

"It did," Alice wept. "Hope you don't have anything important to do for a while," she added as she squeezed him.

THIRTY-TWO

The Escape

THE MENTAL IMAGE of Alice weeping was Noah Lucas' only company while he made his way to Hangar Three. *How could I do that to her? I should have stopped talking the moment Alice finished telling me that she'd just been through something major, something that had her rattled. She must have been shaken really bad too, because she broke right down and we've only seen each other a few times. It doesn't feel that way, though. I felt like I was carving my own heart out.*

He stopped in front of the lift. Trying to ignore how he felt about breaking things off with Alice was almost as hard as forgetting the impact he had on her. It felt like losing a member of his tiny family, and he could only blame himself. Commodore McPatrick ordered him to break ties but he didn't have to call Alice and lie. He couldn't tell her what he was up to, but he could have left her hanging for a little while so he could figure out some way to tell her that he didn't really quit the fleet.

A tug on his shoulder turned him around. "Where are you going?" Pixie asked, looking at his duffel then back up into his eyes. "What happened?"

"Alice and I are over," Noah said. The sound of the notion out loud made him want to find a corner and break down. "Thought I'd go for a ride."

"Then I'm going with you. People shouldn't be alone after breakups," Pixie said, turning towards the lift doors. They opened and she stepped inside.

"Hell no." A thought occurred to him then. "How did you even know I was out of my rack at almost oh-four-hundred? I'm not even in the same berthing as you anymore."

"Um, I was having trouble sleeping and I was curious?"

"Get out of there, I've gotta go," Carnie said.

Pixie crossed her arms and shook her head.

With a sigh, he stepped into the lift and punched the button that would take him down to the secondary hangar doors. "You're not coming with me because I'm not coming back."

"What are you going to run in? Did you get your fighter moved down here somehow? You could be stuck in your cockpit for days, weeks. That's gonna suck."

"Don't worry, I know what I'm doing. If you try to follow me, I'll drop a web round on you," Carnie warned.

"Nah," she said.

The doors opened and a Clever Class Corvette with no name came into view. A crewman and two robots were casually leaving the far end of the hangar, the lights dimmed behind them. "There's my ride," Noah said.

"No way, a factory fresh Clever Class?" Pixie asked in awe. "I heard there were three delivered, but there was a notice that only deck crew were allowed near them."

"You're hacked into the system deeper than you should be," Noah accused in a whisper as he looked around.

"Yeah, I know a guy on the Excalibur who had a few loose high clearance access codes made," Pixie admitted.

It was the first Noah had heard of lax security in the fleet. It was alarming. "What else did you learn using that code?"

"Fine, honesty time: I saw your breakup call with Alice. What the hell are you thinking? Most guys are selfish idiots, I thought you were different, but I guess I was wrong."

"Is that a question or are you so used to butting in where you're not welcome that you have to make sure I hear your opinion?" Noah said, raising his voice just enough to hear it echo across the massive hangar then lowering to a whisper.

"I do not butt in!"

"You're like an annoying little sister: you need to know everything but you're not quite ready to have your own drama yet."

"You're just a..." Pixie was visibly annoyed, but more than anything she looked hurt.

It looked like he struck a nerve, one he didn't know was there, but her silence spoke louder than any screeching retort. "I'm sorry. I just need to do this on my own. I don't have a future in the fleet anymore, but you can work hard and come out of the program as an officer, make something of yourself here."

"Don't go, I'm sure you can get through this too," Pixie said, looking determined again.

"Some people aren't meant to be a part of a crew," Noah said stiffly as he left the lift and tapped the SECURE CLOSE button on the other side. It was a manual control for the deck crew, so they could make sure the lift was closed when they had to depressurize the hangar.

He activated his helmet and strode to the narrow forward ramp. A high-priority personal message notification popped up in his HUD and he blinked it away immediately. It was probably Pixie. He activated the crew ramp and the narrow stair lowered. The security systems weren't set up yet, it really was a factory fresh ship.

While he waited for the ramp to close behind him, he checked the message notification and saw that it wasn't from Pixie, but Alice. CAN'T LEAVE THINGS LIKE THAT. NEED TO TALK BEFORE BATTLEGROUP GOES SILENT IN AN HOUR.

Frozen to the spot, he considered its meaning. In one hour the ship Alice was on and the battlegroup around it would switch to silent running, and they wouldn't be able to use the long range communications systems for hours, maybe days or weeks. More importantly, Alice either didn't accept his goodbye, which wasn't really a breakup as much as it was an attempted one, or she needed to know more. Either way, it was another chance for him to just say 'I'm sorry' and try to mend things. Try to continue things. *None of that matters! I'm supposed to break ties. If I call her right before I steal this ship and run off, I'll be breaking my cover before it's even established.* He thought to himself as he retracted his helmet and started for the cockpit. *But my stomach won't stop churning and my head feels like an overinflated Pongo Ball.*

He realized he was headed the wrong way when he came face to face with gun and equipment cases. The rear compartment was full of them. At a glance, he could see there was enough equipment there to arm and armour at least thirty people. He took the ladder down and saw that there was a manufacturing bay installed. A tap on the pad revealed that only he had full access. Some of the security was set up after all. "I bet the stuff up there is bleeding edge, and this thing is ready to start churning out..." he looked through the list and saw that it was primarily set to produce high quality knock-offs of the most popular combat equipment in the galaxy.

Dropping his duffel, he rushed up the ladder, then to the cockpit where he tapped the tiny command chip to the ship's main console. A hologram of Commodore McPatrick appeared. "Noah, we need you to go deep under cover. You'll be using your own name, your own history. Your mission begins when you leave Hangar Three then escape the main fleet using the quad drive. Your first stop is programmed into the computer already. When you arrive at your destination you will begin the main part of your mission. Using the fabrication technology on this ship you will become an arms dealer, supplying resistance groups and mercenaries that fight against the Order of Eden. You will become their most reliable source of small arms, equipment and armour. The fabrication systems we've installed don't have the patterns for proprietary Haven technology, but they can make tens of thousands of other objects that you may find useful, and your customers will be eager to get their hands on. I don't need to tell you how important it is that you don't let the ship we're giving you fall into enemy hands. Eventually you'll need a crew, and that's what the crew quarters and advanced equipment are intended for. You are not to sell the Haven Fleet military equipment we've loaded onto your ship, use it to protect recruits you trust. When you find a resistance group you think is ready to meet someone from Haven Fleet, contact me using the secure protocol in this message. We'll make sure someone from the fleet encounters them and offers them a place in our organization. You will go on growing your customer base. We will make sure whoever we contact doesn't suspect that you were a part of it. This mission will serve Haven Fleet in two ways. By arming resistance groups, we assist them in their fight against our common ene..." Noah stopped the playback and checked the time. He had nine minutes left to steal the ship before it was oh-five-hundred.

"What the hell? It sounds like this mission will go on for months," he checked the summary on the main display panel and saw the mission duration. "Five to seven years?" he read aloud in shock, backing away from the controls, shaking his head. "I'll be on my own for..." he leaned on his knees trying to catch his breath as he imagined being away from Theodore, Minh-Chu, everyone in Samurai Squadron, and most of all, Alice for five years.

Iora came to mind, the long stretch of time he spent before meeting Theodore, at least it seemed like a long time. He was so lonely that he was willing to risk having a potentially dangerous robot as a companion. Sure, he knew the technical details; that it was unlikely that Theodore could be infected by the Holocaust Virus, but he was infected by the end of his time there. Even after Theodore was reduced to a hunk of junk, he still kept him in the passenger seat. Beyond the details of his solitude on that planet, he recalled the feeling. Creeping loneliness and the inability to trust anyone because there was always a catch, even with the nicest of people. How would the mission he was about to embark on be any different? "No Theo," he answered, looking to the frozen hologram of Commodore McPatrick hovering over the ship's main console.

Straightening up, he paced the short distance between the seats in the small bridge. "I finally felt like I had a family again." His hands ran down his face. "Like I was really a part of something.

Then there's Alice, and I've never had that before. It was new, but, it was..." he trailed off, pacing a few more times. "What do I do?"

He punched the back of the pilot's seat several times. "Dammit! Dammit! Dammit!" That felt good, but it didn't clear his head. There was a short list of people he felt he could go to for advice. Minh-Chu, Theodore and Alice. All three of them would probably have completely different responses if Noah asked them about his situation. "I know who I want to call," he muttered to himself. "But I may have screwed that up."

The hologram of Commodore McPatrick stared at him, and he stared back, his mind blank for a moment as if the gears were momentarily seized. The clock on the console said it was one minute away from oh-five-hundred. He watched it change to oh-five-hundred and an instant later he did something that he knew really would get him in trouble. "Communications," he said to the ship. "Make a secure call to Alice Valent, compress the mission orders I'm playing back right now and send them to her, attach the following statement; 'I just got this mission. I tried to break us up because I was told to cut ties with everyone. I don't want to go. I don't want to leave you behind. Not sure what to do here, but I know that. I'm so sorry about everything I said. Let's make this decision together.' End message, send immediately."

"Sending the message and compressed data as specified," the computer replied in a mundane voice. Several seconds later the communications station stated that the message had been received and opened.

"Let's make this decision together," he muttered to himself. "Cheesy, very cheesy." Seconds, then minutes passed.

At long last, his com-con blinked, indicating that he had a call incoming from Alice and he accepted. "I'm so sorry," he said before she could say anything.

"That's what this was all about?" Alice asked, pulling the shoulder of her uniform vacsuit up and on. "You didn't want to end things?"

"No, hell no," Noah said. "I was ordered to." That was a partial lie that could come back to bite him, and he rushed to correct it. "I was ordered to break ties as though I was leaving the fleet forever."

"Well, good job, flyboy." It looked like she'd been crying. "I can't believe Oz is sending you out solo. I mean, you're the guy for it, but you're also absolutely not the guy for it. Just because you ran solo for a long time before doesn't mean you're ready to do it again."

"He said you inspired the mission, something about you trying to recruit a resistance group?"

"Seriously? That was a disaster. I thought I could walk in there, read everyone, then use that to get people moving in Haven Fleet's direction, but the whole recruitment thing fell apart," Alice explained. It looked like she was putting her sidearm on, but he couldn't be sure since he could only see her from the shoulders up.

"Are you strapping up?" he asked.

"Yeah, the whole ship is on alert. Everyone cleared to carry a weapon has to have one on them unless they're resting in their quarters. Where are you now?"

"Aboard the corvette they loaded up for me. Listen, I saw all this, got the details of my mission and all I could think about was how I didn't want to leave you behind. Then I learned it would be for five years, maybe seven, and I felt like I was about to run out of road and the brakes weren't working. I couldn't leave things the way I did."

Alice looked at him, wiped her eye and started to smile. He could see relief in her tired smile. "Don't ever do that to me again."

"We're back on?" Noah asked.

"We were never off. There was no way I'd let you get away before I was finished with you, I'd hunt you down first," she said with a wink. It was a front; her speech seemed choked.

"That's a little scary, but coming from you, it's cool."

Alice cleared her throat and nodded. "Speaking of hunting, I'm going to go wake my dad up and see what we can do about modifying your mission. It's time to yank on some strings."

"Whoa! I just wanted some advice. This doesn't look like the kind of mission I can turn down, what do I do?" Noah asked, instantly more nervous than he could ever remember being. "I don't want to make a giant fleet-wide issue out of it."

"Well, the only thing you can do that'll keep you from getting into even more trouble is follow through. It's a good mission. If you don't follow through, leaking your mission details to me won't be the only violation they can charge you with. You'll be facing insubordination charges."

"So, you think I should fake-steal this ship and get outta here?" Noah asked, surprised.

"Yeah, just send me a message when you get where you're going and hang tight."

"While you do.... What?" Noah asked, sitting in the pilot's seat.

"Tell my father I'm joining you with the Clever Dream. We've been ordered to rest for now and I have no assignment on the board after that, so he's going to order me to join you in the field."

"Uh, will that..." he struggled to find the right term for a moment before settling on; "Will that work?"

"It's either he orders me to join you in the field and help you with your mission, or Theo and I go after you anyway. One keeps my crew together, the other option leaves whoever isn't willing to go on the deck behind me. It's not ideal, but I get the feeling that half the admiralty expect me to break off on my own any time, so why disappoint?"

"You know I'm crazy about you, right?" Noah said, his heart feeling full and warm as he brought the ship's main systems online. It purred around him as the fusion chain woke up from standby mode.

"You know you drive me crazy, right?" Alice said with a crooked smile. "I'll talk to you soon, Flyboy." The call ended.

"Don't get yourself into more trouble than you can handle," he muttered under his breath as he watched the hangar doors open. It was surprising, the automated departure systems were all set. A ladder that wasn't secured to the deck rushed out before the new atmospheric energy barrier went up. "Oops, should have checked that before the doors opened."

Most of his worries were dulled as he ran through his checklist, looking all the main instrument panels over. He was surprised to see two Uriel fighters latched to the underside of the ship and decided to take a good look at them after he was far away. "Clever Class Corvette Zero Six Three, this is Triton Flight. Power down and secure that ship to the deck immediately." Came the stern female voice over the ship's emergency communications channel.

Noah looked to the Navnet screen, making sure there was nothing in his way, then checked the quad drive system to ensure that his course was already laid in and verified. Everything checked out, so he throttled up. The bridge around him darkened as he left the Triton behind. There were three fighters on their way, moving to cut him off. The navigational system beeped at him, a bright chirp that told him that the quad drive was ready, his course was verified and safe. "I really hope you can pull the right strings so I don't have to do this without you, Alice," he said under his breath as he activated the quad drive.

Space split in front of him, not a tear like the previous generation of drives, but a neat, rippling hole with light pouring through it, and his ship slipped inside. Noah sat back with a sigh, then looked to the hologram of Commodore McPatrick. "I forgot your old friends called you 'Oz,'" he said. "What else do you have to say about this mission?"

"...enemy and we'll be able to review your reports on rebel groups, making sure we only recruit the best of them," the Commodore continued. "Most of the fine details of this mission are in the text section of this record, but I'd like to make a few of the limits and benefits clear before I end this introduction. You can grow your criminal enterprise to any practical size you like. Any actions you take while you're on mission will not be prosecutable by Haven Fleet or the Haven Government. You are immune as long as you can prove your actions served the mission. You are not to directly combat the Order of Eden unless you have no choice. You are not to sell weapons of mass destruction, but you may sell any size of ship you like. Do not pirate non-Order of Eden ships, but all of their allies are fair game. That should provide plenty of opportunity for captures if you get a crew together who can pirate vessels. All proceeds from your work belong to you, and you may sell any leftover equipment that you didn't manufacture using your ship to Haven Fleet for luxury credits. If your ship is captured, the data drives will re-crystalize until they're useless, the quad drives will melt, and the rest of the proprietary systems will self-destruct. This is an incredible opportunity for you to become one of the most important people to our efforts to grow our numbers and win this war against the Order. Make sure you read the text attached to this mission brief. Remember, your mission could be rendered ineffective if people in Haven Fleet discover it's a ruse. The chance of your true purpose being leaked increases as more people find out, so keep this secret. We will control the flow of information coming to the fleet, and you should only contact us at pre-arranged times. Good luck." The hologram faded.

"Oh, he is gonna be pissed when he finds out I brought Alice in on it," Noah chucked, just as worried as he was amused.

THIRTY-THREE

The Hunter

THE MAP of the Kedan Solar System surrounded Admiral Scanlon and Captain Holm. The white sun burned at their feet while the planets and fields of asteroids drifted around them in a high-speed time lapse. "Three large ships are running the operation near Nuaji," the Admiral said, pointing at the now grey-brown world. "Since they began running their rescue operations, smaller ships have moved in to the vessels that we didn't allow to jump to Dulo. They disappeared one by one. We assume the smaller Haven Fleet vessels are extending a cloaking field around them. A few signals escaped their cloak as they performed a hand-off with another, larger ship. From the glimpses we've caught, which were hard-won, requiring hundreds of scanning hours, we suspect that they are loading the ships escaping Nuaji into a massive carrier. It's definitely a vessel we haven't seen Haven Fleet use before."

Captain Holm paused a moment before commenting. Like any good subordinate, he took every word in, making sure he understood everything before asking a question he thought would be obvious. At times it was difficult to concentrate. As an Admiral she was knowledgeable, showed wisdom in her decisions and in the viewing requirements she sent out to everyone under her command. She had a quick mind, and he admired how she brought her staff together to work on one problem after another.

As a woman he found her fascinating. Her beauty seemed effortless, and if it weren't for his own discipline she could become a fixation, a breathtaking infatuation. That wasn't something he'd allow, in fact, he made every effort to make sure she didn't see him notice that she was letting her blonde hair grow back into brunette. That her brown eyes seemed livelier ever since work on the Lance began, ever since he returned from leading the Justicars on their most recent mission. Ever since Tafford was murdered she was closer to the Overlord, closer to Dron, closer to power. He asked his question before he was caught staring. "Why not launch the sensor satellites? Back them up with a coordinated attack in Nuaji orbital space?"

"We can't learn as much from an autopsy as we can a living specimen," Admiral Scanlon said quietly. The Rear Admiral and several of her command crew were talking amongst themselves along the edges of the large hologram. The space between them and the middle of the holographic solar system gave her and the Captain the illusion of privacy. "A phrase one of my instructors in college used to use. If my guess is right, there's a commander orchestrating the rescue operations around Nuaji and they're wondering why we don't attack too. They're tempted by the target the Lance provides. I know I'd want to send an antimatter bomb, maybe a full-on attack at a heavy cruiser while its being refitted light years away from any Order of Eden space dock, while there are no extraordinary defences. That's why we're not aboard that ship, why most of the work is being done robotically. I want to see what that commander does. I don't care if they rescue every living soul on Nuaji and save every ship in orbit. I'd rather they did it so we could watch the work." She looked to her left. "Vice Admiral Jepsen, what do you think of their rescue operation?"

The Vice Admiral, a short fellow who Captain Holm was sure would be promoted the next time a spot for Admiral came up considering his consistently good work, took a few steps into the hologram. "Efficient, they move quickly and covertly. Considering how long it's taken for us to make an assessment, and how few mistakes they make with their cloaking systems, I expect most of the crews are well trained. Most, but not all. There have been errors. We know they are using state-of-the-art ships, technology that outstrips most of our own, and that they ordered the nanobots that were destroying life on the planet to burn out, making them useless to anyone who wants to duplicate them. They've saved over twelve thousand people from the surface since. Those operations happened so quickly that we would have had a very narrow window to attack them while they were taking passengers on board if we had an opportunity at all."

"So overall they have skilled crews and good leadership?" the Admiral asked.

"Overall. The vast majority of their people are highly skilled, yes. As far as leadership, I expect they're experienced. They kept their approach to rescuing the people left on and around Nuaji simple: they treated it like triage."

"Thank you, Rear Admiral." She turned back to Captain Holm

as the Rear Admiral retreated back to a workgroup along the edge of the large space. "We've learned a great deal. Only hours ago we discovered that there was an unauthorized user in our system. We're sure there are more, and we're tracking them down. The signal came from the orbital space around Nuaji. Letting them go about their business has been helpful."

"I applaud your tactics and patience," Captain Holm said.

She took him in, her eyes sweeping down then up. He forgot that he was wearing a fitted suit. It was dark green with the markings of his Order of Eden rank, but it was the same technology Haven Fleet used under their heavy combat armour. Her eyes locked with his for a moment before she quietly said; "Thank you. You don't need to compliment me, Captain." Admiral Scanlon turned back to the hologram, focusing on Nuaji. There were a few locations marked in red around it. Each represented a spot where they suspected there may be a ship. "We still don't know why they hold off from attacking the Lance. It's a prime target, they have a weapon that can get through our best counter-cloaking systems, but we haven't detected any sign of sabotage."

"Maybe they recognize an unofficial truce. Two big predators respecting each other, aware that any conflict would inflict serious injuries on both, regardless of who wins," Captain Holm offered.

"That's come up. It's the best theory, but it makes me wonder who we're dealing with. Valent doesn't seem patient enough. I can't see anyone from the Admiralty putting themselves at risk by coming so far behind our frontline."

"Maybe it's McPatrick? He's one of their most experienced commanders."

"Someone I've done some of the reading on," Admiral Scanlon said, nodding. "It only seems like we know enough about these people. There is so much data out there, but their military has come together so quickly, and it functions well enough. Even with all our records on Freeground and its history, we don't know enough to predict exactly what they'll do, where they'll go. The strikes on our bases and shipyards were sudden, a surprise. It doesn't seem like them, but maybe there's a new mind making plans over there, someone who doesn't care as much about preventing collateral damage. Planet Nuaji is a clear example, but that seems more like a blunder. We've only seen a garbled image of Alice Valent on the planet. Everything we know about her and her family tell us that they wouldn't condone the waste of a planet or so many civilian deaths."

"I'm afraid I wouldn't know," Captain Holm said.

"You haven't watched the files on them?" Admiral Scanlon asked.

Was that amusement? Was his lackadaisical attitude towards her recommended viewing list funny to her? "My people have been practicing in the encounter armour we bought from the British. I've had to design new challenges for them, it's taken up most of my time. I apologize."

"Don't worry about it. There's a reason why it's called a 'recommended viewing list,' but now you and your people will have to catch up. Learn everything there is about the Valents. The Clever Dream, their entanglements, positions in the fleet, and their pasts. I'll have someone put a file together."

"We're going to hunt them down?" The thrill of that challenge made the Captain square his shoulders, even puff his chest up a little.

Admiral Scanlon looked at him, the edges of her lips turning up just enough so he could see her smiling in the half light. "Not directly. Our intelligence tells us that the Clever Dream came here on its own before Nuaji was denuded. The uninvited user who was exploring our network visited the profile of Mary Reed more than once, and we know she was down there on the planet. Our experts expect she's helping resistance groups and suspect that she left Nuaji after a short time. We don't know why, but I have a theory that I'm so certain of that I'm willing to send you to test it. Bring your best, leave the rest of your people with me so they can continue training. You're going to follow our most promising leads to find Mary Reed. I need you to hunt her. Tell me when you find her. Watch her while she meets with resistance leaders. I don't want you to make a move until you see a Valent. Alice or Jacob, it doesn't matter which."

"What about the mother, Ayan?"

"I don't think she'll expose herself, not for this. We know that Remmy Sands was a friend to Mary Reed, they may send him to entice her into joining them, but don't spring your trap until you see a Valent or are sure Reed is about to disappear in to the ranks of Haven Fleet. I'll need detailed reports from you. I trust you to execute this on your own, but the Overlord is eager to capture a Valent. The Edxi are furious at the destruction of Nuaji. We've convinced them that the Valents are at the centre of their failure to take the Haven System and the Nuaji incident, so they'll be satis-fied if we present them with a living Valent and a new, populated solar system to colonize. I don't have to decide on which solar system we're sacrificing yet."

"But you do have to capture a Valent," he added, looking at the red marks on the map. A new one appeared, an old one disap-peared. Their information was three minutes old, who knew what they were really detecting. The signals could be sensor ghosts, decoys, or momentary gaps in the Haven ships' cloaking fields. "If you try to capture the ships around Nuaji, there's a chance they'll all slip away."

"Not only that, but the Merciless may be in orbit. That ship can stand toe-to-toe with one of our heavy cruisers and win. We know the Excalibur may be here as well. The cost of this hunt would be too high, especially if the third ship they have is some kind of super carrier."

"So we watch what they're looking for."

"No one knows I'm sending you on this mission. There may still be unwelcome guests in our system. Officially I'm sending you out on training exercises, a tour of nearby moons. You're joining me in a real conspiracy, Jaden."

Hearing her use his first name for the first time was exciting. It was even sweeter whispered in half-light. Then he remembered how far in debt he was, that she was much more powerful thanks to rank, wealth and political connections. He sunk from the height his heart rose to, stiffened his spine and replied; "I'll bring you a Valent, Admiral."

There was that amused smile again. He returned it this time along with a salute. The Admiral straightened up and returned the gesture, releasing him to begin preparations. An encrypted message appeared on the optical display inside his mechanical eye. It was bio-locked to him, from Admiral Scanlon and it contained the details of his secret mission. He was to depart in three hours.

THIRTY-FOUR

At Last

THERE WERE a lot of complaints running through Alice's head as she left her quarters. Quan met her in the hallway outside, it was still strange seeing him in the black on black uniform of the Merciless. He was a visitor, but ship security put him in the uniform of an able crewman after determining that wearing a suit that made him stand out from the rest of the crew would make him a target to boarders. It almost suited him.

"I sense that you're frustrated," Quan said.

"See, that's what I don't want to turn into," Alice said, turning nose to nose with him, well, it was more like her nose to his chin. "I don't want to walk around my ship telling my crew how they're feeling, playing amateur therapist to the lot of them while they don't feel like they have so much as a private moment. Ever since I woke up it feels like you've been listening to whatever's going on up here."

"I'm sorry, I'm here to help but I'm still figuring out how to do so tactfully."

Iruuk was in the hallway next. The uncertain look he fixed her with made her remember why Quan was so important. He wasn't just there to help her, he was there to protect everyone in case she had a flare up. That was the only reason why he got aboard the Merciless before it jumped far behind enemy lines. "I'm sorry, and yeah, I'm pissed. Is that splashing around? I thought I was containing my emo-spill."

"Emo-spill? Interesting term," Quan said, cracking a little smile. Then he went on more seriously; "No, you're perfectly contained, I sensed it because I was reading beside my door. I'm still highly attuned to you. The mind bridge I made between you and your father left me connected. I hope that's not unsettling, it will fade over time."

"No, I'm getting used to all this somehow." It was irksome, but Alice didn't think telling him would make anything better. It felt like she spent an afternoon with her father, the memory of her being a child at his side was as real as any. It was as if a puzzle piece was created and put into place where she had something missing. Quan was the one who made that possible, and she'd always be grateful.

"You keep forgetting that you can't be deceptive with me," Quan said. "But I sense that you were only trying to spare my feelings."

"See, you keep telling me you're not using telepathy on me, but that's a lot of detail for someone who is only reading emotions," Alice said.

"Emotions can be seen in greater detail than you're aware of just yet. In the vernacular of one of Iruuk's favourite food establish-ments; there are hundreds of flavours of ice cream and every one is waiting for you to try them. What I'm saying is; there are dozens of flavours of frustration, anger, joy and every other feeling you can have. There are spectrums within spectrums."

"Sure, that simplifies everything," Alice said, rolling her eyes. "It's too early for a lesson though, and I'm not broadcasting to the rest of the crew, so you can go back to sleep, or get back to your reading."

"You feel better now that you're calmer, though?" Quan asked.

"Well, yeah, and no," Alice replied, shaking her head before going on. "Listen, I wanted to be pissed, sometimes it helps."

Theodore emerged from her quarters. "Hello, I couldn't help but overhear as my charging cycle completed. It's true, sometimes humans want to be angry. Engaging in aggressive behaviour can help some people process."

"I've read that, it's an interesting phenomenon. Most of my people try to avoid the more violent emotions, they can create a kind of discordance..."

"Holy crap, get out of my head!" Alice exclaimed, throwing her hands up. She was several steps down the hall before she remembered that Iruuk was awake and watching. As soon as she looked over her shoulder at him he rushed to catch up, squeezing past Theodore and Quan, who stared at her dumbly.

"So, you don't want me to go with you?" Theodore called after her.

"It's all right, go check on the Clever Dream. Muster the crew when they wake up," Alice said.

"It's a good thing Iruuk is going with her. He's good for her mental state," Alice heard Quan tell Theodore as she walked away.

"They make a good pair," Theodore agreed. "Have a good rest Quan, I have duties to perform."

"Talk about two people who make a good pair," Alice muttered as the lift arrived and she stepped in with Iruuk at her side.

"You heard that too?" Iruuk asked. "I hear all kinds of things humans don't think I can. It's like no one realizes how good Nafalli hearing is."

"Yeah, I hope my rocky night didn't keep you up," Alice said, a yawn almost interrupting her.

"I slept for nine hours straight, though I had some really screwed up dreams at one point. I don't remember what they were about, but they were really sad."

"Sorry, that was me. Got a late-night call from Noah. We broke up, then when he called again we got back together." With a few taps on her left command and control unit, Alice brought the medical interface up and started a Wake Nine treatment. It was a non-addictive sequence of nonnarcotic drugs that provided the same benefits of ten hours of sleep. It would run over the course of a few minutes, but past what the intended effects were supposed to be, she didn't know much about it. The treatment was new. The world spun for a moment and she leaned against the handrail. "Whoa, they should warn you about that. Pilots are supposed to use this, it could be a problem if you get the spins every time."

"Are you all right?" Iruuk asked.

Her head stopped spinning and Alice straightened in time for the transit pod doors to open. They were already on the bridge level. "Fine, just trying the new patrol drugs."

"Oh, I read the brief about that, the fake sleep stuff," Iruuk said with a nod. "What's it like?"

For a moment Alice felt like she was lifting off the floor, and her thoughts seemed very slow. "A little bumpy, kind of fuzzy," she found herself mumbling. "I'm cloudy like a slow frog sound."

"Oh boy," Iruuk said, holding her up and looking at her closely, too closely. "Your pupils are super dilated. Are you sure we should be on the command level?"

"You're really worried about me, that's sweet," she found herself saying to Iruuk as she patted the side of his face. "That's really soft," Alice breathed, then she came back to her senses. "Whoa, that was a hell of a trip. A short trip, but I feel like I just slept for a week."

"You're okay?" Iruuk asked, surprised.

"I'm fine," she checked the medical display on her command and control unit. TREATMENT COMPLETE, it read. "How long did I go loopy for?"

"About a minute, less actually," Iruuk said as he scanned her then nodded. "Your stress levels are down, and it really looks like you're well rested."

"Enough scanning and probing," Alice told him, gently pushing his arm down. "Let Theodore worry about that."

"Just wanted to make sure you were okay," Iruuk said with a shrug as they left the transit car. It was quiet in the corridors near the bridge, they were still over an hour away from the end of third watch.

"I know, but I'm getting pretty tired of people asking me how I'm feeling, scanning me. The only one who hasn't treated me differently since I took an extra-long nap is Noah."

"I'll stop scanning you, sorry. Oh yeah, and why did you guys have a rocky night? What brought that on?" Iruuk asked.

"Some high ranking dick told him to break all ties and pretend to desert from the fleet, so he followed instructions. That's why he tried to break up with me," she was still angry at him for it, but so much more so at whoever came up with the plan he was following. "We got back together when he 'fessed up to being forced into it by the fleet. That's when I told him to follow orders while I took care of the rest from my end."

"Wait, so he's deserted already?"

Alice nodded as her father's door came into sight. "Along with a clever class corvette and a load of gear. He's supposed to become an arms dealer to resistance groups so he can assess them. Another team is supposed to follow up on good recruit and alliance candidates."

"Us?"

"Definitely not. This isn't in the Special Operations Combat Unit files from what I can see. This is another Intelligence operation."

"Oh, so they..." Iruuk hesitated as they stopped in front of Commodore Jacob Valent's door. "Wait, you think *he* wanted to separate you and Noah?"

"I don't know, but aside from calling Ayan up, I don't know who else to go to with this. If my Dad's behind it, I'm gonna be pissed."

His nose low, almost lowered to his chest, Iruuk asked; "Are you sure I should go in there with you? I mean, he's probably sleeping, you might want to come back later."

"This is worth waking him up for." Alice held the call button down. "Besides, if I'm going to leave the fleet and join Noah, then you should hear the whole conversation that leads up to it. Someone will have to explain why I left."

"Wait, you don't think I'd go with you?" Iruuk asked.

"Of course not, you could make Captain in three years, probably less," Alice said. "I wouldn't ask you to throw that away."

"You wouldn't have to ask," Iruuk said, straightening up.

"It's not a good career move for you. All your hard work would be for nothing and the fleet is better with you in it." She let the call button go, then started tapping it, the intermittent buzzing was barely audible through the door.

"I thought you were finally happy in the fleet, maybe you're the one who should stick around," Iruuk countered. "Noah's trouble could be resolved some other way. There's nothing saying someone couldn't order him to abort his mission and return home. Besides, the Clever Dream needs a new pilot. Ute is going home as soon as we're out of Order space."

The thought of Noah becoming the pilot of the Clever Dream hadn't occurred to her.

"Would you stop leaning on that..." Jake grumbled, his thick vacsuit half way up. "Alice? Everything okay?"

"No," she said, brushing past him. "Noah stole a clever class corvette and left the fleet on Oz's orders."

"Sorry about the buzz-buzz," Iruuk whispered to Jake as he entered meekly, miming the pushing of a button.

"He what?" Jake asked, pulling the rest of his vacsuit on and sealing it. "Access records on Noah Lucas." He walked to the shelf with the beverage dispenser built in and punched the combination that would make a steaming cup of coffee. "Five point fifteen hours of sleep, I've had less," he grumbled as the records appeared in a hologram in front of him. "Okay, no official orders, he's marked as a deserter." He took the steaming hot cup from the shelf along with two peanut butter meal bars and made his way to the middle of the room. "Access all classified files marked level seven and up referencing Noah Lucas and open a call to Commodore Terry Ozark McPatrick."

It was no surprise that Alice's report on Noah was the only highly classified document to appear. "You won't find anything."

"You're probably right, but I've got to check," Jake said. "Close files. Open Intelligence Operations Logs for the last three days. List all orders given to Commodore McPatrick and Noah Lucas." The computer responded with a single red lettered word: RESTRICTED. "Well, looks like someone's made sure no one can access those records. I wish Minh was here, he'd already have a theory about what Fleet wants out of this."

"So, you really didn't know anything about this?" Alice asked.

"No, I was looking forward to seeing how Hal and Noah did in the Pilot's Officer Program. I was hoping that I'd be able to put both of them up for choices as the new pilot for the Clever Dream. Minh was even more excited about it."

"I don't know how well things would work out with Noah as my pilot," Alice said, even though she wanted to have him closer so they could spend more time together for real. The proximity could be a problem though, especially if she couldn't shut her empathic sense down.

"Nothing tests a relationship like being stuck on a ship together," Jake said. He sipped his coffee. "Most of them break though."

He was worried and confused. There was a little anger too, but it wasn't directed at anyone in the room. Alice wished she could turn her sense off as a hologram of Oz yawning appeared. "Jake? Aren't you supposed to go dark in a few minutes?"

"Don't worry, the Merciless is a few days out of sensor range from any Order ships. We can delay our return to Nuaji for a while," Jake said. "I have an irate Captain on my hands this morning. She says you ordered someone to steal a corvette and desert?"

"I was executing someone else's plan. I don't disagree with it, but I can't take full credit," Oz replied.

"Oh, we need a higher power on this," Jake said, bringing a list of contacts up and touching several listings.

"Wait! This is classified at the highest level," Oz said. "Our deserter wasn't supposed to tell anyone."

"Well, if he's a deserter and he got away with a bunch of our tech, we should let the whole admiralty in on it," Jake replied.

Beside Oz's holographic head Ayan and Admiral Doolth's appeared. The Nafalli admiral was still straightening the fur on her broad face and Ayan was burping Laura. "Oh, this is an official call," she said.

"I'm sure Laura won't leak any classified information," Admiral Doolth said in a sweetly pitched voice.

"Sorry for waking you two up. One of our corvettes has been stolen by a deserter," Jake said in a surprisingly casual tone. He was watching Laura and Ayan more than anyone. "So far, I've been able to trace the orders back to Oz, but only unofficially since I got the information third hand."

"Wait, this deserter was ordered to leave the fleet?" Admiral Doolth asked, surprised.

"Ever since Intelligence saw Alice's work on trying to bring a large resistance group closer to full recruitment into Haven Fleet, Lamonthe and other members of Intelligence have been working on a plan to get a few more operatives out into the galaxy who can get similar efforts going," Oz explained. "When they saw several candidates aboard the Triton they came to me and I helped them hammer out some of the details. Noah Lucas was one of the candidates along with every other member of the Pilot's Apex Program. Most were crossed out in the first few days, leaving Noah and a few others. I admit, he was high on my list, but not at the top. I didn't like the idea of isolating Noah, but when the order to send him out as the first operative came down, I executed it."

"I didn't know anything about this," Jake said.

"I brought that up and Lamonthe told me that the integrity of the mission could break down if you were aware of it," Oz said.

"So this is Lamonthe," Admiral Doolth said, glancing at Jake then Ayan. "It's inappropriate. Noah Lucas is part of Samurai Squadron, which is part of the Special Operations Combat Unit and that is completely under Commodore Jacob Valent's control. Did anyone aboard the Merciless know?"

"The only other high ranking officer who might know is Commander Minh-Chu Buu, and I can't ask him because he's on mission right now," Jake said. He was holding his frustration in check well.

"He doesn't know," Oz said. "Not even aides were allowed to see the details of this mission. There's no record of it. I'm disobeying orders right now by discussing it."

"I didn't know about this," Ayan said soothingly to Laura as she slowly lowered the baby into her basinet. "I'm going to restrict Lamonthe's privileges and put him under guard while we investigate this if I can get your support, Nimeen."

"I'll support the action," Admiral Doolth said, stroking the fur under her chin. "Who will serve as interim lead of Intelligence?"

"I'm elevating Commodore McPatrick to my own rank: Founding Admiral. I think it'll only be appropriate if you second that too, since Founder is a Nafalli rank."

"Oh, I second it," Nimeen said with a broad Nafalli smile. "I've read your file and find that your story proves that you are a man of high honour, Admiral McPatrick. Even the killing of Geist is made honourable by your reasoning. I will support your elevation if it is challenged. What about Commodore Valent?" she asked Ayan, her broad, furred head turning. "He is a founder of the fleet as well and quite a tactician."

"We entered him into the fleet at a lower rank because the British Alliance didn't approve," Ayan said. "Now I think he's afraid that a promotion will take him away from commanding a ship and going on missions."

"Our high-ranking officers bolster the soldiers morale by leading missions," Admiral Doolth said. "I propose that he is promoted to the highest rank but with that philosophy in mind. He and his command crew are legendary, I'm sure they can take care of his ship while he's leading his troops."

"I need you, Jake," Ayan said. "Now that we can communicate in real time across the galaxy, you can play a bigger role in fleet leadership while you go on some of the most important missions. I think we can leave SOCU in your hands while Oz takes care of the rest of Fleet Intelligence until we restructure that organization at the top. You can build it however you like and work with us on bigger operations that keep you active out there. I know you don't want to leave that kind of action behind."

Silence hung over the room, and as much as the sudden events were exciting, Alice was still trying to figure out how exactly they would help Noah. Benching Lamonthe was a good thing, his ideas needed to be examined at least, but elevating Oz and Jake to the highest rank in the fleet wouldn't necessarily lead to Noah returning to the fleet.

Admiral Nimeen Doolth cleared her throat. "I advance you, Commodore Jacob Valent to Founder Admiral with the support of Founder Admiral Ayan Anderson."

"You have my support," Ayan said.

"It's about time," Alice muttered.

"All right, so this means I'm a leader in Nafalli and Haven Fleet ranks," Jake said in as serious a manner as Alice could recall seeing him in.

"Exactly right," Nimeen said.

"I'm honoured," he said. "First thing: let's resolve this deserter garbage." He looked to Alice for a moment before turning back to the holographic torsos of Ayan, Oz, and Nimeen. "I've been through Noah's file a few times. He spent enough time alone on Iora, and even when he had a companion, they were on their own and under stress for months. The mission he's been sent on is a good idea, but the execution ignores the family Noah has surrounded himself with, so I'm sending the Clever Dream after him. This act is classified at the highest level because I want it to look like Alice is acting against orders, taking her ship on her own to go after him. That way they can put up whatever front they like if they run into Mary Reed."

"You knew we were looking for her?" Iruuk asked.

"That's how you found the resistance group on Nuaji. You were tracking her and Peter's resistance group was the last Order surveillance linked her to," Jake replied, nodding. "She might know of several resistance groups, how to contact them. We need to use her contacts to give the right fighters support."

"So, the first objective is to get Noah, second is to track Mary Reed and try to work with her," Alice said. For the first time everyone was looking at her, so she decided to push her luck. The feeling of relief coming from her father told her that it was the right time. "Any promotion for me and Fur-Face while you're handing them out?"

Ayan was the first to laugh. "Like rank would stop you from doing anything."

Oz cleared his throat. "I think you're both in the right place for now."

"You're not wrong," Alice sighed. "All right, so you want me to act like going after Noah is my idea?"

"Exactly," Jake said. "We'll put his coordinates behind a high classification rating and we'll make it look like you've stolen them and taken off."

"Bah, you don't have to make it look like they've been stolen," Iruuk said. "I'll just get Lewis to do it." He looked around the room nervously, realizing that he just casually proposed using an artificial intelligence to crack through fleet security. "Awkward," he breathed as four Admirals and a Captain stared at him.

"Tell Lewis I want a report on vulnerabilities in the Haven Fleet network," Oz said.

"Will do," Alice replied. "Well, I have my mission. Now I'll get my hug and storm out of your room like I'm a pissed off teenager planning on stealing the family shuttle."

Jake embraced her for a long moment, he was nervous, she could feel it. "Don't worry, it's a milk run, and I can feel what people are gonna do before they do it," she said against his chest.

"I always thought humans should cuddle more," Nimeed cooed, tilting her head.

"I know, I've said it to several of them but they mostly ignore me," Iruuk told her.

"Good luck, Alice," Ayan said as she watched her and Jake step apart.

"Remember to call your mother," he told Alice, holding her at arm's length.

"Don't get into too much trouble, and take good care of the

crewmembers who don't want to go with me. I'm pretty sure Ute could use a pond in her quarters, but she'll be too polite to ask."

"I'll make sure she gets your quarters," Jake teased.

"Oh, and do I have to call you guys Founder Admiral Mom and Founder Admiral Dad now?" she teased.

"No, actually. That's sort of like saying; Admiral Admiral Valent, since the military title of Warrior Founder is synonymous with admiral in my culture. We only use Founder and Admiral together when we want to say that they rank in the Nafalli part of the fleet and the rest of Haven Fleet," Nimeen explained.

"I don't think she was serious," Ayan explained.

"Oh. I don't always understand sarcasm, my tribe's not good at it."

"Seriously, it's about time you guys were at the head of this thing," Alice said, looking at Ayan, Oz and Jake. "I can't wait to get back and see what you do together."

"Thank you, Alice," Oz said with a nod.

"Wish me luck. Now, go pretend we just had a brutal argument, round up a few of your crew and run off in the Clever Dream. We're crafting high end scuttlebutt here."

"Yes, Father," Alice replied with a crooked grin and a sigh.

"Oh, do I get to be angry too?" Iruuk asked as they turned towards the door.

"Sure, why not?"

Iruuk growled, his head low, hands balled into fists as he stomped out of the room and down the hall beside Alice.

THIRTY-FIVE

Trimming

THE ROUND SEATING in the habitation section of the Clever Dream was filled with the crew that Alice felt she was still just getting to know. They were curious and concerned about her well-being. Jessen, who hadn't spoken to her since she objected to having an empathic captain, was being ruled by guilt, which Knud shared even though he had no reason to.

Utc was more difficult to read, but for the first time Alice could sense the small Mergillian. There was a mixture of hope and sadness, less so the latter. The Nafalli were easy to read. Woone, Noro and Krooke were getting impatient, probably wishing they could get a mission off ship soon but they were also concerned like Faloo, Callum and Yawen. Theodore was a blank as always to Alice, but he sat down around the table at the rear of the Clever Dream with everyone but Iruuk, who stood beside Alice.

"I'm sorry for everything I put you through while I was recovering. I took on more than I can handle, made a mistake or two, and suffered the consequences, but it's not fair that you had to suffer with me," Alice said. It was an apology she composed over the last few days between sessions with Quan and time hanging out with Theodore, Yawen or Iruuk.

"Never you mind," Faloo said first.

"It's all right," Woone offered, the rest of the Nafalli nodding with her.

"No harm done," Callum offered. "Well, except for Ute, maybe."

"No, what happened to me wasn't harm," Ute said, her voice squeaking. "I'm going to have my first..."

"I think they call them tadpoles in English," Theodore whispered.

"Tadpoles, thank you Theo," Ute said. "And I'll spend the next year taking care of them while I tell the stories about what I've seen, done and where I've been. Well, to anyone with clearance, anyway. I'll be returning to my people as a hero explorer, the first to visit another dimension among other things. The adventures I've had will provide days of storytelling, and I'll be called on to tell them over and over again. It's such an honour. I have nothing but gratitude for you."

"Well, I stand corrected," Callum chuckled.

Alice wished Ute was staying aboard, but was happy to see and feel that she was overjoyed. "Good, well, I hope you keep in touch," Alice said. "I'm leaving in a few minutes, so you'll be staying aboard the Merciless. I'm taking the Clever Dream out on personal business. It could take a few days, it could be for a few years."

"Oh, I didn't expect to say goodbye so soon," Ute said sadly. She stepped forward and Alice leaned down so she could hug the best pilot, and one of the kindest people she'd ever met. "Good luck, Alice. I will call you, you know that. You can navigate through a field few understand, an emotional one. Trust yourself and don't be afraid to use all your talents."

"Thank you, Ute," Alice said. "I hope you and your children stay safe and happy."

Ute went around the two-tiered seating saying her goodbyes and dispensing hugs to everyone who wanted one. Meanwhile, Jessen approached Alice quietly, Knud was right behind her. "This trip could get us black marks on our record if it goes wrong?" Jessen asked.

"No. I'm your Captain, I'll be fully accountable. Don't break regulations on your own and follow orders, and you'll be fine," Alice replied quietly. She was surprised to feel the disbelief in Jessen and tried to turn her empathic ability off, but it wasn't happening.

"This has nothing to do with you being an empath," Jessen said, but it was a lie, Alice could feel it. "But I'm going to stay aboard the Merciless. I think I know what this mission is. Noah deserted, you're going after him."

"You're right," Alice replied. "You shouldn't be here then."

Jessen nodded. "My things are already off the Clever Dream. Good luck, Alice." She walked past her Captain into the hallway beyond and was half way to the small lift that would take her to the main ramp leading off the ship when she stopped and looked at Knud. "Are you coming?"

Knud looked at her, then Alice, and finally back to Jessen. There was a rigidity and a feeling of doing the right thing when he said; "I'll see you when our paths cross again. Good luck, Jessen."

After a moment's hesitation, Jessen continued towards the lift. The hurt Alice felt in her was deep. That was mirrored to a lesser degree in Knud, who took consolation in feeling he was doing the right thing. "I'm sorry," Alice said quietly to Knud.

Knud only nodded and sat back down beside Krooke, who was adjusting his goggles after hugging Ute. The Mergillian turned to Alice, gave her one more brief embrace and left with a wave over her shoulder. "Um, she forgot to clear her quarters out," Callum said. "I mean, I don't want to see her go either, but she should have her stuff."

"I'll do it before we leave and make sure someone gets her things to her," Faloo said.

"So, all of you are staying?" Theodore asked.

Nods and short statements of confirmation followed and Alice was surprised. Faith in her crew wasn't in question, but she thought there would be at least a couple more taking their leave. She looked around the circular room at Callum, Knud, Yawen and Krooke who were on the lower tier of the sofa. They were confident in her, ready to hear about what was coming next. Woone, Faloo, and Noro lounged on the upper tier with growing eagerness that didn't show on the surface at all. They relaxed in place like they were watching a holomovie. If it weren't for her gift, Alice would have completely misread them, missing their internal excitement at the prospect of going along with their Captain's personal adventure. "So, uh, where are we going?" Noro asked.

"Ute and Jessen are off the ship," Lewis said over the ship wide audio system. "Would you like me to activate security lockdown while you give us the details?"

"Go ahead," Alice replied as she checked her com-con for Noah's destination.

. . .

SOLAR SYSTEM: DOXAN
  PLANET: DOXAN III
  SETTLEMENT: THESS CITY
  PRIMARY INDUSTRIES: MINING [FMR], BIO CULTI-
VATION [FMR], MILITARY MANPOWER DEVELOPMENT
[FMR]

"ALL THOSE INDUSTRIES are marked as defunct," Woone pointed out. "It sounds like a hole."

"It probably is," Callum said. "But you know what they say at the academy;" He, Yawen and Knud said the last together; "Save your questions until the end."

The image that came up of Thess City was so dark that she thought it was taken at night, but the details revealed that the sun was high in the sky. Some of the tall buildings were almost finished but work was abandoned, most of the others in the city were blackened, even the tall environment processing towers near the centre of the vast metropolis. She looked to Theodore then, who smiled at her a little. "Is this one of the destinations the Order thought Mary might have in mind?"

"One of ninety-one, yes," Theodore replied in a whisper. "I would put the chances of Mary Reed being there at four-point two percent, rounding up. Those are good odds for someone who moves around so much."

"Can you review all the files on Thess and correct me if anything in my briefing is wrong?" Alice asked in a whisper.

"If you haven't reviewed the details regarding our destination, the chances of you being wrong about it are very high. Why don't I do the briefing?"

"I won't be talking about it much," Alice replied, turning back to the rest of her crew. "We're going to the Doxan System. Everything is settled here, the Pelican is safe along with as many people as the Fleet could save."

"And the Order of Eden didn't fire a shot," Callum said. "That's strange, right?"

"Yeah, unless there was something holding them back. At the same time, we haven't interfered with the work on the Lance, the battlecruiser they're refitting in the system, either. Whoever's in charge doesn't think the same way as the rest of the Order's leadership. Anyway, we're leaving," Alice said. "We came here with the best intentions and I screwed it up. The political and ecological fallout will last decades, and I can't be sorry enough for how badly I represented this ship or you as a crew. Your names will be attached to mine when people review what happened here, no matter what I do or say. That's why I want to give you one more chance to leave before I make another big mistake, even though I think I'm about to do the right thing."

"We're not goin anywhere," Yawen said as Callum and most of the crew nodded. "You're stuck with us."

"Okay. Before the Merciless and Rassaaga leave the area, we're going our own way. The Admiralty is having a shakeup that started early this morning," Alice started to say, aware that she was about to present the truth in her own way so she could avoid lying to her crew at all. They could keep secrets, they were smart enough to see why her mission wasn't entirely misguided, and she trusted them. The last thing she wanted to do was lie. "My Father and Oz, I mean, Commodore Terry Ozark McPatrick, have been promoted, skipping the rank of Rear Admiral and going straight to the top. The Nafalli have recognized them officially as well, making them two of three human Admirals with confirmed rank on all sides of the fleet. That affects us right now because they don't approve of a secret mission that Noah Lucas was sent on."

"Oh, so he didn't defect?" Noro asked. "I heard he defected this morning, I have a second cousin on the Triton," he explained to everyone else.

"He pretended to. It's a little complicated, but the important part is that we're going after him. I just found out he's on his way to Thess, a city in the Doxan System that has been mined out, cultivated until it was dead, and was once used for military training and testing. Now it looks like most people have abandoned it, and they don't have any affiliation."

"That is all correct," Theodore said proudly.

"I hope he's well-armed," Yawen said.

"He's flying a new Clever Class Corvette that he's named the Corsair. The cloaking and spoof systems are better than the type installed on the Clever Dream."

"Really?" Lewis asked. "These were just installed, and I've kept the firmware up to date. His are better?"

"Not by much," Alice replied reassuringly.

"Keep in mind, newer isn't always better. Maybe you just meant to say they were newer?" Lewis asked.

"Maybe," Alice replied, rolling her eyes.

"I saw that," Lewis said. "Rolling your eyes at me, bah! If I had eyes to roll, I'd roll them at you too, but..."

"Lewis," Alice interrupted. "Can I finish this?"

"Oh, right. Go on."

"The Corsair isn't set up the same as this ship, it has fighter launch systems and an extended fabrication bay. His original mission was to pretend to be an arms dealer who broke away from

Haven Fleet so he could meet leaders from organizations who the Fleet may want to recruit in the future. We're going to rendezvous with him, make sure he's safe, the technology he has is secure and then join his mission. We'll make contact with Command shortly after."

"So, we're not actually following you on a personal mission?" Woone asked, a little disappointed.

"That was what I wanted anyone leaving the crew to believe, because this mission is classified. The new leadership wants it to look like we took off on our own."

"In case they think that mission could use two ships and more excellent crewmembers," Callum added. "That's how I see this going."

"That's a possibility," Alice confirmed. "That's why I don't know how long this mission will take."

"We could be out there for years, dealing with the criminal element," Woone said with excitement, "selling weapons to the highest bidders, separating the scumbags from the rebels."

"Or we could pick up Noah and tow his ship back to the Fleet," Faloo said with a shrug.

"You are so boring," Woone told her, disappointed. "I can't... it's just... so boring!"

Faloo and most of the crew laughed. To Alice it felt like a weight had been lifted off all their shoulders. "All right," she said as it petered out. "We're leaving in ten minutes, so let's get through the ship checklist. If you left anything on the Merciless, tell Theo and he'll note it in the log so you get it back next time we link up with the fleet."

THIRTY-SIX

Death

IT WAS easy to grow complacent when you were flying something that could hide in plain sight. That was one of Minh-Chu's fears when he discovered that the new Uriel fighters had cloaking systems. Mastering them was easy as long as you were used to looking through checklists, and his pilots were. Even still, he didn't want any of his pilots to grow accustomed to cloaking systems. That was a technological race that cost the loser dearly every time.

Only five people knew about his mission. It was a full test of the cloaking fields. His fighter was outfitted with a bigger power reserve for his shields instead of a jump drive and there was an indent along the bottom where he carried a piece of technology that he wrote one simple word on in white grease pencil: DEATH.

It was a modified Hammerhead Torpedo. It had its own stealth systems but they worked with the Uriel fighter's to make a seamless field around it and his ship. The torpedo had internal shielding that hid the large antimatter reservoir and the system that generated the stuff. If he wasn't sure that the cloaking system hid that and everything else better than anything they had in the fleet, he wouldn't have let anyone launch with the payload or get near the Order of Eden Super Cruiser called the Lance. It was the best cloaking system the fleet had according to all but the most important test, the last one. The one he was flying.

The Merciless, Pelican and Rassaaga were allowed to run rescue operations near Nuaji, but they knew they were being watched. There was no doubt. Jake and Minh agreed: The Order were trying to see whatever they could as the rescues went on. There were scan waves, evidence of highly sensitive detectors a few hundred thousand kilometres away from the planet, a scan array functioning on the Lance, and who knew what else. It was easy to destroy the detectors, a simple long range shot took them out, they were disposable tech. The array aboard the Lance was becoming a problem, though. It had heavy defences and its range was growing every few hours. He was also asking himself if the unspoken truce was their way of seeing how close they could get a ship to the Merciless or Pelican without being detected? A shiver ran down Minh-Chu's spine and he turned his attention back to the matter at hand. His tactical scanner still showed only four destroyers around the Lance, his kilometre-long target. Its outboard systems were fortified, heavy armour plating was still being placed between them, and the launch bays had the same new shield technology that Haven Fleet was installing. Its scanners pulsed three hundred times a second. The stealth systems on his fighter made it look like they weren't there at all, judging from the lack of response from the Cruiser's perimeter guns. He glanced at his relative distance indicator as he closed to within thirty thousand kilometres.

"You're clear so far, Ronin," Jake said. He was on the bridge of the Merciless, probably in that classic pose where he was leaning forward, elbows on his knees, fingers knitted together as he watched his tactical hologram. He most likely didn't realize he was doing it anymore. "You can drop the torpedo any time now."

Ronin looked at the ship, it looked large, but he knew it was still quite far away, over twenty-five thousand kilometres. He couldn't respond to Jake, it might be enough to break his stealthy approach. His communications systems were muted, so nothing he said would be broadcast, but he answered anyway; "Up to one litre of liquid anti-hydrogen. I bet that would make a huge mess of that thing, but I want to make it gone, and to finish testing these cloaking systems. They're our best, so I'm going to get close enough for their collision alert scanners to hit them. Let's see how good they really are."

The throttle was set perfectly, he was moving at the right relative speed to maintain his cloak, not too fast, and not too slow. Normally that didn't matter much, there was a wide margin, but the collision scanners near the Lance's hull were many times more sensitive than its normal combat scanners. They were made to fine tune the aim of the countermeasure systems so rapid-fire weapons could destroy missiles, meteorites, even small projectiles an instant before they struck the hull. It was an old system, but a good way to have redundant scanners built into a ship. He closed to within ten thousand kilometres of the Lance. At two thousand he'd be close enough for the collision scanners to test his cloak. That was when he'd deliver Death, too. There would be nothing they could do about it. If he detonated it at his current distance, most of the Lance would be destroyed. The display of his fighter in the lower left of his HUD drew Minh-Chu's attention. He got a bad feeling and shook his head, returning his attention to his instruments. Almost five thousand kilometres away. He couldn't shake the feeling of dread creeping up on him. It wasn't his cloaking systems that made him wary, it was that thing strapped to the bottom of his fighter. Death. "I don't trust it," he breathed to himself. The math of dropping it within two thousand kilometres of the enemy ship, passing over the Lance, then having it go off behind him precious seconds later added up fine in Minh-Chu's head. There would be enough time to get clear of the worst of the explosion, his shields would protect him from the rest easily, but he still didn't trust it, so he dropped the torpedo and sent it on its way. "Lost my nerve at three thousand, three hundred and twenty-four klicks. We'll let the torpedo test those scanners."

ADMIRAL SCANLON WAS FINALLY GETTING AROUND to some pleasure reading. It was an old exercise, reading a book, moving your eyes across a page, but she loved it. The chaise lounge she read in was in the corner of her standby room. The shelf beside it had her small selection of favourites; Testing The Void, The Time Machine, the most recent version of Unrequited which was a romance novel that the author was still adding to, and a few others that most people never heard of. Above the desk she never sat behind was a holographic math model that was the closest thing her people could come up with to explain Haven Fleet's cloaking systems. From time to time she glanced up from her reading, which was supposed to clear her head and give her mind time to come up with new ideas and looked at it. Her analysts were better physicists than she was by far, but she understood the problems they were having as they tried to break through the cloaking technology.

The Lance was an expensive ship, the space she gave Haven Fleet to operate around Nuaji was controversial since most of the Admiralty thought she should send interdiction ships in and wipe the Haven ships out, but she stuck to her plan. The Overlord trusted her, that's all that mattered. She was just getting back to her book, Founder of Mars: A Biography, when a chime interrupted her. That sound meant there was an urgent communication coming in and she tapped her wrist to answer. "Yes."

"Ma'am, the Lance just detected an object with its Near Field Collision scanners," the officer said in a rush. "Then the ship went dark."

"They finally took the bait. They attacked," she said.

"Yes, but not at long range, from what we can see. This was an antimatter torpedo like the ones that hit our bases and shipyards not long ago. The energy dispersion is the same, but we're still analysing it..."

"So you're not completely certain yet, I understand," Admiral Scanlon said, dropping the hardcover onto her seat, standing and striding to the door. "I'm on my way, start a full analysis now. I want to feed new parameters into our long range scanners as soon as possible."

"Yes, Ma'am, we're working on updating our model."

"Thank you, Stanley," she told the lead analyst.

THE TORPEDO WENT off as Minh-Chu was a little over twenty-five thousand kilometres away from the Lance. The kilometre-long ship was between it and him, but you wouldn't know it. Its hull disappeared in a bloom of white light, and his fighter was sent tumbling end over end as he heard something strike his hull. "That's not good!" Minh-Chu said as he brought it back under control and started checking his systems. His shields were down to twenty-eight percent, but a shard of metal penetrated them. He looked through his cockpit window towards the back then back at his damage panel. The backup energy storage system he brought with him was offline, punctured by whatever hit him. "Good thing I brought those, or it would have hit me right in the cockpit."

"...to Ronin. We are sending a rescue team," Jake said as the signal from the Merciless cleared.

"No need, my ship is still flyable and my shields are back up to thirty percent. I'm coming back uncloaked."

"We can see that. A chunk of material from one of the Lance's reactors is sticking out the back end of your fighter. Are you sure you're all right?" Jake asked.

"Fine, just a trophy for the squad room," he replied.

THE SMALL LIFT at the end of the secure hallway took Admiral Scanlon directly to the workgroup hub, a darkened room where thirty-one scientist worked on the problem of Haven Fleet cloaking devices. Their work was summarized in the middle of the room as a hologram of drifting math, and it was changing quickly. "How are we doing?" she asked as she approached Stanley Edwards. He was skinny, too skinny as far as she was concerned, and had a long, thin chin. He worked too hard, but that could be taken care of after he was finished leading her team.

"We've confirmed that the Lance was destroyed, and we're scanning a Haven Fleet fighter. The stealth systems are still trying to activate, but they're damaged. Part of the ship is obscured while the rest is visible. We're getting great data."

"How close are we to building a new parameter set we can use?"

"Close," he said, looking over his shoulder at two of his senior team members then up at the column of holographic math in the middle of the room. "Minutes before we can get that for you and test it."

"The radiation from the blast is clearing up, we're getting a better scan of that fighter," someone announced from across the room. "Wait, he's turned his cloaking systems off."

"Use the data we collected," Stanley said.

Admiral Scanlon watched as the large team put all their work together, collaborating rapidly with practiced grace. The column of numbers turned green, he smiled a little, then nodded. "We have parameters you can use for a new scan."

"Load them into the array on the dark side of Asteroid Nine Five Three Three One and scan the coordinate range I'm putting into the system, please." She punched coordinates that would scan a huge amount of space, she was sure there was a Haven ship in there somewhere.

"Done, scanning," a technician near the middle of the room said as he changed the main holoprojector to show the results. "Fifty-three second delay."

Everyone in the room watched, quieting down until there was silence. Admiral Scanlon stared at the empty space above the holo-projector, realizing after some time that she was holding her breath. The Lance was destroyed. She would have to use an older command carrier for her flagship. The Order of Eden would feel the expense. Most importantly though, with no reason to remain in the area, the Haven ships would move on and she'd lose them unless...

"Scan data is coming in, we should see something now," the technician running the tactical scanners announced.

Admiral Scanlon began to grin, excitement rising as the shape of a Haven Fleet ship appeared. At first that's all it was, just a dark shape, then there were details, enough details to see that it was the Merciless. "We got it, we can see them!" she exclaimed, the first to clap.

The room erupted with applause as she walked around Stanley's station and gave him a hug that surprised him at first. There were tears in his eyes, and she wiped one away. "Save those scan parameters and encrypt them with my key. You are going on vacation as soon as we start using them."

"Thank you, thank you so much," he said before turning to another member of his team to embrace them.

She waited for the din to die down, then locked all the doors with a quick command on the computer printed on her wrist. "Can I have your attention!" she said, making sure she proceeded with a congratulatory tone. "Thank you all for your hard work, I knew you could do it, I knew all the sacrifices we made would be worth it. Congratulations. Now the hard part begins. You're all being sequestered in this part of the ship. You can move between your quarters and the common room in this section, but that's all, because we have to keep this a secret. I know you're all looking forward to contacting your friends and families, but you'll have to wait a while longer. These computers will not be reconnecting with the fleet database."

"How long are we going to be isolated this time?" asked Tobin, a scruffy blonde analyst several stations down.

"That depends on the best strategic use of this new scanning technique. Someone from security will let you know when we do. You'll be paid twice your rate while you're sequestered, plus a project completion bonus," she replied as several dissenting voices began to rise. She wouldn't have it. "Enough!" she barked, silencing the room. "This is a secret worth burying everyone here for. Do you understand? If you are calm, patient, and no one leaks the fact that we have a way of penetrating Haven cloaking systems, then you'll all be fine. You'll be much wealthier, and opportunities will open up for you. If this leaks, I will have to start taking a close look at each and every one of you for indications that you are a mole. That kind of scrutiny gets people executed. For now, celebrate amongst yourselves, relax, eat something, and keep quiet. There will be a perfect time and place to roll out these new scan parameters, and when that happens, when they're in common use, you'll all be free to talk about how you cracked their cloaking systems all you like." Admiral Scanlon took her leave, wishing she didn't have to dampen their spirits, and hoping that there would be no leaks. There were a lot of mysteries to solve, technologies to analyse in the Haven System, and she wanted to use as much of the same team as she could. It would be a waste if they had to be silenced permanently.

THIRTY-SEVEN

Nuaji's Lessons

ALICE HAD two holographic images running in front of her. To her right was all the information they managed to gather on Mary Reed. She'd been busy, the Order suspected that she organized a meeting between three rebel factions. Where and when it took place were vague, she was good at keeping that kind of information secret. Mary Reed's file was a loop of data that she picked at, didn't focus on past reading and watching it through the first time.

The other image was simpler but more devastating. The Mary Reed file was momentarily forgotten as she watched Peter's final moments. "I love you all," he said wistfully before the nanobots ended his life then started pulling his body apart. It was the first time she'd watched his whole declaration, and as she struggled to keep the outrage, sadness and guilt from spilling out of her head, she wondered if it was still too soon for her to see it.

A chime at the hatch to her quarters sounded. "Come in." The tears were wiped away on her long sleeve, and she shifted on the round seat.

"I'm sorry, I stowed away," Quan said as he stepped inside.

Alice was shocked. "How?"

"Lewis, Faloo, and a little mental shielding," he said sheepishly.

"You sneaky little subroutine," she scolded towards the ceiling.

"Hey, no reason to get nasty," Lewis replied. "Admiral Valent ordered me to hide him aboard. We agreed that there was a fifty-fifty or so chance that you would leave him behind if he made it a choice. I was only following orders. Oh, and I'm a whole program, not a subroutine. Words hurt, you know."

"Sorry," Alice snickered, making a mental note not to use that insult again. "I know."

Quan looked from the ceiling, where most people stared when they were talking to Lewis, back to Alice, seeming uncertain. She slipped off the round seat and hugged him. "I'm glad you're here," she said, amused that he was such an awkward hugger with her as he gently patted her on the back before she released him.

"I can be an annoying companion," he said, looking at the frozen image of Peter's body going limp behind her. "I've been told that a few times when I tried to help people. I felt you might want to talk, though. That's the video the Fleet is afraid of."

"I can see why now," Alice said, sitting back down, nodding. "I can't believe I made that happen. They were just medical nanobots, I didn't think he could use them to make a weapon that would strip his own world."

"I sense that you didn't imagine he'd follow through with that kind of destruction, either," Quan said, sitting beside her. "Oh, that's more comfortable than it looks."

"High-end self-adjusting seating," Alice said, turning back to the frozen image. "You're right, I never thought he'd actually do it." Sadness and fear established a sudden grip on her, and she started shaking.

"You're supressing something," Quan said, putting his arm around her.

"I don't know what, I don't know where this is coming from."

"Look away from that for a moment, you weren't there, that was his decision, not yours," Quan said. "Relax, your body is only telling you that your mind is hiding something. Forget shielding the people around you from what you're feeling, I'll do that for you."

Alice followed his advice, it felt good to let go, and she felt the urge to slip deeper, to let go of consciousness so she could begin to create her own world again. She didn't follow it. "God, I want to hide again. Put a bigger wall around what I'm supressing, just so I don't break down again."

"I won't do that for you, besides, did it ever occur to you that you're not breaking down, you're breaking through?" Quan asked.

The image of Peter the moment before he was completely torn apart was still hanging there when a memory returned to Alice. It was while she was in her dream world, she was escaping, walling her mind up and pretending to be little, young, innocent. A flood of alarm, pain, and terror struck her then as she felt hundreds then thousands and tens of thousands of people at once. "I felt them die," Alice sobbed, feeling the memory of a multitude screaming. "I felt their fear and pain so I made sure I wouldn't have to wake up again."

"Let go of that memory," Quan said. "You've uncovered it, now you can begin to accept it, but you have to let go, you can't live in that moment anymore."

"I..." Alice started, but finishing the statement she wanted to make proved difficult. *I want to hide again? I want to be alone? I want you out of my head? I shouldn't be alive when all those people are gone because I didn't see how crazy Peter was? I can't do anything right.* Remembering the outcry of pain that was so loud that it crossed incredible space, she doubled over.

"I know it feels like it happened seconds ago, but you have to face that it ultimately wasn't your fault and begin to let go. You don't deserve the guilt you've taken on." He rubbed her back soothingly. "You only wanted the best for Peter and his people. You didn't see what he did coming because you are a good person who expects allies to be as good or better than you. You've learned a hard lesson, but don't let it take that away from you entirely. You don't need to suffer anymore. There's still so much good you can do."

He's wrong. Alice thought, then she started remembering what it was like to have Lewis as her only companion. Months where she did odd jobs with him and the Clever Dream, trusting no one, serving herself while she kept an eye open for her father. She realized for the first time that that Alice, the first human Alice wasn't selfish, she was lost. Being lost, having no purpose was as much a feeling as it was a way of being. That was as bad as going to sleep and refusing to wake up, as running away. She could do that, Alice realized, deny the memory of feeling a world die. *But I've run away so many times before.* Noah, Ayan, Jake, her old friends and crew began drifting through her mind then, and facing that memory became easier. "How do I face this?" she asked.

"A little at a time, and it'll get easier every time it crosses your mind. Emotion will turn into knowledge, and pain will become a lesson," Quan said. "You don't have to do it alone, either. Put it aside for now. Your control will come back and you'll feel better."

Believing what he said was difficult at first, and she scoffed. Then she realized it was true. Putting the memory aside, focusing on the moment wasn't easy, but she found herself doing it, straightening up, remembering that she'd be seeing Noah Lucas again in about ten hours.

"What was that? You got control back very quickly just then," Quan asked, smiling a little, wiping a tear of his own away.

"Noah," Alice said shyly, taking a tissue from the drawer built into her seat.

"He was your happy thought," Quan said with a grin.

"Are you teasing me?" Alice asked before blowing her nose.

Quan laughed. "You're a remarkable woman, Alice. Our progress tonight would normally take weeks, months for most people. That's your strength, not his gift to you. It takes fortitude to live through one awful day so you can see what the next holds, even when there's someone you care for waiting to meet you in the future."

"It takes a toll on you, though," she said.

"It's for a greater good, temporary for the most part," he said. "Besides, I have a lot to make up for with you."

"I think you've more than made up for the first time we met," Alice said, remembering how he tried to get into her head then. It was a violation, but she made him pay then, too.

"I still have guilt of my own to work through," he replied.

"Do you think it'll ever go away completely?"

"No," he replied with no hesitation. "But some lessons come with the sting of the rod, and that only serves to remind us so we don't make the same mistake twice."

"Dark," Alice chuckled.

"I suppose so."

"Now, do you mind if we do an exercise? We can practice..."

"Hey, Captain," Faloo said, her audio address coming over the main system. "We're about to start watching an old 'choose the scene' movie. It plays, we pick what happens next. Callum says this one's hilarious."

"Oh, that's perfect," Quan whispered.

"We'll be there in a couple minutes," Alice said. "What exercise?"

"It's the River Stone exercise. You're having trouble turning your gifts off, so you should learn how to withstand the emotional river around you without having to inspect or react to each one. This movie might be perfect, especially if it is funny. All you have to do is relax, accept that everyone will feel what they will, and that you can be passive, non-reactive."

"Why didn't you bring this up before?"

"I brought up a few things that could lead to it, but the focus was on you being able to turn your ability off. Now, perhaps learning to live with it on might be the best way to come at it."

Holy crap, I can't imagine walking around, knowing what everyone is feeling all the time. Alice thought.

"I do," Quan said. "Sorry, I was still listening in, I'll back off."

"It's okay," Alice replied. "How do you not get headaches?"

"I don't try to interact with what I feel from other people. You subconsciously do. Let's train you not to."

"With a comedy night?"

"With a crew you love, and yes, a comedy night."

THIRTY-EIGHT

The Road to Doxan

IT TOOK medication for Noah to get some sleep. Waking up eight hours later, he continued where he left off, chewing a denta-tab, reviewing notes on the ship in the shower, then eating a mocha meal bar after getting a fresh armoured vacsuit on. It felt a few layers thinner, and he realized that there had been advancements. It felt like a more flexible second skin. "Computer, look for Doxan Three in your Stellarnet Archive."

The computer flashed a red; NO RESULTS. ARCHIVE INCOMPLETE notification as he dropped into the pilot's seat. "Don't tell me..." he checked and found that there were no downloads other than system updates in the computer. "You didn't download anything from the Stellarnet before you left?" He checked his command and control unit and shook his head. He didn't have anything on Doxan either. He was in such a rush that he forgot to fetch the information before he entered trans-dimensional space. "Remind me to add that to my pre-mission checklist."

There was no response from the computer. He brought up the mission brief on Doxan, which included several darkened pictures, the name of a suspected gathering place for revolutionaries: Nil, a large bar with gambling and music, according to their nine-year-old advert. There was the information he'd already gone through about Mary Reed, how they had suspicions that the Doxan system was one of the places she visited often. It was high on their list, but their list was long. He'd been through the whole file, thinking that he may as well look into the side mission just in case Alice and SOCU wanted him to follow through with part of his new assignment. Perhaps he wouldn't become an arms dealer, maybe they'd assign her and the Clever Dream crew to join him, or she'd just yank him back to the Merciless and he'd be reassigned, who knew? Even still, it made sense to do something useful while they were in the Doxan system, especially since Alice was the first to start looking for Mary Reed.

He sat back, looking at the pilot and co-pilot controls surrounding him. He had a secondary hologram to his left that had all the communications and engineering systems summarized as well. Everything was fine, but they were running on autopilot, letting the navigation and power systems in the quad drives take care of everything while they were in faster than light transit, skimming the space between dimensions. As soon as the Corsair emerged into normal space, he'd have to run it alone. There was automation, sure, but if he got into trouble he could run into problems. "Activate advanced automation systems interface."

The interface came up, but tall red letters blocked the window:

WAITING FOR ARTIFICIAL INTELLIGENCE INITIALIZATION.

"You mean, this ship isn't using an artificial intelligence yet? What do I do to boot it up?" he asked, looking around the console. The computer was silent. "Can I get a tutorial?"

"The Seventh Generation Clever Class Corvette implements several improvements that captains in previous versions of the ship have made. Not the least of which is the Removable Artificial Intelligence Module, or R.A.I.M. for short," the playback said as a hologram of an armoured data cylinder appeared. "Inspired by Captain Alice Valent, each ship comes with two. One is loaded with an advanced artificial intelligence, the other is empty, made to maintain a backup in the core of the ship. The empty module is preinstalled, the artificial intelligence must be installed by the ship's captain by inserting it into the main console on the bridge of the ship." The hologram showed a slim drawer, then a socket he didn't notice between the pilot and co-pilot stations just below the main console. "Calibration will commence, and your artificial intelligence will guide you through the last steps of the setup process."

"Good tutorial," Noah said to himself as he got out of the pilot's seat and looked beside the hatch, where there were several small drawers with parts and tools inside. "Hey, here it is." The cylinder was heavy for its size, only the length of his palm. "I wonder if it'll be anything like Lewis."

It took a moment for him to figure out how to pinch the two latches in the data slot together so it came free, then he put the cylinder in and re-capped it. The entire console flickered as the false cockpit view disappeared for a moment. "Uh-oh."

It came back on later, a holographic phrase in chromatic letters appearing: ELISE IS CALIBRATING. Noah's command and control units' screens began rapidly scrolling through his entire file, including the extensive report Alice made on him. "Wait, what is it using to calibrate itself?" he asked nervously.

The communication and information hologram appeared to his left again, and the scroll of data ran past so quickly that he could barely see what the system was scanning through. The fleet regulations passed in a second, there was a flash of his latest mission briefing, then a status bar appeared, running from zero to a hundred percent in seconds as everything in the Corsair's standard database scrolled behind it. Aside from the ship systems, manuals, tutorials and updates there was a kind of encyclopaedia that touched on a few million topics. Noah generally found the Standard Galactic Information Resource, the encyclopaedia to be pretty useless and outdated.

The critical consoles re-lit properly, and he checked navigation, communications, engineering, tactical and support. "Okay, that's cool, the quad drives kept the ship moving in the right direction while it was having a chaos minute."

"Chaos minute," a female voice said. "I like that."

"You're my new artificial intelligence?" Noah asked.

"Yes, I'm Elise. I've finished calibrating, so you'll probably find me easy to communicate with, and since you're alone on the ship, I suggest we converse often."

"What did you use to calibrate yourself?" Noah asked as he made sure the autopilot was working properly.

"I reviewed the crew data, which was all about you at this point, the fleet regulations and the file nested in my data module called Primary Directives for Haven Fleet Artificial Intelligences. I synced with the ship so I'll be able to assist you or assume control if needed and ingested the general information database that was available."

"Just wondering: why are you speaking in a female voice?" It was a clear sounding voice that sounded more casual than most artificial intelligences.

"Most of your friends have been women, so I deduced that you'd be more comfortable this way. I could use a male voice, alter my pitch or sound like a person you know, like Alice, for example."

"No, no, you have a good voice, I was just curious," Noah said, leaving the pilot's seat. "Good to meet you. Can you watch things while I get ready to arrive in the Doxan system?"

"I'll be happy to. By 'things' you mean the overall operation of the ship, right?"

"Yeah, sorry."

"Don't worry about it. So, are you preparing for a mission? I see one primary and three secondary missions on your list."

"I'm guessing the primary is all about becoming a Haven Fleet deserter who turns to arms dealing?"

"With the hidden agenda of learning about rebels in the underworld so you can inform a follow-up team about them," she added. "Yes, that's the mission. You're meeting Captain Valent so you can discuss your orders, though."

"Do you have any reservations about that?"

"This ship is technically your property now. I was calibrated to it and you, so your purpose is my purpose. In short: do what you want, Skipper," she said the last as though she was completely laidback, relaxed on the topic.

"That's reassuring," he said.

"So, what are we doing?" she asked.

"Well, you're making sure the ship is running right and the autopilot is working properly, right?"

"Of course, but that takes about point zero zero three percent of my processing power. I'm more interested in what you're doing in the rear section of the ship and what you're planning when we emerge from transit space."

"Well, the Doxan System reminds me of some of the rougher places I've seen, so I'm looking through the weapons inventory for a good sidearm and a backup. I could use some armour and a personal shield too. If I have to land, or dock somewhere and walk around, I want to blend in a little. As much as I like this kind of vacsuit, I look a bit like a pod fresh clone."

"So, that means you won't be wearing heavy combat armour," she said.

"Exactly, but the kind with retraction abilities so I can hide it."

"Two cases down from the one you're about to open you'll find a Model Three Haven Fleet Heavy Pistol. It has a high intimidation factor, has a double magazine design and a variable energy output. In the same case you'll find a pair of personal energy shield emitters that are already fully charged. They're made to match the Model One and Three."

"Never heard of this stuff, is it new?" he asked as he opened the case she recommended, it was bio-locked to him. The weapon inside looked savage, with a clip above with three large suppression shells and one in the grip for slim kinetic rounds. The rest of the weapon's body was dedicated to cooling, firing and energy management. There were two oval discs beside it with stickers that said; MODEL THREE COMPANION SHIELD GENERATOR.

"Yes, your mission file says it's for you and trusted crewmembers only. There's a captain's long coat in the debarkation room for you, too. It's a locked design like the pistol, so you can't make more or scan them into another printer."

"I get it, sell weapons, but not these weapons," Noah said. He picked the pistol up and his vacsuit made a holster for it low on his hip. He holstered it and slipped the shield discs into the spots his suit made for them on his chest.

"So, do you think you'll actually need weaponry when we get to the Doxan System?" she asked, sounding worried.

"Probably not, but if this place is like I think it is, I'd rather have a gun and not need it than need a gun and not have it."

"I see your point."

A trio of skitters carried his long coat down the hall to him. "Aw, you didn't have to get it for me," he said.

Thin arms extended from their small dome bodies, holding the long coat up for him so he could slip his arms in. "Sometimes being nice saves everyone time."

"Thanks," he said, slipping his arms into the sleeves and feeling the welcome weight of the armoured garment. "There's a full suit of combat armour in this thing, right?"

"Yes, and it's latest generation."

"Well, I'm gonna have to make some changes," he said, bringing a hologram of himself wearing the jacket up. He changed his vacsuit's colour to dark purple then altered the V shape of armour slats running down the back of his long coat so they looked chromed. The rest of the coat and his boots were adjusted to matte black, and he made it look like he was wearing a gun belt while making sure all Fleet markings were removed. "Well, I still look like I'm wearing good tech, but most people won't immediately think I'm from Haven Fleet."

"Isn't that part of the story you're building? Oh, we're emerging into normal space in two minutes, by the way," Elise said.

Noah started jogging up the hall to the small bridge. "Well, yeah, if that's the mission I'll be following through on when Alice gets here. Still, if I were actually a deserter, I wouldn't want to look like some kinda Haven Fleet heavy. That kind of thing makes some people nervous and gets the wrong kind of attention. I'd rather look like I'm trying to look like a badass using Haven tech."

"Oh. I don't get it. I'll just watch and learn, Captain Badass."

Noah laughed as he pulled his long coat off then dropped into the pilot's seat. He checked the countdown counter, seeing that they had a minute and ten seconds until they emerged. "I'm starting to really like you, Elise."

"No surprise, I was made to be awesome."

"Okay, how are our systems?" he asked himself as much as Elise while he looked at the consoles around him.

"Everything's ready. Power reserve, shields, and weapon capacitors are all at one hundred percent. Diagnostic results indicate..."

"Is the checklist green?"

"The whole checklist is green," she replied.

"Okay, I'm taking the controls once we emerge. We'll be on the edge of Doxan Three Navnet space, so run active scanners and make sure we're not about to bump into anything."

"Sure thing, boss."

Noah looked from his console to the fake cockpit display ahead. It was exactly what the sensors around the outside of the ship were picking up, translated so he could see it as if he was looking through cockpit windows. The small bridge was actually under thick layers of armour. The energy surrounding the ship whirled as the Corsair passed through it. Blue, green and white light was everywhere as they tunnelled through interdimensional space. A spot of black ahead was growing larger rapidly.

"Noah?" Elise asked quietly.

"Yeah?"

"Thank you for activating me," she said, it was almost a whisper.

"Welcome to the universe; it's complicated, but I like it that way," he replied, wondering what Alice and Lewis would think of his new companion.

THIRTY-NINE

Freighter Honopu

THOUSANDS OF SHIPS littered the navigational display between plain asteroids and planets that had been cracked or drilled until they had few resources left to offer. "Doxan Three doesn't look promising, environmentally speaking," Elise said. "There are a few green spaces but most are privately owned. The penalty for breaching their boarders is slavery or death. I detect three abandoned cities, nine that have active gang wars, and nine more that are ruled by a recently formed government or corporation of some kind. Order of Eden has a satellite in orbit and three recruitment centres, but nothing garrison sized."

"Watch what you download from this place, especially the adverts," Noah told his new artificial intelligence.

"Oh, there are thirty-three advertising only channels, and I've been analysing their streams. I'll stop. Did you know you could get a complete skin purification and pigmentation adjustment for only three platinum if you land in Augustus in the next eleven hours?"

"Uh, no, but thanks. I don't normally go for that pigmentation stuff," Noah replied.

"Also, why do humans favour the; 'Fresh and Smooth' choice of pigmenta... Wait, there's a distress call coming through, it's four minutes and twenty seconds old."

"Put it through. Oh, and change our hull colour so it's dark red and black, then de-cloak. We need to make this ship look like an extended version of the Arcyn Starskipper."

"No problem," Elise said, and the Corsair's hull hummed for a moment before their cloaking systems disengaged. Navnet recognized them and requested that they state their destination.

The distress call began to play and a flashing red marker appeared near the edge of the solar system. "This is the Freighter Honopu. Shlaki Pirates jumped us as soon as we decelerated into the system. They won't negotiate, they're trying to destroy our ship and take the cargo train. Please help, our whole family is aboard. Please, any good Samaritans out there?"

"They've already registered with Navnet as freelance traders carrying medical supplies," Elise said. "Their shields are down to thirty-five percent. Their attackers are flying four Hunter Three Type fighters that have been heavily modified and the lead ship is a Zaugin Systems second generation destroyer which has been heavily modified as well. It's firepower is greatly enhanced, there's a direct connection between some weapons and their reactors."

Noah only needed the few seconds it took Elise to describe what was known of the situation to make up his mind. He turned the Corsair towards the flashing red blip on his tactical screen and brought his thrust up to maximum. The powerful engines at the rear of the ship howled, if it weren't for the dire circumstances, he'd be grinning at the sound. He sent their new course to the main Navnet system in the area. "Contact the pirate ship."

"Their transponder is numerical only and contains twelve threes in a row, it is obviously a fake. I'm targeting their main antenna with our transmission systems."

"Good idea, keep a lock on that so we can jam them if we have to," Noah said.

"They're answering," Elise said, putting the image of something that looked like a human with reflective skin on the main communications holoprojector.

"Don't interfere with the Shlaki, Samaritan," it said. The mouth moved awkwardly, the motions not matching the words as a humans' would.

"Is this the Captain of that ancient destroyer I'm seeing?" Noah asked.

"First Officer. I speak for him. If you interfere with our little salvage operation here, that pretty ship is going to be destroyed."

"Okay, listen, chrome face; break off your attack and I'll spare you and your little fighters. I'll be in sighting range in nine seconds." Noah replied, looking at the shields on the old destroyer. It was a big ship, they had rows of emitters that were fifteen metres long in some places, but old railguns didn't look like much of a threat to the Corsair. "I'm bringing my combat shields online now." He turned the shields all the way up.

"You are spoofing, there's no way your ship has that kind of shielding," the First Officer replied, his eyes going wide before he turned away from his console telling someone behind him; "Take a look at this, Cap, it could be a problem."

"That's a fake reading, they're spoofing, beaming energy at our array," replied a voice.

"In range, last chance to break off your attack. I have your main reactor targeted, your ship will be disabled," Noah said melodically.

"We're sending our pilots after you, moron. Even a Starskipper can't survive our best."

"I warned you." He verified the aim of the Corsair's three stationary railguns and fired five shots each, feeling the vibrations underfoot. "It'll probably be best if you don't use countermeasures on those. I sent fifteen solid rounds your way, they're coming at about fifty-six thousand klicks per second. It'll be a few seconds."

The First Officer leapt out of his seat, moving out of the range of the recorder. Noah watched the shells move across the tactical map. They would all strike the ship's main reactor, a large fusion system that was running near its peak to maintain the ship's mismatched shield system. "Their ship is going to be on emergency power without most of its shielding," Elise said.

"What do you think about that?"

"In terms of the continuation of the human species, killing all of these pirates is a good idea if they're murderers. The First Officer is wanted in this solar system for five killings. Oh, and that's not chrome on his skin, it's a permanent reflective pigmentation shift that deflects small beam weapons."

"I know, I just like calling him that." Noah watched as the destroyer's countermeasures, two shell turrets, managed to hit two of the shells he fired, splintering them into high velocity, deadly shards, then the destroyer was struck. The Corsair's shells put a small hole through the destroyer's hull, penetrating the outer wall of their main reactor. The transmission cut off for a few seconds, and the Corsair was in firing range with the rest of its weapons. He targeted the destroyer's bridge with the Prometheus Beams and set the lock to track so they would maintain their aim while he flew around the ship.

"The fighters are in firing range," Elise said.

"Do they pose a threat?" Noah asked.

"One does, it is carrying electromagnetic pulse missiles. Our countermeasures should be able to take care of them, but he has a group firing mode that can launch nine at a time in a scrambling pattern."

"How'd you learn that?"

"I scanned his ship and analysed the data?" Elise replied as though the answer should be obvious. "I'm not some ninth-generation general artificial intelligence, you know. They're not sure what generation I am, galactically speaking."

"Sorry, I'm just not used to working with someone of your obvious magnificence." Noah said as he piloted the Corsair so he could get behind the fighter trying to get a missile lock on him.

"Was that sarcastic?" she asked.

"Focus," he replied. "How's that destroyer doing?"

"Well, it looked like battery power was about to come online, then there was a burnout at Junction Three, right near the main power distribution centre, so they have to find that before they can get power to weapons, life support or main propulsion."

"The freighter?"

"Their shields are regenerating. There is a breach in the starboard-rear compartment of the hauler, but the crew is not in that section. No casualties."

"So, we got here in time. Is it possible to send a repair drone to their ship to fix that breach?" Noah asked as he lined a fighter up in front of the Corsair.

"Yes, I'll launch one whenever we're on a more stable trajectory. Speaking of which, what are you doing, Noah?"

"Wait, what?" he realized that he was flying the Corsair as if it was a fighter, making sure the other fighters couldn't get a good shot at him, lining his guns up on one opponent while he planned to strike another. His ship had seven hidden turrets and two slots for Uriel fighters that operated as turrets when they were docked. "Holy crap, thanks for reminding me. Open a channel on whatever frequency they're using to talk to each other." He kept one fighter in his sights, following it easily.

"...right behind me! He's gonna hit me with one of those big fricken railgun shells!" the pilot ahead of him was saying.

"Oh, man, you are on your own, buddy. I'm heading back to base," replied one of his wingmen.

"Hey, this is the guy with the big fricken railguns," Noah said. "If you all break off and head home now, I won't unlock my turrets and blow you to dust. I mean, I know I sound like I'm being cocky, but it's a fair warning."

"Yeah, Corsair, we're gone, buddy. This sky's yours," the pilot he was chasing said, turning toward Doxan III and blasting his thrusters. The three fighters with him did the same and Noah let them go.

"This isn't technically a sky, it's open space," Elise said. "Learn science, dumbass."

Noah laughed as he swung the Corsair around so it headed for the destroyer, the few transparent sections were still dark as it listed aimlessly. "Not a bad burn, Elise, close the channel."

"The Shlaki destroyer is launching an armed shuttle at the freighter. There are sixteen people aboard and scans are picking up small arms," Elise said. "I think they plan on boarding the freighter by force, but the turret on the top of the shuttle is pointing at us."

"Activate turret one and lock on to the shuttle's turret."

"It isn't capable of penetrating our shields," she said.

"What do you suggest?" he asked, flying the Corsair close to the destroyer, watching the tactical scanners.

"Maybe we could switch one of the Prometheus Beams to directed electromagnetic interference mode?"

"Sure. Leave Turret One active just in case, but train one of our beams on the shuttle," Noah replied. It was done in seconds. "Corsair to the combat shuttle on it's way to the Freighter Honopu. I see you. Break off or I'll leave you dead in space."

Their turret rattled off its response, sending a barrage of small projectiles in their direction. They disintegrated against the Corsair's shields, costing them less than a percent of their charge.

Noah fired the Prometheus beam for three seconds, hitting the turret first, then drawing a burn line down the hull to the cockpit. The turret stopped turning and the engines went out. "Now you'll suffocate or freeze and die, all squeezed in there like sardines."

Elise laughed. "Canned fish are funny."

"Are you sure you finished calibrating?" Noah asked.

"My creation was carried out perfectly. Do you detect an undesirable element? I mean, I could change a little."

"No, no, I was mostly kidding. Everyone has their own sense of humour," he said. "How's that freighter doing?"

"Well. They're turning towards Doxan Three now, but one of their dorsal thruster pods was damaged, so it's slow."

"What about that destroyer?" he asked.

"There is activity in their launch bay and they have another shuttle. It could be a rescue for the first one or they are going to try to board the freighter again. The majority of the crew are working on the electrical systems, though. None of them are anywhere near Junction Three."

"So, in other words, they're still figuring out the problem and don't have backup power."

"Correct."

"Call the freighter."

"Channel open," Elise said.

"This is Captain Lucas aboard the Corsair. Everyone okay over there?" Noah asked.

"We're good now, Captain," an older woman said as she came on screen. There was a young boy on her shoulders, grinning at him. "Thank you so much for fighting those pirates off."

"It's the least I could do. I used to run with a travelling show, so I know what it's like to get kicked around because people think you're on your own. I have a couple repair drones aboard. I could get them to attach a line to a hard point, get you into the patrolled zone around whatever planet you're on your way to and fix that hole you've got in your side."

"We're grateful for the save, but I'm afraid of what you'll charge us for that on its own. We probably can't afford more services," a younger man answered, turning the holorecorder in his direction.

Noah was stunned. He'd met a couple mercenaries who would save rich looking ships then demand payment before, but he never thought he'd be mistaken for one. "I think she expects us to demand money. How much should she pay?" Elise asked.

"Nothing," he replied.

"Pardon, Captain?" asked the young man.

"Oh, I was just telling my co-pilot that I don't charge for saves. I just couldn't watch pirates take you out. The tow and patch-up are free too."

"We can fix our own ship," he replied.

"Then how about a tow to wherever you're going? I'm new here, Captain..."

The holorecorder turned back to the older woman, who was handing the little boy off to someone else. "Captain Hewett. We'll take the help. I have to ask why you're offering, though."

Noah launched the drones. Loaded with modified skitters, they pulled heavy lines from the Corsair to hard points on the front of the Honopu where they were attached and moved on to repair the rupture in its hull. "I have the tech, and I have a little time to blow before my friends get here," he shrugged.

"And a good deed is its own reward," Elise added cheerily.

"That too." He moved the Corsair into position and gently increased thrust, sending an update to the local Navnet so they could mark them as a rescue effort with a warning to other ships that they weren't particularly manoeuvrable. It asked him for their final destination.

"Well, thank you, I wish there were more people like you in the galaxy."

"There's a bunch. Anyway, what port are you headed to?"

"Angel's Landing Starbase. We were told our cargo would sell well there," she replied.

He looked at the scan data and saw that they were carrying raw nutrient solution and medicine. "That's expensive cargo. Are they always short on the essentials here?"

"From what we were told, yes. The local Stellarnet is telling us we'll get between fifteen and nineteen times what they were worth on Ficelles."

"Well, good luck, we're building some momentum up now and the repairs are almost finished, so maybe I'll see you station-side. I think I'll see what it's like there."

"Oh, you didn't have a destination here?" she asked, surprised.

"No, just meeting some friends who said we'd meet in system. Good luck to you and your crew."

"Thank you again," the angle on their holorecorder widened to reveal a young boy and a girl sharing a woman's lap beside the older Captain. They waved, saying; "Bye, thank you!"

The transmission ended. "Well, I'm sure I'll hear from those pirates if I stick around. Did we ever get the name of that destroyer?"

"No, but I'll start looking for more information using the data we have. By the way, that freighter had four generations of the same family aboard. You saved a lot of people just now."

"We did, actually," he said, ordering the cables to detach. The drones finished printing the patch on the Honopu and were on their way back.

"Do you do that a lot?" she asked.

"Not as much as I'd like. Maybe that'll change if we spend some time here. Do you like saving people? It can get dangerous, you know."

"I think I do. I'd like to do that more often," Elise replied.

FORTY

Slander

TAMMY DERMEN HAD NEVER BEEN MORE TERRIFIED in her life. Two days into her work assignment, taking care of children on the bottom floor of the Everin Building, she found herself surrounded by Order of Eden soldiers in full armour. They put restraints on her then covered her mouth with a patch. It was a sight that terrified the young children in the cramped play room. Their cries were silenced as the door closed behind her and the soldiers.

It was lucky that she wasn't the only one taking care of the kids that day, but that wasn't much consolation as the soldiers rushed her down the corridor, into a transit car then to a shuttle. Standing out from the cliff side like a dark crystal shard, one of the newer buildings in Haven Shore had been taken as the main Order garrison. It was a target for the resistance, but Frost couldn't figure out exactly how they'd do enough damage to make a difference yet. They called it The Shard, a terrible name, she thought.

Fear gripped her even more firmly as she realized the shuttle was headed directly there, to the top landing pad. How did they find out who she was? Samantha and Frost showed her how to avoid the DNA sniffers, it wasn't hard, and she wore her second skin face even more than she ought to. A few pimples were nothing compared to getting taken into custody. For the life of her, she couldn't figure out what she did wrong, how they could identify and catch her. Frost, Samantha and Nigel did the risky things, they hadn't let her do anything yet. Her jobs - helping with the garden in Founder Square and caring for children while their parents were away - kept her out of the way. She'd overheard some soldiers and Order technicians talking, passed the information on to Frost and Samantha, but that couldn't be why she was in trouble.

Looking around the shuttle, she saw that all three of the guards with her had the safeties on their weapons activated. The glow-haze around the edge of one of their visors meant that one was watching a video stream. The other two weren't looking at her. The hatch leading to the cockpit was open. There was a locked cupboard under the seat across from her. It probably had emergency materials inside, including something that could be used as a weapon. Her restraints were Regent Galactic bracelets with an energy binder between them. If she could get close to any other kind of energy emitter that would be easy to overload. It wouldn't burn her much, she'd still be able to use her hands. "Eyes down!" one of the soldiers barked.

Turning her eyes to the floor, she realized he was the most vulnerable one. There was fear in his voice, it sounded like aggression, but that was a cover. He was big, surprise would only get her so far with him, but he was her best target if an opportunity to escape came up. A thought occurred to her then; *my fear is gone. How did that happen?*

The answer to her question came on the heels of that thought. Frost told her everything he knew about her model. She wasn't unique, but designed, a manufactured human. The intention of the designers was to create a charming, beautiful woman who would be underestimated. Her model was supposed to have the hidden capabilities of a deadly assassin, but the extent of Tammy's training was a year of self-defence classes when she was a young girl. How could the potential to be an assassin help her if she was never taught to utilize it?

The shuttle touched down, a final whine of the thrusters was familiar, and she realized that the ship used a xetima fuel source. It was highly explosive. That made the shuttle a bad escape vehicle. Rough hands picked her up by the elbows and forced her off the ship. They were close to the edge, waves crashed against rocks hundreds of metres below.

The doors leading into the building ahead parted and she recognized Wheeler, the man who rescued her so he could play some kind of head game with the leadership in the Haven System. "Duchess! It's so good to see you! Let's get you inside so we can take that hideous mask off. I missed you."

Her response was muffled by the patch over her mouth, and she followed her instincts, turning, ducking low and bashing into the guard on her left. He collided with the guard rail. Tammy lifted his leg, throwing him over the side.

The fearful one hesitated, in shock, and she pulled his sidearm out of its holster and tripped him, folding is knee from behind with her ankle. "Guards! We need help out here!" she heard Wheeler call.

The soldier who was behind her raised her rifle but Tammy fired three times, catching her in the chest twice and disabling the rifle with the third shot. It was a sparking mess. The guard she tripped, the fearful one, grabbed at her ankle. Tammy turned the intensity of her stolen sidearm up and fired at him. The fiery bolt put a hole through his helmet and he was still.

That female guard was still a problem. Tammy shot her again before she could get her sidearm out and she watched her go down, realizing that this conflict was anything but emotional. Tammy felt nothing.

A rush of guards was coming, and Tammy started backing towards the shuttle. It took off in a shot, leaving her on an empty landing platform. The first stun pulse set her nerves on fire, and she was on the ground so fast that she didn't remember falling.

The new batch of soldiers had her up on her knees in another room. The patch over her mouth was gone. "I passed out," Tammy said to herself.

"Oh, she's awake," Wheeler said. "Yes, you passed out." His helmet muffled everything he said, but his face was clearly visible through a large faceplate. "Three stun blasts will do that."

"Where am I?" She caught her reflection in a glossy pillar half way across the room. They'd taken her second skin disguise off. It had been a while since she'd seen her own face, it seemed too young somehow.

"My personal command centre," Wheeler said. There were two other officers around. One was a Captain, his brow was furrowed, worry creased. The other was a Rear Admiral and he looked like he'd rather be anywhere else as he watched the holographic status map of the Haven System in the middle of the room. "Tell me, Tammy, what's the morale like on the ground? What do the people think of their new situation?"

"They hate it. They hate you. You're right to live in armour," she replied.

"After all the opportunities I've given them? Almost everyone is employed, there's enough food, shelter and care to go around."

"You've made everything a debt trap and we all know it'll lead to us serving the Order as blaster fodder or worse. We know we're labour, that all the pay we get is going back into the system. It's just another form of slavery."

"Is that what everyone thinks?" Wheeler asked.

Tammy made eye contact with the Captain, who was trying not to seem interested in the conversation. "It's what people believe, but most of them blame you more than they blame the Order. They know you have history with the founders here."

"Yes, they like to kick me around, blame me for all their hardships. They put a bounty on me through the British Alliance, when I was just playing my part, a working man for Regent Galactic. It was the only way to get my life back after I ended up in stasis for years. All they had to do was own up to their crimes like honest people, but they painted me as the bad guy." Wheeler shook his head. "I'm just stumbling through life in this screwed up galaxy like everyone else. That's how I got here, working for the most powerful force in human history, the Order of Eden. They saw my value and gave me a top spot. Now they resent me for taking that power and trying to make this little piece of the galaxy better, I'm sure. I mean, I'm just here to help while they can't take care of this solar system. As soon as people here realize that I have their best interest in mind, they'll turn around."

"I've never heard anyone stitch together more bullshit in one breath..." Tammy didn't get to finish. Wheeler kicked her in the stomach hard enough to send her onto her back.

She didn't get up, instead she fought for breath, it could have been worse, but she knew there would be deep bruises. This was what Frost warned her about so many times that it became annoying. He told her that she should distance herself from the tiny resistance. No one else made it clearer that tears and entitlement would bring her to a bad end. At first she resented him for it, but then she opened her eyes to what was going on and realized that everyone in Haven Shore was at the bottom, more prisoners than peasants. For most of her life she had been surrounded by people who would get her anything she liked, who would do what she liked, but now she was constantly in danger. That realization prompted her to start asking Frost how to survive. He and Nigel were happy to help, and within days she started seeing her old self as a privileged brat.

Breathing got easier as Wheeler paced around her, and Tammy made eye contact with the Captain again, he looked like he was struggling not to be sympathetic, and she let herself feel hopeless just long enough to let a tear slip. "I'm sorry I did that," Wheeler said. "It's just frustrating when people refuse to see what you're trying to do for them. I'm the lesser evil, if I'm evil at all. I'm keeping families together, making sure Haven Shore is mostly untouched. If someone else was in command this place would be cleared out and Order of Eden officers would be moved in or worse. This was almost a brood world! Do you remember that? The invasion? There are people in the Order who think we should just give it to them, but I see value here. I see the people. Even the Nafalli, who have forced us to isolate them on their poisonous plots of land."

"Sir, the broadcast is about to start," one of the lower ranking people sitting around the large holographic projector said.

"Right," Wheeler said. "Sit her down there."

Tammy was picked up and put in the plush chair Wheeler pointed to. Her stomach hurt more, he'd planted the toes of his boot deep in her middle, it hurt to breathe.

"Now, this broadcast is all about Ayan Anderson, the so-called founder. Everyone knows she wasn't here first though, this place is hundreds of years old. Anyway, everyone is about to see what kind of freak she really is," Wheeler said, dropping into a chair beside Tammy.

"I still don't think anyone will believe this," the Rear Admiral said, gracefully sitting down on the edge of a sofa.

"They will, the recording is real, there's no signs of alteration," Wheeler countered.

"Because you staged it with real objects in a real place, not because the situation is as you present it."

"We'll see," Wheeler muttered.

The tactical hologram of the solar system shrank so a broadcast could take up the centre of the room. A large, silvered OEN logo spun in the middle with ORDER OF EDEN NETWORK written under it. Wheeler appeared, he wasn't in his suit but in an Order of Eden dress uniform, his dark green jacket looked crisp and his hair was perfect. "Citizens. I didn't want to show this to you, but my people inform me that the footage you're about to see will be leaked any day now, so I'd rather you see it here first so I can debunk any lies and confirm the truth. What you're about to see is shocking. Ayan Anderson may be a criminal, but I never suspected that she was a deviant, and ghoulish creature that will soon be known for strange practices. I understand that some misguided people love her, so it wounds me that this has to come to light at all. In my opinion she's mentally ill, a clone gone wrong, but some secrets refuse to stay hidden. Without further warning, here is the footage that was stolen from our digital storage. What you are about to see is the unmodified recording of our soldiers first inspection of Ayan Anderson's private quarters."

Wheeler's image faded. The hologram that followed it was a rough recording from the perspective of a soldier as they finished cutting through the locks on a pair of doors. The space within was sparse, with a fish tank wall separating the living room from the bedroom. "Verden, go left, check the bedroom out with Gusten," came the instructions.

The view seemed to be Verden's as he passed through the arch built into the fish tank wall and crossed into the bedroom. A large hologram of Ayan Rice and Jonas Valent hung projected high over the large bed. They were dancing in fine dress, happy, beautiful. The dress in the hologram was hanging in the corner on a mannequin with Ayan Rice's image etched onto it. Freeground uniforms were hanging in large frames. It looked like one was male, the other was female. Verden got close enough to see the small metal plates on each. SERVICE UNIFORM OF AYAN RICE was etched into one and SERVICE UNIFORM OF JONAS VALENT was etched on the other.

The soldier's inspection took him to the closet, and he opened the door with the press of a button. Near the back was a selection of clothes on hangers, nothing unusual for walk-in closet. "Wait, sensors pick up a hidden door," Verden said. He reached out, pushed the clothes at the back aside and found a button near the bottom of the innermost wall. It slipped aside to reveal a full sized dress box. "It's the same as the one Duchess Tammy gave Ayan before we took over," Verden breathed.

Footage of Ayan opening the metre and a half tall dress box appeared in the bottom right corner of the hologram. It was the one Tammy sent her, but the angle didn't reveal what was inside. Ayan smiled as the box opened, peered inside gratefully, then closed it. The video was roughly how Tammy remembered it, but it seemed shorter.

The soldier looked around the hidden compartment at the back of the closet, scanning. There was a framed portrait of Ayan Rice above the box and little holographic candles around it. "Doesn't look like it's trapped," Verden said. "I'm opening it." He pressed the button on the bottom of the dress box and backed away.

The top split into two doors and opened, revealing a corpse dressed in a while vacsuit. There was a scarf in there with her. "Oh, my God, it scans as Ayan Rice. It's Ayan Rice, the Duchess gave Ayan Anderson the corpse of Ayan Rice. This is screwed up," Verden said, taking another good look before backing out of the closet. "What kind of deal were they making? What the hell?" he turned towards the apartment's main room. "Sarge! You have to see this! Sarge!"

The recording ended and Wheeler reappeared. "I'm sorry you had to see that, we've been hiding it for weeks. We had to show Ayan Anderson for what she is; a poor, mentally ill woman who needs our help. The Order would like to capture her alive so we can treat her. Thank you for your attention. Next time I appear, I'll be announcing good news, you have my word."

The hologram faded, and Tammy focused on the tactical map as it enlarged. There were Haven Fleet ships in the solar system, one was the Sunspire, it was marked in three places along patrol or search patterns. "So, how do you think the people in the Haven System will react to that?"

It wasn't until she looked at him that she realized how much she hated Wheeler. It was a furious, reason disrupting hatred, and she gave into it. Tammy leaped from her chair and got her hands on his helmet. The fear on his face through that ultra-clear visor was almost reward enough. "You're wearing this for a good reason, aren't you?" she asked as she struggled to find the emergency release switches for his headgear.

"Get off!" he shouted, panic on his face. He tried to push her off but only grabbed the side of her jumpsuit, ripping it.

One of her fingers caught on something behind the lip of his faceplate and she pressed it. "Is there something in the air? Is this a signal isolation suit? What are you afraid of, freak?"

That made him angry enough for his panic to disappear, and he punched her in the face. Hands grabbed at her from behind, and she was forced onto her knees a moment later, her hands re-bound behind her back. Wheeler re-attached the hidden clasp for his headgear and got to his feet. "I brought you here for your own protection, you know," he said with a sigh. "That was a favour."

You brought me here so I couldn't tell everyone that I brought Ayan a dress and nothing more. Tammy thought, wishing she could say it aloud, but her eye was already stinging from the blow he dealt her. The suit he was wearing must have had some strength augmentation. "Why would you do me a favour?"

"We had a couple good nights after I rescued you," he said.

"You should have left me in stasis. I'd rather die asleep than look at you for another minute."

"All right," Wheeler said. "Put her in holding. Wait, no: put her in isolation. No one talks to her, no one sees her."

"For how long, Sir?" a soldier asked.

"Until I say otherwise," Wheeler said.

The thought of being alone for days, weeks, maybe more terrified Tammy for the first time since the Order came. "I'm sorry, I'll do whatever you want. If you want me to appear beside you in fancy dresses, keep you company, be like I was before with you, then I'll do it. You're right, you rescued me, I owe you everything."

"Too late, bitch," Wheeler said, drawing his sidearm.

"Wait, just wait!" Tammy shouted the instant before her nerves felt like they caught fire. She was still awake, in agony, but still upright on her knees. "You need someone to watch your back," she slurred, the muscles in her face and mouth weren't cooperating. "These Order people don't like you, I can see it."

"Neither do you," Wheeler said. "Next time you wake up, you'll be in a three by seven box."

A second flash of pain filled her and the world disappeared.

FORTY-ONE

The Tourist

THE SCRAPING and clanking of the docking collar on the rear end of the new ship made Noah Lucas cringe as he waited in the main hold on the lower deck. Ammunition, his handguns, the seal on his suit, status of the armour hidden in his long coat and boots, the integrity of his uplink with Elise, the security systems on his ship were all checked and double checked. "Finally," Elise sighed through the sub-dermal communicator he applied minutes before. The docking collar found a fit and the right shape, making a hard seal with the Corsair's rear hatch.

The pair of doors within the ramp parted, and Noah Lucas stepped through. The ten-metre-long plastic hallway was still shifting as though it was windy outside, leftover motion from it snaking around, trying to find the right fit. The ribs and thin plastic didn't look like match protection from the vacuum beyond it, but he wasn't worried. His suit was better. "This embarkation hallway is pretty low quality," Elise said. "Is that common?"

"It's not a military base, so things aren't quite as high spec," Noah replied. He looked ahead to the inner entrance to the station. "I'm thinking the permanent docking fixtures were probably ripped off or crushed. Maybe they're using these temporary ones until they fix them."

"That makes sense," Elise replied. "I see some evidence of twisting and tearing on some of the other docking ports."

The inner doors opened and Noah was confronted by an officer in a blue and green uniform. HARBOUR PATROL was written on his chest. Two imposing looking androids with white skull faces were flanking him. "Hail, Captain Noah Lucas. Normally you'd be greeted by one of the stations security 'bots and they'd take your docking fee, but you put your nose into someone else's business."

"Are you talking about the pirates or the family who were about to be murdered for their cargo? I mean, I guess I got into all their businesses, technically, but I'm wondering what you're more worried about," Noah asked.

"There's a treaty of non-interference between Doxan Three Harbour Patrol and the Shlaki. They believe you were working on our behalf."

"By the Shlaki, are you talking about those pirates that are still twisting in space out there?" Noah asked.

"Considering your ship is called 'The Corsair,' you're one to talk."

"A name I chose for style and my intentions. I like going after a specific faction of spacer. I didn't pick up any of them aboard your station, so you won't have any trouble from me." One of the tall security bots was starting to look him up and down. "I don't like that bot, though. If it scans me again, I'll turn it to scrap."

"Are you trying to put him at ease, or confuse and alarm him?" Elise asked in a whisper.

"What gives you the right to threaten any security entity on this station?" the officer asked.

Noah activated his personal shield and turned it up to maximum. The field cracked and hummed in the air ominously. "Superior firepower and a low tolerance for bullies," Noah replied, his voice warped as it was distorted by the field.

"Ah, confuse and alarm, gotcha. Your mission doesn't include instructions to visit this station, you realize," Elise said directly into his left ear using his implant. "Oh, and I checked. There are twenty-eight different harbour patrol organizations in the solar system from what I could find so far. He only represents this station and a small sliver of space above Doxan Three."

The officer took three steps back and the androids moved in front of him. "What's your business here, Captain?"

"Just thought I'd land and check it out. I'm a tourist," Noah said, watching the androids. They were menacing enough, but only had handguns. They were probably set so they could disable or kill people, but not harm the station.

"Then why get involved with a boarding action?"

"Where I come from, that would have been an illegal boarding action. Piracy. Those idiots would have been overpowered and imprisoned. I was only doing the decent thing, Officer. If the authority you represent doesn't agree that I did the right thing, then I might have to stick around and see who else needs help. I know I couldn't do much, really, save a freighter here, blast some pirates there, but I have friends coming. I'm sure they'd love to join in."

"Sir, please lower your shields and remove your helmet," the Officer said.

"Do you have a supervisor who I could talk to? I feel like we got off on the wrong foot," Noah sighed.

"I think he is the supervisor," Elise said. "He might want to arrest you because he thinks it'll give him leverage when your friends arrive."

Noah snickered, forgetting that only he could hear Elise for a moment.

"Sir, I have to ask that you deactivate your shield..."

"That's not happening," Noah interrupted. "You know, I'm just gonna go. I feel like this could have been handled better - I said some things and you said some things, so it's not entirely on you - so I'll leave and we can all relax for the rest of the day."

He started to turn, then one of the androids fired on him. In that instant, Noah felt like he was back on Iora. His sidearm was in his hand, firing twice at the central power core low on its middle and twice into its rib cage, destroying the battery array there. The other one got the same treatment. Grey metal armour melted, dust from the battery packs turned to liquid, flowing red from the bot's chests, and both of the menacing machines collapsed. Noah didn't point his sidearm at the officer, dropping it into his holster instead. "The only thing worse than pointing a gun in my direction is sicking your skull bots on me."

"They were set to disable your shield and stun," the Officer explained, backing away. "Are you from the Order?"

Noah stopped dead in his tracks. "Would you believe, I'm one of the good guys? The Order would slag this whole station and move on. Besides, they're the guys I was talking about before."

"Why didn't you say you were from the resistance?" the Officer asked, relieved and surprised at the same time.

"Because I..."

"Aren't we here to find resistance members and sell them guns? Look for Mary Reed, who is probably trying to organize resistance groups?" Elise reminded him so rapidly that it was almost unintelligible.

"...I'm here to join the resistance," Noah finished. "I've got a few things they might want."

"I believe you," the Officer said, glancing at one of the bots. It was cooling down, a cracking and hissing sound drifted up from where the battery solution was re-solidifying as it cooled. "Listen, if I knew, if the management knew, then we wouldn't have tried to take you in." he cocked his head for a moment, listening to something only he could hear. "Yes, Commander," he said, looking back to Noah. "The station Commander wants me to convey his apologies. Your ship will be safe docked here for a while, maybe a few hours before someone tries to steal it."

"Don't worry, she can defend herself. Besides, I don't think I'll be staying very long." Noah reached into his pocket and felt for a thin, rectangular platinum coin. "Do you know where resistance folks meet up? I'd like to start making connections." He handed two of the coins to the officer. "One's for the bots, the other is for the information."

"The Dark Room," he replied. "It's a bar under the reactor, doesn't have any windows, recording devices don't work there," he said. "I'll walk you there."

FORTY-TWO

Departure

THE PELICAN, with the Rassaaga as escort, was on its way out of Order of Eden territory. The planned trajectory of its journey to the War Forge was on the large hologram hovering in the middle of the largest presentation room aboard the Merciless. There were only seventy seats including several boxes high on the sloping circle of sections. Minh-Chu and Jake stood in the highest of the boxes, made for presenters and higher ranking individuals so they were eye level with the huge hologram.

The entire route across three sectors leading from Nuaji to the Zato System, where the fleet was gathering so it could be on the edge of Mergillian territory. "What's the mix of civilians and fighters on the Pelican?" Minh-Chu asked, looking to his right where the hologram of Ayan Anderson started to appear.

"Fifty-eight to forty-two," Jake replied. "Not what anyone was hoping for.

"But in numbers that the War Forge can accommodate. We're building the internal workings for another mobile station, too," Ayan added as her hologram increased resolution. It was almost as if she was right there, between Minh-Chu and Jake, "I'm sorry I'm late, Lamonthe had questions about his new role. Well, complaints, more like. He still wants full control of Intelligence, but we're going with your suggestion, Jake," she said. "More delegation, less compartmentalization with the exception of SOCU. That's all yours now. The only question is, what else do you need?"

"I don't know yet," Jake said, looking at the other lines leading away from Nuaji and the Kedan System. They represented ships that either headed to Dulo or parts unknown. There was a lot less data to go on there, thus those lines were fading as the map aged. Over sixty ships refused to join Haven Fleet, and he understood why. Ayan's hologram followed his eye line to the fading red course lines. "When do you think you'll rejoin the rest of the fleet?" she asked.

"As soon as I know that it's the right move for the Merciless. I ordered the Excalibur to the next rendezvous to fill the gap. They need some help from fleet, too. They have the lowest efficiency and morale rating."

"I know, we're just having trouble moving people around," Ayan said. "Oz is considering turning the Excalibur into a training ship, keeping the adequate members of the crew there as they train up under new leadership while we pull the rest back to the War Forge so they can start all over again."

"Good," Jake said. He was horrified at the reports coming from the Excalibur. There was evidence that everyone from the First

Officer down were making reports that didn't match the accident record in the ship's computer. They were averaging nine major accidents aboard per week, ranging from overloaded capacitor banks to a hangar hatch opening while technicians were working in the bay, resulting in several people being spaced. One of them didn't make it back on board. Getting that crew broken up, reassessed and retrained was the only solution as far as Jake was concerned, and he was happy to hear that it would be in Oz's hands. The Rassaaga, in contrast, had one accident worthy of note on file - a fire in the galley - with no casualties and every report on the incident lined up perfectly. Their efficiency had room for improvement, but Jake had no doubt that the ship, captain and crew were ready for combat.

Those fading red lines leading from Nuaji to several other points recalled his attention, though. He straightened his sleeves, gathering his thoughts. "What's up, Jake?" Minh-Chu asked.

"Most of the people who wouldn't join us were fighters. Every one of those departure points probably represents a resistance cell. The Order let them get away, probably because the notion of fighting us when they didn't have a battlegroup nearby didn't make sense when they have a good chance of catching those cells further down the line."

"A lot about Nuaji doesn't make sense," Minh-Chu said. "I shouldn't have been able to drop a bomb on that cruiser, and when I did, I shouldn't have been able to get away."

"You were being studied," Ayan said. "It's the only thing that answers all the outstanding questions."

"You're right, I've had that thought too. That's one of the reasons why the Merciless hasn't moved on. I want to see what they do with Nuaji next, and if they send bots out to repair or replace the sensor sites we destroyed."

"They haven't repaired anything," Minh-Chu said. "So they were for us. They were trying to detect us."

"Now they've either assumed we've gone, which is mostly true, since the Merciless is watching from outside the solar system, or they have the data they needed," Ayan concluded.

"Either way, watching us cost them," Minh-Chu said, dropping into a chair, letting it swivel all the way around, stopping when he was facing the hologram again.

The courses of the resistance ships that went their own way were wiped out as Jake updated the map. "So, the Merciless will move on in a couple hours. Finn is almost finished looping the rest of our quad drives in, so we should be able to re-join the fleet soon." He shook his head at the travel pattern he saw. The Fleet was only getting further away from the Haven System. "The crew on my ship feel like we're running away. It looks like that from here."

"We are, but only to find a foothold in a more defensible area," Ayan said. "The Mergillians are great allies, but they can't afford to publicly harbour us. More Nafalli will be joining us soon, several thousand fighters who want to train, but they don't have territory or modern fighting ships. The fleet is growing even faster than expected, but it's still going to take time for us to take the Haven System back, if we ever do. We're being forced to look for a longer term solution, for all we know that could be where we settle for a long time."

"What about the people we left behind in Haven?" Jake asked, keeping a level head. It wasn't an argument, it was a strategic meeting, he reminded himself.

"Maybe SOCU could work with Phase Seven and create a plan?" Minh-Chu asked. "Admiral Rice has five Sunspire Class ships ready within an hour of the Haven System along with manned corvettes and nine destroyers. With a battlegroup like that she could do a lot."

Jake nodded. "Our plan to return to the Haven System when the Order's coverage thins out isn't looking as good now, because Wheeler has his own battlegroup with two more for support, and nothing's moving. Admiral Rice's fleet is big, powerful, maybe a few ships could join her and we could get our own people out of Haven Shore if we were quick."

"Stephanie's still hidden, she hasn't missed a check-in with the Sunspire yet," Ayan said. "She says organizing a resistance is slow, though. The Order has a stranglehold on Haven Shore. Outlying cities are being emptied, their people are being taken off world if they pledge to the Order with the leftovers getting moved to Haven Shore so the Order can monitor them more easily," Ayan said.

"So, no matter what we do we'll be abandoning people in the Haven System," Jake said. "I see the wisdom in getting as many people as we can and getting out before we take too many casualties, but the whole fleet could lose heart if it looks like we're leaving the Haven System behind."

"Unless we plant our feet somewhere else, somewhere we can mount a real defence and wave a flag so the galaxy knows the Order can't wipe us out," Ayan said.

With a gesture, Jake brought up the report he just received from Noah Lucas. Using recordings of a conflict with some pirates, and the gratefulness of the family aboard the hauler he saved, Noah explained what his arrival in the Doxan system was like and what he planned to do. Angel's Landing looked like a hundred different drift stations that Jake had seen in his travels, and he was fairly sure Noah could take care of himself. The report ended and Minh-Chu laughed for a moment, clapping his hands a few times. "That's

Carnie; gets into the system with instructions to take a look around while he waits for backup and he ends up making an enemy while he makes a save. The whole system will be talking about that by now."

"Oh, his new artificial intelligence forwarded a local news feature," Jake said, bringing up the Hart News recording. The Corsair flew close to an observation satellite, which recorded him firing at the pirate destroyer, a ship with mismatched armour plating and weapons. Another satellite picked the action up from the opposite angle and zoomed in as the Clever Class Corvette began pursuit of one of the fighters with surprising agility. "This ship, the Corsair, came to the rescue of the Freighter Honopu. Stenob's Pride, a Shlaki pirate ship that has been spotted harassing and capturing ships coming in to the end of the deceleration zones on the edge of the Doxan System, was effectively destroyed thanks to some good shooting by the Corsair using some kind of armour piercing weapon. The Honopu was repaired by drones launched by the Corsair, who helped the freighter get underway. The Stenob's Pride has been abandoned and will be tagged for salvage if it isn't removed in three hours from the time of this broadcast. Hart News had the ship scanned and we can confirm that only the main reactors have been destroyed, effectively scrapping the ship, but there should be plenty of salvage for anyone brave enough to claim it. Stenob's Pride isn't the only destroyer owned by the Shlaki, so this Newscaster advises caution to anyone who wants to board the destroyer. In other news, a Flesh Tech Bio Fabrication Facility inside the Coreward Sector of Obun has been raided, its employees taken. A ransom demand has been issued by an unknown party. If the current pattern holds. This is the third such raid and ransom act in two weeks, with estimated damages near the trillion credit mark.

A representative from Flesh Tech had..." the holographic feed cut out there.

"So, that was Hart News, but for what area?" Ayan asked.

"Local to Doxan. Other affiliates might pick it up," Minh-Chu replied. "One more rescue like that and he'll be famous if a news agency broadcasts it wide."

"Wait, this tells us something about the Doxan system," Jake said. "If answering a distress call and defeating pirates there is so unusual that Hart News covers it for a couple minutes, then that whole system must be a mess. People will be watching him, those pirates are going to be gunning for him, whatever he does next will be noticed."

"Yeah," Minh-Chu said. "His artificial intelligence, Elise, says he's going to a local bar so he can start looking for a resistance group. I would have let things cool down, waited for Alice to get there first."

"You know, I'd like to think I would too, but..." Jake shook his head.

"But you'd do exactly what Noah's doing, start exploring," Ayan said. "Because you'd be restless after getting turned around a few times by command."

"You know me too well," Jake snickered. He sobered then, there was a good idea behind what Noah was doing. "All this could get him in a position to be known, to start his arms dealing career. The most reckless rebels will approach him first, and he can sell them everything they can afford. Maybe even cut them a deal since he's just getting into the trade. They'll hit Order targets using new fire-power, maybe tell him what their next target is."

"Once they trust him, the more strategic groups may approach him," Ayan said.

"Right." Jake brought up the map outlining the departure routes of the ships from Nuaji carrying people who didn't want to join Haven Fleet. "No matter what Alaka told them, they weren't sticking around to join us. They wanted to fight in their own way, going after targets that they chose. We didn't stop them, it's not our place, but we could have armed them better than we did. Sure, we sent them off with a few hundred guns that were a few generations behind, a couple thousand armoured vacsuits, but we could have done more. Real armour, a few ships missing our proprietary tech, and some real firepower that has been out there for ages. Most of the stuff they were fighting with wasn't military grade." He pulled a shield disc from his pocket and put it on the railing's edge. "This tech is easy for us to reproduce, but it'll burn the fabrication heads out on non-Haven ships after getting through most of one. Even still, there isn't a bit of tech in this little shield emitter disc that isn't known."

"But the difficulty in making them makes them expensive," Minh-Chu said. "Unless the fabricator on the Corsair is churning them out. He could probably do twenty an hour using some water and a few ounces of heavy metal, right?"

"Easily, and it wouldn't wear out the heads on his fabrication system because they'll regenerate for months," Ayan said. "But I think you have a bigger point to make?"

"Right. There will always be a certain type of freedom fighter who wants to sign up with Haven Fleet," Jake said. "They'll come looking for us if we score a major public victory against the Order soon. More importantly to Carnie are the people who want to fight, but don't want to sign up. Sure, we won't get to control them, but if he and Alice could work as a team, they could find resistance groups who are fighting the Order for the right reasons and equip them for a discount. The rest, well, Noah doesn't have to deal with them. If Noah and Alice do this right, there could be tens of thousands or more very dangerous rebels tearing the Order apart. Imagine hundreds of groups with real firepower going after their own Order targets, raiding, destroying, disrupting their operations in ways that are more difficult to predict than anything we do."

"Maybe we could even coordinate with a few after a while," Ayan said.

"Exactly, and there's a good chance that Mary Reed will surface eventually. If Noah and Alice become the best arms dealers in the sector, she'll have to meet with them sometime, especially if we send Remmy Sands to work with them. Let him be a visible figure," Jake said. "I'll build SOCU up from within while they're gone so it's a full-fledged unit and I'll make sure they have support."

"This operation is getting bigger by the second," Ayan said, sounding unsure.

"It'll cost the fleet one destroyer," Jake said. "One with a full fabrication system installed so it can make a few fighters at a time or even a corvette class ship, just not one of ours. We'll rip off a good manufacturer's design or use one of the last designs Freeground put out before they merged with our fleet."

"I can spare that, we have a destroyer with no crew in the War Forge. It would take about eight hours to build the kind of fabrication system you need inside and we can rig it to have a crew of nine, minimum," Ayan said, brightening a little. "You'll want more, though. I'm sure Oz can send us some promising trainees who won't take advantage of a command structure with a relaxed attitude."

"All right, if you could get someone on that, Minh and I can put some kind of plan together for Alice and Noah. I want them to run this their way, it's their boots on the ground, but it'll help if they know what kind of backup they can get if they need it. While we wait for their destroyer, I'll have someone brief Remmy and the Merciless will..." A red bloom appeared on the holographic map in orbit around Nuaji. "Wait, there's a trans-dimensional gate opening in orbit around Nuaji right now," Jake said.

"I see it, but that's not our signature, it's not Edxian either," Ayan said. Five ships nearly half a kilometre long emerged, three of them increased speed towards the surface of the planet. Each of the ships was heavily armoured, their scanners were high powered, reaching out in all directions. "We're checking their profiles now, but I think I know what they are. We found a ship similar to those near an abandoned moon base in the system we just left. It sent encrypted transmissions though wormholes, but it was old, dormant for well over a century as far as we could tell."

"The Merciless is cloaked and well out of scan range. Our relay is sending this information back to us," Jake said.

Minh-Chu got to his feet. "I'll get my guys ready, just in case we have to launch."

"Sir, this is the bridge," Liara said, her hologram appearing on the railing in front of him. "One of the new ships is scanning our sensor relay and breaking off from the main group. Tactical believes it means to capture it."

"Activate the self-destruct," Jake said.

The hologram of Nuaji and the area around it froze as sensor data stopped travelling between the sensor relay. "The signal went through, the probe is destroyed," Liara reported.

"Thank you, it's time for the Merciless to move on."

"I'll link you to the Captain," Liara said.

Agameg appeared in her place. "Sir, should we investigate the ships around Nuaji?"

Jake took a look at the holographic map and zoomed in on the brown and black planet. At the time their sensor relay was destroyed, the ships were entering the atmosphere. Large scoops were opening along the sides, and a broad energy beam was extending to the ground. "What is that for?"

"We have a theory here," Agameg said. "It's a directed gravitational beam. The area of ground its targeting is covered with nanobots that self-destructed."

"The ones that tore the surface of the planet apart," Jake nodded. "They're taking them?"

"We can't tell for certain, but it looks that way," Agameg said. "There is a small chance that they could piece the technology together from the remains of thousands of nanobots."

"Was our scan relay probe cloaked when one of their ships broke off and headed in its direction?"

"Yes, but it was transmitting to us using a micro-wormhole, so the cloak was not at full effectiveness," Agameg replied.

"So, we know they have high-end scanning technology," Jake said.

"And they have multiple high gain antennae," Ayan added. "Just like the ship we encountered at our end. There is a chance that it detected the transmission of a report on Nuaji. It was encrypted, but the Triton was receiving it while they were in pursuit of their old ship. We've confirmed that the configuration is similar enough for them both to be of a similar origin."

"So these could be the same people," Jake said. "Are they using our trans-dimensional technology?"

"No, definitely not. Our working theory is that it was stolen or traded from the Edxi," Ayan said. "It's slower, but the fact that they can navigate through trans-dimensional space says something about the sophistication of their science. The Order tried and failed to figure it out and we needed Lorander to get us started. If they did it on their own, or were able to get the Edxi to teach them how to use it, then they could be dangerous. Do you think we should approach them?"

"I'm going to try," Jake said. "But I'm going to be careful. Captain Agameg, put the ship on full alert."

FORTY-THREE

The Encounter

AGAMEG RAN the ship from the captain's chair. It was his place, he'd earned it in more than one way. His leadership of a strike-and-fade defence team when the Triton was boarded was still legendary. He guided his own education since then, following everything Jacob and several other captains did as the fleet grew, examining their victories and failures while he completed every qualification examination that he could. If there was a captain Jake hoped to never face off against, it was Captain Agameg Price. He thought like most aquatically based people, in multiple dimensions at once, could keep track of several complex situations at a time for long periods, and he didn't fatigue for weeks, even longer if he had time to rest every day. After being with humans for years, he finally mastered the art of sleeping two to three hours a night so he no longer had to hibernate for several days in one stretch each month.

He still enjoyed that kind of deep rejuvenation, but it wasn't necessary anymore.

Looking up to Agameg, where he sat in the best seat on the Merciless' bridge only added to Jake's confidence as he split his attention between the communications and scanning and sciences stations. The Merciless slipped into position several hundreds of thousands of kilometres away from Nuaji, letting the intense scanning pulses from the newcomer's ships do the work for them. The passive scanning systems aboard the Merciless were getting plenty of data from the second hand energy as it penetrated and bounced off everything in that region of the solar system, including one of the newcomer ships. "What facts do we have so far?" Jake asked Kadri as she worked at her console. There were six other scanning crew around her, busy running the data from the sensors through analysis software as it came in, examining the results.

"These are definitely the same android type as the ones that the fleet encountered," Kadri said, bringing up a cross-section of the one that was taken aboard the War Forge after it was briefly activated. With a flick of her hand another cross section appeared. "It took a lot of raw scan data to put this second image together, but we got a complete picture of one of them. I'd say the original, the one aboard the War Forge, is about two hundred years old. The tech is still amazing, they're analysing it, everyone wants samples and scan time, but it's an older version of artificial neural tissue technology." She focused in on the heads of both of them, pointing to a thick strip of brain that was interconnected with a cybernetic casing. "Here there are actual wires, they're made of some kind of neural chain materials, so they're not like wires we use. No, they have built in buffering, they can sense electrical fields, feed data to the synthetic brain and store overflow. It's like they're super-wires, providing something like a sixth sense. That was two hundred years ago."

"The new version looks different, no wires," Jake said, looking at the scan of the new android from the nearest newcomer ship. The synthetic neural tissue looked more like half chewed gum that had been tied and twisted into waves and knots. It was submerged in a blue and green fluid inside a thick case.

Kadri looked over her shoulder at a dark-haired young Nafalli. He smacked his lips nervously, but pushed on to explain what they were looking at. "Admiral Valent," he started. "Yes, um, yes, the new brain is denser. You can see in its shape, but you'd expect that after two centuries. The liquid around it is conductive, we're still analysing the solution. It's like a neural fluid that makes connections and does everything those wires that weren't just wires in the older version did. So, there's extra processing power, memory, and all kinds of other stuff in that gel. By 'stuff' I mean, well, a lot, like a solution that protects the neural tissue from disease, nanowires that form and dissolve as they're needed, and we have to assume that the ability to feel different types of energy carried forward to this, more current model, because there's no way I'd leave a whole new sense behind after having it in a previous version. I mean, would you? Anyway, these things, these androids are fascinating. There are two sub-processor clusters under the synthetic tissue brain, our best theory is that they work in tandem, assisting with locomotion, sensation, even communicating with the entity inside. They could be supplementary computing power, but the way they're connected suggests more of a companion computer like our command and control units than a secondary processing system."

"So they would have a mental connection to their command and control systems," Jake said.

"Exactly. Like the nervous system interface that's in all our com-con units, only this can answer your questions, communicate and show you data at the speed of thought. I might be getting ahead of myself, here, but I don't think these people see reality the way we do. I believe they can see sensor data the way we see everything around us. These secondary processor nodes also connect to exterior ports, so there's every reason to believe that they connect to their computers directly."

"That does extend through their nervous system," Kadri said. "By touching an active surface with their finger, they could make a direct mental connection with a computer, or a whole ship, if the Ensign is right. I think he is."

"Right. For all the advancements, though, they still use a rather primitive set of servos, power unit and skin. They don't have much of a sense of smell, taste or touch as far as we can tell, all those synthetic systems are primitive. The nerve conductivity is at human speed, too, at least, away from the brain, which suggests a few things that I don't want to speculate on just yet," the Ensign said.

"Thank you, this is good, this is a lot of information," Jake said. "What about their ship?"

"Their weaponry isn't elegant, they use pulse cannons and a couple rapid fire rail guns, but their missile systems are brilliant. They're rapid fire, they can empty a bay of thirty missiles registering at three tons each in five seconds or less," Kadri said. "Each one of those missiles carries between three and ninety projectiles, depending on the load. Two of their ships could take the Merciless down. Their thruster technology is primitive, so they're not manoeuvrable, but their shields are tough, using three quarters of the energy they generate on board to maintain. It's a sloppy, outdated barrier type technology, but as long as their reactors are running we wouldn't get through with most of our weapons."

"Any other stand-out differences?" Jake asked.

"The antenna and sensor receptors are plates that run the length of the ship. They're impossible to pick out with the naked eye. There are thousands of armoured plates sensitive to all kinds of energy, they're probably part of their power generation system, too, we just haven't gotten enough data to determine that. There are a hundred fifty androids on each ship exactly, they move like humans and still use verbal speech. Everything else is speculation now, but we're getting more data every second, so we'll learn more."

"Wait, isn't this some kind of antenna?" Jake asked, pointing at the new and old versions of the androids. There was a conspicuous wire running down the necks of each out to their left shoulder under their skin.

"We're still confirming that," Kadri said. "But we suspect it is."

A high priority communication prompted Jake to look at his command and control unit, where he found Ayan, who was aboard the War Forge, opening a call to Quan, who was aboard the Clever Dream. It started, and Jake turned on privacy mode as he found a seat in the communications station. "Jake, I wanted you to listen in on this," Ayan said as Quan's face appeared opposite hers.

"I'm listening," Jake said.

"Quan, I tried talking to the Lorander leadership aboard the War Forge, but they shut up as soon as I showed them an image of the ships the Merciless is about to open communications with. That's when I put the call out and you signalled that you knew something about these people?"

"We don't have a name for them," Quan said. Deep lines of worry creased his face. Alice sat down behind him in the seat above in the Clever Dream's gathering space. "My people call them Raiders. They send expeditions into areas where there's some kind of technology or resource that they don't have and steal whatever they can, killing anything that gets in their way. We've been able to fight them off when we were prepared, but they're dedicated and fearless."

"So, they steal technology? That's what they're after?" Jake asked.

"Yes, and other items of value. Certain rare raw materials that are difficult to produce synthetically are particularly important to them. I know of one world that had whole continents stripped down to bedrock for Omirdom, a material that formed in swamp land there. I'm sure there's a lot I'm forgetting, but that example stands out. An aquatic species much like the Mergillians were wiped out completely for that resource," Quan said. "There's one thing that I believe informs everything else, though. The Raiders are not people. They are things. Like a mechanic uses a spanner, the people behind the Raiders use their androids. We've detected signs of live communication between Raider ships and androids extending into trans-dimensional space. We've cut that off, thinking that the Raiders would be unable to function without the live link, and it failed. I don't know how, exactly, but we learned that every Raider android has a whole mind uploaded into it. The Raiders start out as empty androids, then their faces and body shapes change to suit the mind that's uploaded. Whoever controls them are masters at copying a consciousness into a complex synthetic brain, and when a Raider is successful, their ship departs for a place we haven't seen. The theory is that the people, probably humans or human like, put the captured technologies and resources to work for them, but that's not important. The most important..."

"Admiral, something is detecting the signal from the quad drive," Liara said, quietly alarmed. "They're tracking the communication back to us."

"...thing to know is that Raiders don't care if they die. That's what makes them dangerous," Quan finished in a rush.

Jake disconnected from the call and looked to Agameg. "Reset all quad drives immediately."

Agameg nodded at Finn, who was beside him. "Resetting now," Finn replied.

"Thank you," Jake said to Liara. "Who was tracing that signal?"

"The new ships, that one in particular, number three," she pointed at the tactical display at the front of the bridge. "They probably knew where we were for a few seconds."

Ashley was already piloting the Merciless out of the area using a jagged, difficult to predict course. Jake made his way to the command seating and pushed Agameg back down in the captain's seat when he started to stand. He sat to his left instead. "I need you to prepare our simplest drone," Jake said. "I'll record a message into it, we'll launch it then see what happens when it broadcasts from a distance."

Agameg nodded at the tactical station, and two crewmembers got to work on it right away. He turned back to Jake. "Admiral, I'd like to mention that we are operating under the assumption that our cloaking systems are working. That may not be the case. Scanning rays have swept through our location five times. Our readings indicate that our cloaking systems worked, but..."

"Operate however you see fit," Jake said in a whisper. "If you think we've been detected, then act accordingly."

"We're ready for you to record your message," Liara said.

Jake stood and took his place in the middle of the bridge.

"Record holographic, video and audio data isolating me. Do not include visual or audio background information." A holographic pointer appeared in front of him, focused on his face. It turned red. "Greetings from Haven Fleet. I am Admiral Jacob Valent and would like to open a dialogue. We are not the dominant power in the area and will be leaving soon, but we are in search of allies. With that in mind, I'd like to discuss a trade or cultural alliance. We are at war with the Order of Eden, Regent Galactic and their subsidiaries. You can contact us using the drone I've sent towards Nuaji, the planet your ships are currently orbiting." He nodded, and Liara deactivated the recording. "Good, send that to the drone, make sure it's not carrying any other important information, and launch."

"Yes, Sir," Agameg said. "That was carried out exactly as regulations suggest."

Jake sat down beside Agameg. "I haven't had the most reliable track record with diplomacy. May as well follow the rulebook, see how that works."

"Ready to launch the drone," Lieutenant Commander Huun announced from the tactical station.

"When the drone is launched, we will retreat to the asteroid I've selected," Agameg said. "Do it your way, Ashley."

"Yes, Captain," she replied. "Course plotted and ready."

"Fire the drone, Lieutenant Commander," Agameg said. "Be ready to set all shields to a high cycle rate, just in case."

The drone launched and the Merciless took a drastic turn away, rotating so its narrowest edge was facing the newcomer ships. Intense energy beams focused on the drone, then waved around it, looking for the origin point. "Scanning beams," Kadri said. "More intense than anything I've ever seen. One just passed over us."

The beam tried to keep up with the Merciless, trying to predict its trajectory, but failed as Ashley took them into a jagged turn upwards. "That beam detected something," Jake said. "Enough so they knew to keep looking, at least."

"The drone is playing your message," Liara said.

"Both the newcomer ships that were collecting nanobots on the planet surface are leaving, making best speed off Nuaji towards the drone, towards us," Huun said. "Generally."

"Ship Four has launched a missile with a grabber on the end towards the drone," Kadri said.

"Impact in seven seconds," Huun said.

"Is there any tech aboard that drone that's better than what they have?" Jake asked.

"Micro-servos and the battery," Kadri said, everyone at the sciences station nodding.

"Would they have gotten everything they needed from a scan to learn about those technologies?" Agameg asked.

"No, the drones have shielding," Kadri said.

"Activate its self-destruct," Jake ordered.

Huun pressed three sections of his control panel and the drone exploded an instant before the missile grappled with it. "Nothing remains."

Three of the newcomer ships opened missile bays and fired a barrage of barrel shaped projectiles. They accelerated at an incredible pace. "They're destroying the asteroid," Ashley said. "They're getting rid of our cover."

"Time to go," Jake said.

"I agree, Admiral," Agameg said, turning to the helm. "Ashley, open a wormhole that will take us out of the solar system and begin plotting a trans-dimensional course back over the Order of Eden territorial line."

"Aye," Ashley replied, two members of the sciences team joined her navigator so they could assist with the calculations as the Merciless turned away from the asteroid. The first of the newcomer missiles activated, beginning a chain of nuclear explosions that pummelled the asteroid, enveloping it in light.

"These are definitely the Raiders Quan was talking about," Jake said.

"Admiral, I could use you at tactical, if you would do us the honour," Agameg said in a hurry.

Jake stood and took Huun's place at his station. "Orders?"

"Those three Raider ships are coming. As I suspected, they're using the high energy pulses from the nuclear explosions to find us," Agameg said.

There was less then point three percent damage to the shields, Jake noted, but that only meant that they were close enough to catch some of the blast. It might have been enough for the Raider ships to detect them. "How much force do you want me to use if they open fire on us?"

"Admiral's discretion," Agameg said. "How are you doing on that wormhole, Ashley?"

"We need a few more seconds, there's a lot of energy dissipating out there," she replied.

The three Raider ships launched ten torpedoes each. They accelerated quickly. Jake saw the scan results and shook his head. Each of them had hundreds of small missiles made to send millions of grains of iron in all directions when they exploded. It was the simplest system he'd ever seen to detect cloaking devices. If they went off and the grains were energized, they would definitely be revealed. "They're going to detect us," Jake said. "They have a system." The torpedoes were slowly closing, using solid fuel they had an advantage.

"Are you certain? We may only need a minute," Agameg said, looking at the trajectory of the Merciless as it accelerated away from Nuaji. The torpedoes were going to miss, but not by much.

"I'm sure," Jake said.

"Then we will be detected on our terms," Agameg said. "Ashley, we are opening a trans-dimensional portal as soon as possible, abandoning the step of using a wormhole. I believe the risk of them learning from our quad drive system is lesser than the risk we take by prolonging our stay."

"Yes, Sir, we'll be out of here in twenty seconds," Ashley replied.

"Admiral, fire at will at the torpedoes. If the ships fire on us again, then use whatever force you deem necessary to ensure our escape."

Jake ordered the heavy railgun turrets along the bottom of the hull to aim at the Raider ships. Locking the beam weapons on the torpedoes was automatic, as simple as selecting his targets then setting the power to full, enough to melt through the hull of an Order of Eden destroyer in less than a second, before activating them. Lines of perfect white light were drawn between the beam emitters and the torpedoes as the Merciless's precision weapons obliterated them.

All three Raider ships opened up with pulse weapons and cannons. Gravitational shielding slowed the projectiles down while acting as a lens, reducing the effectiveness of the energy weapons. The barrier shields took the rest of the damage, some sections at the rear were battered down to eighty-four percent before Finn increased the power.

The Merciless' heavy railguns opened up, twin barrels rapid firing tons of energized metal at the lead Raider ship first. The Raider's shields held for several seconds, and Jake watched as the Merciless' rear shields started to fail, falling from eighty-four to seventy-seven, then to seventy, and finally sixty-three before he drew energy from the reserve capacitors, bringing them back up to eighty-five.

The lead Raider ship's shields continued to stop the barrage of railgun fire, and Jake pointed the beam weapons at it. They were at full charge.

"Tactical, report?" Agameg asked.

"Their shielding is holding," Jake said. "But I have a theory. The bubble is about to pop." He activated the beam weapons, focusing in on a pinpoint. Dense metal battered the Raider ship's shields, a steady pummelling that even Frost would be proud of from the ship's heavy lower guns. The beam weapons finished firing, the capacitors down ten percent.

"Jake?" Agameg asked, worried as the Merciless' rear shield took a sudden dip below seventy percent.

All at once the lead Raider ship's shields disappeared, and its thick but bare hull was hammered by tons of high speed metal. The vessel turned away, the ships flanking it moved into the path of the Merciless' firepower as they followed. "Their shields are tied directly into a reactor," Jake said. "They don't lose integrity until they burn out completely."

The Merciless slipped into trans-dimensional space and was hundreds of thousands of kilometres away seconds later. "I'm happy you were right," Agameg said, his green eyes wide. "Huun, did you learn anything?"

"Yes," the Nafalli Tactical Officer said. "Thank you, Admiral."

"There's a more important lesson here," Jake said as he stepped aside and gestured for Lieutenant Commander Huun to take his place. "That was how much firepower the Raiders use when they want to learn about something. They were going light on us, trying to stop us from leaving." He pointed to the segments of their rear shielding that took the most damage. "Every shot they took was aimed at our main thrusters. If they wanted to kill us they would have had a chance."

"I hope they don't appear outside of Order Space," Finn said.

"That's where we encountered them first," Jake replied. "I have a feeling these guys will be a problem for everyone. Liara," Jake said, walking down to the communications section of the bridge. "I'm going to need your help. We're drafting a message to the Order of Eden. We're going to send the data we collected on these people and warn them."

"Wait," Ashley said. "We should just leave them here, hope that these Raiders start messing them up."

Jake brought up the incomplete scan they had of one of the Raider ships. "Look at it, half the ship is dedicated to weaponry or defence. The rest is reserved for launch craft including fighters and these combat shuttles. Power generation, communications, sensors, and the other essentials are all so well integrated that they take up almost no room. They don't have sleeping quarters from what we can tell from this scan, they don't have a leisure area, not even a galley."

"Nor should there be one," Kadri said. "Haven Sciences confirms: the two-hundred-year-old android can survive on nine calories a day and doesn't have to recharge for two hundred hours. I'm sure the newer version's requirements are even lower. Oh, and they can survive in space for years."

"The point I'm making is that these androids and their ships are made to fight. We have some simulations to run, and I'd like your help, Ash, but I bet one of those ships could take out a pair of Order destroyers without a scratch. We had to use more firepower than those same destroyers would have to scare one off."

"So, the Order would get wrecked," Ashley said with a shrug. "We'd have a while to power up, get ready."

"Maybe," Jake said. "But maybe not. We don't know how many of them there are. They could come after our tech while they pick a few things up from the Order, or just skip them entirely. If it were me, I'd steal their data and find out where I could find Haven Fleet tech. Ship to ship, we have the best technology by far, and if Lorander's people have trouble with these Raiders in another galaxy, then we're in trouble. My hope is that the Order of Eden gets distracted, puts the Raiders down or drives them out. It could give us a good opening. The better their chances are, the less we have to worry about these Raiders ourselves."

"That makes sense," Ashley said. "Sorry Cap, I mean Admiral."

"I think it's about time you started calling me Jake," he whispered as he passed by on his way to his quarters. "I'll see you and Minh at the end of your duty shift."

FORTY-FOUR

Introductions

THE SMELL of burnt electronics barely hid the stench of sweat and whatever else the variety of species that visited the Dark Room. It wasn't the kind of place Noah Lucas would go if he had a choice. All were not welcome. If someone was having too much fun, which included dancing, yelling, or drawing any attention to themselves, they were hushed by their friends. The whole place looked like thousands had been through there since it opened with a pile of broken chairs in the corner, booths made of hard plastic, tables that no amount of wiping would clean completely, and a pockmarked floor. He hoped he was stepping on snacks from the bar when he felt something crunching underfoot while he put his drink order in.

If it were up to him, the bar would be clean, invite people who were there for a good time, have a dance floor and drink service that didn't only offer pre-sealed manufactured beverages. Instead of flashy, flirty clothing people who went to the Dark Room were in spacer clothes or armour. He snickered to himself as he pictured a Sigren in a miniskirt. The creature had an oval torso with a head stalk, not a neck, and she didn't have arms, but three fingers that extended a metre from each side of her body with many joints. She did have legs, but they were larger versions of her arms, extending below from a hip that was split high up the middle. He could tell it was a female because she was missing the outrageously coloured fins along her neck and shoulders. The males were the flamboyant ones.

Three Surge Gulp energy drinks in, and no one from the station or the resistance had so much as nibbled on the bait he threw out when he boarded. Noah knew he was being too obvious. Asking the security guard where the resistance met up was a bit like asking a cop where he could hire a hitman. Sure, there were cities where he'd get a straight answer if he dropped a few credits in the cop's palm, but it wasn't the best move. He was too clean and his armour didn't look like anything you could get on the open market. For anyone who knew, they could probably pick him out as someone from Haven Shore, the desertion story would only get him into more trouble if he started spreading it around too early. A man alone with all kinds of amazing tech could find himself cornered quickly.

He still wanted to accomplish something while he waited for Alice to catch up, though. Noah looked forward to a reunion so much that he couldn't focus if he let himself think about it. Her advice would go a long way, he was sure, but that wasn't the main reason why he wanted her there. An apology was owed, and he wanted to see how things had changed since his breakup and turnabout. It was worrying, not knowing. For all he knew he could have smothered whatever magic they had.

Shaking his head, he opened the last tall can of Surge Gulp. The stuff claimed to sharpen senses and keep energy levels high. It did so, but only just enough so he could tell. Noah drank it because it tasted like tangerine, not that he'd had one before, but that's the flavour that was written on the can. Noah sat back and looked at the bar's main attraction. A transparent section of the ceiling allowed the patrons to see the circle of white fire in the station's main fusion reactor. There was some kind of filter in place, otherwise it would be too bright to look at, but the light of the reactor illuminated most of the space.

Noah was on the edge of the light. He avoided a bad move by choosing a seat that wasn't in shadow. Those darkened booths and tables in the far corners were great places to get trapped by a few heavily armed thugs. "You keep looking up at that," Elise said through his subdermal communicator. "Is it pretty?"

"Yeah, I like it. It's not every day you can see a fusion reaction with the naked eye, even if it is through a metre and a half of transparesteel."

"It's not a very efficient reaction, that's why the pattern of the flame is so random, with those white plumes and surges."

"Beauty and efficiency don't always have much in common. One's subjective, the other isn't.," Noah replied.

"Oh, a lot of things make more sense now. Alice is superficially beautiful, but her efficiency comes from smart work and preparation," Elise concluded. "Is her intelligence as attractive to you as her appearance?"

"If we didn't get along, or I didn't like her attitude, I wouldn't find her very attractive at all," Noah said. "I've met really attractive people who were closed minded or mean and I just didn't see them as pretty anymore. I guess it depends on what you value, though. Like this place. It's a pit: dirty, the bartender is a row of vending machines, the people here aren't what I'd call social, and people don't have fun here."

"The electronic noise is so bad there that I have to burst broadcast on the Z Band to get through to you," Elise added. "I suspect I'd lose contact with you entirely if they turned the reactor up."

"Right, but if I start making good memories here and I keep coming back, then I could get attached to this place. This stinking pit could become like a second home," he said, leaning back in his chair.

"Oh, so association can change perception. I'm capable of that, it's programmed in. I don't think I'd look at the Dark Room as anything but a noisy, disease ridden converted storage space, though."

"Am I catching something here?" Noah asked.

"You would be if it weren't for the nano-medical package in your breastbone. It's taken care of, though."

"You mean there's no trace of the disease left, or I'm symptom free?" Noah asked, knowing that computerized medical systems didn't always have the same priorities as their patients.

"Oh, the Nabaren Phage is completely gone. It's not that bad for humans, though. Once the affected area sloughs off the phage is gone. There are a couple other patrons who are in for a rough month or two when it really takes hold, though."

"Maybe I should cut my losses, this place isn't as entertaining as I thought it would be," Noah said. As soon as he started standing, one of the better dressed patrons at the bar looked his way. Three of his fellows looked as well. They were the muscle, one of them moved like he had cybernetic enhancements from hips to fingertips. It was that too-smooth, computer assisted kind of motion he'd seen a few times. He sat back down, nodding at the well-dressed fellow in a coat that flared out at the bottom like a short cape. He was one of the cleaner people there, a lot of them sat at the bar or the tables nearby, and there was plenty of muscle around. "I think I have a bite."

"I detect no parasites or insects interested in human. The radiation probably killed them," Elise replied.

Noah made himself more at home in his seat. "I mean, someone's coming over to talk to me. It's either trouble or what I'm looking for."

"Hey, there, Heavy," the well-dressed gentleman said, sitting down. His jacket parted enough to reveal a thin, skin coloured shirt that had the gleam of a dense, thin armoured under suit. It was better than a standard non-military vacsuit, but Noah had only ever seen one in videos. He wondered if they still cost hundreds of thousands of platinum.

"I guess I deserve the nickname since I blasted two bots on my way through customs," Noah said, gesturing to the free seat across from him. "Most people call me Carnie."

"Customs? You didn't give them a reading, not a look. You got past and came here. Better to check in at the Dark Room anyway. I call you Heavy because of that killer ship. Arcyn Starskipper that's not a Starskipper. Can't scan it, wouldn't dare try to crack it. Probably a better, new improved Starskipper. The Corsair," he finished with breathy reverence, spreading his hands out over his head as if he was putting the name up in lights.

There was something familiar about that banter. Noah focused on how he sounded his words out carefully. The accent was off, and it sounded a little like he learned New English from advertising, not like most humans. "It's a special ship. What's your interest?"

"Admiration," he said. "Administrator asked for me to get the data on you. There's not much news, no one's got a flash on you."

"What is he saying?" Elise asked. "I was keeping up, then he lost me."

Noah smiled a little at her confusion. His companion smiled back, leaning back in his chair. "Meaning no one knows where I'm from, where I got my tech, and you can't really guess why I'm here. A few people probably tried to make something up, though, right?"

"Fake words for a greasy palm," the pretend human said. "I don't drop credit for bad news flashes."

"Yeah, no fooling you, so you're coming to the source. I told that guard all I really care to. I'm looking to hook up with the resistance. Big, small, I don't care about the size of the group."

"Resistance against the Order of Eden. Hate fate. That's what they say. Why do you want them?"

"I'd like to help. I have some discount guns and other goods."

"Big sale, today only!" the fellow said, grinning and laughing. "Guns! Guns! guns!"

"Something like that," Noah nodded, wishing he wasn't the centre of attention for half the bar. "Only for the resistance."

"I could be resistance, if there are low, low prices."

"Okay," Noah sighed, letting all signs of amusement drain from his face. It was easy to play people like him. They watched every micro expression, studied human faces so they could pick up convincing tricks for their shapeshifting. He could be Issyrian, Tuzon, or a couple other shapeshifting races he'd heard of but never seen. It didn't matter which. If he showed obvious, increasing displeasure, he'd get a real reaction from the guy. "I knew this would happen. You'd pretend to be a three-legged dog if it would get you guns and information. If there's no reason for me to be here, I'll find the nearest airlock and get my ship to pick me up."

"Whoa, Space Ranger," the fellow said, alarmed at the discussion turning sour. "I was just tickling your funny bone."

There were several Space Ranger shows over the years, most of them were exaggerated comedies about a high tech adventurer, and Noah wondered how many episodes the creature across from him saw. "I'm all frothy ale and good times until you threaten to waste my summer home," he said, imitating the over-the-top heroic styling of the main character in an episode that was probably four times older than him. A tentacle alien was threatening to demolish a moon where Space Ranger had built a cabin by a lake.

The shape changer across from Noah's eyes went too wide and he laughed with two voices at once before he regained his composure. "That episode was banned on most nets, too much talk about his hallucinogenic 'ale.' I thought I'd never meet anyone who saw it."

"I'm a big Space Ranger fan, especially when he gets wacky on the good spice," Noah said, letting himself smile again. "You got a name, cadet?"

"Rikan. I wheel and deal for the station," he said. "You have old Space Ranger episodes?"

"I know a guy who has thousands," Carnie said, remembering that Remmy was his most recent source when he looked to replace a bunch of data he lost. "You must have your own collection, though."

"I haven't seen Space Ranger since the fall. Mad bots cleared everything out, It was on a human network," he said.

"Well, you hook me up with a contact for the real rebels and I'll set you up," Noah said.

"I need something for the man," he said, pointing up.

"The administrator needs to see you make a deal," Noah said, watching Rikan. "Let me talk to my associate." He closed his helmet and set it to opaque. Rikan's jaw dropped as he watched the plates rapidly move up and into place from Noah's collar. "I'm wondering, can our manufacturing bay make something like the bots I slagged?" he asked Elise.

"I've scanned their security bots and we can print four an hour. I'd need some basic raw materials, but there are plenty of abandoned asteroids and other bodies around the system that would do. I could also make several improvements that wouldn't cost me anything."

"So, storage is our biggest problem," he said.

"Yes, we could fit twenty bots in the lower hold without interfering in operations down there. If we used quarters for storage we could fit another thirty-two, but that's with you sleeping on the bridge."

"That's actually not bad. What's the price of those bots on system?"

"Twenty-eight thousand platinum apiece reconditioned on average. There are no new models available. Oh, and I can program them, too, by the way. They're dullards. They're good at security and some other basic care tasks, but they're not terribly dynamic. The software I just wrote for them is better than what the bots you blasted were running, and it's still not a general artificial intelligence. Oh, and it'll be compatible with their primitive operating system."

"All right, thanks. Tool up to make a bunch of those. Oh, how do they measure up against someone in Haven Fleet heavy armour?"

"Without significant weaponry in hand they couldn't harm

heavy armour. You'd be safe indefinitely. I could design and print one that could, though."

"We'll talk about that later. The version we can make copies of would be good for this base's defence, though?"

"They're excellent when using standard weaponry. Do you want me to set the manufacturing system up for that, too?"

"No, just the bots."

"All right, I'll begin tooling and calibration."

Noah retracted his helmet. "Is your base low on defence androids? The type I blasted when I came aboard?"

"Yes, you have stock?" Rikan looked surprised. It was an intentional expression.

"I don't have any used or reconditioned models, just new, so I don't know if your administration wants to pay the premium."

"New KA-Twelves?"

"These would be KA-Fifteens," Elise corrected in Noah's ear. "I found enough data about them online to manufacture the latest model, the one that was rolling out before the fall."

"KA-Fifteens," Noah said. "They'll be thirty-five thousand plat each. Can you guys afford that? I'm cutting you a deal."

"How many do you have?" Rikan asked, the ends of his fingers shifted, the definition of his fingernails failing for a moment.

Now, that was a clear sign that the shapeshifter was excited. "You introduce me to a group who is really fighting against the Order of Eden and make sure the Shlaki pirates I pissed off don't get aboard at the same time I'm here, and I'll sell you fifty."

"Fifty!" Rikan whooped.

"What? Too many? Not enough?" Noah asked calmly, leaning back in his chair.

"You could sell more? We could have real security from you?"

"No, from the bots I sell you. I can get more, too. No previous owners, factory fresh with clean programming. But you have to agree to my other terms too, or I'm moving on to another station."

"I need to talk to them," Rikan said. "I can introduce you to Underground. As for pirates, that is a problem of the chicken or the egg."

"Ah, you don't have the security to keep them out but you will once I sell you the bots," Noah interpreted.

Rikan pointed to his nose and to Noah as he nodded. "Give the man a prize."

"Well, then that part of our agreement will kick in once you buy fifty bots. I can have a sample in your airlock in..."

"An hour and a half," Elise answered in his ear.

"An hour and a half," Noah said, starting to his feet, extending his hand.

"You have to go on your ship to do that?" Rikan asked.

"No, you don't, but I'd feel better if you were aboard where I could protect you," Elise said.

"I don't, why?" Noah asked.

"There are people waiting for you to leave. People who are after your cash and prizes," Rikan whispered. "I'll bring my protection over, we can have a few beverages on me then leave with them. I might be able to get someone from the Underground here too."

It would be unlikely that he'd need any protection. The weapons he scanned on his way through could damage his shields, but they wouldn't win in a real firefight, not compared to the hardware he had. Even still, it was better to avoid more shooting, especially since most of the galaxy didn't know what Haven Fleet technology could do, something he had to remind himself of often. "Yeah, I'll take you up on that, Space Cadet," he said.

"Good, make yourself at home, Space Ranger."

As Rikan moved off and started sending his security detail in his direction, Noah started imagining all the ways the shape shifter could screw him over. There was always the hope that things could stay straightforward, that he could create a safe harbour at least for a while and engage in a little simple commerce, but Noah Lucas stopped trusting his luck on Iora.

FORTY-FIVE

Catching Up

THE DOXAN SYSTEM reminded Alice of several off-trade route stops she made while she was in hiding. That felt like a previous life until she saw the list of stations, ruined ports and competing outposts that populated the system map. She tapped her finger on the edge of the navigation console, listening to the Hart News Report for the third time. Woone was flying, it was her third time in the pilot's seat. The only outward sign of nervousness was how she licked her chops every once in a while, that pink tongue running from her nose then back along the length of her jaws before it disappeared. Her anxiety was plain to Alice, though, and she wished she could reach out and turn it down for her, but she had to depend on old-fashioned reassurances. "Remember, Lewis has you on easy mode. He's running the flight assist program," Alice told her.

"I know, I know," Woone said quietly as she guided the Clever

Dream towards Doxan III. They would have moved faster if Alice was at the controls, mostly because she'd have the ship on autopilot, but the absence of Ute was keenly felt. There was only one person experienced at flying the Clever Dream with her gone. Inexperienced pilots had trouble training aboard her ship. It had the agility of a fighter along with the sensitive controls but there was a lot more to account for. Even Alice depended on flight assist software to smooth some of the jagged edges of her flying out, something she'd have to work on.

Quan was muttering with impatience to at the communications panel as he struggled with a few of the finer details of the system while Faloo was taking instruction from Iruuk at the sensors and sciences station. She'd manned it before, but he was teaching her a new level of detail that she hadn't started training on. At least that seemed to be going well.

Yawen popped into the bridge hatch, leaning in. "Look at all the learning going on here." They could hear her smile if they didn't bother to look up at her. "How's it going?"

"Pretty good." Alice could feel Yawen's eagerness. Whatever feelings the woman had were pushed aside by the urge to get off the ship and explore.

"Woone has promise as a pilot," Lewis said. "She needs a little more patience, but I've barely had to assist her. True competence will require practice, but I see qualifications in her future. Quan does not like the live directory system and is easily frustrated by junk advertising. I could help, but I find his quiet frustration amusing. Faloo is smarter and faster than I anticipated, her general inability to read detailed scans without me translating them will be corrected soon."

"Thank you?" Faloo snickered.

"Oh, it was a compliment. Most people can't learn how to read scan data at that detail level so quickly. Your intelligence easily makes up for your shedding habits."

"Still feel like that was less compliment and more criticism there," Faloo snickered, holding her nose for a moment.

"Shedding is not a habit," Iruuk said. "We must shed."

"I disagree. There are grooming machines, and shaving is a valid..."

"Lewis," Alice interrupted. "Remember that conversation we had about hygiene and privacy?"

"Right. How people keep themselves is their business," Lewis sighed. "Bringing me to the status of our Captain. Alice seems uncharacteristically impatient and on edge. I have a feeling it has something to do with her impending reunion with Noah Lucas."

"Yeah, about that," Yawen said. "I took a look at the floorplan and specs of Angel's Landing. The main station is a great spoke design, like some of the older astronomy hotels, but the drift that grew off its starboard side is a mess. Security wise it can handle the rabble, and compartmentalization is good, but against military hardware it's a joke. We can do whatever we want there. Maybe that's why Noah picked this spot to start reaching out to resistance groups?"

"He didn't so much pick the place," a light, clear voice said. "It was a convenient spot to explore while we waited for you."

"Who's that?" Alice asked Quan.

Quan looked over his shoulder at her, a helpless expression on his face. Confusion and frustration mingled in his head. "It's not coming through the communication system as far as I can see."

"That is Elise, I've been speaking to her since we arrived on the edge of the system," Lewis said. "She's my counterpart on the Corsair."

"I thought you said communications weren't possible with Noah right now," Alice said.

"That is true. He's a few metres below the main fusion reactor for the station. It's old, the shielding isn't as good as what you'd expect from a modern system, but he's safe, and the people in the bar beneath enjoy the inability to communicate or make clear recordings," Elise explained. "I was able to communicate with your ship, though, and Lewis answered my call. We've been talking, it's been interesting. Theodore said he was going to tell you, he's been in on the conversation for several minutes."

"How long has the conversation been going on?" Yawen asked.

"Three minutes, five seconds, fifty-three milliseconds," Lewis said. "It has been lively."

"So, what is Noah up to right now?" Alice said, glancing at the Navnet hologram. They would be in a direct line to scan Angel's Landing in less than a minute, able to dock in fourteen. With a few gestures she requested to be reassigned a more direct route to the station. The Navnet system responded, giving them a route that would allow them to dock in just over five minutes.

"I am printing the first batch of KA-Fifteens for the station. They're human analogue security bots that Noah sold to the station in trade for a meeting with The Underground, a prominent resistance group in the Doxan System."

"He works fast," Yawen said.

"Are the station owners members of the Underground or any other resistance group?" Alice asked.

"Not that we know of."

"He's going against orders then?" Iruuk asked. "Wasn't he only supposed to sell to resistance groups?"

There was a part of Alice that agreed with Iruuk, those were his orders, even if he was encouraged to improvise. That part of her thinking came from her time in the Academy during the first Apex Program. It might not have lasted long, but that was a formative time that she remembered fondly.

The rebellious, improvisational side of her appreciated what he was doing though, and she knew him well enough to be fairly sure that he wasn't doing something that would bite them in the ass later. "It's not like this mission would benefit from me putting him on report. He probably had to get the door open." Alice looked the robots he sold up on a hologram to her right and nodded. "These things aren't dangerous to us unless you put serious hardware into their hands. Skitters are smarter."

"I know, I think that's why he wasn't reluctant to sell them. I did print a New Type Haven Shore Guardian for myself, too. That one will not be for sale, but I had to have security aboard since the Fifteens I'm printing are walking out the airlock and a few lookie-loos have gathered to watch from the nearest hub."

"Can I talk to him?" Alice asked.

"The reactor has been turned up, our communications have been basic and intermittent for over an hour. I can verify that his suit is reporting good health and low stress, however," Elise said.

"Lewis, take over," Alice said. "Get docked with the station. Iruuk; you're on watch. Yawen, Knud, Theo and Krooke; you're with me. What are the docking fees here?"

"Three platinum per hour," Quan replied. "That seems high."

"That's all right, we're only getting dropped off, then the Clever Dream will orbit the station." The navigation station showed that they were cleared to dock at Angel's Landing, and Alice locked it. "We're going with our hoods up, no one gets to see our faces. Personal shields will be on, we will be fully armed, but our heavy suits will not be deployed."

"Rifles and secondary weapons?" Yawen asked. "You realize we can blow holes in any part of that station if we turn them up, right? This isn't a military installation."

"We're putting on a show." Alice could feel Yawen's excitement, Iruuk and Woone's disappointment at not being allowed to join them, and she tried to muffle her empathic sense. It worked a little, the people around her didn't seem as intense. "I don't know what kind of narrative Noah's building, so we're going to join him as his personal security force."

"That's wise, Captain Valent," Elise said. "He's building a solo operator legend, very similar to what I've seen in the training manuals. There's a little Robin Hood in there, too, but it gets a little screwy considering how much platinum he's making on this deal. If you go in as his protection, then his work will remain intact. I'll send him a text message so he knows you're coming."

"Don't include our names, just in case someone demands to see the message. Call us The Muscle," Alice said. Elise was surprisingly similar to Lewis, she even liked to talk, choosing a friendlier tact instead of the most efficient one. Only time would tell if she actually liked the artificial intelligence, though.

"Wise, again. I feel I'm going to learn a lot from you, Captain Valent," Elise said warmly.

"Sensors off, newbie. That's my Captain," Lewis grumbled.

"Sorry, I'll defer to your judgement in terms of access and exposure, since you are the artificial intelligence assigned to the Clever Dream."

Alice and Yawen made their way down to the embarkation compartment. "Tell me everything about Noah's deal, Elise."

While Knud, Yawen, Theodore, Krooke and Alice got ready, Elise told her every detail, playing parts of the conversation back as needed. They removed all emblems from their thick military vacsuits and changed their colours. Alice went with powder blue, Yawen's was yellow, Theodore's was green, Knud's was a startling silver, and Krooke's was turned glossy black. The vacsuit detail was turned all the way up so his fur looked like spikes coated with dark steel. Alice's heavy armour captain's long coat was styled the same as Noah's, the V shape of the armour slats were chromed. Her boots and the rest of the jacket were a matte navy blue.

The changes happened fast, and Alice barely paid attention as she smiled at Noah's simple negotiations. Waiting around took patience, and investing in the station management was a risk, but they would definitely be meeting with someone today.

YOUR MUSCLE IS COMING, SIR. FIRST DELIVERY OF 10 ANDROIDS IS COMPLETE. THE CORSAIR IS SECURE said the text message on Noah's wrist.

"What's that? You get communication down here?" asked Onir, the Mergillian in power armour across the table from him. He was a representative from the Underground, so he said, but if the ragtag trio he arrived with was any indication, they were barely in shape for a fight.

"Yeah," Noah said, enlarging the text on his arm and showing it to him. "More of my people are arriving, things are going well on the station."

"Good, good, so what weapons are you selling? Do you have anything today?" he asked.

"I could use some armour, how much does that under suit cost? I can't even scan through it at two metres," one of his human companions asked.

"Hang on," Noah said, smiling. "Rikan didn't say I'd be meeting anyone named Onir, and you still haven't answered my question. How did you get on board the station?"

"We are freedom fighters with the Underground. They dropped us off," Onir shrugged.

"What kind of muscle is coming?" asked one of Onir's men. He had a shell treatment on his head and shoulders that made him look like he was coated in violet metal. It moved with him, making him look more like some cartoon character than something Noah found intimidating.

Noah disregarded the violet man's question. "Okay, but I don't see any Order of Eden fighters here. This is a backwater to a back-water of a station, why would the Underground drop such fine, capable members off here?"

"That is not your business," Violet said.

"Right, not your business," Onir agreed. "Now, what guns?"

"I'm here to meet with and sell to resistance fighters. I mean, maybe I'll branch out someday, but stock is limited. I could spare some polish or something if Violet there wants to shine his dome a little, but no guns unless I see you are true freedom fighters against the Order."

"How do we prove that, simian?" Violet asked.

"Show me footage. Maybe some important stolen Order of Eden data. I mean, even a black box from one of their combat shuttles or fighters would do as long as it verified that your ship shot it down or you pirated the ship somehow. There are plenty of ways. If you're a resistance fighter, you'll be able to confirm it somehow."

"You can read Eden black box?" Violet asked.

"Sure, can't you?" Noah asked. He could have sold the thugs a bunch of hardware that was just a hair better than what they had, but Elise would run out of resources in two hours, so her printing capabilities were limited. They'd have to go gather some raw materials and soon. "Listen, if you're from the Underground, then you can get out of this reactor's jamming range, contact someone from them with negotiation power, and come back with proof of who you are. As it is, you're not who Rikan said I'd be meeting, so this is all a bit sketchy."

"Sketchy?" asked Onir the Mergillian. "What is 'sketchy?'"

"He's not going to sell to us," Violet said. "We take him for Nore then."

The double doors across from Noah opened, revealing five armoured figures carrying rifles that were more powerful than weapons found on most of the starfighters in the solar system. He guessed Alice was in the lead in form fitted powder blue and a captain's jacket like his own. Knud and one of the thick bodied Nafalli crewmembers towered in the rear, while Yawen and a human male beside her were in the middle. He wondered if it was Theodore, that would be his guess since his stature was absolutely average. He was the only one without a rifle. "There's that muscle you were asking about. Move along." He was relieved to see them. A firefight was coming, and he'd win unless someone was hiding a grenade or two, but he didn't want to cause trouble on his first day of negotiations.

Violet, Onir and everyone else in the bar looked over their shoulders as Alice led her group of five across the large space.

Muted white light from the reactor above flickered throughout the place as they marched to his side. The group at Noah's table slipped away quietly. Alice and the rest of her people arranged themselves behind him, the sound of their boots ringing out as dozens of patrons looked on. A laser link symbol appeared on Noah's command and control unit. "Hope we didn't screw up negotiations," Alice said, her voice welcome in his ear.

"No, they were the third group to have a seat since word got out that I was the latest arms dealer brave enough to sell to anyone other than gangsters. I think they were about to try to put me in restraints and sell me to Shlaki, the pirate group I pissed off, not that I'd let them. Your timing was perfect. Oh, and you look amazing in the blue suit, but you probably already knew that."

Krooke snickered, his black coated spiky head looking more sinister than he realized, Noah was sure. "We can all hear you, she made a laser link net."

"Oh, he means the new colour enhances her attractive figure," Theodore said. "You know, that gets confusing with slang and how attractiveness is so subjective."

"Good to hear you, Theo," Noah said with a smile, still not looking back at him. "I'd give you a great big hug but I don't want to spoil the cool image I've built up over the last few hours. That goes for all of you."

"That's good to hear, my empathy is so muffled right now that I feel almost normal," Alice said.

"I'm crazy happy to see you," Noah said under his breath, casually covering his mouth. "In case you were wondering."

"She was, she definitely was," Krooke whispered. "Pretending that we're all your stiff-necked guards, showing no emotion must be driving her nuts. Everyone wants to see what happens next in your mating ritual."

"I believe that was inappropriate," Theodore said. "Or at least embarrassing."

Noah lost his composure, laughing not only at the antics of the Clever Dream crew, but with relief at not being alone. Then he spotted Rikan as he entered. He smiled at a group in the corner booth to his left. They got to their feet and fell into step. The three of them were wearing helmets that covered their faces down to their upper lips that matched the plate and environment suit armour they wore. Patches of yellow and red were visible on the flexible parts of their suits where wear and tear had rubbed the green and black coating off. Noah recognized the prismatic quality to the over-coat paint they put on their armour. It was made to reflect beam weapons and dissipate stunner blasts. "Welcome," Noah said as they approached.

One of them, he wasn't sure if it was a man or a woman, sat down and held out a small, high resolution holographic projector. An image appeared of an Order of Eden Customs Corvette. "Rikan said you needed proof," said the petitioner, her voice was disguised, electronically lowered and rasped.

Cannon fire to either side of the view made it plain that he was watching footage from a ship's nose recorder as rounds raked the customs corvette. Target indicators along the bottom of the holographic recording showed that its shields were failing, and in a jarring, sudden move, the ship made contact with the Order vessel. Audio of creaking metal and plasma drills proceeded to switch to the first-person view of a helmet camera.

The soldier in the lead moved through a shattered airlock door, blasting Order of Eden troops as he went. His kinetic rifle rattled rounds off at the defenders as they were torn up by the explosive impacts. The soldier who was providing the point of view had to change magazines every few seconds, and the group behind him made sure that he was covered as he did so. It seemed they all had to do the same, perhaps their rounds were powerful, but large so they had to reload constantly. Even still, Noah watched as the footage detailed how they killed several Order of Eden soldiers, none were Knights, but it was still impressive. Fourteen were gunned down as they made their way to the nearest access point to the ship's data core and cracked the security by hooking it up to a computer the size of a keg. It was old fashioned piracy, done well, but at great risk and expense. "My system can verify that there are no signs of doctoring in that recording," Alice said. "Now you just have to figure out if it's hers." Only Noah could hear her, and it was good to hear her voice even though he was sure there would be a serious discussion about how many enemies he might have made on his way into the system and how over-exposed he and the Corsair were. Maybe she was right, but he hoped it would be worth it, he hoped he was actually meeting with leadership from a real resistance group without setting foot on Doxan III.

The holographic recording ended with the pirates inputting the new name and owner of the ship using their battered terminal. The name of the ship was the Razpa, her new captain was Majan Lor. "The Razpa is docked to pylon nine," the woman said as the small holoprojector deactivated. "I am Majan, one of the Captains with the Underground. Do you need a tour? More holos of what we've used my ship for since?"

Noah sat back, he knew Alice had been right where he was before in many ways. She'd given technology to someone who took things in a direction she couldn't have predicted. In her place, he didn't think he could have done any better, and he wasn't going to agree to anything until she had her say.

"Lewis just reported that he's spotted the Razpa. It's a modified Order of Eden Customs Corvette, registered to her, and her DNA has been detected on the bridge. Order records report the ship being pirated then disappearing three weeks ago on the edge of the Godan System," Alice said. "She's wanted by the Order for piracy, grand theft, the murder of five officers, unlawful imprisonment, and destruction of military property. If she isn't a rebel, she's a pirate and a killer who really likes messing the Order up. I'd take this to the next step."

"All right, Majan," Noah said. "I think you qualify for my special freedom fighter discount. Have a seat and tell me what you need. The Corsair Arms Dealership is open for business."

EPILOGUE

It was maddening. After taking several side-excursions to parts unknown, Admiral Hadlee of the British Alliance sent Ayan a coded message with a simple title. SUPPORT MUST BE WITH-DRAWN. It was straightforward and clear. Even so, Ayan had to watch the rest of the message then forward it on to the rest of the admiralty.

Most of them were scattered throughout the fleet, which included fifteen lumbering Nafalli ships along with a constellation of smaller support and secondary vessels of their own. There were tens of thousands of newcomers from tree tribes, plains tribes and under tribes who were eager to join Haven Fleet officially. Three new Mergillian Cruiser-Carriers, which were even larger, were on their way behind Remmy Sands, who was approached by several politicians who wanted to offer real military support for Haven Fleet.

So many of them had been wronged by Regent Galactic and the Order of Eden. One of the largest tribes of Nafalli were driven from their home world by a variant of the holocaust virus when a small part of the Eden Fleet recognized them as enemies. No one was ready. Millions were killed, and while they wanted revenge, they also saw a glimmer of hope in Haven Fleet, because a story had begun to spread further than anyone expected. Haven Fleet was once tasked with defending the Haven System. That wasn't the most important part of the new story that was reaching distant stars though. That was the second part of the story, where the Haven Fleet had technology, ships, a need for warriors so they could return to Haven, take it back and give the people who needed a place to settle land, protection and peace.

The Mergillians asked Remmy about it over and over when he visited one of their well populated colonies. When they looked upon him there was hope, an expectation in their eyes that reminded him and his team why they were fighting more than anything. After the news reached Ayan, she, Oz and Lamonthe, who would be working alongside her old friend on training and intelligence, stated developing a plan with the Nafalli to train thousands. When the War Forge settled into its new hiding place, it would begin building large and medium ships again. They would need them, it was a good feeling, but it would still take weeks to train most of the newcomers on the essentials.

Then there was this message from the British Alliance. Ayan got to her feet when Leon and Lamonthe entered the darkened room. "So the British gave us the brush-off?" Lamonthe asked quietly.

Ayan nodded, looking around at the furniture for another moment. "Officially, I assume. I haven't run the playback yet." The space was remarkable, a room built for resting Nafalli Tree Tribe people. There were bars along the ceiling with durable textures made to simulate bark, soft resting platforms hanging down, and large adjustable seats like the one she just abandoned that could fit three humans or one full grown Tree Tribe Nafalli. Two if they were familiar. There was also a corner specifically designed for a group of them to build what the designers started calling a 'rest nest' where they would all bring their own furs and blankets then relax in a pile. She'd seen the Murlen family all piled up in their quarters in Haven once, and the memory of that large mound of fur made her smile.

Standing in quarters that would be filled by a Nafalli family or social group the next day, seeing how comfortable it seemed already, even if not for her because everything was far too large, gave her even more encouragement. Ayan knew that Lamonthe would probably never see the space, so she had Leon bring him to her, it was a good a place as any while it was still empty. "Well, I'm ready for a little bad news," Lamonthe said. "First, I have to thank you. When Admiral Valent and McPatrick were promoted I was sure I'd be permanently shut out. I'm still surprised that some of my more controversial plans are going through, with a few modifications, and that I'm still in the Admiralty. Even more so now that I'm back in Intelligence again, working with Admiral McPatrick. I think we'll work well together, especially since I'm running the security for the new recruits. I knew I would have a meaningful place in the fleet when he offered that role to me right away. I think this is the right balance. Intelligence and training could go well together in this organization, and our staffs can cooperate. Most of all, I want to thank you for keeping me useful."

"Welcome to the family," Ayan said, glad that there was no sign of bitterness in him. "You should thank Jake most of all, though. He saw something no one else did; that you were drowning in responsibility. Even after delegating huge parts of your workload, you still had more going on than any one person should have to handle. He thought putting you with someone who knows how to delegate would be the right way to fix the problem. Oz has more command training than all of us."

"I already thanked Jake and... Oz." It was obvious that calling Admiral Terry Ozark McPatrick by his nickname was new, even awkward for Lamonthe. It may have been the first time he'd done it, for all Ayan knew, but it made him lighten up a little.

"Good," Ayan said. "Ready for some bad news?"

"I suppose there has to be some on a relatively good day like this one. There's that balance the universe likes to push on us," Lamonthe sighed.

Ayan activated the recording and British Alliance Admiral Hadlee appeared in an isolated full-length, full-sized holographic image. "Former Defence Minister, Admiral Ayan Anderson. It pains me to convey this message from the British Alliance Military. It is the opinion of this body that rectifying the situation in the Haven System is not a cause the British Alliance sees as a worthwhile pursuit. Furthermore: the persistance of Haven Fleet, despite its superior technology, is no longer seen as just or rational. The loss of life and resources is regrettable, but past is prologue, and the British Alliance does not believe that Haven Fleet's strategy will lead to any kind of meaningful victory against the Order of Eden. As for reparations for technology acquired during our cooperation, the British Alliance has decided that any settlement will be indefinitely suspended. It is the recommendation of the British Alliance that Haven Fleet leave the sector for unexplored space, since they have the transportation technology to make the journey quickly. Once there, you should settle on a suitable world and become self-sufficient, pursue your goal of growing and developing a peaceful society. Once such a pursuit is well under way and the Haven Fleet is removed from negative diplomatic entanglements, you will be welcome to contact us again." Admiral Hadlee nodded to herself and cleared her throat before continuing in a less chiselled tone. "I'll catch hell for this, Admiral Anderson, but I have to add that joining you during the invasion of the Haven System was the most right-eous thing I've done during my service. No call to battle has ever been as just as one made by people defending their home. I regret that I have to leave, and believe my people are making a mistake by abandoning your people. I hope to see you again, God speed."

"She really didn't want to go," Leon said.

"There will be a lot of time for her to think about what she's seen here on the way back home. It'll take her weeks," Lamonthe said. "I have to wonder, though; why did she bother adding her personal statements at the end? They didn't accomplish anything."

Hadlee's parting statements would land her in a world of trou-ble, Ayan was sure. She didn't have much time to spend with Haven Fleet, but she was pleasant while she was around. "We must have made an impression," Ayan said. "Even still, maybe your code breakers could run through the message for a while. She could have been trying to give us a tip on the way out."

"Good thinking," Lamonthe said. "I'll put a few people on it."

"Ma'am," Leon said. "Councillor Malsen is about to board her transit shuttle with the rest of the Lorander Delegation."

"Open communications through the internal holonet," Ayan said and a moment later, the small group of five Lorander delegates appeared in front of her, Lamonthe and Leon. The Councillor looked as sour as ever, her pale brow heavy. "Hello again, I was hoping you would reconsider negotiating a fairer sharing of knowledge before you left. There's still time to forge a real bond between the Lorander Corporation and Haven Fleet." They had refused to trade so much as a word of history, even about the Raiders when they were shown images of them and their ships, even when Ayan put data on their new intelligent plating on the table to sweeten the deal, the Lorander representatives were silent.

"You insulted me, limited our access, cut us off from our people and imprisoned us for weeks and you expect me to change my mind?" The Councillor asked. "You people are eternally greedy, and it makes you foolish. No, it's worse, it twists your expectations, pulls you out of line with reality. Your whole fleet is doomed. I'll be surprised if this glorified pod you're sending us off in makes it out of the solar system, but at least we'll be away. Good-bye."

"That transit ship we made you is a Lorander Corporation design, one of the best. I'm sure you'll be comfortable," Ayan said. "I made sure we didn't deviate, so it's safe, your flight crew will find that it's familiar. I am wondering something, though; do you really represent all Lorander people? We've found out that the Lorander name represents two completely different things. One is Lorander Corporation, and according to every record we could find on you and your group, that's who you're representing, and the other is Lorander the culture, the society, and we couldn't find much in our system, but from what we can tell, you don't represent them. Can you confirm that? How big is Lorander Corporation compared to the Lorander people?"

Councillor Malsen turned away and moved on, passing into the airlock then walking onto the transit ship. One of her aides fell behind. When the rest of his fellows were out of sight, he looked to the holo recorder, it seemed like he was peering directly at Ayan, Lamonthe and Leon. "The Lorander Corporation is less than one-

one-thousandth the size of the Lorander people proper. Keep looking through the Lorander Corporation data you have, you'll find a way to contact my people. They are as varied as all the stars in your sky in attitude, appearance, and aspiration. Good luck, little fleet." He passed through the airlock, it closed and the view switched to the slender transit ship as it decoupled from War Forge Mobile Station.

The trio watched as it glided away, opening a blue-white wormhole then slipping in, disappearing with the fading of the light. A signal from Navnet Control flashed on Ayan's command and control unit. The fleet was ready to begin preparations to move on to their next destination. "So, we make for the next star," Ayan said as she tapped the order to get the fleet moving on her wrist.

"With more questions than ever," Lamonthe said.

"We'll find the answers. Until then, I think we can show the Order of Eden that winning this war will be more difficult than they thought." The notion of her daughter, Alice along with trusted friends arming rebel groups far, far away, close to the Order borders, the small fleet of ships that were hiding in and near the Haven System, and the plan Jake was putting together with his Special Operations Combat Unit made her feel like Haven Fleet was about to have a great effect. The recruitment effort wasn't going as expected, she thought there would be more humans than they could handle coming aboard, but they had thousands of new friends who wanted to sign up regardless. Then there were the rebels and families they were about to meet, almost all human, all from Nuaji, and ready to join Haven Fleet after being ferried out of Order of Eden territory by the Pelican. They would be waiting at the fleet's next destination. The thought of so many humans, Nafalli, Mergillians and people from other races filling the War Forge gave her more hope than anything, and she wanted to show them that the future would be brighter than the horror and fear they left behind. The fight may not be easy, but Ayan would make sure that it was worth the cost and that everyone could see that it led to a better place.

SPINWARD FRINGE BROADCAST 14: REBEL PREVIEW

ONE

Angel's Landing Station

THE MEETING with Majan Lor went better than Alice expected. A few crates of rifles, military grade handguns, a new shield generator that would be compatible with her ship - a pirated Order of Eden Customs Corvette - military vacsuits and five sets of generation two Freeground Armour. The equipment was better than what the Order had, but several steps behind Haven Fleet's systems.

Watching, listening, commenting on a closed channel to Noah Lucas as he made the deal was more relaxing than being the brains and the negotiator at the same time. He was good at putting a deal together, showing that there were limits without letting the situation become negative. Every time Majan Lor, the Captain of the Razpa, tried to ask for ship weapons or a starfighter, Noah turned her to something else like a new shield generator and specifications for emitter upgrades or intelligence on the supply lines for the

Order of Eden only a couple light years away. The generators came at a cost, but the intelligence was free. He lit a fire in Majan by telling her that she was the first to get the information, but he was going to be sharing it with everyone, so she only had a limited time to get to a wormhole emergence point and make her move on whatever Order of Eden freight delivery she could catch.

That wasn't the only thing that was free. When their business was about to conclude, and Majan had already agreed to pay one point four million platinum for the equipment and weapons that was on the table, Noah told her that he was throwing two new forma processors, three tons of the high-grade food for them and a month's worth of meal bars for her and her crew. "A revolution fights better on a full stomach," he told her with a smile that melted the hardened Captain.

With a promise that she'd tell the members of the Underground she knew that he was trustworthy as soon as he made good on the deal, she and her crewmembers departed. Alice wished she could have gotten a clear read on her with her empathic abilities, but they still felt supressed by the reactor over their heads. Her suit said it was some kind of electronic interference that made most communication and some other systems unreliable as well. It was one of the reasons why the place was appealing to its clientele, and the ambience was helped a great deal by the rolling blue-white light shining through the partially shielded transparent ceiling that separated the establishment from the fusion flame above.

Moments after the deal was closed and a delivery date was agreed on, Noah got up from his seat. He looked to Alice and the others behind him. "Ready to go?" She was in the lead in form fitted powder blue vacsuit and a captain's jacket like his own. Knud and one of the thick bodied Nafalli crewmembers towered in the rear, while Yawen and a human male beside her were in the middle. That was Theodore, who he was overjoyed to see. They were all in full helmets which were a new design. They still used metal slats over a sealed frame, but they were pointed down from the chin, broader at the top with a blacked-out faceplate that was tapered, giving them a serious, almost menacing look.

Alice nodded, and they followed him out of the bar. There were at least four other groups of people who stared at him or tried to approach him as though they wanted to strike up a conversation. To her surprise, he strode past without giving them a seconds' notice. "One of those groups could be from a resistance cell," Alice said, communicating from her suit to his suit using a laser link.

"If they were, they'd know that we wanted to talk to them by now, and they'd get right in front of us," Noah said, activating his own helmet. "They'd have the confidence of someone who already knows we want to talk to them. That is, unless there's another resistance outfit that isn't ready to approach us. In that case, I'd rather see them when they've decided I'm worth their time."

"I would add that, if they can't get real attention from an arms dealer, they probably aren't very good rebels," Theodore added. "It takes a kind of ruthlessness to attack an Order Ship or installation."

They passed into the lift and Alice felt her empathic abilities start to open up again. The general sense in the elevator car was that people were pleased, but her focus hadn't returned. Before it did, there was something she wanted to do, a risk she wanted to take. With an eye gesture at her heads' up display, she ordered her helmet to retract.

"Hey, there she is," Noah said, opening his helmet a moment later, revealing a smile that summoned hers in an instant.

"Wow, you really are bald," Alice laughed, reaching up and running her hand over the prickly stubble on his scalp.

"Yeah, part of the whole Apex thing I was ordered to run away from. I could stimulate it, but..." he looked down into her eyes unflinching.

The elevator car was much cleaner than the bar they just left, but it still smelled of sweat and something that had burned a long time ago, something biological. Alice ignored it as her fingertips made their way down to his cheek, where the stubble ended, becoming perfectly smooth skin. "I would have come even if I didn't have orders, you know," she said softly, not looking away from those eyes, that smile.

"I'm glad I'm not alone, I'm happy you're here." It sounded like a confession, something he was saying only for her.

"Are you sure you wouldn't rather they sent Remmy? He has a more experienced crew." It was a joke, of course, something to cover her nervousness, the rare uncertainty of not really knowing how he was feeling yet. It was exciting, normal, like old times before the extra sense kicked in. Alice was sure he understood the jest, her raised eyebrow and lopsided smile would telegraph at least that. Her fingers moving under his chin, gently drawing him down while she started pushing herself up on her toes would suggest something else.

"Maybe, but he'd definitely get a different welco..."

"Someone is trying to pirate me! Help!" Elise said from where she was installed on the Corsair, the message crackling into clarity. "I just got past their jamming signals, but I'm afraid the whole station is hearing this."

The opportunity to have a normal moment with Noah without her empathic abilities letting her cheat or giving her a reason to retreat was gone. She could feel that he was overjoyed to see her, he liked the way she looked in that powder blue vacsuit, he was feeling a little insecure about his negotiation, and it took a lot of effort for him to restrain his joy at being near her again. His positive reaction was reassuring, more encouraging than she would admit to anyone but him, but it felt like she'd skipped to the end of a story she wanted to experience from the very beginning. The reaction he was having to her was disappearing under his alarm at more pressing concerns. Alice reactivated her helmet. "Hey, Lewis," she said, watching her comm signal get lost in the jamming noise.

"I can't get a signal out," Noah said, the slats of his helmet coming together.

"There's someone with a generator on his back using a beam weapon on the airlock," Elise explained. "They're not making too much progress, and they'll have to get through my armour plating once they're finished depleting that shield, but it's alarming. They could get through if they keep at it for another nine hours and three minutes, give or take a few seconds."

Noah sighed with relief. "Okay, it's not as bad as I thought."

"You may want to have a short conversation with her about exhibiting the appropriate degree of alarm for different situations," Theodore added. "Also, the elevator is no longer in motion. It stopped while you two were focused on each other, so I thought it could wait. Could the two events be connected? The pirate attempt and the elevator stopping?"

"I'm thinking, yeah," Alice said. "Can you hack it?"

Theodore looked at the control panel. "I'd have to damage the control surface, but once I get past that, probably."

"Please." Noah gestured at the small interface panel, the digital buttons were surrounded by a swirling ad that was telling them to order a can of Gan-Gan but to 'Imbibe responsibly.' "I'll reduce the station's bill a few plat to cover the damage."

"If you insist," Theodore said, poking a tiny hole that was less than half a centimetre wide in the corner of the display then pushing a miniature arm that extended from his finger inside. "Oh, that ruins the whole aesthetic."

"I think they'll get over it," Yawen snickered.

A moment later Theodore shook his head. "The problem is not software, it's mechanical. Something is blocking the old cable mechanism from working."

Alice looked at Knud and pointed up. Without hesitation, he reached up and pushed the hatch in the roof open. "Okay, armour up, shields up. We're flying the last nine levels then sixteen frames over," she said.

"WAIT, uh, I only took one advanced qualifier for flying in this armour," Noah said, nervous as he activated his entire suit. Slats of metal spread up from his boots and around him from his captain's coat. "You know, the fun one where you fly through rings, shoot the little boxes that come drifting through that try to knock you off course."

"What's your best time?" Noro, the thick-bodied shorter Nafalli asked.

"Nine minutes, thirty-five and change, no collisions," he replied, hoping it wasn't too bad.

"Damn, that's really good," the Nafalli replied, covering his nose. "How many attempts?"

"Well, it took me a while to get used to the way the emitters in the suit..."

"So, you can fly," Alice said. The slats on the bottom half of her suit flared a couple times, lifting her feet off the floor for a moment. Knud was already up on top of the elevator car, and Theodore hopped up easily. "Just take it easy and you'll get there without punching a hole in the side of the transit shaft, flyboy." He could hear her grinning, this was fun for her.

"Have you logged much time flying in these suits?" he asked, happy that they were on laser link communications, only the crewmembers in a direct line of sight could hear him. "In gravity? Outside of a simulation?" Alice asked. "Just about none. I qualified then had a few hours of fun in the sim. I've done a lot of time in zero-G, though. Still, you won't be the only one taking it slow." With a burst of light beneath the slats of her armour, and a "Woo!" she launched up through the hatch.

When he stepped under it he was just in time to see her slow her thrust down so she was hovering ten metres above the top of the car, listening to her laugh at her overshoot was enough to make him grin. He reached up and let the strength enhancement kick in so he had an easy time pulling himself through the hatch. Knud and Noro picked him up like he was feather-light toddler and a map of their route through the transit tube appeared on his HUD.

The elevator shaft walls were host to cables, pipes and tubes that ranged from manufacturer original to new and improvised with signs of hasty repair everywhere. "Well, there's our problem," Knud said, looking up to an open door above and a clamp that had been wrapped around the cables, keeping them from moving. "Someone's been watching us."

"This might be the pirates I messed with when I came into the system. They could have paid the admin of the station off, gotten some extra access so they could try to take me out? Take my stuff? Probably both," Noah said.

" Are you sure the station management would burn you like that?" Alice asked.

"Might not be them, that's true, the security here is kind of a joke. We'll see if someone from Angel's Landing already paid me. I don't really care past that. I think someone trying to screw you over in this area of space is like their version of hazing, I'm just glad I'm ready for it."

"Well, we just have to get to the Corsair or an airlock for now. Let's go," Alice said enthusiastically. Her emitters flared, blue light pulsing under her armours slats as she course corrected with her hand against the wall of the transit shaft before ascending.

He followed behind Knud, who was flying with his fists raised over his head like some ancient super-hero. The path outlined in Noah's heads up display was easy to follow; straight up for many levels, then to a horizontal transit shaft that would take them to an emergency airlock. Even flying at less than ten percent thrust, they moved fast, over ninety kilometres per hour straight up at first, and Noah stayed within the section of shaft that was reserved for their elevator.

Noro didn't. "Yikes!" he yiped as he narrowly dodged an elevator car coming down to Noah's right.

"We're in military grade power armour," Alice said as she waited at the entry to the horizontal shaft. "No one else on this station is, so if you smash through a wall, or into an elevator car, you'll also smash through whoever's unlucky enough to be in your way."

"Sorry," Noro said. "I'm just eager to get out of here. A bad smell got into my helmet from that bar. I'll watch out."

They were at the end of the horizontal passage and at the

airlock door in no time. There were bands of metal welded to the inner door. "I would say someone tried to disable this," Theodore said, gingerly touching a thick metal bar. "It was years ago, though, so probably not the angry pirates."

"Station management probably trying to stop people from boarding the station without going through customs," Noah said. "I could cut through it."

"Step aside," Knud said as he and Noro pointed their side arms at the bands, carefully but efficiently cutting through the metal braces. Theodore plugged into the smashed terminal beside it and fed power to the door. It opened, and they gathered inside the airlock chamber, there was no room left to move, Alice was pressed against him, her chest against his. "This could be fun if we weren't in power armour."

"I can't quite reach the outer door panel," Theodore said as the inner door closed. "I couldn't stay connected to the other door so we're trapped in here until we shift around or someone gets impatient and tears through the wall."

What came next was an awkward shuffle as everyone carefully shifted, moving Theodore to the outer door, trying not to damage the airlock walls. "They don't use this thing, what's the point in being careful?" Asked Noro.

"If we poke a hole in their airlock, they may not find it until there's an emergency and someone has to escape," Yawen replied.

"Don't they have escape pods for that?"

"Lewis said they only had fifteen aboard, and those were for the high-end suites," Alice replied as Theodore got into position.

The outer door beeped loudly, then popped open, sending Theodore and Noro out into space where they drifted away slowly. "I can see the Clever Dream from here," Noro chuckled.

The Clever Dream decelerated into view, turning so their aft section faced them as its main embarkation ramp was lowered, and Theodore led the way from the airlock. "Welcome aboard," Lewis said to Noah as soon as he set foot on the ship.

"Thanks." The main doors closed and the cabin began to repressurize. "How are the Corsair and Elise doing?"

"She's doing well now that I reassured her that I'd expedite your release from that junk drift the Angel's Landing staff have the nerve to call 'a station.'"

"Who's attacking her?" Noah asked, deactivating his helmet as the green light and indication on his HUD told him it was safe. The rest of the crew did the same.

A hologram of the Corsair, the twin of the Clever Dream, and the long, flexible docking hall affixed to its side appeared in front of them, following as Alice led the way to the bridge. Noah could see the fellow in heavy environment armour firing a drilling laser at the entrance to his ship. There was a line of other crewmen in rough armour behind him, as if they expected him to get through any minute. "There is no immediate danger to the Corsair, since Elise is reporting that the shield... oh, never mind, I'll let her tell you," Lewis said, his tone was that of someone who was giving in. "She really wants to talk to you anyway, I have her on laser-link now."

"Like he was saying," Elise continued, her voice coming through the ship wide address system. "It'll be over nine hours before they break through, then they have to deal with my hull, so I admit I might have over reacted when I sent you that emergency transmission. Crying was definitely too much, I won't do that again."

"Sorry, I didn't hear that," Noah said. "I think I missed a lot of your communications, whoever's jamming this area has a hell of a transmitter."

"Oh, okay. I'm happy you heard enough to know that you should come get me. I've tried to open a dialogue using high-volume emitters in the docking tunnel, but they just laughed and kept drilling. It really looks like they think they'll get through."

"Okay, next time someone starts trying to cut through your shielding, separate from the docking collar and fly around. Cloak if you have to."

"I was going to do that in a few hours, when things got a little desperate, but I didn't know if you had another solution yet," Elise replied.

Alice dropped into the pilot's seat and brought up the tactical interface. "Lewis, will there be any damage to the station if the Corsair rips free of the docking tunnel?"

"Well, that cheap plastic docking tunnel will come apart, decompressing suddenly and sending the seven pirates into space, but I expect the station will have the tunnel replaced within the hour. My scanners picked up several backups in their storage area when we arrived. As for the pirates, well, there's a chance a few of their suits would lose integrity."

"Your ship, your call," Alice said, looking to Noah, gesturing to the co-pilots seat.

"Pull away from the docking collar. Use the mooring cutters and hard shield first," Noah ordered.

"Or you could do it that way, minimizing damage and making repair even easier," Lewis commented. "It won't be as much fun, though."

"Cutting the collar's mooring clamps and activating shield now," Elise said. The Corsair thrust away from the docking collar, which was dislodged so cleanly that they couldn't see the damage. The ship moved away horizontally so it was several metres away from the end. The plastic boarding tunnel flapped and writhed for a moment as the air inside was released in a rush, sending the pirates out of the end. All but two collided with the side of the Corsair at high speed then pinwheeled away.

"All right, let's get out of here before Noah pisses off more pirates," Alice said. "We'll fly out of the system then cloak, listen for anyone who wants to talk to us."

"After hours in that bar, I could use a break," Noah said. He looked around, coming eye-to-eye with Iruuk, who looked like he was happy to see him. "Hey, man, glad you could make it."

Iruuk gave him a big hug from behind the chair, his long arms crossing his chest and pressing him into the cushioning. "Glad you're here," he said, his low Nafalli voice rumbling. "She really missed you," Iruuk said as he let go, pointing at Alice.

TWO

Preoccupied

THE WEIGHT of the occupation changed everything in Haven Shore. Nigel was new to the place, he didn't know what it looked like when people were free, but he could feel discontent and worry start to turn to anger and hate faster after they pulled the statue of Ayan Anderson down. Footage of her denying that she wanted to be called Queen at all played often, it was part of the smear campaign the Order of Eden ran, but to most of the people he knew, that's what she was.

There were people on Tamber before she and the rest of the Freeground Originals arrived. Most of them were from some other government called the Carthans, and they sounded worse than the Order. Their soldiers were serving punitive sentences, unable to disobey orders. The other residents that predated the Originals were dregs, castaways and opportunists who wanted to live in a place no one knew. It wasn't even a planet, but a moon used to test the ecosystem that was going to be reproduced to a partially hollowed giant; Kambis. If he saw it on a star chart, he wouldn't have even stopped in out of curiosity. There were some functional ruins, a few interesting wrecks, tropical areas, but there were also contaminated fields that were supposed to be terraformed but turned toxic instead. He would have definitely passed it by. Ayan was credited with bringing democracy, new progress, and some culture to the place. There were safe areas to live in, jobs, even a government that would take care of you regardless of whether you were an artist, an engineer, or soldier if they had room. Looking around at the hundreds of workers headed back to the Everin Building with him, it seemed like they'd taken a lot of people in. The picker shift he was headed back with represented less than a hundredth of people that the Order crammed into the finished buildings in Haven Shore.

Questions were the most important thing during the occupation. You had to know when not to ask them, who you could trust for the answers, and what the most important ones were. His uncle Frost was building a resistance. It wasn't like the open one that sung songs, shouted obvious phrases of dissent like; "Order go home!" or "Hate fate!" which was his favourite useless sentiment. One of the first popular speeches given by an Order leader ended with; "It is our fate to make this life eternal. Our fate to bring this chaotic existence under control whether it's the governing of ourselves or the entire galaxy. Embrace your fate! Join the Order of Eden!"

He'd seen that speech a dozen times, given by a little boy they called the Child Prophet who came and went before the whole financial ladder theory was big in the Order of Eden. He knew he could ask any soldier about that crap, a lot of them liked to educate the people under their control endlessly as though they were bringing literacy to the unwashed masses or something. Nigel hated every one of them but prompting them to gab about their glorious fate was better than working, it was better than getting a beating because he shot one of them a defiant look. Shouting; "Hate fate!" was a quick way to earn yourself one of those. Nigel didn't have to, though. His height earned him six or seven - he wasn't sure how many exactly - baton thrashings because he was taller than most of the soldiers.

He tried to keep his brow high, to look friendly and harmless. It was hard to make sure he didn't seem like he was looking over one of their heads or scowling all the time. He learned to hunch. It felt like he was giving in.

Every picker around him had their piece of fruit. It was a reward for meeting the quota that day, something that got harder as they moved deeper into the jungle surrounding the city. They were encountering more territorial wild life. Giant cats, predator birds that would pluck you off a tree and carry you off if you were unlucky, and snakes that were so thick that they could be mistaken for fallen logs. He listened to his uncle's advice about being a picker; never go first. They weren't allowed to have weapons or more protective clothing than their flimsy jumpsuits, so the only way to make sure you didn't get killed was to be in the middle of the pack and make sure someone else got it first. He forgot sometimes and ended up climbing above the pack in a tree, or wandering, but he'd been lucky every time so far. He was saving his orange for Samantha.

How could he know why she joined him to cuddle several nights ago when he was falling asleep on his bedroll? She did. He made her laugh, made her comfortable, listened to her even if he didn't completely understand some of the science at times, and that seemed to be more than enough to keep her coming back so far. He enjoyed her visits because it always felt like her attention was a gift, like she was taking time out of being smart, independent and well liked so she could be vulnerable with him.

That orange, worth a hundred-forty-seven credits, would go to her. Seeing her smile would be the height of his day. Most of the people there would sell their fruit to someone else, often a guard. The rest would share it with their kids, but it was the best offering he could give. After moving through the jungle, climbing trees, picking fruit for sixteen hours and walking for one, he wanted to hand it to her and fall down on his bed.

The broad doors to the Everin Building awaited, and Nigel stooped low as he passed through. They were twice his height, there was no problem there, but the line of soldiers and guards who watched the scanning stations were looking for people who stood out, and he didn't want to get picked out of the line again. He passed through, and when the crowd thinned out he had an easier time getting to the first-floor dwelling that he, his uncle and Samantha called home. All four of the others, including Tammy, had been taken. She was in isolation, but no one knew where the rest were.

Nigel stepped through the door. "I'm home, you lucky, lucky people!" he exclaimed as the door closed behind him. Samantha, Frost and David looked up from the table, their expressions stony.

"Come in quietly," Frost said. "We have a visitor."

"Yeah, hey Dave," Nigel said, extending his hand.

"Good to see you," he replied, smiling warmly. He looked more like Frost's nephew than Nigel did. They were almost equally stocky and broad shouldered.

"No, not him," Frost said with a smirk.

"I don't see anyone else," he said.

A shimmer in the air preceded the appearance of Stephanie, who was standing at the opposite end of the table. "Surprise."

He went around and hugged her. "Aunt Steph!" he said with a squeeze. "How are you doing? I didn't think we'd see you until the occupation ended."

"I have to make some deliveries. It's good to see you," she said, tapping a finger to his earlobe lightly. "There, now we can always hear each other."

"What?"

"I just planted a communication device on you that's indistinguishable from skin. It uses a mesh network I made so we can communicate. You turn it on and off with a thought, it's new tech from the Fleet."

"Cool, wouldn't they detect a mesh network, though?"

"It works by disguising our communications so well that you can't tell the difference between them and ambient static. Their equipment can't even tell we're transmitting," Stephanie said.

"Cool, cool," Nigel said. "Thank you, but, how are you?"

"Good," Stephanie said, offering a rare and brief smile. "It was hard, hiding out in isolation for a while, but I've been keeping myself in a safe place. I'm hoping that the occupation will be over soon, but we still have a long way ahead of us."

"The Order probably knows I'm here," Frost said. "This disguising tech isn't as good as we thought. That leaves you and Sam there to carry out an important part of our plan."

"We're finally doing something?" Nigel asked, excited and afraid at the same time.

"It's time," David said. "You're in the wrong place, we were hoping they'd put you somewhere other than on a picking crew, but Stephanie has found a way to make the plan work."

"Good, I need to be a part of this. I've seen enough of these power tripping assholes. So, what's the plan?"

"Well, a lot of this is going to sound like bad news," Stephanie said. "Frost is leaving."

"I'm getting in a cloak suit, doing some damage, then I'll be getting out. I wish I could stay, but it's only a matter of time before they pick me up and I go the way of the rest of our friends. If they haven't scanned me and seen that I'm wearing a mask yet, then it's going to happen soon."

"He'll join me, where I'm in communication with Phase Seven, the nearest battlegroup," Stephanie said.

"What happens to Sam, Dave and me after this plan?" Nigel asked.

"I'd love to say that you get snatched up so you can hide out with us, but that's not certain," Stephanie replied. Her expression was darkening by the second.

The feeling in the room was grim, it was like everyone expected to lose and it made Nigel uneasy. "So, we're not supposed to get caught. That's part of the plan."

"If everything goes well, then you won't have to worry about that for long. The Phase Seven fleet has doubled in size and most of the command structure is in Haven Shore right now. Wheeler has moved Order Knights and several of his commanders down here because things haven't gone well since he released that footage of Ayan's apartment," Stephanie said.

It was impossible to miss what she was talking about. When Wheeler aired the footage of soldiers finding a freakish shrine to Ayan Rice, which included her corpse, and no one believed it. Even when they let independent members of the press analyse the video and visit the site for themselves, people didn't believe it was what it seemed to be. They hated Wheeler for orchestrating the whole thing. No one liked it when someone tried to trick them, but it was even worse that he went after their queen with such grisly evidence. It was ghoulish, and residents were insulted. Nigel found himself wondering if things would have been different if Wheeler revealed the queen as some secret glutton, or as an embezzler with hidden riches, but it didn't matter. The damage was done and the citizens were starting to notice signs of Wheeler's paranoia. The shimmer of a shield around him when he appeared in public and his unwillingness to open his containment suit when he was in the open air were just a start. He'd started travelling with a crowd of soldiers and his public appearance had been rescheduled twice. "Are we finally going to kill him?" Nigel asked, everyone knew who he meant.

"No," Stephanie replied. "We'd rather deal with a known incompetent than the commander they have in the wings. Someone new is taking control of the Cluster, and we expect the Order of Eden to start attacking the Mergillian and other free worlds within the month. If we remove Wheeler, she may come here first, and I know what I'd do if I were facing a rebellion in Haven Shore."

"Burn it all down," Samantha said under her breath. She was still in her work uniform: dark trousers and a jacket with the markings of a Supervising Engineer. Her knowledge of manufacturing materials put her near the top of the command chain in the fabrication plant.

"That's right. Most of the people the Haven Government and the Rangers saved then resettled have been moved here. They're all seen as sympathizers to Haven, so Wheeler has been trying to convert as many as possible to the Order way, get them climbing the ladder. It's a good way for them to keep an eye on us, too," David said.

"And if we make too much trouble, you know, kill our mentally unbalanced overlord, we'll be easy to wipe out," Frost added. "No, we're going to make him shake a little, give him another reason to keep one eye open, but he'll be whole by the end. The real plan will use the ships we have waiting. It's something they won't expect, and it starts with these." He put a thick stack of reprogrammable communication strips on the table. There must have been a hundred of them. Soldiers gave them out to people with their ident codes on them so people could call them to borrow money or rack up charges by using them to call other people. Everyone had a couple on them, some people even used them as intended. The Order confiscated anything that could be used to reprogram them, but Stephanie had a pair of command and control bracers with her, among other things, and she scanned them. "There are three bad ones in that stack, leaving us with ninety-eight we can use. I'll reprogram these while you fill Nigel and Samantha in on what comes next."

Nigel listened closely as a plan that eventually had him grinning was laid out in whispers by David and Frost. It would be dangerous, but it would be worth it, especially since the Merciless had returned to the Haven System, and they would not be sitting idle.

THREE

The Tour

IT DIDN'T TAKE LONG for the crew of the Clever Dream to find asteroids with leftover heavy metals for the Corsair to harvest so it could finish manufacturing security androids for the station and start working on Captain Majan Lor's order. It was a strange thing, not worrying about being detected. The small group of asteroids were slowly drifting away from the Doxan System, plenty of ships were passing within scanning range, and they had two military class artificial intelligences on watch using the best scanners in the solar system to see danger coming. Elise and Lewis were their first line guardians, and it didn't take much effort on their part.

The Corsair used an advanced version of the maxjack system Frost built for the Samson to cut some of the best parts of the asteroid away, grab it, then break it down while it was stored in an expandable compartment along the bottom of the ship. The manufacturing systems picked the material up from there, breaking it down further, refining the better substances it found then converting the remainder to bulk that would be converted into useful but lighter metals and other construction materials. Alice knew how it worked, she'd done the reading, qualified on an earlier version of the system, but it still boggled her sometimes, how rough stone and raw metals could come out minutes later as something useful. It was technological alchemy.

It was good to have a quiet time when people could rest and hang out. Yawen was in charge on the Clever Dream, and the crew were on alert just in case an Order ship or over ambitious pirates showed up, but they could relax, socialize and watch a few local holographic live shows, which were rare finds in any great quantity. Doxan had hundreds of live channels, even a pirate one that celebrated a more base and brutal type of programming that Noro, Knud, Yawen and Krooke were glued to as the pirates replayed recordings of them playing vicious pranks on each other, like affixing a thruster to one of their friends that went off as soon as he stood up from his chair at an outdoor café. They changed the channel when the pirates started executing ransom victims who weren't paid for in time.

Spending time out of armour and heavy boots felt good to Alice and most of the human crew, especially since she knew there would be long days in full armour ahead. She kept the powder blue suit as it was when it was time to join Noah on the Corsair so they could get to work then spend some time. The brief rise of attraction she felt from Noah when he saw her in it was verification that he liked it.

They had the most work to get through, and it was slow going for Noah and Alice. There were several appeals from people who wanted to meet him, but none had known ties to Mary Reed or claimed to be members of the Underground. A few claimed to know people in resistance groups, but there was no one who could actually say they fought or preyed on the Order of Eden in any way so far.

The number of contacts approaching them through the local network was cut down by Elise and Lewis, even more so by Theodore, but the two captains still had to go through the remainder. There was also syncing up to do between the ships, which required access code swapping and more system checks than either of them cared to do, especially since Alice was feeling distracted. Their reunion was slowed by discipline and duty. There was a lot to do, none of it the kind of thing they wanted to do before taking time for each other, but that was exactly why they decided to get through the least exciting stuff first.

It was difficult. Alice could sense how he felt, on the verge of excitement about her being there even after they calmed down and focused on the task at hand. Noah did get serious, he was good at staying on task, but when he took moments to glimpse at her the excitement resurged, and Alice wondered if it was all him or if she was adding her own elation to the mix. Either way, it made it hard for her to concentrate.

While they were looking through people trying to set a meeting to buy arms, Alice closed her eyes and tried to meditate for a moment. Life was simpler when she didn't feel everyone else's emotions more than her own, and she tried to raise the wall around her mind. Noah had that quiet mind set she felt from people when they were idling a little while they were working or watching something. He was feeling impatient as he watched a pre-recorded message from a polite petitioner she could overhear; "...I ask that you ignore my criminal record, I am not the thief the authorities think I am. I transport goods that most materializers can't produce without breaking down regularly, like so many others, and I'd like to expand my business but I require the means to better defend my concerns," the fellow went on, going into details about his operations and why he needed military grade ship weaponry. Even though there was plenty of boredom and a little impatience, there was an underlying hum of happiness, and she smiled, her eyes still closed as she felt it was inspired by her.

Wait, I'm supposed to be closing the outside off, I want to be uncontaminated by what other people are feeling. Alice thought to herself, trying to pull away from the sense that made her more open than she thought anyone could be. The hum coming from Noah changed, like there was a hiccup, then she felt his concern. "You okay? I mean, we're almost finished, I could watch the last few messages."

With a shake of her head, Alice opened her eyes. He was taking her hand, and she knit her fingers between his. "I'm fine, I just couldn't look at this guy much longer." A nod directed his gaze at the petitioner she was supposed to pay attention to, a man with a thin third nostril in the middle of his nose between the normal pair and an extra set of cybernetic eyes above the human ones. "...need a retailer on the ground, on Doxan Four. The atmosphere is toxic to most humans, but I have the mods, I can breathe the air. I could sell to the races who land here for you if you advance me the first gun shipment. I could sell shields too, you know, and other stuff."

"I see what you mean. He's a little hard to look at. Which eyes do you focus on? The ones he got installed or the factory originals? How much input can you wire into one brain?" Noah asked, cringing at the question as soon as he finished talking. "I'm sorry, I mean cybernetics, not, uh."

Alice put a finger across his lips and paused the playback. "It's fine, I'm not offended. I think we found something though," she reversed the recording for a moment then played it back. "...and other stuff," the cyborg said. "I shouldn't say this on this transmission, but I know there are people who take on the Order here, I see their ships every once in a while from my bunker. Those things are repainted, but I know Order fighters and corvettes when I see them. I know they stole 'em, and I can get to that market for you." Alice paused the recording. "Maybe he's actually got contacts," she said.

"That's why Lewis and I agreed to forward it to you. He attached several recordings of Order of Eden combat shuttles, a gunship and two corvettes. We have his location on Doxan Four as well, but he advises that he will be communication dark for another forty-one hours from now. If he sends outgoing signals his bunker will be discovered by the authorities," Elise said. "Which authorities he's talking about, and why they would care about his bunker are things we couldn't determine. Theodore suggests that he's paranoid, perhaps a little delusional."

"All right, then we follow up on his terms. We should have time to check Doxan Three out in the meantime," Alice said.

"Sounds good," Noah agreed. "Let's get through the last three messages." He was eager, and a little anxious.

They watched them together, fingers still intertwined as they held hands in the pilot and co-pilot seats on the small bridge. They were all just thugs looking to buy guns, one of them spat a few times during her recording, repeating; "I hate the Order, hate them!" but there was no proof that she had done anything to fight them in the past. Alice was stretching in her seat as the last one played, and she noticed a spike in his excitement as he stole a glance. "Can I get a tour?" she asked, sending him a little knowing smile.

"Oh, yeah, sure," Noah said, getting out of his seat. She wasn't far behind, still trying to close her empathic ability off as she followed him through the crew quarters. They were the same as the ones in the Clever Dream, except the first mate's quarters were a storage area instead, and the furniture was collapsed down into its smallest configuration so they could be used for storage too. He was proud of his ship, it was fun to watch him get excited about it, even though most of the features he showed her were already aboard the Clever Dream.

A few of the crew quarters already had security androids standing idle in them, ready for delivery to Angel's Landing. "I'm going to hold off on final delivery until I get a few answers from the administration there," Noah explained. "They paid me, I've got the platinum in the hold, but I want to put the screws to them a little, find out how much they had to do with the trouble we had there before I deliver."

"Makes sense," Alice agreed. "How good are these bots?"

"They're great for civilian security, but not great against the military." He closed the hatch and they moved on.

The round seat she enjoyed so much was absent from the Captain's quarters, but everything else was the same. It had its own food production fabricator, drink mixing machine, hidden refrigeration, roll-out work table, and a great big, luxurious sleeping area with a huge bed.

They both stared at it for a moment before he cleared his throat and led the way out of the room; "Onward! There's a whole other deck!"

The lower deck had a larger hold than the Clever Dream, and

she could see where a couple fighters were installed to act like turrets until they launched. It was a solid improvement over the pair of turrets and automated weapons she had aboard the Clever Dreams' underside. The hold had a few of the bots within, but then she noticed one that looked a little different. "What's this?"

"Oh, that's the militarized android that Elise built. It has an upgraded artificial intelligence, all the materials are to Haven Fleet standard, and there are a few surprises built in. It can follow us in that crazy heavy armour we put on."

"It can fly?"

"Yeah, some antigravity tech along with barrier thrusters, not quite the same as our armour, because there isn't much need to protect from g-forces."

"It is a superior security android design. Military class with an obedient but advanced artificial intelligence with all the limitations set to conform to Fleet Security standards. I have three," Elise added proudly.

"And why didn't you activate them when the pirates tried to drill through your shields?" Noah asked.

"I didn't see the need. If the situation was more urgent I would have used them, but I had plenty of time to consult with you first."

"Give them a trial run next time, okay? If you're unsure, use non-lethal measures first."

"Oh, I'll install some. Right now, they're using an FDH-3 module as their primary offensive weapon. It's adjustable."

"It's a starfighter cannon," Alice snickered. "I can't even see where you put it in."

"It's hidden. The modules run off the micro-fusion power plant and use concealed hand emitters. Do you want me to remove them?"

"No, you just need to add more flexibility to these guys. I mean, blowing people in half makes a statement, but it's not the one we want to make all the time, not on this mission at least," Noah said, wide-eyed but amused.

"I'll add a non-lethal option or two, my boys are a work in progress," Elise said.

"Consult with Lewis and Theo, they'll probably have some good suggestions," Alice said. It was fun watching a highly intelligent but new artificial intelligence learn, Lewis had mostly outgrown that phase.

"And I'm afraid that's the tour, unless you want to take a walk on the hull," Noah said, raising his arms like a showman.

Alice could feel his nervousness like a storm rolling through her head, and she tried not to wince. With the tour over, but hours ahead of them to relax on the ship together, alone, he was nearly overcome with uncertainty.

"I know," Noah sighed. "There really isn't much difference between this and the Clever Dream, which is a more interesting ship on the inside." He paused a moment. "Hey, are you okay?"

"I'm just having trouble," Alice replied. "It's not painful or anything, there's nothing you can do, it's just... I wish I could only be aware of my feelings."

"What's going on in there?" Noah asked, taking her hand and turning to face her. "Or in here?" he pointed at his own temple.

"Nervous," Alice responded. "You're nervous because we haven't been alone together like this."

"All that?" he asked. "The feels and the why's of it too?"

"No, just the feelings, I guess the rest is an assumption," she admitted.

"What if I'm nervous about what you think of my ship?" he

asked, his voice growing quieter. "I mean, it's not just my pride on the line, here, there's Elise too."

Alice laughed a little and shook her head. The wave of nervousness from him was beginning to recede, there was affection beneath, it felt good, but it was still almost too much. Blushing, shaking a little as she looked up at him, Noah had confidence that she faintly remembered having herself in a different life as his lips turned up into a little smile. "It's a great ship," she said. "That's not why you're nervous, I bet. There's such a mix of things going on in you, it's not confusing, though. Everything goes together, even the nervousness."

"You're an amazing, complicated woman," Noah said. "Of course I'm a little anxious, but are you sure that's all coming from me? I don't know much about what's going on in there," he caressed her cheek lightly. "But I know I wasn't so nervous that I looked like I was about to fall over. You're blushing, I'm not, and I know I can turn red sometimes, trust me."

"Maybe I'm feeling both of us," she said, the explanation resounding through her thoughts.

Laying a hand on the chest of his dark vacsuit, something she did unconsciously, she became aware of how good it looked on him. He spoke to her softly, blue eyes peering into hers. "Could there be some way to tell the difference between feelings I'm having and your own? Excitement can't feel exactly the same from one person to the next. Maybe it's like when someone describes something to two different people and they try to draw it, but the drawings come out looking different."

"Perception. Interpretation. Nuance," Alice whispered, investigating the wave moving through her mind, and then she found it. There was a sense, an underlying tone under everything he was exuding that marked emotions as his and his alone. There was that confidence again, a little nervousness, sure, but so much more affection. "I can feel..." she grinned, blushing deeply, "...you. It's like knowing your name, but so much more. I feel better, I feel..." Nervous! She was so nervous about everything going on! His fingertips gently tracing the edge of her jaw, how they were standing so close, how she hoped they could meet the expectations she had, what might happen, and most of all; whether seeing her go through all this would make him think she was a freak. There was a deeper cause for the anxiety, though, and it was what made her blush; the growing passion she had for him. Their emotions were separated in her mind, and that breakthrough, having it right when she really needed it to happen made her so happy that she hopped on her heels a little. "I know now, what's mine and yours."

"You feel better?" he asked, his head lowering, lips drawing closer.

"So much..." they connected, lip to lip. A thousand butterflies in her stomach dissipated as they started slowly. When his hands lowered to her waist, feeling big but light as they rested there, she invited him to stay and start a warm, enthusiastic lip-lock. Her hands drifted up from his chest to his shoulders, feeling their way to the back of his neck, then up the stubble on the back of his head. As she ran her fingers down his scalp Alice realized he liked that, and she made that the playground for her digits while their kiss continued, warm amorous sensations rising in them both.

A squeak against the deck behind him drew her attention, and she opened her lids a crack in time to see the custom security bot frozen in a sneaking position behind Noah, looking at her. She could swear it looked worried, unhappy that it made any noise at all, and she snickered.

Noah straightened, looked at her, then behind him. The

android waved, then resumed its sneaking. "I'm controlling that, I'm so sorry," Elise said. "I didn't mean to interrupt but I thought it would be better to add the modifications to the security bots I designed sooner rather than later just in case. I really didn't mean to interrupt, it looked like you were having such a good time."

After a moment of snickering that quickly grew into outright laughter, Noah nodded. "It's okay, I'm surprised we noticed."

"Oh, good, I really didn't want to break that fascinating display up," Elise said.

"Crew lounge?" Alice offered, taking his hand.

"Yeah. Wait, it's full of equipment cases, stuff reserved for whoever joins my crew," he replied.

"Then bedroom," she said, feeling anticipation and anxiety spike in him. "But I want to take it slow, flyboy," she added with a raised eyebrow. "It's not about the destination, but the journey."

Noah nodded, happy about the stipulation.

"Could you clarify that statement at all, Alice?" Elise asked.

Alice ran for the lift, Noah close behind, and he caught her in an embrace when he arrived. "Nope, too distracted, Elise, sorry." They couldn't resist resuming their kiss, even though the lift ride was less than ten seconds long.

"Humans. It's amazing you get anything done with all those pheromones wafting around," Elise sighed.

AFTERWORD

Thank you for buying and reading Spinward Fringe Broadcast 13: Warriors, it's been great having you aboard. The Spinward Fringe series has led me to one of the most satisfying periods in my life, and I'm happy to continue the journey with you.

After the tenth anniversary of the series, an opportunity for improvement came along. Patreon offered a platform where I could serialize new novels as they're written. That suits this modern age, offering an option for people who don't want to wait six months to a year for a book to be finished. Subscribers can read two chapters a week, see them months before the Ebook comes out. Thanks to that assured pace of story telling, two Spinward Fringe Ebooks will hit the digital shelves every year for the foreseeable future. The days of one book a year are over.

Spinward Fringe has been my full-time job for eleven years now, and I look forward to writing it now more than I have since the early days. Thank you for embarking on this adventure, I hope to see you again.

Randolph Lalonde

www.patreon.com/randolphlalonde
www.randolphlalonde.com